King Solomon's Pilot

A novel of Africa

JEROLD RICHERT

Previously printed as *The Pilot*

JLR Publishing

ISBN: 978-0-9871622-3-6

for Lorna Rose
My wife, my shield, my arrow
my love

Also by Jerold Richert

NOVELS OF AFRICA SERIES

DANCE OF THE FIREBIRDS

BRACELET OF THE MORNING

INTO THE SUN

FOREWORD

*And they came to Ophir, and fetched from
thence gold, four hundred and twenty talents,
and brought it to King Solomon*

1 Kings 10:28

*For the king had at sea a navy of Tarshish
With the navy of Hiram: once in three years
Came the navy of Tarshish, bringing gold
And silver, ivory, and apes, and peacocks.*

1 Kings 11:22

THE MONSOONAL WIND SYSTEMS
USED BY ANCIENT MARINERS
BETWEEN THE MAIN PORTS AND
LANDFALLS OF ANTIQUITY

Alone man leading a shaggy brown horse came out from the dark mountain forest into the bright sunshine of the valley floor. His clothes were bloodstained and filthy. Dry blood and dirt streaked the exposed flesh of his face and arms, and drying blood had stiffened the tangled mass of his hair. Across the horse's back lay the carcass of a wild sheep and the man's weapons, and once through the cold shadow of the slopes he paused to adjust the precarious load with fingers still clumsy and numb from exposure. He removed the weathered skin blanket that had covered his shoulders against the bitter morning chill, adding it to the pile before continuing unhurriedly across the valley towards the bluff and sea. With the worst now over he breathed deep and thankfully of the tangy salt air, revelling in restored life and the rejuvenating warmth of the sun.

The night had been the coldest he had ever suffered in the mountains. Low cloud and darkness had trapped him on an exposed peak at the end of the hunt. With his blanket still with the horse below he had sheltered in a narrow crevice away from the icy north wind, crawling into the tight space then dragging the carcass of the sheep on top, embalming himself in its long fleece with his bare hands and arms buried in the freshly opened stomach cavity amongst the steaming entrails.

He stopped near the top of the bluff to search the shimmering expanse of the Great Sea that stretched beyond. It remained empty. No sail had breached the horizon for all of the long winter past, and he was beginning to believe that none ever would. Immediately below the bluff, but still out of view, lay the small harbour village of Lamos and home. A thread of smoke in the clear sky confirmed his father and older brother were already at work in the potting shed, and he suffered a moment of guilt as he coaxed the mare away from the main path to the village and led her down a steep track leading to a secluded cove. But the guilt was quickly subdued. Fresh meat, he reasoned, was a fair trade for one more day away from the drudgery of the potting shed and the unpleasant sensation of slimy clay oozing between his toes as he paddled it.

Protected from the wind, the tumble of boulders in the cove, many the size of small houses, trapped the sun and held its warmth. The ideal place to wash and catch up on some badly needed sleep. He tethered Piko at the base of the cliff in the shade of a boulder and relieved her of her load. He gave her a drink, pouring cold mountain water from his soft leather canteen into his bowl and scolding her gently as he held it firm under her impatiently thrusting muzzle.

At the water's edge he stripped off his filthy clothes and dropped them into the surging waves between the rocks. He first washed his weapons, scouring the blades of his knife and two javelins in the coarse sand and shell detritus of the beach until the bronze heads gleamed. He laid them aside and picked up the smock, prolonging the pleasure of his own wash, even though his body now felt as if it had been infested by a thousand fleas and the smell of it was beginning to attract a growing number of flies.

Working quickly, he rinsed the smock and breeches then laid them over a rock to dry. He took his first step into the water for the long awaited swim, then a sound from behind made him pause. It had been a small, secretive sound, like that of an urgent whisper quickly stifled. He held his breath, listening carefully, then above the rising and falling rustle of the sea came the unmistakeable crunch of a foot on broken shells. He turned quickly to glimpse a flash of blue in a gap between the boulders.

Years of hunting alone in the mountain forests had imbued Hallam with the reflexes and agility of the wild animals he hunted. He snatched up his two javelins and leaped towards the gap. If it was children again from the village he would give them a scare to remember, but it was not unknown for outcasts or thieves from other villages to scavenge around Lamos for easy pickings, and Piko, his most prized possession, was tethered out of sight with his other belongings a short distance away. Hallam bounded through the gap with one of the javelins raised and a fearsome yell on his lips. He skidded to a halt in the sand as he almost collided with two women.

Both women screeched and fell back against the boulder behind which they had been hiding. One held a hand forward, as if to ward off the raised javelin. The other cowered away, covering her face with her hands.

Hallam stared at them with the yell dying in his throat. They were strangers. Rich strangers, for their robes were finely embroidered and bracelets of gold and silver adorned their arms.

The elder of the two recovered first. With her hand still protectively outstretched, she spoke in a voice made hoarse and breathless with fear. 'Please... do not harm us.' .

But Hallam's attention was fixed on the other, much younger woman. She had partly lowered her hands to reveal a face so strange he could only gape in awe. Wide, frightened eyes pleaded with his. Eyes that were painted around with blue; the brilliant iridescent blue of a kingfisher's wing, the paint extending in a sensual curve to her temples, ending there in points to give her the look of yet another exotic bird. The nails of her fingers that she held to her face were also painted blue. Hair the colour of glowing embers cascaded in fiery curls behind her back.

After several moments of shocked silence, the old woman drew herself haughtily erect. 'Who are you?' she demanded in a croaking voice. 'Why do you threaten us in such a rude manner?' She tugged a square of white silk from the sleeve of her robe and held it to her nose, turning aside with deliberate disdain.

Hallam ignored her, continuing to stare into the wide eyes of the young woman as if in a trance. He had heard that in Egypt and Tyre there were women who painted their faces, but had never imagined the effect would be so enchanting. No woman in Lamos had ever dared such a thing, or had ever exposed so much of their breasts. Lustrous as giant pearls, they heaved rapidly to the rhythm of her breathing. She was wondrous in every way; as enchanting as the figures of the goddess Astarte his mother painted on the vases and urns. Hallam realised suddenly that she may even *be* the goddess Astarte, and his already racing pulse quickened.

Transfixed by his thoughts and her astonishing beauty, Hallam was slow to respond when her eyes suddenly darkened and shifted to look over his shoulder. He spun around, but not soon enough. A jarring blow on the shaft of the still raised javelin sent it flying from his grasp, then a heavy blow between the shoulders sent him stumbling across the ground. He fell, sprawling, managing to flip onto his back, but with his second javelin trapped beneath him. Stunned by the unexpected assault, Hallam looked up at his attacker, a soldier, who now stood looking down at him, a triumphant grin on his face, and the thick shaft of a battle spear in his hands.

It was a face far different to the one that had so recently entranced him. This was a dark, bearded face, and the eyes were fixed on the centre of Hallam's chest, the mouth cruelly contorting as the soldier raised the spear and gathered strength for the downward plunge.

With a shock Hallam realised he was only moments away from death. He steeled himself, and yet needed, desperately, to protest, not ready yet, to contemplate dying. A sound escaped his frozen lips. A husky, choking from deep within his throat.

The young woman screamed.

Her scream was short and sharp, and cut through the silence with a suddenness that caused the soldier to hesitate. He turned his head to glance at the women, perhaps thinking there was more than one attacker to deal with, and Hallam did not waste the opportunity. He lashed out with both feet at the man's legs, sending him stumbling back.

Hallam rolled and sprang to his feet, scooping up the javelin in a single fluid motion, spinning to face the soldier and drawing back his arm for the throw, and the woman screamed again. 'No!'

Hallam stopped, but remained with arm drawn back and his legs braced, poised in readiness, watching the soldier recovering from his stumble, and realising with a surge of elation and relief that he now had the advantage, their positions reversed in a few thudding heartbeats. Time to think. He had no idea who they were or why they were there, but they were certainly not thieves or gods. The soldier obviously there to protect them.

And it was a responsibility the man took seriously. He had recovered and was drawing a short sword from his belt.

Now the dark face was bloated with anger and humiliation, and Hallam tensed, feeling a stab of uncertainty replace the giddiness of relief. The man was a trained killer. Killing had been on his face and in his eyes as he had stood above with the spear raised in both hands. No question of mercy. Had the woman not screamed the soldier would certainly have killed him. And he still may, Hallam realised, for the short leather skirt and sleeveless jerkin revealed muscular limbs matted with dark hair, the shoulders hunching and the rugged face hardening into resolve.

Few could better Hallam in wrestling matches at the village, but against this man he knew he would be as a child. He could not allow him to get close. At this range Hallam was confident of his ability, and he still held the advantage, but with this adversary it could soon change. He had all but made up his mind to throw the javelin and be done with it when the young woman called out again.

'Please! No killing! Parak, stop! Let the man speak.' Her voice was unsteady, and although it was a plea, still there was authority in her tone.

'It is a madman, Lady Philippa, and I doubt he can speak. He lives in his own filth and goes unclothed in front of noble women. He is a stinking animal that should be killed and thrown into the sea for the fish.'

It was not until then that Hallam became fully aware of his condition. It had all happened so fast. The blood still raced in his veins and beat urgently at his temples, demanding action, and he drew in a deep breath to calm himself. And with the breath came the stench of his own body. Moistened by fear and matured by three days of unwashed sweat and sheep gore, the smell in the hot airless cove enveloped him like a sulphurous cloud. He suffered a moment of confusion, unwilling to accept the smell as his own and not that of some long dead sea creature rotting amongst the seaweed and rocks. That he could do nothing about his smell or his nakedness in front of the women only fuelled his frustration, and he vowed that if the ape moved he would kill him.

'Who are you?' the old woman demanded again. 'Are you a madman?'

He did not take his eyes from the soldier. 'Tell your pet ape to stop or I'll spike him.'

'You stinking animal,' the soldier snarled, but in the face of the menacing javelin he made no move to come closer.

'Parak is our guard. You should not have threatened us.'

'You were hiding like thieves.'

'*Thieves?*' The old woman's voice sharpened with indignation. 'How dare you accuse us of such a thing! I am the sister of King Khiram and we are guests of Governor Nathan!'

'I doubt the mad fool understands, my lady. If you move to safety I will deal with him.' He took another step forward. 'Come,' he challenged Hallam, 'throw your puny stick.'

'Parak, no!' the young woman cried, but the soldier paid no attention, and began a strange ducking and weaving motion, prancing from side to side in a surprisingly dainty, almost dance-like movement that had the situation been different, would have caused Hallam to laugh out loud. But he was in enough trouble already and did not want to fight. The news that the old woman was a relative of King Khiram was sobering. No king, except perhaps Solomon, was more powerful. Governor Nathan would not look kindly on having such important guests threatened, no matter how innocent the circumstances. He wanted to do as she asked and leave, but he sensed the soldier did not. The man had lost face, and given the chance Hallam was sure he would try to reclaim it. Nevertheless, he lowered his javelin and partly turned away. 'I meant no harm. I will leave now,' he said, loud enough for all to hear, and moved slowly to where his second javelin lay on the sand.

The soldier stopped his prancing, and for a moment Hallam believed his move towards conciliation had worked, but as he stooped to pick up the javelin the soldier charged. He came with the sword held high and the spear thrust forward, dancing around the rocks, and Hallam threw his javelin.

Facing the wrong way, and with no time for aiming, he threw instinctively, with a quick underhand flick of his wrist

13

from his stooped over position. But with the second javelin now safely in his other hand he could afford to take the risk.

The slender hunting javelin flew like an arrow, too swift for his opponent's parry. It struck him in the fleshy upper part of his sword arm and stuck there, held by the single barb.

The soldier bellowed in shock and rage, but kept coming, the shaft of the javelin clattering amongst the rocks, and he would have continued had not the shaft caught between two boulders and jerked him to a halt. He bellowed again at the wrenching and dropped the heavy spear to clutch at the javelin, lifting the shaft and trying to pull it free, but it refused to come, and he cried out more sharply as the pain took hold against the cruel pulling and twisting.

But still the soldier was not about to submit, and Hallam felt a grudging respect when the man left the javelin to hang and, after wiping the perspiration from his face with a forearm, took the sword in his left hand. 'Now...' the soldier snarled, '... throw the other one.'

It was too much for the women. Pulling and pushing each other they stumbled away to safety behind the boulders..

Hallam did not throw the second javelin. He leaped onto a rock, then onto another as the soldier raged after him, leaping from one to another with the sure-footed agility of a mountain ram, going higher with each leap until finally he stood on a tall boulder well out of the soldier's reach.

'Get down and fight!' the soldier roared. He flung the sword in frustration, but it was with his left hand and against the painful restriction of the javelin. The sword spun harmlessly over Hallam's head and splashed into the sea behind.

Standing poised with the javelin raised, Hallam looked down at the fuming soldier. From where he stood he could kill him easily, but his anger had gone and the man was now unarmed. The full length of his arm glistened with blood. It trickled from his fingers in a steady stream, and the quantity of it made Hallam uneasy. If the fool died from the loss of his own blood it would be his own doing. He felt no sympathy, but he was the one they would hunt down. It was not his fault, and he did not want the responsibility for it. The soldier had stupidly forced him into defending himself.

The man was now showing signs of increasing distress. Ignoring the threat of the javelin from above, he kneeled on the sand and tried again to remove the head, gasping with the pain his futile actions were causing

Hallam looked for the women. They were standing near his horse, at the bottom of the path. 'Your soldier needs help!' he called to them.

They seemed reluctant, whispering to each other at length before the old woman answered. 'If you move your horse from the path and promise no harm we will call someone.'

Her foolish reply angered Hallam. 'Stupid woman! Order him to submit and I will remove the javelin myself.'

'Never!' the soldier roared. 'If you come down I will kill you!'

Hallam laughed scornfully. 'You have no weapon, and with no blood it is you who will soon die.'

The young woman left her mother and came towards them. She glanced up quickly at Hallam before looking away. 'What must we do?' she asked stiffly.

'Order him to submit,' He turned his back and clambered quickly down the boulder. It was not the soldier's welfare that concerned Hallam so much as retrieving his javelin. Going home was now out of the question. He would have to return to the mountains to avoid the governor's wrath, and would need all of his weapons.

The soldier was on his knees, pleading with the woman. 'Please, my lady, if you will help... the shaft... I cannot lift...'

'Leave it alone,' Hallam advised, 'you will only make it worse. I will do it.'

'Stay away from me, you foul stinking animal!'

The young woman spoke sharply. 'Parak! Be quiet and do as he says'

'But My Lady, if you will…'

'I order you, Parak!' the demand was delivered with a stamped foot, and with such unfeminine vehemence and authority that Hallam could not help but give her a startled look. It had a similar effect on the soldier, for he lay back on the sand with a groan and with his head turned away so he did not have to look at his unwelcome benefactor.

'Stand there… on his arm,' Hallam directed her, pointing to the soldier's bloodied forearm. 'You have to keep it still.'

She gave him a sharp look, but said nothing and hoisted her robe to remove her sandals, revealing slim ankles and the promise of shapely legs beyond. 'I'm not sure…'

'It's only ape's blood and will easily wash off,' Hallam said. Perhaps it was because he was now in control of the situation, or it may have been the euphoria of having survived after staring at what he believed was certain death, but Hallam suddenly found he was enjoying himself.

She flushed. 'It is not what I mean. You have rude manners... whoever you are.'

Hallam placed his knee in the crook of the soldiers elbow, pressing it firmly into the sand as he lifted the shaft of the javelin. 'My name is Hallam.'

He studied her feet as she placed them cautiously on the arm. The toenails were painted blue, the toes wriggling as she struggled to hold her balance. Slender and unblemished, with a fine net of blue veins, they were feet clearly unaccustomed to carrying more than the slight weight of their owner and looked obscenely out of place on the blood matted coarse black hair of the soldier's arm.

Hallam gripped the base of the shaft and looked up to indicate he was ready.

Her attention had been elsewhere. Her eyes shifted quickly towards his at the question, then flicked away, her cheeks flushing, and Hallam smiled. A noble with the look of a goddess but with the mind of a common woman.

Gripping the shaft firmly in one hand, he found the notches cut into the base of the javelin that lined up with the barbed head. He turned the shaft quickly to match the notches with the gash in the arm and pulled the javelin free, unavoidably ripping out a strip of bloodied flesh and skin.

The soldier bellowed and jerked upright, lashing about in reflex at Hallam with his uninjured arm before falling back to clasp at his wound and squirm in agony.

Hallam leaped back instinctively, dodging the flying fist, but crashing into Lady Philippa. She fell back and Hallam reacted automatically, jumping to catch her. She clung to him as she regained her footing, for a brief moment looking close into his eyes, then she uttered a low cry and pushed away from him.

With the soft feel of her still on his hands, Hallam gathered his weapons, including the soldiers heavy spear, and started towards the sea.

'What of the blood?' she called out. 'Can you not stop the blood? I fear he will die if it is not stopped.'

Hallam paused to look. The soldier was unconscious, the arm bleeding freely. 'I will get my knife.'

He returned to cut a long strip from the hem of the soldiers tunic and wrap it around the wound several times, binding it firmly. Lady Philippa stood uncertainly, watching, until Hallam had finished, then moved aside hastily as he strode past her towards the sea. He could do no more. The luxury of a leisurely swim and lazy day was now out of the question. It would not take the women long to reach the village and report what had happened, and by then he intended to be well into the forest and safe from retribution.

Scooping up handfuls of the coarse sand from the bottom, Hallam scoured his body until it tingled, then he dived in search of the sword. He found the shiny blade easily in the clear water and carried it back, but left it and the spear concealed in an underwater crevice for collection at a later date. An iron sword was rare enough to fetch a good price, and would be some compensation for not being able to return home until the soldier and his noble employers left the island.

He need not have hurried. They were still where he had left them, the soldier conscious but unmoving. The old woman had joined her daughter. Hallam struggled into his wet and clinging breeches and gathered his weapons. 'I thought you would go for help, 'he said as he approached .

'We cannot leave him here like this, 'Lady Philippa replied. He may die before help arrives. Parak is not a bad man. He was only trying to protect us. You must take him to the village on your horse.'

'On my horse?' Hallam laughed. Despite being the most wondrous creature, the arrogant assumption affronted him. 'No… my lady.' The title came off his tongue with difficulty. I am not one of your slaves, only a rude mannered fool who goes unclothed in front of noble women. But I am not so foolish as to return to the village to be arrested.

'No, I will explain to my husband what has happened and that the fault was not yours. If you help us I give my word you will not be arrested.'

The news that she had a husband triggered a sardonic laugh from Hallam, and suddenly he felt even less inclined to help. 'I think not. Your ape tried to kill me. If he dies the fault will be his alone. And I wish him a slow and painful departure.'

She reproached him with silence and a look akin to disappointment, and Hallam instantly regretted his words. He opened his mouth to take them back, but was too late. She turned away and he stared after her. Even her walk was a thing of sensual beauty, and he sighed in resignation. No man could fail to be aroused by such a walk and still call himself a man. He called after her. 'If you stay with him and give your word I will not be arrested I will go for help.'

She stopped and turned. 'I give you my word, but can you not take him on your horse?'

'No, he is much too heavy to lift.' It was a lie. He had long ago taught Piko to kneel like a camel, or even prostrate herself to facilitate the loading of animal carcasses or logs for the kiln, as he was about to do with the sheep carcass once they was out of sight behind the boulder. To put the man who tried to kill him, and who still would if given the chance, on Piko's back was unthinkable. And now not necessary. She had given her word he would not be arrested if he went for help, that is all that mattered. The soldier could take his chances. Live or die. It made no difference.

When he reached the top and was leading Piko along the path to Lamos, Hallam saw the masts of two Tyrian boats that had previously been hidden by the rise of the bluff. He went closer to the edge of the cliff for a better look.

One of the boats was large, larger than any boat he had ever seen, with a pitch blackened deck and a mast thicker than the man standing beside it. The massive sail hung in bunched swathes from the single spar, the sun-bleached material streaked brown with timber stain. Glimpses of an embroidered design in yellow showed amongst the folds. The other, much smaller boat was moored close alongside, it's hull curved and sleek as a gull's neck. A yellow awning was strung forward of the mast and the railings were thin and decorative. No doubt the private boat on which the nobles had travelled from Tyre, Hallam surmised.

A sailor straddled one end of the long spar of the large boat, working on ropes, and although Hallam could not catch the words, the sailor's voice carried clearly as he bantered with his shipmates on the deck below. Another group of men sat on the wharf, the iron heads of their spears glinting in the sunlight.

Hallam continued on with a turmoil of mixed feelings. Seeing the boats stirred vague longings inside him. Not that he particularly liked boats. He preferred horses as transport, but they had limitations when you lived on an island. The visual reality of the boats also brought home with a rush of uneasiness the predicament he was in. He had probably killed the bodyguard of King Hiram's sister, a woman he had called stupid, and all he had between himself and certain death was the word of her beautiful daughter, and that given only to get his reluctant cooperation. And although she had given her word he would not be arrested, she could not speak for the bodyguard's friends. Dead or alive they would discover the truth and seek revenge. He would not be able to visit the boats or the tavern to hear what news it brought of the outside world.

Lamos was not a wealthy town, and mainly survived because of the governor's copper mine and the tavern. A wall of stone had once protected the rear of the village from marauding bands of thieves, but had long since been abandoned, the stones used for building of houses and other works. Hallam had used part of a still intact section as a stable for Piko, building a secure enclosure and roofing one end against the weather.

When he stopped there to offload the carcass and hide his weapons before going to the tavern for help, Hallam again considered his untenable situation and came reluctantly to the decision that he would have to leave Lamos again for the mountains as soon as possible, and stay away at least until the boats had left. With the woman having given her word, it would probably be safe providing he stayed away from the wharf, but he was not going to take any chances. Everyone knew you could not trust a Tyrian or a woman, and the beautiful Lady Philippa was both. He would get one good meal and a sleep at least, then leave at daybreak.

The group of Tyrian soldiers sprawled in the shade of the

tavern wall regarded Hallam with suspicion when he told them that the women's bodyguard had been injured in the cove and that he had been sent by Lady Philippa to get their help.

'Captain Parak was injured? How was he injured?' The soldier who spoke had a similar dark complexion to that of the bodyguard, Parak, and the same red tabs on his tunic indicating he was also a leader. His tone was aggressive and disbelieving. None of the men had bothered to rise

Their attitude angered Hallam, particularly that of the man with the questions. The worst night he had experienced was now the worst day. He was tired and hungry and still trying to catch up with everything that had happened. He spoke directly to the man. 'Why don't you ask him yourself? I only bring a message. He has lost blood and needs help. He is too weak to walk. If he dies while you sit here and talk like women the fault will be yours.' Not waiting for a reaction, good or otherwise, Hallam turned Piko aside and rode away.

He was salting and pegging out the sheep skin behind the pottery shed late that afternoon when the soldiers came to arrest him.

Sitting with her knees tucked under her chin, Philippa dipped the plover's quill into the silver cosmetic box at her side and applied the violet paste to her toenail with a practiced twirl of her fingers. Her mother sat opposite, seeding the pods she had collected from the carob tree overhead into her lap, and going over yet again their frightening ordeal at the cove.

'He displayed himself in the most disgusting manner, Philippa, and he called me stupid! Him, of all people!' She paused in her seeding to give her daughter a look of shocked outrage. 'Do you realise what could have happened if Parak had not been there? He could easily have ravaged and killed us both! He could have thrown us in the sea and no one would ever have known. It is only right he should be arrested.'

'But he did us no harm, Mother, and he did help Parak. Ari should have respected our promise.'

'*Your* promise, Philippa, and Ari is your husband. He has a right to be angry.'

Philippa grunted her disagreement. It was not right. And what Ari and the governor intended doing was not right either. The man had been crude and insolent and had smelled worse than the sheep he had killed, but he had done what she asked because she had given her word. But then the word of a woman never did account for much, especially with her husband.

Other than a few servants and a guard at the gate, Philippa and her mother were alone at the house. It was cramped and airless, and by Tyrian noble standards, more suited to a stable than a governor's residence, which is why they spent much of their time outside. Governor Nathan had been forced to send his wife and children to stay with friends in order to accommodate his guests.

Lord Arumah and the governor had left early that morning to inspect the copper mine. Before leaving, and despite Philippa's explanation the night before about what had happened at the cove, Ari and the governor had gone to visit Parak at the tavern to get his side of the story. Then they had immediately ordered the arrest of the man from the cove.

Philippa had first heard about it when she took a package of food to give to her husband and the governor as they were preparing to leave. Hidden from their view by the stable wall as she approached, she had overheard Governor Nathan talking,

'... that such a thing will happen again. Perhaps a sound

flogging in the square will teach the lout some manners, and also give notice to the villagers that your women should be treated with respect. I hope it will not...' He fell silent when he saw Philippa and busied himself with the thongs of his leggings.

Philippa had taken an instant dislike to the governor. He was a strutting bald man with a demanding voice that reminded her of her uncle Khiram, and his eyes seemed able to look clear through a robe. She suspected the governor was trying to impress her husband to prove he had control over the villagers who would work the mine if Ari bought it.

'You are going to flog the man even though I gave my word?' Philippa asked, struggling to keep her voice even.

Lord Arumah cautioned her with a frown, warning her not to discuss the matter in the presence of the governor. Yet he placed no such restriction upon himself. 'It was not yours to give,' he stated bluntly. 'Your protection is my responsibility.'

'My word is not my own?' It was so ludicrous that Philippa could only stare in bewilderment, not sure if it was a joke.

'It is not a matter you need concern yourself with.'

'But my own word does concern me, Husband.'

'And It concerns me, W*ife*, that you show so little respect. Why is it you show less interest in the welfare of the guard who tried to protect you than the man who attacked you? Why did you not tell us the peasant exposed himself to you?'

'He did not expose himself to me... or attack us. He was washing his clothes, which is why he was uncovered. He also helped Parak as I asked.'

'No man should expose himself to women,' the governor boomed righteously. 'Especially noble women. He should have taken the time to cover himself first.'

About to protest further, Philippa clamped her jaw. She had already said too much. Whatever she said in defence of the man, especially in the presence of the governor, would only act against him - and her. She had purposely not mentioned the man's nakedness to Ari because she knew it would anger him. It had been a mistake. He now saw more in the omission. She should also have realised that Parak would not miss the opportunity of embellishing his story to excuse his failure.

'I know this fellow well,' the governor said, filling the silence. 'He's a troublemaker. His father is our master potter, and a good man, but he has no control over his eldest son. The lout is a wencher and needs to be given a lesson.'

'In Tyre...' Lord Arumah said ominously, pausing to give Philippa a meaningful glare. 'A man who did such a thing would not be flogged. He would be gelded.'

Philippa was aghast. Even the governor's ruddy complexion paled.

'No... you cannot!' Philippa cried. 'That would not be right! I have already told you it was not his fault! Why will you not believe me?'

'It is not a matter of believing you,' Lord Arumah said. 'It is a matter of doing what is fitting for the crime.' He signalled impatiently for the stable slave to assist him with mounting. Turning away from Philippa, he spoke curtly to the governor. 'See to it, Nathan... and soon... before we leave.'

Governor Nathan nodded rapidly several times to cover his discomfiture. He scratched at a scab on his bald head, causing it to bleed unnoticed. 'Of course, my lord... if that is your wish...'

Tight-lipped, Philippa thrust the package of food into the governor's hands and strode stiffly away. Much of her anger was with herself, for she knew her husband well enough to realise she should not have spoken out. Ari's possessive jealousy was close to insanity. He would have the man gelded simply because she had seen him naked. It also did little for her peace of mind to know that Ari would not so much be giving a lesson to the man as he would be giving a lesson to her.

Aware that she would get no support from her mother, Philippa had not mentioned what punishment had been suggested by her husband. Her mother would agree with him, as she always did, and there was still a chance Ari would reconsider. Philippa prayed to Ashtoreth that he would. Of all the gods, surely the goddess of fertility would be the one to understand.

Sitting under the carob tree, Philippa took her frustration out on her mother. 'I'm tired of hearing about it, Mother. Can you not speak of anything else?'

'But I can't get it out of my mind,' her mother persisted. 'All that blood! I thought I was going to be sick. I have never been so frightened!'

'There was a dead sheep by the horse, he must have killed it in the mountains.'

'With his teeth? It was all over his face!'

Philippa had to admit she had never been so frightened either. The raised spear and his eyes bloodshot and glaring at her through the mass of hair. It had frozen her all the way through.

And she thought he was going to die too, when Parak had him helpless on the ground. The awful choking sound he made... like a dying animal. Her scream had surprised even herself. It had probably saved his life. At least that was something in her favour.

Merely thinking about it sent a shiver through Philippa's body and she paused with the plover's feather held away from her toe until the shudder had passed. 'I have blood on my robe,' she said. 'I'll have to throw it away.'

'I don't know why you allowed yourself to get so close. We should have gone for help. Did you not see the way he kept staring at you?

Philippa *had* noticed. But she was used to men staring at her. What she was not accustomed to was staring back. And she had done that more than a few times.

'I nearly screamed when he grabbed you,' her mother said. 'I thought he was going to have you right in front of me.'

'Mother!'

'Well, that's what I thought. He was *naked,* Philippa!'

'Yes, Mother, I noticed.'

From all she had heard she had expected it to be different – larger and more threatening. And he had caught her looking! Strangely, she had not been afraid when he knocked her over. Not for a moment did she think he was going to harm her, even though he held her so close she could feel the heat of his breath. Only concern had been in his eyes. Brown eyes... and gold. The same colour as his body.

'I'm surprised it doesn't bother you more.'

'There was no time to think about it. Parak needed help.'

But Philippa knew in her heart it was more than that. It did bother her, but not in the way her mother thought it should. No point in trying to fool herself, Philippa conceded. It was not the whole frightening experience that bothered her so much as the image of him standing on the boulder against the clear blue of the sky. A lithe, naked male body, poised and glistening, perfectly still and taught except for his heaving chest, the javelin raised and wild hair shaggy as a lion's mane. A trickle of blood running down one buttock from where he had fallen on his javelin. The image would not go away. She had gone to bed with it, and woken up with it.

She had not realised that a man's body could be so beautiful. When she was a girl her uncle had taken her to watch the games between the soldiers. The men wore only loincloths, and she remembered how she had admired their bodies and been awed by their strength and prowess, but she never remembered thinking of them as beautiful - and never as desirable. Maybe now she was older it would be different, but since Ari had forbidden her to attend the games there was little chance of finding out.

Philippa shifted uncomfortably and, not for the first time since she had thought of that golden body, frowned at the disturbing response of her own. That was also a new experience - and a revelation. She had not realised it could happen so easily.

Philippa straightened her leg and wriggled her toes, viewing the results of her work with a critical tilt of her head. Then she licked her thumb and began furiously rubbing the paste off.

Her mother stopped to watch in surprise. 'What are you doing?'

'I hate it. I'm not doing it any more, I keep seeing it when I walk.'

'It will look odd if you only paint your finger nails and eyes.'

'I'm not doing them either. It makes my skin itch.'

'Ari won't be pleased, you know how he likes you to wear it.'

Philippa stood up. 'I don't care what he thinks. I'm going to rest.'

That's all she was to her husband Philippa thought as she crossed the courtyard. A painted ornament to be put on display. It gave him pleasure to see the envy and desire in the eyes of stronger, but less powerful men. There was no love in their marriage, or even lust. Only his degrading perversions. Ari's lust was for wealth and power, and she still recalled with shame the day he had taken her as a wife, when she was fifteen years old and still innocent. Suspicious as ever, and before agreeing to take her, he had insisted on proving her worth, as if testing the authenticity of a new acquisition before parting with his gold.

And a dirty acquisition too, it seemed, for after he had finished his painful probing of her womanhood he had scrubbed his fingers so thoroughly the knuckles had turned red. It was a relief he never showed any desire to touch her there again and was content merely to disrobe her - while he himself always remained fully clothed - then fondle and suckle on her empty breasts like a starving infant.

Preoccupied with her disturbing thoughts, Philippa was startled when she saw a shadow in her path and looked up to see a soldier standing to attention before her.

'May the gods provide for you, Mistress Philippa,' he greeted her. 'Captain Parak has ordered me to attend you until he is recovered.' The guard also appeared to have been in a fight. One eye was partly closed and a bruise showed on his cheek.

But it was not his injuries that caught Philippa's attention. 'Where did you get that?' she demanded, pointing to the medallion he wore around his neck.

'This, Mistress Philippa?' He lifted the medallion to squint at it. 'Spoils of war, Mistress.' He grinned and pointed to his eye. 'In payment for this.'

Philippa did not return his smile. 'I asked where.'

The guard's smile vanished at her tone. 'From the man we arrested. The one who wounded Captain Parak.'

'Who ordered his arrest?'

The guard looked nonplussed. 'The governor, mistress, after he and Lord Arumah had spoken with Captain Parak.'

'Was he harmed?'

'It will take more than a peasant's javelin to put the captain down, mistress. He is saying he will be back on duty tomorrow.'

'I'm talking about the man you arrested.'

'He gave us a fight, mistress. We had to beat him down and tie him.'

'What have you done with him?'

'We have him locked in the hold of the ship, mistress, as Lord Arumah ordered.'

Philippa held out her hand. 'We are not at war with these people on the island, and looting here is forbidden, as you well know. Give it to me. I will see it is returned, and if you have taken other things you had better give them to me as well.'

The guard hastily removed the medallion and placed it in her hand. 'Nothing else, Mistress, I swear it. Only that. It was ripped off in the fight by accident.'

Philippa examined the medallion in the privacy of her room. It was unusually attractive. Jewellery abounded in Tyre, but she had never seen anything quite like this piece. It was black, with a pattern of holes that did not appear at the surface, only below it, and it had the smooth look and feel of glass, but it was wonderfully clear around the centre, whereas glass was not clear. It looked like frozen black water.

Philippa washed her face, removing the colour she had applied earlier, then she massaged the sensitive skin around her eyes with a thin smear of palm oil. She held the silver mirror to catch the light, checking carefully to be certain she had left no unsightly streaks, then she took the blue robe from under the pile of clothes in her chest. It was Ari's favourite.

She examined the bloodstains. Particularly one at the back which showed a smudged handprint with splayed fingers. She gazed at it for a moment, then laid her hand over the top, measuring her own small hand against it. The fine silk was stiff with dry blood. Parak's blood. She removed her hand hastily.

Philippa put her foot into the neck of the garment and tugged with both hands until it ripped across. She rolled it into a ball and stuffed both it and the medallion back under the pile of clothes, then she threw herself angrily down on the mattress.

By diplomatic questioning of the woman who did the cooking, Philippa had learned that the name of the man at the cove was Hallam, and she had also established that although he did have a reputation in the village as a man quick to pick up the scent of a wandering female, he was not quite the scoundrel the governor had made him out to be.

'Hallam has supplied more than one hind-quarter for the governor's dinner,' the cook had informed Philippa. 'I hope nothing bad happens to him because of what he done. I'm sure he didn't mean harm to you or your soldier.'

It confirmed Philippa's suspicion the governor was only trying to impress her husband. That was good. It made the plan she had spent the afternoon devising that much simpler.

Governor Nathan and her husband returned late in the afternoon. When she saw Ari coming alone from the stable, she seized the opportunity and hurried to meet him, putting on a welcoming smile. It made her jaw ache in protest, but if her plan was to succeed it was important she act as if nothing had happened between them that morning.

Her strained smile turned to a frown of concern however when she saw her husband was limping. 'Ari! What have you done?'

'These sandals and the accursed mountain are poor companions. I have sores and aching feet.'

She took his arm, clicking her tongue in sympathy. 'You should have insisted they carry you,' she scolded. 'Come, we'll soak them, then I'll tend them with balsam. Was your journey worth such an affliction?'

'Perhaps, but Nathan will have to build a better track if he wants me to buy his mine.'

Philippa fussed over him, questioning him further about

his trip as she washed his feet in a bowl of warm water scented with her special oils. Then while he soaked them she fixed him his favourite drink of hot wine and honey and he settled back with a sigh of contentment.

Philippa hurried out, going to the stable where she could hear the governor shouting abuse at his slave.

Governor Nathan was sitting on a bench, holding a leather helmet in one hand and rubbing with a cloth at his bald head. The slave was kneeling at his feet, trying, apparently with little success, to remove the governor's leggings.

When he saw her approaching, Governor Nathan kicked the slave away. 'Get a knife, you fool!' He threw his helmet after the departing man then smiled at Philippa. 'Ah, my lady, each time I see you my pleasure is greater than before. I believe our fine weather has smiled favourably upon you. It shows in your lovely cheeks.'

'It is not the weather that I wished to talk to you about, Governor.'

Governor Nathan's smile weakened. 'I hope his lordship has not been too badly afflicted by the mountain. As you can see, even I have suffered, and I am much younger with more strength.'

'He is quite well, Governor, and stronger than you may think, but that's not the reason I am here either. I wish to talk to you on a matter of business.'

The slave returned with a knife and Governor Nathan scowled down as he cut the leggings free. He dismissed the slave with an impatient wave and stood to lift a leg onto the bench. He rubbed gently at the plump calf muscle, prolonging his response, and Philippa's lips firmed at the deliberate snub.

'Business, is it?' the governor said finally. 'What business could interest such a pretty head?'

'It concerns the man you intend to punish.' Philippa replied evenly. 'It is my belief that you do not really want to do what my husband suggests.'

The governor paused in his rubbing to look up with both eyebrows raised. 'But, my lady! Did not Lord Arumah say it is not something to concern yourself with? You do not have to attend the punishment, of course. No women should be encouraged to witness such crude exhibitions. I will forbid my own women to attend.' The governor replaced his foot on the ground and turned the ankle experimentally. 'I swear... the great god Baal shall have my own worthy balls in sacrifice before I wear such cursed things again.' Kicking and flexing his legs, Governor Nathan adjusted his crotch in the tight breeches then grinned at Philippa. 'Forgive me, my lady, I forget myself in your presence.'

Philippa had met such men before, and suffered similar clumsy posturing to impress or embarrass her. It did nothing but strengthen her position. She had learned much from watching and listening to her husband. Ari was an expert in manipulating men and finding their weakness, and the governor had many. And something else Philippa had inherited from her uncle Khiram other than his red hair, was his temper.

'Then you had better remember yourself quickly,' she said coldly. 'That is, if you wish my husband to buy your worthless mine. And you had better show me respect for the same reason. I am not one of your servants.'

'My Lady Philippa...'

'To you, Governor, I may only be a woman, but be warned, if I tell my husband of your crude advances and the way you stare at me when he isn't looking, you can say farewell to your mine, and maybe even your life!'

The governor gaped at Philippa in shock. His complexion first paled, then deepened in hue, the colour spreading over his baldness until his head resembled a well boiled joint of meat. No woman had ever spoken to him like that before. 'My Lady Philippa! You are mistaken! I meant no...'

'My husband is not really interested in your mine, Governor. From what he tells me it is in a difficult place. A smelter and track needs to be built first, and he is not sure if he can wait. He has other mines in mind that are much easier to reach.' It was a lie, but the governor was not to know. 'Do what I say and I will convince him that yours is the best because of your good harbour.'

'Yes, yes, the harbour...' The governor sat down and mopped at his head. It had resumed some of its normal colour, but glistened wetly. A small trickle of blood ran from the scab to his ear. He dabbed at it with the cloth. 'What is it you expect of me?'

'I gave my word to the man he would not be arrested. I want you to make sure my word is kept.'

'But he has already been arrested, and your husband...'

'I know you are doing it because you think you must prove to my husband you can control people, but it is not necessary. 'You must release the man.

'I don't know, Lady Philippa... what can I tell Lord Arumah? It is already arranged.'

'Tell him the truth,' Philippa said. 'Tell him the man is not so bad as you made out, and that you were only doing it to impress him. My husband is a jealous man, Governor, not a violent one, and anything but a fool. He will respect you more for your honesty than your grovelling. He gets that all the time.'

'If we speak to your husband together...'

'No, I must say nothing. If I speak in favour of the man it will only make it worse.'

The governor examined the spots of blood on his cloth at length before answering in a resigned voice 'I fear I have badly misjudged you, Lady Philippa. I beg your forgiveness for my crude behaviour. My weakness for beauty betrays me. I will not deny my interest.' He squinted up at her. 'I did not realise you were also astute. What you say is true. Hallam is wild, but does not deserve such punishment, and I am more inclined to believe you than your soldier, but I will have to give some punishment or lose respect from the villagers. It will have to be a flogging at least.'

Philippa was almost as taken aback as the governor had been at the sudden change in attitude. But she was not about to let the compliment weaken her resolve. 'No, I gave my word, and I do not believe your people will want him punished either. They will remember your injustice longer than your loss of face. Can you not arrange his escape?'

The governor raised his hands in a gesture of helplessness. 'He is being held on your ship by your own soldiers. What can I possibly do?'

Philippa hesitated. She did not want to push the governor too far and lose what she had already gained. But the scent of victory was in the air, and for Ari to say her word was not her own was the final indignity. She had little else that was her own. All her life she had been treated as a possession. Everything was done for her. She was fed, dressed, protected, and relieved of all responsibility except for the way she looked. She had little joy in her life, and with Ari incapable of siring children, even that pleasure was denied her. She could not go out without a guard following like a dog, visit friends, or even speak to Ari's business associates without being spoken to first, and then only when he was present. She was invariably bored to exhaustion. To overcome it she forced herself to listen and learn, and one of the things she had learned was that she was not stupid. She was constantly told she was beautiful, but the governor calling her astute was the greatest compliment he could have paid her. No one had ever acknowledged she had a brain, and the governor was the last person she would have expected to hear it from. It softened her attitude towards him.

Philippa took the cloth from his hand and dabbed at the bleeding scab. 'You must not pick it,' she advised. 'Wait here while I go and fetch some balsam, and to see if my husband is in need of anything.'

Thankfully, Ari was snoring in his chair. She found the balsam and took the medallion from her clothes chest before returning, slowly, to the stable. She wanted to give the governor ample time to consider his options. And she needed the respite to calm herself. She could hardly believe what she had done. Never before had she spoken to a man of authority in such a manner.

'Have you seen this before, Governor?' she asked, handing him the medallion.

He examined it without interest while she applied the balsam to his head. 'No, I have little experience with trinkets.'

'One of the soldiers took it from the man when they arrested him. 'It is very unusual, don't you think? It has the look of glass but is clear like water.'

'It does have an unusual look, but as I say, I know little of such things.'

'Well I know about them,' Philippa said. 'My husband owns a glass factory. I have never seen anything like this. There could be a good profit in making them. I think Ari would be interested to see it.'

'I don't understand what you are suggesting, my lady. How can that change what is already done?'

'Have you spoken to this man... to ask his side of the story?'

There has not been time.'

'Maybe there is time now, before you speak to my husband. You have heard my side, and that of Parak. Is it not only right that you hear what this man... Hallam... has to say in defence? And when you do...' Philippa continued quickly, not giving the governor time to back out, 'you can ask him about the medallion. My husband can be more easily persuaded to change his mind if there is a profit to be made. When you return it will be best if you see me first, so we can discuss what to do next.'

'And if I do all you ask, Lady Philippa. You will persuade your husband to buy the mine?'

Philippa was thoughtful. In her place, Ari would agree without hesitation, but she did not have his ruthless nature, and there was no point in being dishonest with the governor. He had no choice. He would do it anyway.

'No one can convince my husband to do anything he doesn't want to do, Governor, but I give you my word I will try.' She stepped back to give the governor a disarming smile. 'And you know how strongly I value that now, don't you Governor?'

Hallam could do little in the gloom below the deck of the hollow black ship except think, and he was more inclined towards action than thinking. He would have preferred sleep, but that was made impossible with the constant thumping of bare feet close overhead and, as the day progressed, the suffocating heat.

It was made worse when they closed the single hatch after he had tried to escape through it. He would have succeeded had the guard posted above to prevent such an occurrence not woken at the wrong moment and skulled him with the butt of his spear. The blow adding yet another bruise to those sustained during his fight with the arresting soldiers

The only reprieve from the heat, the bitter tang of copper ore, and the sour sweet stench of sweat and urine impregnated timbers, came from the open oar ports beside the rowing benches. Unfortunately, they were too small to accommodate his body. He sat beside one of them after clearing a space on the bench by shoving a crate of ore off it with his feet. The resulting crash sent a shudder through the boat that resulted in the thumping of feet increasing to stampede proportions, followed immediately by dire threats to his well-being.

From the open port he breathed fresh air tinged with the familiar smoked fish smells of the harbour, and watched the activity on the wharf. Not much seemed to be going on. At irregular intervals more of the ore crates from the governor's mine were carried onto the wharf by men from the village and stacked beside the ship, ready for loading.

Some of the men Hallam knew, and once he called out to one of them. 'Amik! It's me, Hallam! Take a message to my father. Tell him he must see the governor!' But Amik only looked startled at hearing his name called then scurried away. The villagers must have been warned not to speak to him, and Hallam discovered the truth of this a few moments later when the butt of a spear crashed against the port, almost catching his fingers.

It didn't matter anyway. By now everyone would have heard what happened and know where he was, including his father. What they wouldn't know was the truth. The soldier would have lied - as the women must have lied. The truth of their duplicity depressed Hallam more than he wished to admit. He could understand it of the old hag, but not Lady Philippa, against whose pledge he had wagered his life. But he had lost wagers before, and it was commonly known that the word of a Tyrian was not worth the breath it took to give. Still, when he thought of her, it was not with anger.

Hallam counted only five soldiers, not including the ape who was still recovering in the tavern. The majority of the men were sailors, and from what he saw and heard, little friendship was shared between the two groups. It seemed the sailors did all the work while the soldiers did all the joking.

Hallam received his share of their wit at noon when the hatch was opened and a soldier called out invitingly, 'Some cool water for you!'

37

When Hallam went to collect it the pail of water was dumped on his head. 'What a wasteful scum you are!' the soldier laughed. 'You'll be needing that after Captain Parak has peeled off your hide.'

The water was not all wasted. It helped soothe the bruises and bump on his head, and soon after the soldier had left, a small tub scraped against the hull near where Hallam was sitting and a sailor passed a mug of water and a round of bread through the port. 'Compliments of the pilot,' the sailor said. 'And he asks that you please do not drop any more crates, for you may put a hole in the bottom and you will be first to drown.'

Governor Nathan came at dusk.

Hallam was summoned from below and a rope was tied around his ankle while a soldier held him at spear point. 'Jump over the side now, if you wish,' the soldier invited, laughing. The other end of the rope was tied to the rail, leaving enough slack so he could move around freely.

Hallam was not feeling all that well disposed to the governor, whom he didn't particularly like anyway, but he spoke politely as the governor walked him out of earshot of the soldiers. 'I don't know why I have been arrested, Governor. It was all a mistake.'

'It's why I am here... to hear what you have to say.'

Hallam told him from the beginning, and the governor nodded throughout, as if it was what he had expected to hear, so Hallam was surprised when, at the end of his story, the governor said, 'It is not how the soldier tells it.'

'He is lying to save face, Governor. He tried to kill me and I got the best of him. I only acted in defence of myself. The women must also have lied or I would not be here.'

'Speak of them with respect,' the governor said testily.

'I don't mean disrespect, Governor, but the Lady Philippa gave her word that if I helped the soldier I would not be arrested.'

The governor waved his hand impatiently. 'Yes, yes, but it doesn't matter what they say or what I believe. It is Lord Arumah you have to worry about. He believes the soldier and wants you gelded for exposing yourself to his wife.'

Hallam laughed. 'I have been listening to bad jokes all day about what was going to happen to me, Governor, but yours is by far the worst.'

The governor's face remained impassive, and in his uncomfortable silence, Hallam felt as if the blood was slowly draining from his body. Punishment had barely entered his head. He had fully expected to be released once the governor heard the truth of what had happened. It was impossible that he could be gelded for such a trivial matter, which wasn't even his fault. It was beyond understanding. They may as well execute him.

'I see you are taking your situation seriously at last.'

'With respect Governor,' Hallam said grimly. 'This is not Tyre. You are the governor here, not Lord... whatever his name is, so even if I was guilty, how can he order me... punished?' He could not bring himself to say the other word.

The governor nodded. 'Yes, yes, of course, I am the governor, but Lord Arumah is here to buy the mine. It will mean prosperity for the whole village. I don't want to lose the sale because of your stupidity.'

'Hallam laughed scornfully. 'Forgive me, Governor, but I am not interested in copper or prosperity, only my balls. I intend to keep them. Does Lord Arumah not have any of his own?'

'You fool! I am trying to help and all you can do is make jokes! Lord Arumah means what he says. He can do what he likes, and I am in no position to stop him. He could take the village and the mine by force if he wished, including your balls... *and* mine!'

Hallam bit down on the sarcastic retort that sprang automatically to his lips. The governor was usually full of pomp and bluster. He had never heard him talk like this before. 'Then how can you help?'

'Maybe I can't, it depends on Lord Arumah, but we may be able to persuade him to change his mind.' The governor took the medallion from his pouch. 'Tell me about this... what is it made of?'

'It's glass. One of the soldiers stole it from me. How did you get it?'

'Never mind that. If it's glass, why is it clear? Glass is not clear. How is it made?'

Hallam shrugged. 'I don't know. Why... is it important?'

'Where did you get it?'

'It was given to me by my mother. It came from my ancestors in Crete.'

'You don't know how it is made?'

'No.'

The governor screwed his face in disappointment. 'Then I don't know. She thought it would help.'

'She?'

The governor waved aside his question. 'Lord Arumah owns a glass factory in Tyre. If you knew how to make the medallions, we may have been able to persuade him to forego your punishment in return for you going to Tyre and making them for sale.'

Hallam laughed sardonically. 'Hardly a fair exchange, Governor, my balls are worth more than my medallion. But I don't even know how to make a clay jar. That skill belongs to my father and brother. All I know is how to walk in the pit and squash the clay with my feet. His lordship will have to be content with my balls hanging around his painted wife's pretty neck instead.'

The governor's response was both sudden and dramatic. He leaped forward with fists flying and one struck Hallam cleanly on the ear with a force that set his head to clanging. The sheer weight and unexpected ferocity of the governor's attack sent Hallam reeling back until his tethered leg pulled him up and he sprawled on the deck. He rolled swiftly to avoid a kick aimed at his head.

'Ignorant pig!' the governor spat. 'I should kick your stupid head off!'

Alarmed by the scuffle, the two guards ran forward, and Hallam decided it was more prudent to remain lying where he was. He had no intention of responding to the governor's attack. He was more surprised than anything, and also felt a little foolish. He rubbed at his ear and grinned up at the red bloated face of the governor. 'That's a solid fist you have, Governor.'

'I'm warning you,' the governor spluttered. 'If I lose the sale of the mine because of you...'

'Is all well, Governor?' asked one of the soldiers.

'No. Lock the fool up again. 'If he gives any trouble, flog him.'

The soldier grinned at Hallam. 'It will be a pleasure, Governor.'

There had never been a gelding or execution in Lamos. Even floggings were rare. Those deserving of such extreme punishments were either cast out to fend for themselves in the inhospitable mountains - where they usually died of hunger or exposure - or they were dealt with directly by the victims of the crime.

Gelding was a Canaanite and Egyptian penalty. Most of the villagers did not even know what it was, and only the tavern keeper knew how it was done. He explained the procedure to a group of locals in a corner of the tavern where they could not be overheard by the Tyrian sailors.

'There are two methods,' the tavern keeper explained knowledgeably, and the group leaned close to listen attentively. 'You can either cut them off with a sharp knife then seal the wound with hot pitch, or you can use a specially made gelding iron which does both operations at the same time. The iron is similar to the coppersmith's tongs.' The tavern keeper used his fingers to demonstrate the pincer action. 'The tongs have to be very hot though, and you must be careful to spread the man's legs wide or they will get burned as well.'

'Suffering gods!' murmured one of the group in the awed silence that followed. 'And they're going to do that to Hallam?'

'I still don't believe it,' said one of the others. 'Hallam is no rapist, and you only have the word of that Tyrian captain in your bed.'

'And the governor's stable slave who heard the Tyrian merchant promise it,' said another.

'I can understand if Hallam did try to get under her robe. She's a tasty looking piece of meat.'

'Who will be next, I wonder, once the governor has learned how to do this gelding?'

'I've seen you sniffing the air around the governor's daughter, Kethid, maybe it will be you.'

'We should talk to the governor,' someone suggested, and there was a rumble of agreement. Hallam was a wild fool, but he was one of their own.

When the governor left the boat after talking to Hallam, several of the locals confronted him on the wharf and voiced their concern.

'Get out of my way!' the governor snarled at them. 'If he loses his balls it will be his own fault!'

But with the advantage of numbers, and with their courage further bolstered by wine, the governor was unable to shake them off. The group of villagers followed him all the way to his house, asking questions he ignored. By the time he reached his gate the governor was sweating profusely, and not entirely because of the brisk walk. He had also heard several threatening, although anonymous, insults.

Governor Nathan had no soldiers to call on. The men of the village were his strength, and without their support he was nothing. He gave them work, but that was all, and if they refused to work there was nothing he could do except starve along with them. He could not call on the Tyrians for help either, for when they left he would be worse off than before.

The governor turned at his gate to face them. 'All right, men,' he called in a conciliatory tone. 'This is our village and we are all in this together. If Lord Arumah refuses to buy the mine because of what Hallam did, we will all suffer hardship, but if you do not want him punished, so be it. We will starve together.'

'If we suffer because of Hallam,' one of the villagers said. 'We will punish him ourselves. Is that not the way we have always done it?'

'What do you say, Thadus?' the governor asked one of the older men. 'He is your son, you have a right to speak.'

'I stand for him, of course,' Thadus answered. 'He told me what happened, and for all his faults and quick mouth Hallam is not a liar.'

'We'll work harder if we have to, Governor, but no Tyrian pedlar is going to tell us what to do.'

There was a chorus of assent and the governor held up a hand to still it. 'All right men, I will talk to Lord Arumah and do my best for you, as I have always done, but I ask that you keep your own council. We want no trouble with the Tyrians.'

'That we will, Governor, there are too many of them, and we thank you for hearing us.'

Governor Nathan stopped at the horse trough to wash his sweating head before going into the house, giving himself time to gather his thoughts before facing Lady Philippa and her husband. He hoped they had gone to their beds, for he was not in the mood for discussing the matter further. He could do no more than he already had.

Fortunately, the steep climb had been too much for the old merchant and he had retired, but Lady Philippa was talking to the cook in the courtyard kitchen at the back of the house. They fell silent as he stomped in and sat himself at the table. He answered Philippa's silent question with a sigh and shake of the head.

Lady Philippa said nothing. She stood for a while, as if undecided, a thoughtful frown crinkling her brow, then she turned and went into the house.

The cook sliced a large chunk from the succulent roast leg on the spit and placed it on a silver platter already piled with steaming rice cakes and wild spinach. 'I hope you enjoy it, master,' she murmured, 'it is from the sheep killed by Hallam... the man you are going to cruelly torture.' She placed the platter down heavily in front of the governor then bustled away with an eloquent sniff.

Sleeping arrangements were primitive aboard the boats. The men slept on the open deck, placing their sleeping mats on scraps of old sail to protect them from the black pitch that became sticky with heat. The soldiers, who had little authority on the boats, slept in the same manner on the smaller boat. The pilot, a wiry, sea-ravaged man with a sardonic sense of humour and a penchant for sacrificing to his gods, was in charge.

When darkness fell and the sailors set up their mats, the pilot dismissed the soldier guarding Hallam with an airy wave. 'Have no fear,' he reassured the guard. 'We will take good care of him.'

And they did, passing down wine and food and telling him the latest news on his plight. Some had made friends with the locals and it did not take long for word to get around in Lamos. They even knew, almost word for word, what had been said at the governor's gate.

Hallam accepted the contributions gratefully. However, that was not before he had satisfied them, and particularly the deck captain - a man whose size caused even the boat to tremble at his passing - as to what had really happened at the cove, and convinced them his actions toward Lady Philippa had been honourable.

'From what we heard,' the deck captain said, 'we did not think you had tried anything like that or I would have had your sack already cured and filled with my flints.'

'Sounds more like something Parak himself would do,' commented one of the crew. 'Your biggest mistake was that you didn't kill the Cilician pig.'

Hallam learned much from listening to the sailors talk. They were rough in looks as well as in manner and speech, and they came in several colours, but they all had one thing in common. They adored Lady Philippa and disliked Lord Arumah, whom they referred to as 'old copper-bags'.

Hallam listened morosely to their tales of the places they had been, not only in the Great Sea, but also in the Narrow Sea that lay between Egypt and Arabia. It made him aware of how small was his own world. He had never even been to Paphos, which was only at the other end of the island.

It made him feel no better that his mother's family had come from Crete. She had spoken of her heritage often and with pride, and had insisted he learn to read and write script, which she had taught him herself. He remembered her telling him how the Cretans were the greatest sailors and navigators in the world. 'Every boat you see out there,' she had boasted, 'whether it be from Tyre, Sidon, Byblos, or even those of the Sea-People, has a Cretan shipbuilder to thank for its shape and its strength.'

Hallam had never had much interest in boats or the sea. He had sailed with friends who were fishermen, and had enjoyed the sailing well enough, but he found the fishing itself a bore. Hunting was his passion, and occasionally he speared fish with his javelin, which was interesting, but he could not see well enough under water, or stay down long enough to make it really worthwhile.

When the sailors finally went to their sleeping mats, they left Hallam with much on his mind and, despite the wine, he could not sleep. He lay on the rowing bench with his head near the open port where he could see the stars and contemplated his future. It did not look good. That such a thing could be happening to him seemed incredible, and he was still unable to accept the reality of it, so he felt no fear, only a nagging uncertainty. But of one thing he *was* certain. He would not accept gelding. They would have to kill him first.

Even the governor's visit and the talk of the sailors failed to convince him he should be afraid, and he tried to think why that should be. The village was with him, and many of the sailors, and from what they implied - perhaps even Lady Philippa - but he knew they would be powerless to intervene if Lord Arumah insisted, so he should be afraid. He had never thought of the village as a community before, only as the place he lived. It surprised him that the village should give him support and that they were willing to sacrifice prosperity to protect him. He could think of nothing he had done to deserve such loyalty.

It was a humbling experience for Hallam. Too humbling. When he heard the sailors stirring at dawn he called out to one of them and asked to speak to the pilot. When he came, Hallam passed him the medallion. 'I beg a favour, Pilot. I need someone to take this to the governor with a message.'

'What message?'

'To tell him that if it will help and is not too late, I will agree to do what he asked.'

'And what is that?'

'I have no idea, Pilot,' Hallam answered truthfully.

Lord Arumah nodded dubiously as he examined the medallion. 'Interesting, but I doubt it is glass, and even if it is, there will be no market for them. Tyre is already filled with glass trinkets.' He handed the medallion back to the governor. 'However, if he agrees to make them, and also sell himself into slavery for a full year, I will respect the wishes of your people and forego the insult to my wife.'

'Thank you, my lord.' Governor Nathan breathed an inward sigh of relief. He had not mentioned to Lord Arumah that Hallam had agreed to go only if the deal with the mine went through. Such a foolish demand was unthinkable.

'Of course,' Lord Arumah continued. 'If I purchase your mine I will expect your people to exhibit more discipline in future, and work extra hard to make it a success.'

This time the governor could not restrain the smile. 'Of course, my lord. I will insist upon it.'

'Also,' Lord Arumah said. 'They must build a better road to the mine and provide all the labour for building the smelter.'

'I will have them start immediately, my lord.'

'And you must extend your house so there will be sufficient room when I come to inspect progress.'

The governor's smile had weakened under the increasing demands, but he answered promptly. 'I will start on that right away too, my lord. Do you wish to make any further inspections of the mine?'

'No. The pilot tells me we should sail soon and my feet still trouble me. Now will be a good time to sit and record the details of our agreement.'

I t was not until he received the ntews of his reprieve, delivered personally by the governor, that Hallam realised how close to the surface had lurked his fear. His relief was so great he could have kissed not only the governor's feet, but also those of everyone in the village, including the tavern keeper's pig. He vowed he would find some way to repay their support.

He was not sad to leave the village though. The talk of far places by the sailors had sparked a yearning for change, and although he would rather his visit to Tyre had been optional, he was looking forward to seeing the famous city. His father and brother would not miss his reluctant presence in the pottery shed, and he certainly would not miss the unpleasant sensation of clay squishing between his toes. His brother had promised to look after his horse, Piko, in his absence.

Not knowing how to make the glass medallions did not concern him overmuch. He would try, but there were many reasons he could give for failing. It would take time, and hopefully, by then he would have thought of something else. What concerned him more was the governors insistence he remain a prisoner on the boat until it sailed.

'But I have things to do,' Hallam complained. 'I have family and friends to bid farewell, and would like to thank the people of the village. My horse...'

'I will arrange for you to have visitors.'

'Do you not trust me, Governor?'
'No.' Governor Nathan replied.

They sailed with the morning tide. Pilot Meldek stood by the two steering oars with his fist held aloft and the seven crew responsible for the brails - one man to each - watched and waited for the signal to release their ropes and drop the sail. The fishing tubs that had towed the heavy boat clear of the harbour had already moved away and, as the stern of the black boat swung ponderously into the wind, Pilot Meldek lowered his fist.

The freed ropes sped across the surface of the unfurling sail with a sound like that of quills striking across feathers and, like the unfolding of a wing, the sail crackled and billowed to the breeze.

Hallam braced himself against the forestay as the bows thrust into the swell, and watched, fascinated, as the crew scampered about the deck and up the tall mast in response to the pilot's signals.

A smaller crew was going through much the same exercise on the boat carrying the nobles. It was faster than the large boat and followed with a shortened sail, skipping along in Pilot Meldek's wake like a lagging but energetic offspring.

To Hallam's relief all the soldiers travelled on the smaller boat, including the wounded Captain Parak. Hallam had not seen him, but had learned that Parak had since been demoted because of his failure to adequately protect Lady Philippa and her mother. Apparently it was a responsibility the Cilician had retained jealously for himself. The sailors reacted gleefully to his demotion, but Hallam did not share in their enthusiasm. It gave the Cilician one more reason to hate him.

That morning before they sailed was the first time Hallam had seen Lady Philippa since their meeting at the cove. He was talking to his father when he noticed her being helped aboard the smaller boat by two attentive soldiers. She was accompanied by her mother and an old man Hallam automatically assumed was her father until Thadus informed him it was Lord Arumah. Hallam gave him a quizzical look of disbelief, and his father gave him a cynical smile in return. 'Anything is possible if you have enough gold, my son, even that.' Then his father had added his only words of advice. 'It will pay you well to remember you have none.'

She did not see him, and Hallam wondered if she even knew he was on the boat. It seemed unlikely. She would have other things on her mind than one of her doddering old husband's free slaves.

The weather held fair. Other than the occasional adjusting of braces in response to a shift in the wind, there was little to occupy the crew once the sail had been set and trimmed, the cargo secured and the deck cleared. It was a situation the big deck captain was quick to rectify.

'Fifty coppers for the first team up and around!' he called out, and the crew groaned in unison.

'Not that one again, Captain. How about something different for a change.'

'What does up and around mean?' Hallam asked the man beside him.

'It means up the cursed mast, along the twice cursed spar and down the thrice cursed brace,' the sailor answered tiredly. 'I would gladly forfeit my share of the winnings to sit here and watch.'

'On your feet and in your teams!' the deck captain bellowed. 'Too much sitting around will flatten your brains.'

With more groans and protests, the crew formed into two teams of five.

'You'll have to count me out, Captain,' said the last man in one of the lines. 'We have one too many on this team. Mesha has gone over to the king's boat.'

'I'll join that side,' Hallam offered spontaneously. Ten coppers for climbing a pole that looked no more difficult than many of the trees he had climbed in the forest was too good an opportunity.

'That's not fair, Captain, he's not done it before.'

'Always a first time,' the captain replied.' Go last and watch the men,' he said to Hallam. 'The important thing is to swing your legs when you cross the spar. And don't try sliding down the brace. You'll rip the skin off your hands.'

Hallam's team was a full two body lengths behind when it came to his turn. His opponent was already a third of the way up the mast, but the short lengths of rope encircling it at half cubit intervals made it easy. By the time the man reached the spar, Hallam was slapping at his heels.

Already resigned to losing, his team mates began cheering him on enthusiastically, and their encouragement spurred Hallam to even greater efforts, keen to prove his worth and increase his growing circle of friends.

'A share of mine if you beat him, Hallam!'

'And mine!'

'By the gods! He climbs like an ape!'

They started out along the spar at the same time. Hallam's opponent took the starboard side and Hallam the port, facing away from each other so that neither could see the progress of the other. But from the sudden lull in the shouting, Hallam knew he was losing ground. This was different from climbing, and the swaying of the mast - which had been almost unnoticeable from the deck - was so pronounced at this height he could almost believe he was flying.

'Swing, man! Swing your legs and hop!'

Hallam tried, but the movement was awkward, for each time he swung his legs, they collided with the brail ropes angling down to the deck on one side, or caught the billowing sail on the other. On the mast had been the fixed pieces of rope to help with purchase, but on the spar there was no such security. Where the ropes ran over the spar they rolled and slid beneath him, and the spar itself was no thicker than his thigh, making balancing against the movement of the boat difficult.

Until the moment Hallam knew he was losing, his attention had been focused on the area immediately to his front, nothing else had existed, but now he looked ahead to the end of the spar and his spirits sank. It was still a long way. He stopped, twisting around to look back at his opponent. The man was already halfway along.

'Keep going, you fool!'

'Don't look back! Swing your legs!'

'Whatever you say,' Hallam muttered. Gripping firmly onto the spar in front, he swung his legs forward then quickly back, at the same time shifting his weight so both feet landed atop the spar.

Watching from his station at the tiller, Meldek cursed and steadied the boat. 'Don't do it you fool,' he said quietly, 'it's not worth it.'

Unaware of the sudden hush below, Hallam waited, getting his balance against the movement of the boat, timing it. Then, as the boat reached the bottom of the trough, and before it began to lift on the swell, he stood upright and ran along the spar.

'He'll never make it!'

'By Zeus! If he does, I'll kiss his feet! Go, Hallam! Go!

Even the opposing team began screaming their encouragement.

Committed as he was, Hallam knew his only chance of success was to trust his judgement and keep moving. With the motion of the boat, even the smallest hesitation would cause him to lose the rhythm. He held his arms outstretched for balance and picked his stepping places between the brail ropes well ahead, focusing on the narrow lengths of bare timber between and trying to ignore the dizzying distance to the deck.

Then suddenly he was at the end and there was nothing to focus on but the heaving sea far below, and he came near to panic. He caught his balance and turned sideways, preparing to lower himself to the spar, but could not resist a quick glance to see how his opponent was doing.

It was a mistake. The rope he stood on skidded along the spar and he lost his footing. He spun around, attempting to fall towards the brace line at the end of the spar, but he could not quite reach it, and the next moment he was in the air, falling.

Meldek saw Hallam teetering on the end of the spar, saw him lose his fight against balance, and he acted before Hallam fell. He pulled hard on one tiller handle and pushed with equal strength on the other, causing the boat to heel as it entered the turn.

It was only a small movement, but enough to save Hallam's life. He passed so close to the deck rail that the fingers of his out flung hand slapped against it as he passed.

Tucked into a ball, with his face covered, he struck the water shoulders first and plunged deep below the surface.

Stunned, more by the shock of falling than the shock of the impact, Hallam remained tucked into his ball until he was sure he was still alive. It came as a mild surprise to discover he was not even hurt. Through a veil of bubbles he saw the sea around was wonderfully clear. The solid dark bulk of the boat glided overhead, floating in a silver sky, but below his feet was dark and forbidding, full of the unknown. He struck out urgently.

Hallam surfaced a short distance from the stern of the

boat. He gulped air, shook the hair from his eyes, and swam after it, but the boat was moving away faster than he could swim. A line of faces stared at him from the rail. Someone threw a rope, but it fell short, then the deck captain's bellow rang out: 'Haul sail!'

The boat drifted away and Hallam was left bobbing around in the wake, but the king's vessel was close behind. Another line of faces stared down at him, one of them that of Lady Philippa. Her face looked pale without the paint. A purple head cloth concealed her fiery hair.

A rope splashed alongside and Hallam caught hold of it.

'You trying to kill yourself?' the helmsman demanded grumpily as Hallam came aboard.

Hallam grinned sheepishly. 'Sorry, I slipped.'

The helmsman spoke to the sailor who had thrown the rope. 'He'll have to stay. Find him a place and a spare blanket.'

Hallam looked past the helmsman to the group of soldiers standing by the mast. They were turned his way, talking amongst themselves, and Parak, with his arm in a sling, was doing most of the talking. 'No,' Hallam said. 'I thank you for your trouble, but there is no need.' With the sail of his own boat now hauled, the gap between the two vessels had closed to not more than a hundred cubits. He jumped onto the rail and dived over before the helmsman could stop him.

Hallam closed the distance rapidly, mostly underwater, using a powerful sweeping motion of arms and legs. The deck captain threw a rope and several sailors reached down and hauled him aboard.

'You are obviously not injured,' the deck captain growled. 'Though I have a mind to change that by scuffing your ear.'

Hallam grinned. 'Did we win, Captain?'

'No, you fool. You did not finish, so how could you win?'

Hallam held up his grazed knuckles. 'But I touched the rail. Is that not the rule?'

'That's right, Captain! He was first down.'

'We'll argue the rules once you get the boat under way. Get to the ropes, men! And you...,' the deck captain pointed to Hallam, '...can go and help them. And for the sake of the gods at least, try not to fall over the side again or we'll leave you behind.'

The argument over the rules persisted well into the afternoon. It was finally resolved by the pilot.

'Although you can argue that I assisted him by heeling the boat,' Meldek stated. 'If I had not done so, he would have struck the rail anyway, so even though he would be dead, he would have won.'

'Is that a new rule, Pilot?' one of the crew asked.

'No, you dolt. In my opinion you should call it a draw and share the copper.'

Both teams agreed. 'I'd lose ten coppers to see a stunt like that anytime,' said one of the opposing crew.

'And if anyone tries it again,' Meldek warned, scowling at Hallam. 'I will have him bound and soundly thrashed at the mast.'

Philippa watched the contest aboard the large boat with only mild interest. She had seen them several times before, but there was little to occupy her on the boat. Any diversion, no matter how boring, was welcome. Her interest quickened though when she saw a man stand up on the spar. She had never seen anyone do that before.

She was not the only one to notice. 'He must be drunk!' one of the crew called out behind her.

'Who is it, Amos?' asked another.

'A madman.'

Philippa knew who it was as soon as he started to run

forward, even before the crew on the other boat began chanting his name, and her breath caught in her throat. It was the way he stood, poised with arms outstretched, his long hair blowing in the wind. An unexpected fear clutched at her chest and she held her hands to her face. 'No,' she breathed. 'Please, no...'

When he slipped she covered her face and cried out loud. 'No!'

Her cry seemed to silence the boat. No sound but the rustling of water and, for Philippa, the sound of her heart thudding in her ears.

Then after long, agonising moments, came a welcome call. 'He's swimming!'

'Throw a line, we'll pick him up,' the helmsman ordered.

Philippa looked down as he floated alongside, grinning up at them as if nothing had happened, and she felt an unreasonable and resentful anger that she should have felt such fear for him.

'Is that not our new slave?' her husband asked.

Her mother answered. 'Did I not tell you he was a dangerous fool?'

They were still standing at the rail when he dived back into the sea, and Philippa's anger was quickly displaced as her inexplicable fear returned. It was not that long since she had thrown food scraps to the two sharks which had been following the boat. She watched breathlessly until he had been safely hauled aboard, then turned away to see her husband looking at her strangely.

'What is it, Philippa... are you not well?'

She gave him a weak smile. 'It is nothing, husband, only the women's curse.' It had become her favourite excuse.

Meldek was one of only a few pilots with the courage and knowledge to sail not only out of sight of land, but also at night. The knowledge he had acquired from a lifetime of experience, but his courage came from a life devoted to his gods.

Each evening, a small fire was made in the fire tray forward of the mast downwind of the sail. On behalf of all aboard, Meldek spoke his words of appeasement and offered a sacrifice to Baal who, in addition to his many other responsibilities, was also the god of storms. The first night it was a fish, the second, a sizeable portion of the hindquarter Hallam's father had given the pilot in the hope it would dispose him kindly towards his son.

Meldek burned it to cinders while they all stood around shielding the flames and inhaling the delicious aroma. Then the fire was extinguished and they ate their own food cold, for piety dictated that food for mortals could not share the same flame as offerings to the gods.

Coming from a people who did not sacrifice, Hallam hoped Baal appreciated his hot meal. Cold greasy meat and lentil pulp was certainly not one of his own favourites.

On the third morning the horizon ahead showed a discouraging grey. 'The curse of Tyre,' explained one of the sailors. 'Smoke and stench. You'll smell it when we get closer.'

Early in the afternoon the smoke and smell of rotting

molluscs from the dye factories lifted with the freshening sea breeze and Tyre loomed clear and close. The king's boat lowered her sail and skipped ahead, soon losing herself in the melee of other sailing craft that speckled the sea like a swarm of grey butterflies.

As their own boat approached, the deck captain gave the order for the sail to be hauled and they drifted amongst them. A slender galley boat, bristling with oars and looking like a giant water spider, skimmed across the harbour to meet them. A line was passed and the boat towed towards the beach.

Hallam felt as if he were entering another world. A world dominated by a towering wall that appeared to have risen straight from the sea. No land could be seen around it other than a few half submerged rocks, and no city buildings other than the roof of the three-storied palace. High above the roof fluttered the yellow and purple banner of King Khiram.

Seaward of the island city, lying in a great half circle like a protecting reef, were anchored the war galleys. Easily twice the length of their own boat, and with two tiers of galley ports. Their swanlike prows reared up to support the squadron emblems of horse heads, dolphins, hawks and serpents. Fearsome painted eyes glared from the bows. Below them, lurking partly submerged like foraging snouts, were the bronze tipped ramming spikes used for disembowelling enemy ships.

No one had ever told Hallam that Tyre was an island, and he looked upon it, and listened to the sailor's explanations with awe. The narrow seaway between the city and the shore was crowded with boats of every conceivable design, from simple ferry rafts crammed with people, goods and animals, to sleek galleys, gaulos and fishing boats with reed sails. The smoke they had seen from far out at sea came from the coastal plain. From the sprawl of slave compounds, army bivouacs, factories and farms.

It was late in the afternoon when they began offloading. A

seemingly endless line of slaves floated the ore crates ashore on rafts then loaded them onto mule sledges, which delivered them to Lord Arumah's foundries. Meldek and a few sailors remained on board to move the boat at daybreak, and Hallam was to stay with them.

'The glass factory is on the mainland,' Meldek explained. 'But Lord Arumah has ordered me to take you into the city and introduce you to the glassmaker. He has a stall in King Street near the palace.'

'I would much prefer you keep me on as a sailor,' Hallam suggested hopefully. The idea of working in a glass factory was becoming less appealing with each passing moment, and he was beginning to make friends and to enjoy the life of a sailor.

'You may have the makings of a sailor,' Meldek said, 'but you have already been chosen as a glassmaker. Perhaps in a year, once your debt to Lord Arumah has been paid.'

A fire was made on the beach and after a delicious hot meal of smoked fish and barley cakes, a wine-seller was summoned and several skins of wine purchased with the fifty coppers shared by the two teams. The season's vintage was a particularly good one and some mild grumbling ensued when Meldek insisted that a portion from each skin be poured onto the sand in libation.

'Do you sacrifice to mighty Baal only when you have something to fear?' he berated those who protested. 'Or is it your wish to wager your safe return from our next journey against the length of his memory?'

Not accustomed to drinking strong wine, Hallam was reluctant until persuaded by the deck captain. 'It is the only known cure for Tyrian fever,' the captain solemnly informed him. Oblivious to the knowing smiles and elbow digging, Hallam drank his share and was soon cavorting on the sand with the best of them.

Suffering his first hangover - which an unsympathetic

Meldek informed him was, in fact, the Tyrian fever he had been warned against - Hallam accompanied the pilot to the city next morning. He repeated his vow not to drink again as soon as the tub in which they were being rowed lifted on the first small wave. Being as it came from the stomach and not the heart, it is doubtful Baal would have been impressed by the sour libation deposited into the sea. Certainly the helmsman was not. He made Hallam squeeze in behind him and lean over the stern; a station at which he was forced to remain until they arrived at the wharf.

Hallam was surprised to learn that Tyre was not open to the general public. Anyone going in had to have either good reason or good copper to spend. Beggars and sightseers without means were not welcome, and the burly Cilician guards manning the gate ensured they stayed out. Slaves not accompanied by their owners were required to provide identification by means of a small clay token imprinted with their owners mark. Those without letters of authority, tokens, or copper minas to the value of at least one silver minas, were turned away, or, if persistent, simply thrown bodily from the wharf into the sea.

It had not always been so, Meldek explained as they waited in the crush outside the city's only gate. He still remembered the days when all had been welcome in Tyre, if not to buy, then at least to take away the experience to share with others. And there was much to tell, for he himself had shipped in many of the exotic wares that lured the visitors. But the city had become so crowded that restrictions had to be made.

'Even now there are still too many,' Meldek complained. 'If Tyre did not have double walls of stone, I swear it would burst open and spill its guts into the sea.'

They were passed through after Hallam had submitted his bag to a search and surrendered his knife. Unauthorised weapons were also banned in Tyre. Outside had been bad enough. Inside was chaos. Every narrow street squirmed with people. Tiny stalls, some so makeshift as to appear already collapsed, cluttered the street edges and narrow alleyways like flood debris. Goods were displayed like decorations; hanging on lines strung above the narrow streets between poles, on the poles themselves, on the precarious walls and roofs of the stalls, and draped over the arms, shoulders, legs and even the heads of the merchants. Bulkier goods were piled on rugs and reed mats, around which Hallam had to step carefully or suffer abuse - often delivered in a foreign tongue.

King Street was at the far end of the city, and almost deserted by comparison. Along it, with their backs hard against the great wall, stood the three-storied palace and fine stone houses of the nobility. On the opposite side stretched an unbroken row of exclusive stalls, effectively isolating the street from the unseemly clamour of the bazaars.

As if dictated by royal decree, the stalls were almost identical, even to the white colour, and no goods hung from lines or cluttered the street. Double wooden shutters opened onto the street like moving walls to display the wares neatly arranged inside.

Meldek stopped at a stall filled with a dazzling array of coloured glassware. He introduced Hallam to an emaciated Egyptian with cracked brown skin almost indistinguishable from his stained leather apron. The Egyptian looked suspiciously at Hallam as Meldek explained why he was there.

'Show Jabez your medallion,' Meldek instructed.

The glassmaker studied it at length before handing it back and admitting he did not know how it was made.

'Then you have not seen glass such as this before?' Hallam asked.

'Glass? Surely you must be mistaken. No glass has such clarity.'

'It is glass.' Hallam said defensively. 'What else could it

be?'

The glassmaker ignored him, directing his answer to Meldek. 'A stone perhaps, or the clear gum of a tree which has somehow been made hard.' He glanced at Hallam, as if expecting to be contradicted.

'I'm sure you will work it out between you,' Meldek said, impatient to be away. He spoke authoritatively to the glassmaker. 'Lord Arumah will give you further instructions. Meanwhile, you must provide Hallam with a gate token and a place to sleep, and you must teach him what you know of glassmaking.'

After a few moments of surprised hesitation, during which his eyes actually stopped moving, Jabez nodded. 'I will take him to the factory as soon as I have closed the stall.'

After wishing Hallam a pleasant stay, Meldek hurried away and Hallam watched him go with misgivings. He had come to like and admire the pilot.

When he turned to face the glassmaker, Hallam's misgivings were proved well founded. The expression on the Egyptian's cracked face held such undisguised contempt it caused Hallam to stiffen in surprise. Then he smiled pleasantly. Maybe he was mistaken.

But he was not. The bloodshot eyes of the Egyptian told him that clearly, and to emphasise his feelings, Jabez spat on the floor before turning away and pushing through a reed curtain. 'Wait outside!' he called from behind it.

After only ten days in the glass factory Hallam knew from whence came Jabez's bloodshot eyes, and also knew with certainty he would never last the full year.

The glass furnace spewed fiery particles from its domed opening like an erupting volcano. At noon, with the sun beating directly down, the whole area inside the stone walled compound became an oven. Perspiration was sucked away before it could dampen the skin, and eyeballs grated as if the sockets had been filled with sand.

The Egyptian refused to teach him anything: 'You will learn nothing from me,' he told Hallam defiantly. 'Tell Lord Arumah if you wish. I do not care. I will say in return that you are too lazy and stupid.'

And Zabudesha, the ugly, one-eyed and one-eared slave he had to work with treated him like a sworn enemy: 'All Judeans are dogs,' he declared the first time they were alone together, glaring malevolently through his one eye as if issuing a challenge. 'So are their friends and all their gods.'

Their distrust, the poor food, and appalling heat all contributed to Hallam's despondency, but what wore him down most of all was the drudgery. Every long day was the same as the one before, even to the weather, and the nights were as long as the days.

The work had taken a terrible toll on Hallam. Where his dry skin was not scorched from the furnace, it was burned by the sun or freckled with the splatter of molten glass and flying embers. His hair had become as dry as kindling and his eyes raw from dryness and the glare of the white sand stockpiled around the compound.

Only swimming broke the monotony. The sea was brown with filth, but at least it was refreshing, and Hallam swam at the end of each day, floating on his back in company with the discarded rubbish of the city. Lying there, he dreamed of hunting in the mountains of Lamos and planned escapes he knew would never happen. There was nowhere to go. He made no attempt to make the medallions. The rigid routine left no time for experimenting, and the Egyptian's refusal to teach him had given him the perfect excuse.

Unlike Zabudesha, who was required to sleep in one of the slave compounds - which were guarded at night by mercenaries - Hallam, as a free slave, was allowed the dubious privilege of being able to sleep unguarded at the factory. He set up his mattress on the rock wall surrounding it so he could enjoy what little breeze wafted ashore, and he lay naked and sleepless, cursing all those responsible for his being there, including himself.

It was only a year, he kept telling himself, and he had worked with pots and kilns before, but in these conditions he knew he could not last that long – even one more day seemed unlikely. What he didn't know was what he could do about it.

Protected from neck to ankle by a leather apron, his feet and head bound with wet cloths, Hallam signalled the slave pumping the bellows and the wheezing stopped. While water was being poured over the steaming ox hides of the bellows to protect them, Hallam removed the plugs at the base of the furnace and pushed the crucible containing the glass paste out with a pole. He attached a wooden yolk and, together with the slave, carried the crucible across to the moulds and filled them, tamping as they poured to settle the syrupy mixture.

When the last of the moulds had been filled Hallam smoothed over the stiffening paste with a wooden spatula then stripped off his apron. 'That's me for today,' he said. 'I'm going for a swim.'

The slave glared at him through his bloodshot eye. 'Again? But we have not finished the quota.'

'We'll finish it tomorrow.'

'That is what you said yesterday, and Jabez is coming tomorrow. He will expect the blue jars to be ready for the stone polisher.'

Hallam tossed his apron and protecting head cloths irritably into the soaking tub. 'Too bad, I'm going for a swim.'

'You will get us both into trouble.'

'We are already in trouble.'

Zabudesha laughed bitterly. 'What do you know of trouble, a free slave who still has his ear? You know nothing! In one year you will be gone, while I have already been here for seven!'

'You speak as if you are proud of it. Every day I hear you complain and curse the Judeans for taking your country and your ear, but that is all you do. If it were me, I would have gone long ago.'

'Then you would have been dead long ago. A weakling like you would be captured in a day. It is not so easy to escape when you are marked as a slave. Even so, when the time is right, I will return to Edom.'

'You have probably been saying that for the past seven years,' Hallam muttered, retreating from the slave's anger. He had no quarrel with the cantankerous Edomite, and he could ill afford one. Zabudesha was already half mad - probably from the heat - and years of pumping the ox-bladder bellows had given him the strength of the ox.

It was dark by the time Hallam returned from his swim, and the slave had already gone. Before leaving, Zabudesha had transformed the furnace into a kiln for the moulds, plugging the top so the residue of heat was directed through a clay tunnel to a pottery chamber where they could slow bake overnight.

The slave had also taken on the task of unpacking the kiln in the morning, but the next day, in an effort to make amends and speed things up so they could reach their quota, Hallam took on the task for himself. When he opened the kiln he discovered the slave had a small enterprise going. One he was obviously trying to keep secret. Pushed far to the back of the tunnel were a number of small flat disks. They had been glazed and propped upside down, and when Hallam pulled them out and saw what they were, he grinned. The slave had more imagination than he had given him credit for.

When Zabudesha arrived Hallam pointed to the disks arranged neatly on the bench in rows. 'Your gate tokens are ready.'

Zabudesha ignored him, quickly scooping the tokens into a bag.

'I kept one,' Hallam said. 'In case I lost mine.'

'Then you owe me five coppers.'

'I'll try to remember, but is there not a law that says they can only be made in the king's token factory?'

Zabudesha snorted derisively.

'What if you are caught?'.

The slave drew a finger across his throat. With his one eye bloodshot and glaring, and the socket of the other stretched to reveal the raw pink interior, he looked more than capable of cutting a few throats of his own.

'You don't have to worry,' Hallam reassured him. 'I will not tell, but if you are caught, they will assume that I helped.'

'Then you must be careful to see I am not caught.'

Hallam laughed. 'You have a strange way of winning a friend.'

'I have no need of friends, especially foolish ones.'

'But I do,' Hallam persisted. 'I would prefer one less ugly, but I need a friend who will help me convince Jabez to either reduce the quota or return the slave who was here before me. The work is too much for only two men.'

'Jabez will not agree. There has always been two.'

'He will when I have my hands around his neck,' Hallam growled.

'Brave words for one who sold himself for the price of his

balls.'

Hallam's roar of laughter took the slave by surprise. He scowled furiously, as if taking the laugh as an insult, then, when he realised it was genuine, his lips began twitching with the suspicion of a smile. It did not quite develop, but it was enough to encourage Hallam. He thrust forward his hand. 'If not friends, then at least not enemies. We both have enough of those already.'

Zabudesha glared dubiously at the outstretched hand for a moment, then wordlessly clasped it in his own.

After another six days of pushing hard to get ahead of their quota, Hallam was so exhausted he could barely summon the energy to walk the short distance to the beach for his swim. All he wanted was sleep. He had already slept through the night, and now he intended to sleep through his day off.

He returned from his swim to find an old black man waiting for him. 'Are you the glassmaker who is called Hallam?' the man asked.

'Who wants to know?'

'I can speak only if it is you they call Hallam.'

Hallam eyed him curiously. 'Then speak. I am Hallam. Who are you?'

The old man peered hard at him with eyes that were silver glazed with the blind disease. 'A friend wishes to see you in the city.'

Hallam's interest quickened. 'Did he give you a name?'

'He did not give me a name, only that he was a friend.'

'Why does he not come to see me here?' Hallam asked.

The old black man looked puzzled, as if trying to

remember. 'He said that he could not come here, but that I must take you to him.'

'What does he look like... this man?'

The black pointed to his eyes. 'I do not see much.'

Hallam glanced longingly at his mattress on the wall and sighed. 'Wait. I will have to get changed.'

He knew of no one in the city who would want to see him, except perhaps Meldek or one of the sailors, but they would not be so secretive. It could only be someone from home, his brother, or one of his friends, and if so, it was a long way to come without good reason. And good reason could only mean bad news.

The old black acted even more secretively when they reached the crowded gate. 'We must not be seen together,' he cautioned. 'I will go first and wait inside.'

Hallam had not been into the city since the day he arrived. Not for lack of interest, but for lack of time. He kept a sharp lookout for the Cilician guard, Parak. That was one acquaintance he was in no hurry to renew. He did not see the guard, and it suddenly occurred to him that it could be Parak who had sent the black man. He shrugged the thought off. If Parak was going to kill him he would want an audience.

The old man was waiting inside as promised. Hallam followed him through the maze of bazaars with growing enthusiasm. He had promised himself a day in the city and today would be as good a day as any. He still had the silver his father had given him, and perhaps he could take along the friend - whoever he was - to help spend it.

Suddenly Hallam found himself alone. He had looked away for only an instant, distracted by a merchant trying to call attention to his stall, but in that instant the black man had vanished. Hallam looked around in confusion. He was taller than almost everyone around him by at least a head, so he could see a fair distance, but he could see no sign of the old man. With his senses prickling to attention, he walked slowly along the stalls, feigning interest in the displays while his eyes scanned the crowd for anything out of the ordinary.

When he felt an urgent tugging on his breeches Hallam spun quickly, knocking over a black child. The boy scrambled up and ran with robe flapping down a narrow alley between the stalls. He disappeared, only to reappear a few moments later and beckon furiously.

Hallam entered the alley then stopped. He could think of no friend that would go to such mysterious lengths. He turned to retrace his steps, only to be confronted by the broad back of another black man who was blocking the entrance. A huge young man with a shaved head and no neck.

The old man called from behind. 'Come, there is nothing to fear. Kabul is there only to stop anyone entering. Please, your friend is waiting.'

Still wary, but also curious, Hallam allowed himself to be led to a flimsy door of laced poles. The black pushed it open and indicated Hallam should enter. 'You first,' Hallam said.

The child scampered out as he entered, closely followed by a young black woman. The old man also left, partly closing the door and leaving Hallam alone in the small gloomy room with the only other occupant; a figure in a dark robe with a hood that shadowed the face. Pale hands lifted up to throw back the hood and Hallam started with surprise, moving quickly away from the door.

'There is no need to be alarmed. I am alone.'

It was not alarm that quickened Hallam's blood and returned the hollow feeling to his belly. The sweet sound of her voice, her presence, sent the blood racing, singing through his veins. He took a long, deep breath. 'You are the last person I expected to see, Lady Philippa. I was expecting a man... a friend.'

'Yes, forgive me. I had to be careful. I'm pleased that you came. I was afraid you would not.'

'Why, my lady... why are you here?'

'I wanted to apologise... for what happened.'

Hallam smiled cynically, unable to help himself. 'Thank you, my lady, but it is already done and a bit late for changing.'

'You don't understand. I could do nothing. I tried to explain that it was not your fault. I said I had given my word you would not be arrested, but that only made it worse.' Her tone became bitter. 'My husband can be a very difficult man. He does not believe that my word... or the word of any woman has any worth.'

'A wise man, your husband.'

She stood silent for long moments before answering in a voice gone cold. 'You have not changed. I should have known I would be wasting my time.'

All the frustration Hallam felt at his predicament; the long days of hard work and heat, his failure and helplessness at not being able to do anything about it; and his futile infatuation with her, came bubbling to the surface in a froth of self pity.

'No, Lady Philippa, you have not been wasting your time. You wanted to make yourself feel better. Now you can forget all about it and go back to your comfortable life. And the ungrateful slave can go back to his stinking hole!'

Hallam flung open the door and stepped angrily into the alley, pushing aside the terrified young black woman standing outside. He shoved past the bald man at the end of the alley and stormed his way into the crowd.

Philippa sat trembling as Milcah fussed around her. 'He gave me such a fright, mistress! I thought you were harmed. Such a terrible man, and such terrible things he said to you!'

'You were not supposed to be listening, Milcah.'

'I couldn't help it, mistress! And him just a slave too! You should have him whipped!'

'He's not a slave, Milcah.'

'Well he should be, mistress, and he shouldn't speak to you like he was a noble. It isn't right!'

'Did anyone else hear? Your father, or Kabul...'

'No, mistress.'

'You must never repeat what you heard... to anyone. Do you understand?'

'Of course, mistress! You have my word I will say nothing, even to my own dead mother. Do you want to leave now?'

'I hope your word is worth more than mine,' Philippa murmured.

'Mistress?'

'We will leave in a little while, Milcah.' Philippa took a small bag from her pocket and removed a gold disk with the seal of Lord Arumah stamped on one side. 'Take this and go and buy everyone some of that sour sherbet. I would like to be alone for a while.'

'But mistress, it's *gold*!'

Philippa looked at the disk with a puzzled frown, then she remembered. Gold could only be traded in King Street. 'Yes, I forgot.' She replaced it in the bag. 'Never mind, just leave me alone.'

Philippa sat looking distractedly around the gloomy room. Coming had been a mistake. It had not meant to happen like that. Not his anger, and not her own. Especially after spending so many anxious days thinking and planning exactly what she would say. He was right. She should have stayed at home where she belonged. Secure in her comfortable life.

But the thought of it made her thoroughly miserable.

N o more,' Zabudesha stated firmly. 'If you want more, you must do them yourself.'

'I wish you would make up your mind,' Hallam grated. 'First you say I do too little, then you say I do too much.'

'If you hate the Egyptian so much, why do you wish to make him happy by doing more? Maybe it is you who should make up his mind.'

'Why don't you put your head in the furnace.'

'What angers you? Would she not give it freely? If you tell me which of your gods is in control of such matters, I will pray she does so I do not share the blame.'

'You should rather pray for a brain,' Hallam snarled.

Zabby ignored him for the rest of the day. By the end of it, Hallam's mood had simmered down to resignation and he realised he was in danger of losing the only friend he had. And he was sure Zabby would understand if he explained. He must have suffered the same frustration and helplessness during his captivity, and many times had spoken openly of his disdain for privileged nobles.

While Zabby was packing the kiln, Hallam went in search of a roving wine-seller and purchased a skin, then he asked Zabby to share it with him after they had finished for the day.

'It is against the law to drink here,' Zabby said shortly, but his eyebrow had raised up in surprise at seeing the skin and he seemed in no hurry to leave.

'Who will tell?'

'Not me,' Zabby said.

'Then I will drink to a friend, if you will do the same.'

'An angry friend?'

'A foolish one.'

'Who foolishly tries to buy friendship with cheap wine,'

Zabby said, reaching for the skin. 'Tell me of this woman who refused you her favours… if it does not pain you too much, that is.'

'You have the enquiring nose of a hungry dog, Zabby, but a cunning one. It does have something to do with a woman.'

Hallam told Zabby about the old black man's visit and what had transpired thereafter, and Zabby's 'I told you so' smirk gradually changed to open-mouthed astonishment.

'Snivelling gods!' he spluttered. 'Are you mad? And all day you have been crabbing around here like you had the Tyrian fever when you should have been running instead. Maybe I should cut your throat now and save you from a more painful death.'

'I don't think she will report what happened.'

Zabby snorted with derision. 'You don't think? How would you know what nobles think?' He took a long swig and grimaced before passing the skin. 'Especially noble women. Drink now while you are still able to swallow, then you had better tell me more about this black man. I must find him and tell him I had nothing to do with your stupidity.'

'I've never seen him before, but there were others. A black nurse and a big black man with a bald head. I think he was called Kabul?'

'The woodcutter?'

'You know him?'

'He is not from my compound, but he has carried wood here before.'

'I can't see any reason to look for the old black,' Hallam said. 'What's done is done, and if she was going to do anything about it I would have known by now. Anyway, I don't think you have anything to worry about.'

'I worry about all this thinking of yours,' Zabby said. He retrieved the skin to take another long swig before returning it and standing to leave. 'Drink, my foolish friend. I think your need is greater than mine… and even with no brain my thinking is still greater than yours. I will see what I can find out.'

Zabby greeted Hallam next morning with a smirk. 'I can tell by the dullness of your eyes and the stillness of your tongue that you finished the wine.'

Hallam groaned. 'Did you find the black?'

'Of course.'

'Well? What did he say, or is it a secret?'

'Only that I had a fool for a friend, and that she is the reason you still have your balls.'

'I'm in no mood for jokes, Zabby.'

'And with good reason, my friend. For what they are worth, she saved them for you, and if there is a man in Tyre who would not give one of his own for the privilege of having her just think about them, he would be a lesser man than I.'

The lack of humour in his tone caused Hallam to look sharply at Zabby, and the equally serious eye that met his invoked a dawning premonition. 'What do you mean… she saved them?'

'Just what I said. The old man who came here is the father of the young black woman you saw. She's a children's nurse at the palace. I got the feeling there isn't much the blacks wouldn't do for your noble Lady Philippa, including finishing what had been threatened by old copperbags.'

'You haven't answered my question. What do you mean she saved them… what did they say?'

'Nothing much. That Kabul looked like he wanted to have mine as well just for knowing you. I had to stop asking questions for fear he would consider them worth chewing. He didn't look all that fussy to me. Fortunately, my brainless questioning had already told me what I wanted to know.'

'What?'

Zabby smiled craftily. 'The old black refused to talk… that is, until my small brain told me to offer to cut your throat myself. I told him Lady Philippa only had to say the word and I would do it.'

'Oh?'

'You don't have to look so worried. I said that only to feel him out, although there have been times…'

'What did he say, Zabby?'

'Only that he didn't think she would want me to do that after going to so much trouble to save them

. He was disgusted that she should care. It seems she took some sort of risk with the governor in Lamos on your behalf, but he didn't say what it was. I don't think he knew.'

Hallam stared morosely at Zabby, recalling Governor Nathan's solid left hand on his ear after he had made a bad joke about what she could hang around her neck, and he also remembered, with a sudden stab of guilt, the governor's words: "She's trying to help you". He should have listened, instead of trying to be smart. And he should also have listened to what she had been saying in the room, instead of letting anger take control of his tongue. He had the uneasy feeling he had made even more of a fool of himself than he had thought.

'I think I do, Zabby. I have to see her again. Will you ask the old man to pass a message?'

'You want me to help send a message so you can insult her again?' Zabby shook his head and slapped at his mutilated ear. 'I think the loss of my ear has made me half deaf.'

'Not to insult her, to make amends.'

'Even to ask her would be an insult… and dangerous. Better you forget about it and think yourself lucky she has not already sent the Cilician pigs to arrest you.'

'I'm going to see her again whether you help or not,' Hallam said firmly. 'You don't have to be involved, just tell me where to find the old man.'

'You are serious?'

'Never more.'

Zabby lifted his hands in resignation. 'And just when I

was beginning to think you had found a brain of your own.'

It was another three days before the old black man came to see Hallam at the factory, and he was openly hostile, refusing the request outright. Not even a bribe would change his mind, and the only thing that did was a threat.

'If you do not ask your daughter to give Lady Philippa my message,' Hallam warned. 'I will find someone else, and they may not be as trustworthy as your daughter.'

Hallam waited anxiously for the reply, but not as nervously as Zabudesha, who even went to the extent of bribing a child from the slave compound to wait near the factory to warn of the approach of any Cilician guards.

When the old man finally returned four days later with the news she would see him the next day, it was difficult to tell who was the more relieved. But Zabby's relief was tempered with suspicion. 'I wouldn't trust her if I were you,' he cautioned. 'Not after what you did. Nobles think differently to us. It could be a trap.'

Hallam went alone as instructed, following the same procedure as before. The only difference being the role of the child, which the woodcutter, Kabul, filled himself. He showed Hallam into the alley with a scowl that left nothing to the imagination. The young black girl gave him a prettier scowl as she let him in through the door, but the message it conveyed was the same.

Lady Philippa wore the same bulky robe and hood, and did not remove it as she stood waiting for him to speak.

'Thank you for seeing me.' Hallam said. He nearly added, 'I was afraid you would not,' then remembered it was what she had said. He shrugged helplessly instead. 'It is now me who wishes to ask forgiveness.'

'Why?' It was little more than a whisper.

'I was angry. I spoke rudely and have not been able to forgive myself for insulting you.'

'And you are no longer angry?'

Hallam thought carefully before answering. This was no ordinary person facing him. 'I mean no disrespect, Lady Philippa, but yes, I am still angry, but not with you, and it is not my anger I apologise for but my rudeness.'

'You have a right to be angry. I gave my word.'

'Yes, but it was not you fault you were unable to keep it. You tried to help me. I did not know.'

'I'm glad you understand. It is not easy being a woman.'

Hallam smiled. 'Even a beautiful one?' He regretted the slip immediately. It was no time for levity. But she did not seem to take offence.

'Especially that. My life would be much easier if my looks were plain. Maybe then I would be treated as a person instead of an object.'

Hallam was struck by the truth of her words. He had thought of her like that himself. Not as a person, only as a beautiful woman; a painting of a goddess on a vase. He excused his guilt though, for he had never had the opportunity to know her as a person. Talking to her was easier with the hood covering her distracting looks. He was beginning to like the person behind them.

'Lady Philippa. Maybe you will think me a... well...' Hallam smiled to soften his presumption, '... an ignorant oaf, but I am hoping you will not take offence if I were to do what you say and speak plainly and truthfully to you... to treat you like a person and not like a noble.'

He could not see her smile, but it was in her voice when she answered. 'Is that a way of asking if it's all right to insult me again?'

Hallam laughed, delighted she had wit as well as beauty. 'No, of course not.'

'Then how can I take offence at my own words? But in return you must allow me to do the same.'

'You? But you are a noble, you can say what you please.'

'No, you are wrong, Master Hallam, I cannot say what I

please. I am not treated as an individual, even by my husband or those who say they are my friends. I cannot be Philippa, the woman, only Lady Philippa, wife of Lord Arumah and niece of the king.'

She became gradually more agitated as she talked, and Hallam watched her moving about in consternation, hoping her anger would not extend to include him.

'In many ways, Master Hallam, I am no less a free slave than you. It may be a comfortable life, but it is not always a pleasant one. In fact, I hate it!' She stopped and her tone softened. 'Forgive me. I say things I should not.'

'I feel honoured that you do, my lady,' Hallam said with sincerity.

'Will you not call me Philippa, the woman, and not Lady Philippa, the noble?'

'I would much prefer Philippa, my friend.' And this time Hallam saw the gleam of the smile he had been waiting for.

'You have an unusual way with words, Master Hallam. 'I had first taken you for a rude peasant, yet you do not talk like one. I have met few noblemen who speak as well.'

'You must blame my mother. She took me by the ear and taught me to read and write the script.'

'I wish I had a mother as wise. Will you share a mug of sherbet with me, Friend Hallam?'

'I never refuse a drink from a friend, Philippa, but it is difficult to drink with a friend you cannot see.'

She removed the hood and shook her hair free. Even in the semi-dark of the room it shone like burnished copper. Her face was clean of paint, and Hallam smiled his approval. She was even more beautiful than he remembered. About to tell her how well she looked, he suddenly remembered his new role and changed course. Instead, he feigned a great sigh of resignation, then nodded sagely. 'Yes, I can see now why you would want to hide such an unfortunate face.'

She laughed. Music that sent a shiver of pleasure through

Hallam.

'Now you mock me.' She said.

'Yes, but only to hear you laugh.'

'Your hair is shorter than before,' she said. 'It suits you well.'

'I had to cut it. There was danger of it catching on fire.'

They sat a reed mat on the floor, Philippa sipping her sherbet with studied delicacy, Hallam with frowning concentration, unsure in this novel, and as yet untested truce.

'Why don't you tell me about your life,' Hallam suggested, forestalling the chance of the silence lengthening into distance. 'Tell me as you would a friend, and I will tell you about mine. Is that not what friends do?'

They talked well into the afternoon, with only the occasional intrusion of the black girl, Milcah, who brought them a bowl of sweetmeats and passed anxious looks through the open doorway.

In the beginning they spoke only of mundane things. Hallam told her of the peculiar habits of his horse, Piko, making the accounts funny so he could hear the music of her laughter, and she told of her first experience with riding. She showed him the thin scar on her forearm from when she had fallen, and he touched it cautiously, tenderly, as if it were still raw and painful.

At Hallam's insistence she told him briefly what had transpired with Governor Nathan and how she had managed to persuade him to talk to her husband, and Hallam's respect for her grew. And so did his guilt. 'I wish the governor had told me,' he said, 'but more than that I wish I had held my foolish tongue. My apology comes with a thousand others.'

She answered with a shrug and a self-conscious smile. 'I don't know where I found the courage.'

Then as the day progressed their conversation became more intimate, each unconsciously probing deeper, and the short silences were no longer empty. Neither were the looks that passed between them. Looks that were filled with expression that could not be voiced. It was too soon for that, and their friendship too fragile a thing to risk destroying with clumsy words.

When the black girl interrupted for the third time to warn Philippa it was time to leave, Hallam took her hand and helped her up. He continued to hold it as he asked the question he had been putting off. 'So, do we meet again, Friend?'

Philippa made no attempt to remove her hand. 'You said you had not yet seen the city. I can show you.'

Her suggestion startled Hallam. 'Will that not be dangerous?'

'Was it not dangerous to run on the spar of the boat?'

'That was different. And look what happened.'

'I know the city well, we will not go where there is risk.'

'I can think of nothing I would like more, but I cannot afford to lose any friends.'

She squeezed his hand before reclaiming her own. 'I will disguise myself well.'

Zabby's single eye bulged partly from its socket as he fixed it on Hallam. 'That is the most stupid idea I ever heard. Your madness spreads even more quickly than the red spot disease. I have caught it, and now her. Only a mad person would suggest such a thing!'

'She said there will be no risk.'

'The city is full of spies who will betray you for the price of a jug! It is bad enough you met her in the slave's hovel, but to walk around the streets is begging to be executed!'

'You're envious.' Hallam replied lightly, but Zabby's

words only echoed what he had been thinking himself. It *was* madness, but it would also be madness not to see her. 'Anyway,' he added. 'She will be well disguised.'

'Good idea,' Zabby sneered. 'You can punch her in the face until her eyes are black and her nose is flattened. Then you can pull out all her hair. Don't you know what will happen if you are caught? She will be strangled, and you will be spiked outside the gate for the children to play with. You will not believe the things that amuse them.'

Zabby's words, and his own sobering thoughts, almost convinced Hallam he should cancel their meeting, but the undercurrent of excitement they had shared - the nervous expectancy that had filled the space between them with promise - far outweighed the peril of their situation for Hallam. He worried instead that she would change her mind.

But it was still there. Even more so, and Hallam knew she felt it too. It showed in the shortness of her breath and the trembling of her fingers as she tried to knot a head cloth around her hair before covering it again with the hood. He tied it for her. 'If there is risk we should not go. We can talk here.'

She shook her head. 'No, I would like to show you.'

Hallam produced a piece of charcoal brought from the furnace. 'Close your eyes,' he ordered. He darkened her light eyebrows and gently put charcoal onto her lids and sockets, then he darkened the hollow below her fine cheek bones and above her chin. He licked his thumb and smudged the charcoal to an even finish. 'No peasant would dare venture out without a hairy lip,' he said.

'No!'

'Yes... hold still... There! What do you think, Milcah?'

Milcah giggled. 'Oh, mistress! You look terrible!'

'Thank you, Milcah.'

'Hands and feet next,' Hallam said.

'Them too? I wore my oldest sandals...'

'Master Hallam is right, mistress. Your skin is too clean. I will have water ready for washing when you come back.'

The black girl's attitude towards Hallam had changed dramatically since their first meeting. Aware that her co-operation and loyalty was vital, Hallam had gone out of his way to win her over.

'You be careful, master and mistress,' Milcah cautioned them. 'Kabul will be close if there is trouble, but remember not to talk to no one, mistress... except master Hallam, of course.'

Parak scrutinised the grubby document before him and cursed the day he had learned to read. Because of it, and since his demotion, he had been assigned to the gate, which meant sitting in the gate master's booth day after day checking entry credentials. It was even worse than checking gate tokens. At least with that you could walk around and have the other guards to talk to, and when boredom struck, the pleasant diversion of searching the women was always available. In the gate master's booth all you could do was listen to the stupid excuses of thieving merchants - like the one now standing before him.

Parak tossed the document contemptuously back at the merchant. 'What did you do... wipe your backside with it? Take it away. It is impossible to read and has no mark of a noble.'

'But Gate master, you must let me in! I have travelled many days to be here! If I do not return with the oil I will not be able to trade for the wine. It is all explained in this document.'

'Must we make special rules only for you? Copper to

the value of at least one silver minas, a gate token, or a proper document with the mark of a noble, such as these.' Parak waved his hand over the scattered array of papyrus documents and clay tablets littering his table. 'You have no copper so you stay out. We have too many beggars and thieves already. Now go, others are waiting.'

The merchant clutched at his head in despair. 'I used all my copper for food and passage on the caravan, and the oil is already paid for. If I do not return with it I will be ruined.'

'You will be ruined if you do not go away,' Parak growled ominously.

'No, I cannot go... please, I beg you!'

Parak called one of the guards and they dragged the protesting merchant through the crowd to the end of the wharf and pushed him over. They stood for a while, watching as he floundered in his heavy robes towards the rocks and safety. 'One of the lucky ones,' Parak said with a grin.

The next man waiting to see him was even more disreputable looking, but he had the right credentials. 'He went in,' the man told Parak. 'Only a short time before you came on duty.'

'You followed him again like I instructed?'

'Yes, captain. He went to the same place as before. He was still there when I left to come here.'

Parak smiled. So he had been right to have him followed. He knew a fool like that would not be able to keep out of trouble for long. It would be interesting to find out what he was up to. 'What about the woodcutter?'

'He was there too, captain, like before.'

'And the black girl?'

'She also, but I did not see the old man.'

Parak was thoughtful. Why would he go to the same place three times and nowhere else? And why would the woodcutter be stopping anyone from going into the alley if there was nothing suspicious going on? 'Did you see anyone else?'

'No captain.'

'Go back,' Parak ordered. 'When he leaves, don't follow him. Stay and keep watch.

In the centre of the city was an open square surrounding the temple of Ashtoreth. It was crowded with live merchandise; slaves of all colours, shaggy Togarman horses much like Hallam's own, goats, chickens and, on the temple steps, lambs, first born calves, and thigh bones of oxen, all of which could be bought for sacrifice. Camels and other large animals, Philippa informed Hallam, could be purchased on the mainland. She also told him the temple was frequented by nobles and guards so it would be best if they did not venture in.

In the bazaars she showed him bronze vessels from Meshech, purple garnets, brocade, fine linen, red jasper and black coral from Edom. From Minnith came balsam, from Damascus and Izalia sweet wine, and from Dedan, woollen saddlecloths that Hallam fingered with especial interest. There seemed no end to it, and her knowledge left Hallam breathless with admiration.

He held her hand, ostensibly as a precaution against being separated in the crush, but in reality to feel her touch, and he was acutely aware of every slight twitch of her fingers. When she spoke he put his ear close, not so much to prevent her from raising her voice, as to feel on his cheek the delicious warmth of her almond scented breath. The reality of her being there was almost impossible to accept, and more than once he found himself staring to convince himself it was really her.

She had an irresistible habit of rolling her eyes to express her feelings, conveying instant messages of surprise, disbelief, disgust or pleasure, and Hallam soon found himself emulating her.

Before starting out, Philippa had pressed two silver minas into his palm. 'Spend it on whatever you wish,' she said. 'And I have many more if you need them.' But Hallam had refused. He had silver of his own to spend, and he did not like the idea of Lord Arumah financing their day out. He wanted no reminder of her husband. For this day at least, he wanted her all to himself.

But they spent little, content to simply immerse themselves in the novelty and excitement of their forbidden wanderings. She bought him a strip of purple cloth to replace his plain headband, and he bought tasty delicacies, which he insisted on feeding to her so she did not have to expose her hands; inserting them between her parted lips to feel their softness before licking his fingers for their imagined taste.

As they made their way slowly back to the room in the alley, Hallam became increasingly more nervous. Not for fear of being discovered - that had diminished soon after they had started out - but because of the small intimacies they had shared throughout the day. It had been building towards only one thing, as far as he was concerned, and that was the kiss he intended bestowing on those delicious lips.

Milcah had a bowl of water waiting and, after Philippa had removed the hood and washed her face, he washed her feet, taking much longer than was necessary, caressing, and remembering the last time he had studied them. Then suddenly it was all done.

'I'll see if everything is all right outside for leaving,' Milcah said, and Hallam could have kissed her as well.

'I must see you again,' Hallam said when Milcah had gone. She nodded rapidly, seeming in a hurry. 'I will send a message.'

He could think of nothing to do but reach for her, and she came freely and quickly into his arms. Her kiss was woefully inexpert. She pressed her closed lips hard against his, and he coaxed them open gently until he could feel the sleek warmth of her tongue, and she shuddered against him.

'Oh, Hallam... this has been such a happy day.' She smiled up at him, flushed and breathless, and he kissed her again, holding her close and hard, and all too briefly. He could not bring himself to speak in return.

'We should go now, mistress,' Milcah called softly, and Hallam let her go reluctantly. She paused in the doorway to give him one final, radiant smile, then she replaced her hood and stepped into the alley.

Philippa had planned in advance what would be her excuse in the unlikely event they were discovered. Depending on whether they were coming or going from the room, she would say she was either going to, or returning from, the temple. The disguise, she would say, was to prevent being troubled by beggars, and the presence of Milcah and her cousin Kabul was a precaution against being accosted by men or thieves. As an added safeguard, she had gone to the temple to pray before meeting Hallam, giving the priest a piece of silver in lieu of a sacrifice so he would be sure to remember. Not even Ari would dare question her right to pray to Ashtoreth.

But the need for caution had gone now that she and Milcah were alone. They took the shortest route back to King Street, Kabul walking slightly ahead, using his intimidating bulk to clear a path, and Philippa could barely restrain herself from stepping on his heels so great was her excitement. She would have preferred to run, so as to keep pace with her racing heart.

'I can't believe he actually *kissed* me, Milcah! Did you see? Oh, what a day it has been! He made me laugh so much I was afraid my face would get all streaked, and he wouldn't allow me to do *anything* for myself! He even fed me!'

'I saw, mistress, I saw, and I think he's a very nice man, but you must be careful. It is very dangerous what you are doing. I fear for you.'

Philippa sobered instantly at Milcah's words. Her joy had been so great she had forgotten for a moment who she really was. 'I will, Milcah, thank you.' It did not lessen her happiness though, and her racing heart skipped along lightly, refusing to slow down.

A sudden commotion behind made them turn. A man had fallen to the ground and lay writhing and choking. Another man was stooped over him, apparently trying to help. 'Stand back!' the man warned the curious onlookers. 'He has been struck by demons!'

The crowd of onlookers moved hastily back from the stricken man. It did indeed look as if he had been struck by demons. His eyes bulged red, and he clutched at his throat, making horrible rasping sounds.

'Call a priest,' someone suggested, and the man who had warned them detached himself from the crowd, going towards the temple.

Milcah tugged urgently at Philippa's sleeve. 'Come, mistress, we should leave.'

Hallam felt the blood leaving his face. 'Suffering gods, Zabby, I owe you my life.'

'Two lives,' Zabby corrected.

'How did you know they were being followed?'

'Because I was looking for someone to do just that. I saw him as soon as we returned to the alley. He was so obvious, I nearly...'

'We? You mean you were following us too?'

Zabby shrugged. 'I had nothing better to do. Anyway, it was worth it just to see you making a fool of yourself. Hovering over her like a mother bird, and even *feeding* her like one. I almost gave myself away laughing.'

Hallam grinned sheepishly. 'I even gave her a few pecks on the mouth, what do you think about that!'

'I think you're mad. I also think you're both going to end up dead, and maybe you will think so too when I tell you what happened after I had stopped the man. I waited until...'

'You didn't kill him did you?'

'You think I'm also mad? And if you let me finish, I'll tell you. I gave him a punch in the gut and a jab in the throat, that's all, and I thought those dumb women were going to wait around until he recovered enough to follow them again. I waited out of sight until the man recovered, then I followed him. Guess where he went?'

Hallam stared at Zabby.

'He went straight to the gate, and who do you think he saw there?'

'Is this some kind of a game? Get on with it Zabby, it's important. Who did he see there?'

'Your good friend, Captain Parak.'

Hallam gritted his teeth. 'I should have left the swine to die. Do you think he knows?'

'I don't think so. He was angry with the man and sent him away. He was only there for a short while.'

Hallam lowered his head into his hands. 'I can't believe I

was so selfish that I allowed her to risk her life.'

'Did I not tell you the city was full of spies?'

'I don't know how I can ever repay such a debt.'

'You rate yourself too highly, my friend. I did it for me, not you. If you remember it was me who was asking the questions. If you were caught it would have been my life as well.'

'I don't care what you say, Zabby. I owe you our lives, and as the gods are my witness, one day I will find a way to repay you.'

'You had first better find a way of telling her it is finished,' Zabby replied, 'or those same gods will get drunk on your blood.'

'I can't Zabby, I love her. How can I tell her that?'

'Because you love her,' Zabby said, and for that Hallam could find no answer.

The annual festival of Ethanim celebrated the reaping of the barley harvest and marked the end of summer. All who worked and lived in Tyre were expected to attend the celebrations, and listen to the speeches of the priests and city elders. Commercial activity was suspended. Stalls were closed and the temple square and surrounding streets cleared to accommodate the influx of people from the mainland.

For Hallam, the festival meant two days of welcome relief from the monotony of the furnace, and maybe a chance to see Philippa, even if it was from a distance. At Zabby's suggestion he had sent a message to her via Milcah and the woodcutter, Kabul, telling her of the danger, and that it would be best if they didn't see each other, but he had received no message in return, and he worried that she had misunderstood. He tried to forget her, throwing himself into work, but as tired as he was, the nights were sleepless and long.

Slaves were not included in the celebrations of Ethanim, but could attend if they wished, and Hallam persuaded Zabby to go with him.

'I have better things to do than listen to the blabbering of god grovelling whore masters,' Zabby declared. 'To dull my senses it will cost you a jar of barley wine. For two I may even hold your hand and feed you tasty morsels.'

Hallam accepted gratefully, but wary of Zabby's cunning powers of persuasion, he left the bulk of his remaining silver and copper hidden at the factory. Despite a steady demand for his black market tokens, Zabby never had copper to spare, and Hallam suspected it was because he bartered it in the slave compounds for black market wine.

'I thought slaves were not permitted to drink.'

'Who will tell?'

'Not me,' Hallam assured him.

It was in the temple square that Hallam saw Philippa for the first time since their tour of the city. Her hair made her stand out like a flower in a field of weeds.

At Hallam's insistence, and against his better judgement, Zabby had found them a place near the front and he could see her clearly not ten paces away. She stood in a group of noblewomen at the base of the steps, separated from the crowd by a line of Cilician guards. The city elders, including Lord Arumah, stood at the top, flanking King Khiram.

Hallam had not seen the king before but he paid him scant attention, noticing only that he was shorter than anyone else in the group and had a fringe of red hair encircling a bald head. A priest was giving a speech about the harvest and what was expected by way of sacrifice. Hallam was not paying any attention to him either.

She wore a robe of plain white trimmed in the yellow

and purple colours of the King, her face fresh looking and unblemished by paint. She turned his way to whisper something to her mother, and Hallam ducked quickly out of view behind the broad shoulders of Zabby.

He did not want her to see him. And now he wished that he had not seen her either. It was like the painful reopening of a healing wound. He yearned to speak to her one more time, to tell her how much he loved her, and how much it had cost him to stay away, but he knew that just one of her smiles could be the death of them both. He would never find the strength to stay away a second time. They could never be lovers. They could not even be friends. She was one of the elite, isolated and protected, while he was only one of the sweating crowd. He did not want her to see him like that. He pulled Zabby farther back into the crowd.

'Forget her,' Zabby said, removing the skin of wine from within the folds of his tattered robe and slipping it under Hallam's tunic. 'Hold it under your arm and squeeze. Don't forget to suck at the same time. It is guaranteed to dull the heads of even mad people.'

Remembering his last experience with Tyrian wine, Hallam took a cautious sip and shuddered at the sour taste. 'It needs more honey.'

'Pure camel piss, but it's all they have... drink slowly, it also has the kick of a camel.'

The taste improved after the first few sips and the warmth it left helped fill the hollow. Zabby was right, he had to forget her, and he should not feel guilty. He had done what was best for them both. It was only a dream. She was as unobtainable as Astarte herself.

In the heat of the day it was not long before Hallam was seeing two priests on the steps instead of one. Both were saying the same thing.

'Washeshay Shabby?'

Zabby looked at him in alarm. 'Already? I told you to

drink slowly. Give me the skin. If you get drunk here the guards will arrest you, and with your friend Parak in charge, who do you think will be gaining the most pleasure?'

Hallam's protests were ignored. Zabby stubbornly refused to give him another drink until all the speeches were over. By then Hallam's senses had settled to a pleasant glow that Zabby was able to maintain by judicious rationing.

Philippa left with the rest of the King's party, but it did not bother Hallam. Other women were more available, and suddenly he was in the mood. He could not remember being more in the mood than he was right now, and what better way to forget?

''What happens, Shab... Zabby, if you are not a believer? Spear doesn't fall off at the firsht change of moon, does it? All lies, isn't it?'

Zabby frowned at Hallam in bewilderment. 'What?'

Hallam swayed forward and put a hand on Zabby's shoulder. 'Come with me, Zabby, we'll get drunk and go together.'

'We're already drunk.. go where?'

'Red door. I'll pay... how much it cost?'

'One ear slaves are not permitted to use the temple whores.'

'Sorry, I forgot you were a slave. You don't look like a slave to me, Shabby. You look more like a friend. A good friend, Shabby, one of the best friends I ever had.' Hallam removed the pouch from his belt and emptied the coppers on the dusty ground between his feet. He kneeled to slowly divide them into separate piles. 'I only have er...'

'Twenty eight.' Zabby said.

Twenty eight.' Hallam echoed.

Frowning, Zabby did some rough calculating. The price of wine played a vital role in the process. 'Ten is the least they will take,' he stated positively. He separated them and scooped up the remainder before Hallam could object. 'When you are done you will be in need of more camel piss.'

The red door was doing a brisk trade, but the queue moved steadily. Hallam did not have to wait too long - which was as well, for he was beginning to have second thoughts. He gave Zabby a final weak grin then stumbled through the door.

'Ten coppers,' he said boldly to the priest inside, reciting what he had been told. 'And may the Goddessh Ashtoresh accept my ah... seed and bring it to harvest so... so...' Hallam faltered, forgetting what came next. He glanced anxiously at the priest.

'So the fruit may in turn...' the priest prompted.

'So the fruit may in turn...'

'Be sacrificed...'

'Be sacrificed...'

The priest gave a sigh of resignation. 'For the fruitfulness of her people.' He pointed to yet another queue - the shortest of several in the open courtyard. 'Put the coppers in the bag and wait there.'

Smiling stiffly, Hallam joined the end of the queue and stared at the dirty neck of the man in front of him. He had a strange feeling that he was waiting in line to be executed.

As each man emerged from the door - either foolishly grinning or self-consciously frowning - Hallam's mouth became drier. By the time he reached the front he would gladly have given his place for a single mouthful of wine. But it was too late. The door opened and the man behind nudged him forward.

Another priest led him past a row of screened cubicles from which emanated a startling variety of sounds. The priest stopped at a partly drawn reed curtain. 'You must not take longer than necessary,' the priest cautioned. Pulling aside the curtain the priest directed Hallam in.

A mattress on the floor, a stool, and the prostitute herself all but filled the tiny cubicle. She was old, fat, and naked, and stood with one foot lifted on the stool as she applied a thick yellow substance to her genitals. She glanced up as the curtain was drawn, the hand with its yellow glob pausing briefly on its journey while she took in her latest customer. It was the only acknowledgment she gave of his presence. She applied the yellow substance, lowered her foot, and wiped the residue from her fingers across a quivering buttock.

'Front or back?' she enquired blandly.

Hallam could only gape in astonishment. The sight of so much naked female flesh, displayed in such a candid manner filled him with dismay. It was not at all what he had expected. Pendulous breasts sagged into the folds of a bulging stomach, and coarse black hair sprouted from every junction of limb and torso.

When no answer came, she turned her back and lowered herself to kneel on the mattress. Grunting with the effort, she spread her legs then collapsed heavily onto her forearms, presenting him with the twin mountains of her buttocks and a deep valley of tangled forest. Stringy globs of cream, like venomous yellow vines, clung to the foliage. A hand appeared from between the legs to part the forest and reveal the orchid nestled deep within the undergrowth.

'You must be quick.' she wheezed.

Hallam could only stare.

When nothing appeared to be happening, she clambered awkwardly back to her hands and knees and turned to face him. 'You cannot expect a virgin for ten coppers.' she said, beckoning him forward.

Hallam fought his way through the reed curtain and escaped into the passage without looking back.

Zabby was sitting on the ground beside the red door. 'It seems to have taken much strength to bloody your spear,' he leered when Hallam came stumbling towards him. 'I trust you left her mortally wounded?'

'Give me the wine, I need a drink.'

'Did I not tell you? But sadly, it is finished. I think much of it must have spilled....'

'We'll get more. God's grief, Zabby! You don't know how much I need it!'

But the wine failed to come up to expectations. Hallam stopped drinking and followed Zabby around in a state of befuddled despondency. The acrobats and conjurers failed to amuse.

When the drum started beating to announce the return of the king to the temple, Hallam thought his head must be exploding. He summoned up sufficient interest to search the royal gathering for Philippa, but was unable to focus clearly enough to make out the features of anyone not stationary or standing immediately in front.

King Khiram had a booming voice that reminded Hallam of Governor Nathan. His mind turned away drowsily from the speech. He began sagging lower until a murmur running through the crowd and a sharp nudge from Zabby jerked him upright. He leaned heavily against Zabby, squinting hard to see what was happening.

Four prisoners were being led onto the steps; three men and a woman. The hands of the men were tied and they were linked to each other by a rope around their necks. The woman was pushed forward separately.

'Criminals to be executed.' Zabudesha explained.

King Khiram called out the charges in short bursts. The council of elders, he reported, had found the prisoners guilty of serious crimes. Two Assyrian spies had been captured and would be spiked outside the gate to warn others. The third man, a one-ear slave, had attempted to murder his owner, a prominent bread maker, after being caught in the act of copulating with the bread maker's wife. He would be strung in the square and the wife given over to the priests to be used as a prostitute. A condition was added. She would be available to one-ear slaves only, and no more than the price of one round of bread would be charged for the service. The punishments were to be carried out immediately.

A priest went forward and stripped away the woman's clothing. Naked and wailing, she was exposed to the jeering crowd, then taken into the temple. The same treatment was given the men. They were stripped and dragged away by the guards. The crowd started moving. Some pushed towards the gate, others towards the tall pole in the centre of the square, and still others - all one-ear slaves - stampeded to the rear of the temple.

'For the lend of a copper I will repay you with two.' Zabudesha said, holding out his hand.

Hallam was aghast. 'You would have that poor woman?'

'I will not be alone, and unlike some...' he glared accusingly at Hallam. 'My spear remains sharp and thirsty.' He wriggled his fingers impatiently.

Unable to refuse, Hallam grudgingly gave him the copper and Zabudesha hurried away.

Hallam watched the stringing of the slave from the fringe of the crowd with the same morbid detachment he had watched the acrobats. A rope was attached to the cord binding the slave's arms and he was hauled to the top of a tall pole, doubled over and screaming abuse. The rope was released and the slave fell freely until the end of the slack, when he was jerked to a stop. Against the weight of his body his arms were wrenched backwards above his head, dislocating both shoulders. The screams of abuse changed to shrieks of agony.

On the second drop the bones were torn completely free of the sockets with a sound like the crackling of twigs. After the third he was left to hang, sobbing in great gulps and writhing feebly halfway up the pole, supported only by his grotesquely stretched muscles and tendons.

'He does not look to have the strength of the last one.' Hallam heard someone say. 'In this heat I wager one day at the most.'

Loud cheers were coming from the direction of the gate

where the Assyrian spies had been taken, but Hallam did not follow the crowd. He found a vacant spot against the wall of a building, and it was there Zabby found him, asleep with his head on the empty wine skin. Zabby pulled it from under his head to wake him.

'I was too late, ' Zabby growled. He drank the last few dregs of wine and grimaced. 'Here is your copper. Add three more and we can fill the skin.'

The drum began to beat again at nightfall and the crowd gathered to witness the final and most important event of the festival; the sacrificial offerings.

Two bronze sacrificial braziers, each as wide across as the length of a tall man, burned fiercely on the temple portico, their flames bringing to life the stone alter of the goddess Ashtoreth that had been placed between them. The High Priest, now wearing the conical white headdress of the sacrificial functionary, gave another speech, praising the goddess. It ended with ominous overtones.

'As we raise our hands in gratitude, so must we also lower ourselves and plead for the acceptance of our meagre tally in return. For through us, great Baal has sent a message...'

A ripple of unease passed through the crowd. Messages relayed from all powerful Baal through the medium of the priests were seldom benign in the matter of sacrifice.

'...The red spot disease that took many of our new-born infants in the month of Abib was not the making of beloved Ashtoreth, but that of the Philistine god, Dagon who wishes to prove to our goddess the unworthiness of us, her people. Such a test must not go unchallenged.'

The High Priest raised his arms. 'Hear us, Ashtoreth! Hear what bounty will be given by your people to show their gratitude and worth.'

'Hear us!' the crowd responded, and for the next hour listened with increasing restlessness as the priest told them what he expected in the way of sacrifice - over and above the sixty one infants who had survived the disease. Offerings as modest as eggs and chickens from the poor, and ending with one hecatomb of first born calves promised by the king.

'Praise the king!' the crowd shouted with more enthusiasm. It was a generous sacrifice, and would go a long way towards appeasing the goddess. 'May our king live forever!'.

The Prostitutes with their infants had been assembled inside the temple. At a double beat of the drum the infants were carried out one at a time and delivered to the attending priests. The swaddling cloth was removed, and the naked child calmed with an opiate given by the high priest before being presented aloft. It was the cue for the gathering to prostrate themselves.

'Hear us, Ashtoreth! We return to your womb this offering in gratitude and praise of your bounty!'

'Ashtoreth, hear us!' the crowd intoned.

The infant was laid face down on the altar. While a second priest lifted and held its head firm, the High Priest plunged the sharp point of the sacrificial knife into the soft throat below the ear and cut deftly through, severing the jugular.

After the first rush of bright blood had drained into the alter gutter and movement had stopped, the infant was lifted and placed in a shallow basket on a bed of dry barley and frankincense. The second priest carried it to the first of the bronze sacrificial braziers and held it poised above the burning coals.

'Ashtoreth, hear us!' the crowd chanted.

The priest dropped the offering into the coals and it exploded into flame, burning in a cloud of aromatic white smoke, and a crackling and sparking of barley husks.

The drum was struck twice and another infant was brought forward.

Hallam saw nothing of the ceremony. Held against the wall in a kneeling position by Zabby to avoid detection from the guards, he twitched spasmodically each time the drum was struck but otherwise remained oblivious. When the ceremony ended, Zabby used the cover of the dispersing crowd to carry Hallam through the dark alleyways and away from the square. More than a little drunk himself, he could not risk going through the gate under the eyes of the guards.

Fortunately, Jabez had told him he was staying with a relative for the period of the festival so the stall in King Street would be vacant. Zabby carried Hallam to the back entrance and forced open the door. He dumped his snoring burden on the glassmaker's mattress, then found a place of his own under the display table in the front. Within a few moments he was snoring himself.

For long moments Hallam lay unmoving, his brain groping through the remnants of alcoholic fog as he tried to grasp where he was and what had happened. He was aware, first, of pain. Pain filling the inside of the head and leaking out through the eyes. He blinked them several times, rubbing gently at the lids before testing them again on the blurred image of something with vertical lines. The image gradually formed into what looked to be a reed curtain.

Finding no immediate answer for its presence, he concentrated instead on more basic information, such as the straw mattress he was lying on. It was lumpy and unfamiliar. Walls closed in on either side - as in a cubicle - and unfamiliar clothes hung immediately above his head; draped over a sagging pole.

Hallam returned his attention to the reed curtain. Something about it nudged his memory. He closed his eyes. Behind the lids a drum was beating, echoing through his head with every heartbeat; two strong thumps at a time; steady and deep and reverberating. His senses began to swirl. He opened his eyes and sat up quickly. When the dizziness passed he looked around then breathed out with relief. He was alone.

Leaning against the wall he pulled himself up slowly and moved to the curtain. Without touching it he peered apprehensively through the gaps, half expecting to see the shadowy form of a priest, but he saw only the outlines of jars, urns and bowls on a table. Shafts of sunlight streaked from between the cracks of pole shutters.

Something about the bowls and jars was also familiar. Where a beam of sunlight struck the one closest to him it glowed a dark blue. They were glass jars. And the shapes were ....

Hallam stepped back in alarm. Comprehension expanded rapidly. Not only was he in the glassmaker's stall, but in the sleeping cubicle. He had been sleeping on the Egyptian's bed!

He spun around to look, but the sudden motion was too much for his stomach. With a hand clamped to his mouth he clattered through the reed curtain and vomited into a bowl on the table.

Leaning between the glass jars and urns, gasping, spitting and staring through watering eyes at the unbelievable contents of the bowl, he was unprepared for what followed.

From below the table came a snort like that of a startled animal. Something bumped against his leg and Hallam jerked away with an involuntary croak of alarm. His elbow knocked the blue jar from the table and it fell to the floor, shattering amongst other jars standing below, knocking them over against still others, and setting off a brittle clamour like the clanging of a thousand chimes.

The sound provoked an urgent increase in the scuffling from below.

'Godsnotting camel rut...' Zabby emerged on hands and knees. He lurched groggily to his feet, lost his balance, and fell heavily back against the table, sending two more jars crashing to the floor.

'Clumsy fool! Be careful!'

It was some time before Zabby was able to speak. He looked around in bewilderment, then glared at Hallam through an eye the colour of Damascus wine. 'Clumsy? It was not I who knocked them over!'

'It was...'

'And kicked a man in his sleep!'

'I did not... you... '

'I carry you here and in reward you kick me like a dog while I sleep!'

'What are you…?'

'I could more easily have left you in the dirt for the Cilician pigs! Then you place on me the blame for this....' His voice trailed off and they both looked around at the shattered jars in dismay.

'What are you... we doing here?' Hallam croaked. 'Where is Jabez?'

'Visiting. I could not risk the gate.'

'That stinking wine... my head....'

They both turned again to stare silently at the shambles.

Hallam recognised a tall urn with slender curved handles. It had been a particularly difficult moulding. One handle had broken off. 'Suffering gods...'

'We have to get out of here.'

'Before that slimy Jabez...'

'No one has seen us. He will think it was a thief.'

Hallam groaned. 'A sick thief.'

The shafts of light coming into the stall flickered with the movement of people outside. Heavy banging rattled the shutters.

'Quickly, out the back!'

Hallam hesitated, his brain sluggish. 'They know someone is here, they must have heard.'

'God's milk! of course they heard! But there is time.'

They scrambled towards the rear door. Zabby went first, disappearing quickly into the maze of alleyways. Hallam was not so lucky. He tripped coming out, sprawling in the filth behind the stall. By the time he recovered Zabby had gone and a guard was running down one of the alleys towards him.

'Hold there!' the guard shouted.

Hallam retreated into the stall. He had to try and bluff it out. He picked his way unsteadily through the scattered glassware towards the insistent banging that was threatening the shutters. 'Be patient, I am coming!' he rasped.

'Who is there?'

'It is me, the glassmaker's assistant. Why are you banging?'

'Open and show yourself!'

Hallam lifted the wooden bar from its slot and the shutters creaked open at the same time as the guard came through the stall behind him. Another confronted him on the street. 'What is the matter?' Hallam asked, squinting against the bright sunlight.'

'We heard noise in here.'

'I tripped and knocked over a jar, it is nothing.'

'Why did you try to run away?'

'I didn't, I was...'

Do you know him?' one of the guards asked the other.

The second guard shook his head, not taking his eyes off Hallam. His face twisted into a grimace of distaste 'You do not look like a glassmaker,' he said, leaning forward to peer through Hallam's hair to his ears. 'More like a latrine slave.'

Hallam looked down at himself. His breeches were caked with filth and his tunic was stained brown all the way down the front from spilled wine - and what looked suspiciously like vomit. One sandal was missing. 'I have not yet had time to wash,' he excused lamely.

'Who is the owner of this stall?'

The second guard opened his mouth to answer, but closed it again at the raised hand of his companion. They both fixed Hallam with expectant stares.

'It belongs to Lord Arumah.'

'Show us your gate token.'

Hallam reached for it and was dismayed to discover it was missing. He turned to look in the stall. 'It's in there... somewhere...'

'Where is the glassmaker? He will have to speak up for you.'

'He is away... visiting a relative.'

The guards looked at each other, sharing their disbelief. 'We will hold you until he returns.'

'But what about the stall?' Hallam protested. 'I should clean it and repair the damage, and the shutter.'

'It is not your concern. Put out your arms and cross your wrists.' A leather thong was produced and Hallam's wrists quickly and expertly tied. He glanced across the street at the house of Lord Arumah. Thankfully, both it and the street were quiet. It took no urging from the guards to get him to move. To be seen by her now in his present state, even though it would no doubt result in his release, was too mortifying to contemplate.

'If you run it will be with my spear in your back,' the guard warned.

The loss of his sandal caused Hallam to adopt an undignified limp. He stopped to remove the remaining one after they were clear of King Street, receiving a sharp prod in a buttock as he stooped to take it off.

It was the longest walk of his life. People stared and looked away quickly if he glanced in their direction. Those in front scurried from his path, as if afraid he was about to take them by the throat.

When they reached the gate, Parak could hardly believe his eyes. He rushed from his booth to inspect Hallam with an expression of astonished delight. 'Well look who we have! And I thought the gods had forsaken me!'

'How is the dancing?' Hallam asked. He was pleased to see the arm was still bound, with strips of grubby cloth.

'Do you know him?' asked one of the guards. 'He says he is the assistant of Lord Arumah's glassmaker.'

Parak feigned surprise. 'Does he? And how did you come to arrest him?'

The guard explained the circumstances and Parak smiled and shook his head in wonder. 'I think the offal is lying. Pole him with the rest until I have a chance to question him.'

'He knows me,' Hallam said to the guards. 'Ask him who put the hole in his arm then stupidly saved his worthless life.'

Parak's left backhand struck Hallam in the mouth. 'We will see whose life is worthless, Offal!'

Hallam wiped away the blood with his bound hands. 'Hitting me with my hands tied is the only way you will ever win, you cowardly ape.'

The two guards hurriedly dragged Hallam back as Parak stepped forward to strike him again. 'Maybe now is not the time, captain,' said one of them, looking pointedly at the growing crowd of onlookers, and Parak glared at them before turning his anger on the crowd.

'What are you staring at?' he shouted. 'Get about your business!'

The two guards took the opportunity to push Hallam out through the gate to a row of poles. Several were already in use. They stopped beside a vacant pole and one laid his spear on the ground. 'Face the pole and stand on the spear,' he ordered.

With one at each end of the spear they lifted Hallam to

waist height while he leaned against the pole for support.

'Arms over the top.'

Hallam placed his bound wrists over the top of the pole and the guards pulled the spear from under his feet. He slithered to the bottom.

'Was it really you who gave Parak the hole in his arm?' one of them asked.

'It should have been in his throat,' Hallam growled, and the guards laughed, looking at each other knowingly.

The stout pole allowed little movement. With his arms forcefully spread, the binding became painfully tight. All Hallam could do was shuffle around in a circle, sit down, or stand up. The prisoner nearest him was sitting with a leg either side, so Hallam followed his example, pressing himself hard against the pole to take the strain off his wrists. He looked around and saw the Assyrians.

They had no movement. Their poles were taller, and they hung from a single iron spike driven through their overlapping hands. Their feet had received similar treatment, spiked through the ankles; one either side of the pole. The heads of both hung forward and they appeared to be dead but, as Hallam stared in horror, one gave a spasmodic jerk and uttered a low cry, as if in the middle of a bad dream. Blood, urine and faeces stained the poles beneath them, and a moving shadow of flies hovered around their naked bodies.

Except for a group of small boys making a game of tossing pebbles and poking with sticks, the people coming and going from the gate gave the Assyrians a wide berth.

Hallam shuffled around the pole so he did not have to face them, swallowing against a throat gone suddenly tight. He looked out instead across the water towards the hills. They were barely visible behind the haze of dust and smoke, but seeing them brought a sudden and intense longing. If he survived the day he would sell the medallion and buy passage home on a pedlar boat. They would not find him.

He could survive in the mountains of Lamos. He could not survive in the city of Tyre.

The thought helped sustain him through the long and pain-filled day. He moved around the pole to stay in its shadow and tried to sleep as much as possible and, in that respect, his hangover helped considerably.

Parak came several times to gloat and question. His first question- delivered with a kick on the leg - jolted Hallam from his doze. 'How did you enjoy your little black bitch?'

'I don't know what you're talking about.'

Parak kicked him again. 'Don't lie to me, Offal. I had someone follow you. He saw you with her.'

'So what?'

'So who does she belong to? Slaves are not permitted to whore themselves.'

'I don't know, I just met her. I didn't pay her.'

'Liar. Another woman was with her. Who was she?'

'Her sister... how about some water?'

Parak chuckled. 'I don't mind two whores at the same time myself. I might pay them a visit, now that I know where they live.'

Fortunately, Parak was called back to his booth before Hallam could respond. He promised himself he would control his tongue. Antagonising the ape could only make his situation more painful. He was in no doubt that Parak would kill him when given the chance. All that could be stopping him now was the knowledge he was the property of Lord Arumah.

During Parak's other brief visits Hallam remained unresponsive, taking the kicks, slaps and abuse, and giving Parak no satisfaction. The time would come, he consoled himself, and then he would repay with interest.

At dusk, iron braziers were lit either side of the gate to provide light and the guards were changed, Parak among them. He paid Hallam one final visit before leaving.

'I have ordered you stay here until tomorrow, Offal, so we can have some more fun. I'll tell you then about your two little whores and how I enjoyed them.'

Soon after Parak had left, a guard brought both good news and bad. He was to be released, but was to report immediately to Lord Arumah at his house.

It was disturbing news. Hallam's first thought was that he might see Philippa, but as thrilling a prospect as that was, he did not want her to witness his degradation in front of her husband. As for the stall and broken glassware, he could soon think up some excuse for being there, but he could not think of an excuse for looking like a latrine slave.

'I first need to go to the factory so I can wash and change,' Hallam said.

The guard was unsympathetic. 'You cannot keep his lordship waiting, and it is best he sees you for what you are. With luck he will return you to us and we will have a new slave for slop duty in the cells.'

As they passed close to the edge of the wharf Hallam swung away and dived into the sea.

'Get back here!' the guard shouted from the edge, threatening with his spear.

Hallam swam to the rocks and, while the guard stood glowering from above, removed his filthy tunic and scrubbed it. He also washed his hair. He could not do much with the breeches, but at least they would be cleaner than before.

The guard scowled ferociously as Hallam climbed back up the wall and Hallam returned a pleasant smile. 'You should try it sometime,' he suggested.

Only the gates, the temple and King Street were illuminated at night. A brazier was placed beside the gate of every nobleman's house, and several were scattered around the palace. One glowed on the roof-garden, from where also came the drone of voices. It seemed the king was having a feast.

Hallam stayed in the shadows on the far side of the deserted street, walking boldly so as not to arouse the suspicions of any palace guards who may be watching. He felt vaguely disappointed, but also more confident knowing that Philippa would be at the palace and would not see him.

Lord Arumah had two braziers burning. One on the street beside the gate, and another in the courtyard close to the house. Hallam crossed the street and went in. The house itself showed no light from within. He took a deep breath and slapped three times on the door with the flat of his hand, then stepped back to wait, thinking furiously of what he would say. Sickness seemed the best excuse. He had become too sick to return to the factory and had gone to the stall to recover. The proof was in the bowl.

When no one answered he tried again. After the third attempt he moved back into the shadows, relieved. Lord Arumah must also be enjoying the king's hospitality.

The garden roof of the palace was hidden from where he stood, but the rumble of voices and occasional bellows of laughter were clear in the mild evening. To interrupt was unthinkable. Hallam moved farther back in the shadows and sat on the low wall of a well. From there he was hidden from view, but could still see the courtyard gate, through which they would have to come. Meanwhile, he could make good use of the well.

He filled the pail and drank from it. The water was cold and deliciously refreshing. He drank until he could drink no more, then sat on the wall to wait, plucking leaves from a pomegranate tree alongside and chewing on them to freshen the taste in his mouth.

There must have been a way to the palace other than from the street. The springing of a branch made Hallam turn quickly to see her coming alone through the trees and his heart tripped. She wore the same white robe with the purple trim as she had on the temple steps. She stopped near the brazier to look around, uncertain, her hair glowing, and Hallam stood and moved slowly into the light, wanting, yet still reluctant to be seen.

She started with surprise, then came swiftly towards him. She did not stop but took him by the wrist and pulled him back into the shadows behind the well.

'I missed you,' she said, making it sound like an accusation. Her breath was short, as if she had been running. She slid her hand down into his and Hallam's uncertainty vanished. Nothing had changed.

He smiled his relief. 'Not so much as me.'

Her face was thinner, and it may only have been the shadows, but a darkness he had not remembered showed beneath her eyes. Her eyes shone though, and her teeth flashed in a smile.

'I was afraid you...' She broke off, frowning, and leaned closer to inspect his face. 'You have a cut on your lip. Were you badly treated?'

'I have suffered more for not seeing you.' Hallam said. 'But you must take care. I'm here because Lord Arumah sent for me.' The word "husband" was too unpleasant a word to say.

She shook her head. 'No, It was me who sent a message to the guards. If your friend had not sent one to Milcah I would not have known you had been arrested.'

'Lord Arumah doesn't know?'

'No, I don't think so. I don't care. You are here with me, that is all that matters.'

Hallam's spirits soared with her words, but he had to keep his head. 'No, Philippa, listen to me. Milcah is in danger from Parak. He knows where the room is and believes she is the woman I have been seeing. He boasted that he will pay her a visit tonight.'

She rolled her eyes, showing distaste. 'That pig! But it's all right. He will only find Zabul and the old man there. Milcah lives at the palace to be close to the children.'

Hallam chuckled. 'I'd like to see how Zabul treats his advances.'

He told her about what had happened with Zabby and the man that had followed them, and she listened with the frown still in place, her eyes searching his with such intensity he found it difficult to concentrate.

'I didn't know we had been followed.'

'If it wasn't for Zabby...' Hallam did not finish. It was not the time for talk of death. Zabby was accruing debt at an alarming rate. 'You must believe me, my love. Not seeing you was the hardest thing I have ever done.'

She gazed up at him, the smile showing only in her eyes. 'You called me your love...'

'You are my goddess. I have sacrificed and prayed to you every day.'

The smile reached her lips, becoming coquettish. 'To me, or *for* me?'

Hallam laughed. 'Did you hear them?'

'Yes, and I answered. I also prayed you would kiss me again.'

He tasted the sweetness of honeyed wine on her lips. It was all the tonic he needed to strengthen his resolve to stay in Tyre - and weaken the one to leave. Somehow, he would find a way.

She removed herself gently from his arms. 'You're all wet and cold!'

'And making you wet as well,' Hallam apologised. 'My clothes were filthy, I had to wash them in the sea.'

'If you put your tunic by the fire it will dry.'

'Is it safe here?'

'My husband and Uncle Khiram have important guests. They will be talking for a long time. I told them I was not feeling well and had to rest. Milcah was watching for you.'

'Tell her a grateful kiss is on the way.'

'If it arrives I will have her beaten. Now, will you take it off so my robe is not spoiled... or would you rather I didn't come close?'

'Wine has put you in a teasing mood, I see.'

'Only a small goblet, to give me courage. And because Ari doesn't approve.'

'I could have done with a few myself.'

Hallam removed his tunic and tossed it over a branch near the brazier, and she came close to lay her warm hands on his chest, inspecting and caressing the hard muscles shyly, as if discovering something new and wonderful, then she slipped her arms around and pulled herself fiercely against him.

'My own Hallam. For a while, I almost hated you. I wish I had known.'

He stroked her hair, running it through his fingers all the way to the end. 'I will never change my mind. You are my goddess of love.'

She lifted her face to be kissed, then put her hands on his shoulders to push him down. 'Sit here,' she said breathlessly, 'on the wall.'

Hallam sat and she took a silver comb from her pocket and began combing his hair, tugging gently on the knots. 'You made a mess of it,' she murmured. 'If only we could find time I would cut it for you.'

'We'll find a way,' Hallam said with more confidence than he felt. 'I won't let that ape come between us. Neither will I allow you to be in danger, my love, even if it means not seeing you. You mean too much to me.'

'Do I, Hallam? I thought it was because you had changed your mind... about us being friends.'

'Never.'

She replaced her comb and entwined her fingers in his hair, undoing all her work, then she pulled his head gently against her breasts. 'Please, my Hallam,' she whispered from above. 'I want so much for you to feel me too. Will you?'

Hallam could find no voice to answer.

She removed a hand to fumble at a clasp in the front of her robe and suddenly her breasts were free. 'Kiss them,' she whispered. 'Hold them and kiss them....'

Hallam obeyed his goddess, his hands and lips moving indecisively between one delicious breast and the other, revelling, yet feeling with concern the rasp of his callused hands on her delicate skin, surprised at the firmness of her nipples, and she held his head to them, leaning back with her eyes closed, groaning softly.

The sound of her quiet mewling, the sweet almond and honey scent and taste of her, and the feel of her, was too much for Hallam to absorb all at once. He pulled back to marvel at what he held; seeing them pale and gleaming like pearls in the subdued glow of the brazier, swelling warm and alive, the firm dark nipples glistening from the touch of his tongue. No dream, this, he told himself over and over. He removed one of his coarse brown hands to lift her hair and lay it across her breasts, framing them with fiery strands, encircling them, and gazing, uplifted and lost in wonder.

'Yes,' she whispered, 'they are yours.'

Hallam looked up to see her eyes shining down at him. 'I will treasure them forever.'

Silently they looked at each other, letting their eyes say what no words could express. From another, distant world came the sound of laughter. Male laughter from the palace roof, mocking in its gaiety, and he saw a shadow pass over her eyes, as if a cloud had suddenly obscured the stars.

'My Philippa...' he said huskily, looking down to hide his torment. 'What will we do?'

She tilted back his head to hold his eyes with her own, then she lowered one hand to lift up her robe, revealing the sleek paleness of her legs. 'We will love each other,' she whispered.

She lifted the robe higher and, with a flash of naked thigh, smoothly straddled his lap. 'All of me is yours, my Hallam. I want you to have everything of me.' She reached for the cord of his breeches and together they tore at the knot.

She lifted up slightly to give him room. 'Yes... hurry...'

It sprang free into urgent fingers, probing desperately, and she flinched, her nails digging as it found the way, and Hallam hesitated, holding back, but she clung firmly to him. 'No... it's all right, my love...' She eased herself gently, then slowly relaxed her grip, and they held to each other, blissfully joined and unmoving.

No other world existed for Hallam. No sound but her unsteady breathing, and no sensation other than the exquisite, all encompassing one of his love goddess. A world he could have lived in forever.

Then cautiously, she began to move, rocking gently, her fingers entwined and pulling on his hair, leaning back and moaning softly, and it was too much for Hallam. His senses dissolved into ecstasy, barely aware that her moving had all but stopped, and that what remained had become suddenly hard and demanding, debilitating in its intensity, or that her soft moans had become a single restrained whimper, as if the pain was too excruciating to bear. As it eased they held to each other with breath mingling hot and damp, their lips searching, and their worlds joined and drifting into the sweet unknown.

Philippa was the first to find her voice. 'Oh, my love, what a feeling that was... like no other I have known. I felt as if I was melting.'

She leaned back to look at him, eyes shining. 'Now you are my man... my first and my last, and I am your woman.

Nothing can change it. Oh, mother of gods, forgive me... I wanted you so much...'

Hallam kissed her eyes, tasting the saltiness. 'My woman,' he said gruffly. 'If only I could find the words...'

Suddenly Philippa jerked up with a short gasp and pushed away from him. She whispered hoarsely, urgently. 'Go, Hallam! Go quickly! Run!' She fell back with a small cry of anguish, pale legs flailing as she fought to regain her feet against the restriction of her robe.

Taken by surprise Hallam nearly fell backwards into the well. He caught his balance and called after her. 'Philippa... what?'

She did not answer, and he watched with a feeling of bewilderment and dismay as she ran through the trees towards the house, struggling with the front of her robe, stumbling over the dead branches, tripping on the hem of her robe and falling, scrambling quickly to her feet.

Hallam stood to go to her aid, holding together his breeches.

Someone else called her name: 'Philippa!'

Footsteps hurried through the gate. 'What is it? Why is she running... what happened?'

'I don't know... I heard a voice... '

Hallam dived for the cover of the trees.

'There... by Zeus! Get him!'

'Guards!'

Hallam ran through the grove of pomegranate trees like a panicked hare, one hand holding up his breeches, unaware of the lashing of branches on his bare skin or the spiking of twigs to his bare feet. He ran to the side of the house, away from the gate and the shouting, as behind him came the sounds of pursuit.

'Follow him! Follow him!' A thin querulous voice rising high in outrage. 'Warn the palace guards he is coming their way!'

Hallam almost ran into a stone wall. At the last moment he saw the solid bulk of it and swerved aside, falling and crashing through a tangle of bushes.

'There! Cut him off!'

Hallam searched desperately for an opening in the wall, but came instead to another wall and a corner. He hesitated. The wall ran towards the house. It was too high to scale.

'He is heading for the gate behind the house!'

Alerted by the information Hallam found a loose rock at the base of the wall and hurled it into the bushes ahead - towards the area behind the house - then he ducked low in the shadows of the corner.

'Over there!'

His pursuers cut across the corner and Hallam moved stealthily back the way he had come. The gate was deserted, but beyond the wall he could hear the slapping of sandals approaching fast along the street. He ran to the well and lowered himself in as two guards came rushing through the gate.

The holding well was so shallow he had to lie down in the water to remain in the shadow. Anyone looking in would see him immediately. He listened to the sounds. The search seemed to be concentrating on the area behind the house and towards the rear of the palace. The street was quiet. He had to make a run for it before the search spread. And he had to get out of the city before daylight or it would be impossible. With the main gate so well guarded, only one other way was possible.

One of the sailors had spoken of the King's Gate - a narrow canal next to the palace leading out through the wall to the open sea; an emergency exit for the king's boat should the need ever arise.

Hallam pulled himself from the well and ran, streaming water, for the courtyard gate. He paused to check the street was clear then sped along it, his bare feet making only a soft slapping on the stone paving. The light from the braziers threw his shadow far ahead. The gods would have to be with him.

He skidded around the corner of the palace and ran along the canal, past the boat to where the canal widened before the sea-gate. He took a moment to tie the knot on his breeches, then slid into the water, pulling himself along on the slimy rocks in the deep shadow.

When he entered the gap between the overlap of the high walls, Hallam stopped in confusion. Where there should have been an opening was only solid shadow. Treading water he turned in a circle, but it was no mistake. The sea-gate was closed. Closer inspection showed that great logs, lying one atop the other, filled the gap. By feeling with his feet he discovered the logs went far down. The gaps between were too narrow to accommodate even a foothold.

He took several deep breaths and dived deep, but still he could not reach to the bottom of the logs. His breeches were holding him back. Taking them off was a desperate measure, and he had left his tunic hanging on the branch beside the brazier. If he made it to the other side he would be completely naked. But he had no choice.

He paddled across to the jumble of boulders at the side of the gate and sat on one while he worked on the knot of his breeches, now made even more stubborn by being wet. The boulder moved beneath him and he slid off. He felt around, testing its weight. It was heavy, but desperation gave him the strength. He rolled it into his arms and pushed hard away from the wall.

The dark water closed over his head and he sank rapidly. When the pain in his ears became unbearable he let the rock go and kicked towards where he thought was the gate, groping blindly ahead for the logs, but he felt none and kicked for the surface with the last of his breath. Gulping air, he opened his eyes and saw the log wall directly in front of him, less than an arm's length away.

Hallam beat against the logs with his fists, venting his anger and frustration in a flurry of kicks and punches until the pain forced him to stop. He pulled himself across to the rocks and lay against them, giving his exhausted body over to the gentle rocking of the swell. He did not think he had the strength to try again.

The gentle lap and gurgle of water through the rocks had a soothing effect, but his body was beset with pain. His ears from the dive, his fists and toes from the logs, his ribs and legs from Parak's kicks, and every other part felt as if it had suffered a deck captain's lashing. A stinging behind his shoulders puzzled him until he remembered the clutching of Philippa's fingers, and suddenly the pain seemed less.

He began to think about what had happened. He had dreamed of it so often he could almost believe he was dreaming again. He had possessed what he thought was impossible. Could it really have happened? And she said it was the first time, but how could that be? Did she mean it was the first time with him, or the first time with a man other than her husband? She had spoken of her pleasure, but there had also been pain, and remembering brought a stab of guilt. If only there had been more time.

She had obviously seen them coming through the gate, and they had seen her running to the house and him standing half naked, holding up his breeches. Only two conclusions could have been reached and, thankfully, they had chosen incorrectly. They had assumed Philippa had been attacked.

Even had he not been recognised in the shadows, and even if she told them she didn't know who it was had attacked her, they would soon find out. The guard had sent him there, and his tunic was hanging on the tree. If they caught him they would kill him. More than likely string him from the same pole in the square as they had strung the slave, or worse, spike him as they had the Assyrians.

And what of Philippa? She had arranged his release. He could only hope she had not done it openly and that she did not try and protect him with the truth. It would make no difference as far as he was concerned. She had been lucky to see them when she did. She could have done nothing else in the circumstances.

Hallam decided to give the logs one more try. He felt around for another loose rock, determined that this time he would hold on longer through the pain and force himself to swim farther out before coming up.

But the boulders were too large even to move. He pulled himself across to the other side, but it was the same there. In desperation he stood on one and worked again on the obstinate knot holding up his breeches

He was beginning to make some progress when a larger than normal wave washed him off the boulder. He looked at the water around him. It seemed rougher than before. He looked farther out and stiffened with surprise. Where the dark shape of the king's boat had been was now the dark shape of another boat - a much larger boat - and beyond that another. And beyond that, shimmering under the stars, was the open sea.

Philippa stood breathless and shaking in the darkness of the house, listening with heart thumping to the shouting and crashing sounds outside. She closed her eyes, fighting off the all but overwhelming desire to panic and run herself. She had to stay calm and think. Ari would come soon. She could not believe what had happened, how she could have been so careless.

All she could do was pretend she had been attacked and

hope Hallam got away, and with her fists and eyes screwed tightly closed she murmured her desire aloud. 'Run Hallam, run, my love... help him, Mother Rhea, I beg you... help my man escape.'

Philippa hurried to the sleeping room, her mind in a whirl. If they caught him and he told the truth, Ari would have her strangled and her uncle would not protect her. But Hallam would not be caught, and he would not betray her. She knew it.

A tallow candle burned in the outstretched palm of a figurine by the doorway. Philippa used it to light the larger candle on the wall then examined herself. The gold butterfly clasp that held together the front of her robe was missing, and her breasts showed blotchy red marks from Hallam's rough hands. She slipped the robe from her shoulders and let it fall to the ground, wincing as the material scraped against a grazed elbow. The white cloth of her robe was stained with dirt. She would have to change.

Standing naked Philippa became aware of a moistness between her legs. She looked down and gasped. The insides of her thighs glistened with the blended juices of their passion. She snatched up the robe to wipe it away then stopped. Ari would be suspicious if she changed, and he was not beyond checking. She lowered her head and wiped it away with her hair, bunching it in her fist and scrubbing furiously until she was thoroughly dry, then she hastily pulled up the robe.

'Philippa?' Ari's footsteps sounded at the front door and a thin wail of despair escaped Philippa's lips as she ran for her clothes chest.

Yes, we are certain, my lord,' the guard reported. 'He is no longer in the courtyard or behind the house.'

'He did not pass through the rear gate,' said another guard. 'He must have jumped over the wall.'

'Impossible! He would have been seen. Did anyone see his face?

'No, my lord.'

'Where are my guests?'

'Returned to the palace, my lord.' The guard's eyes shifted uneasily and Lord Arumah's thin face hardened, knowing what they were thinking.

'Who was watching the front after you came in?' he demanded.

The guards looked at each other in silence.

'You ignorant fools! By now he will have escaped into the city. Search it. Warn the guards at the main gate. I want him caught... and alive!'

Another guard ran towards them. 'I found this, my lord, hanging from a branch. It's wet.'

'Wet?' Lord Arumah took it from the guard and examined it closely, his frail body shaking with agitation. The tunic gave no clues as to the owner, only that it was of poor quality and could not have belonged to any of the guests. He flung it angrily at the guard. 'Why are you all standing there? Find the owner! If he escapes the city I will have you all on the galleys... Go! ' He waited to see them off before striding towards the house.

Philippa sat amongst her cushions in the shadows at the far end of the room, her arms crossed in front to hold together the gaping robe.

'Are you harmed, Philippa?' Lord Arumah lifted the candle from the wall and went to her.

'Is he gone, Husband? Did you catch him?'

'We will,' Lord Arumah said grimly. 'What happened, Philippa... did he harm you?'

'Oh, I'm so glad you came when you did. He was so strong! I was helpless in his hold... and so afraid I could not...' She covered her face, the robe falling to expose her breasts, and Lord Arumah sucked in his breath when he saw the red marks.

'It seems he did harm you, Philippa.'

She shook her head. 'No... only broke the clasp on my robe when he tried to rip it open.'

'He did them no damage? Let me see.' He kneeled beside her and held the light close while he carefully examined each breast, lifting them gently in turn. 'Some redness only, and one flower a little swollen. There is no pain?'

'No.'

'Who was he? Did you see his face?'

'It was dark. He came from behind.'

'You did not cry for help?

'I... I can't remember.. I think I did... it was so sudden...'

'Your lips are a little swollen and red. Did he perhaps hold a hand to your mouth?'

'Yes... I think so. I remember his hands being rough.'

'Lie down.' Lord Arumah patted one of the cushions beside her. 'You look quite pale with the shock.' He took her arm and gently but firmly eased her down. He adjusted the cushion comfortably under her head. 'I saw you leave. You were gone a long time and I came to see if you needed help, and to bring some guests who wished to see my collection of goblets.'

'Forgive me, husband. I think it was the wine and my moon together. It made my head turn.'

'Your moon?'

'Yes. I sat by the well to bathe my face in the cold water... I spilled some on my robe. It was while I was sitting there that he attacked me.'

'The well!' Lord Arumah exclaimed softly. 'That is why it was wet!

Philippa sat up. 'What are you saying, Husband? What was wet?'

'We found...' Lord Arumah hesitated. 'Never mind, it is nothing. Lie down, my dear, while I remove this dirty robe. It's ruined, I fear, but we shall buy another.'

'No. There is no need. You should return to the palace and your guests. I will change and join you there.'

'I will help you. Lift up your hips, Philippa.'

Philippa resisted, holding onto her robe as he tried to remove it. 'Please, husband, you must not. You should leave now, your guests will be waiting.'

'Remove it.'

'Why do you do this, Ari?'

'Your purity is the only demand I make of you, Philippa, and the measure of belief is more conveniently weighed in your favour. Show me the blood of your moon and I will let you be. It is a small thing I ask.'

Instead of pulling the robe down against her hold, he pulled it up from the bottom as far as her waist, and Philippa turned away her head. 'You shame me, Ari.'

Lord Arumah looked at the arrangement of ribbons that crossed his wife's sweetly curving hips. They were tied in a bow at her waist, holding in place the wad of raw cotton wrapped in silk that had become the fashion amongst women of nobility. They concealed unsightly hair and the bright colours of the silk made an attractive and tantalising curtain to the gates of paradise. Philippa's were a rich purple.

'Remove it please, I wish to see.'

'It is not for men to see.'

Lord Arumah was tempted to leave. She was a great asset, and the implications of proving her a liar were many. He weighed them carefully as his eyes roved the smooth contours of her beautiful young body, and not for the first time he suffered the shame and bitterness of his incapability. She was so beautiful. A firm and perfectly formed fruit that was right for plucking, and although he had no appetite himself, he had seen the hunger in the eyes of other men.

It would have been for her own good, as well as his, if the stem of her flower had been clipped in her youth. He had always been afraid the day would come when her ripeness would cause her to fall. And now, because he had foolishly checked her purity on the day of their marriage, he had no way of knowing if a bite had been taken. And her moon seemed to come with suspicious frequency these days.

Seeing the blood of her moon would not be conclusive. If hunger was strong enough it would not wait, but it was all he could do. If the culprit was caught and his confession told she had not been attacked, it would not prevent him from upholding the law. A spoiled fruit was worse than none.

Lord Arumah loosened the bow on her stomach and, with the candle held above, lifted one end of the silk covered pad. He stared for a moment then gently replaced it. Without any word he returned the candle to the wall and left the room.

Philippa felt sick. When she heard Ari calling to the guards outside she kneeled and hurriedly removed the pad. There had not been time to check when she had put it on. She held the pad towards the light. It did not look at all convincing to her, but the blood taken from her grazed elbow had left a smear and she sagged with relief. She started to replace the pad and ribbons, then dropped them to snatch up the discarded robe, and vomit into the folds.

Well away from the sea-gate and the boats, and for the moment secure in the dark, Hallam did nothing but float on his back and look up at the stars, gaining strength from their steadfast familiarity, then he began to consider ways of making his freedom more permanent.

He was still in desperate trouble. No place near Tyre would be safe. He could not risk returning to the factory to get clothes or pick up his silver. It would be the first place they would look. But without the means to buy food he would have no chance of going anywhere, and he could not float about for much longer either. He would be seen as soon as it became light.

Stealing a boat was the only way. He could sail it home to Lamos and hide out in the mountains for as long as he liked. It was not the ideal life, but better than none. And if not Lamos, then anywhere the wind blew him that was a long way from Tyre.

Hallam paddled in to the section of the shore used by the fishing boats. Most had been beached, but a few had been conveniently anchored a short way out in shallow water. He peered cautiously over the stern of one. It was empty, but stank of rotting fish. The smell nearly changed his mind, but he was in no position to be fussy. He lifted the anchor stone and untied the rope, then he towed the boat slowly out to sea, hoping that if anyone noticed they would think it was drifting.

Only when he could no longer see the beach clearly did Hallam climb aboard to take stock. It had little. A sail made from tattered strips of linen and reed matting was bundled untidily around its spar, and two paddles lay in the bottom, rocking gently in a wash of slimy water, fish gut and scales.

A single pole laid across from one side to the other served as a crude bench. There was no steering oar.

And no breeze. Setting up the sail would be futile, he decided, which in any case would make the boat more visible. He rested a while then eased back into the water and towed the boat some more, repeating the drill several times during the dark hours before dawn.

The breeze arrived shortly before the sun. Hallam saw it approaching as he was resting between tows. The sea shivered as the first tentative fingers crossed the glassy surface, then ruffled as it grew steadily in strength. It wafted gently in his face, adding the rich smell of rotting molluscs from the dye factories to the cloying stench of the bottom swill.

Hallam raised the dilapidated sail and watched apprehensively as the material flapped and shook, but it held together and filled out, bringing the boat under way. He took the handle of the makeshift steering oar - made by tying one of the paddles to the transom with the stubborn cord of his breeches - and watched with relief as the shoreline faded into the horizon.

It was vvimpossible to estimate how far he had come. The breeze blowing from the land lasted until mid morning, when it suddenly stopped, leaving the boat drifting on a calm sea. At noon the breeze returned, stronger than before, but the smoke from Tyre had disappeared in a surrounding haze that covered all but the empty sea, and with the sun directly overhead, Hallam could not tell in what direction it blew. He stood on the pole to get above the smell from the boat and sniffed at the wind, reaching hopefully for the stench of rotting molluscs, but tasted only the freshness of the sea. The same smell as when he had lain on the factory wall to catch the afternoon sea breeze.

Reluctantly, he lowered the sail then lay in the bottom of the boat to sleep, but below the reach of the breeze the heat and the smell was more than he could stomach. He removed his breeches and used them to protect his head and neck from the sun. Drowsy and thirsty, he sat on the pole bench to wait for a favourable wind.

It did not come, and the afternoon sun finally confirmed what he already feared. The wind was blowing towards Tyre. It increased steadily throughout the afternoon and into the evening, and Hallam peered anxiously towards the setting sun, expecting at any moment to see the glow of fires.

When the stars appeared he found the bright one low down in the sky to the north, which Meldek had told him was used by sailors to steer by, and he tried to hold it on his starboard bow, but the sail flapped alarmingly and the boat refused to stay where he pointed it. Only when he had the star astern would the sail fill, taking him neither towards Tyre or Lamos, but someplace far out into the Great Sea, where, no doubt, he would drift forever.

But as long as he was not going towards Tyre he didn't care. Cold and tired, and no longer bothered by the putrid smell, he dozed hunched down in the stern with the fish slime swilling around his drawn up feet.

Several times in the night he was jolted awake by the flapping of the sail and violent rocking of the boat, but each time it stopped by itself when the sail filled, so he let it have its way.

Dawn revealed no answer, only fog. The sail hung limp and the slapping of waves and creaking of the spar sounded loud in the stillness. Hallam sat drowsily on the pole bench, wondering how he could have forgotten to bring water. He had not even given it a thought. He could go without food, but not water for the four or five days it would take to reach

Lamos, and then only if he managed to get a favourable wind. He could not last even another day. Whatever the risk he would have to go in with the sea breeze and find water ashore.

Gloomily he pondered the difference between dying of thirst and drowning.

An eerie groaning in the brightening fog jerked Hallam awake. He stood listening, holding the end of the spar to stop its creaking. The sound continued, getting louder, and the hairs on his neck prickled as he stared towards the direction it came. An area of fog ahead was getting steadily darker, forming slowly into the grotesquely twisted, grimacing face of Baal. Angry red eyes glared down at him.

More shapes appeared, coming at him from all sides; one of them the raised up head of a sea serpent. The mouth gaped open, the long red tongue poking out between jagged fangs. The fog drifted, revealing more of the sea and, looming ominously, the forbidding rock walls of Tyre.

Hallam leaned heavily against the mast as the boat drifted amongst the war galleys. Baal wanted him. There could be no mistake. Had the gruesome image of the great god actually spoken the words, the meaning could not have been clearer. Baal wanted him captured and put to a horrible death because he refused to sacrifice. It was certain, only a matter of time, and not much time, for already the beach itself was becoming visible.

Hallam lowered himself into the water and, using the last of the wispy fog as cover, swam away from the boat and the war galleys, towards an area of the beach where he thought he may have a chance of going ashore unseen.

But the great god Baal was quick to make amends for his short lapse. He blew away the last tendrils of fog to reveal Hallam's bobbing head, and a few moments later a shout of alarm rang out across the water.

The day following the king's feast was one of crisis and agonising uncertainty for Philippa. Ari remained cool towards her despite her best efforts to humour him, and the attitude of his two guests, once they learned the details of her experience, was also disturbing. They seemed more embarrassed than sympathetic, exchanging sly glances, and allowing their eyes to wander more freely than before. Even the guards seemed to look at her differently. She could feel their smirks as sharply as arrows in her back as she passed.

When the courtyard was deserted, Philippa searched for her gold butterfly clasp and found it amongst the dry leaves where they had been together. She knelt there for a while, in the exact same spot, smiling as she recalled every wonderful moment. Memories that gave her some measure of relief from the uncertainty. At least the love they shared was certain.

It was not until Jabez came to report the damage to the stall that Philippa suddenly remembered it was she who had ordered Hallam to be released - and to report to the house at a suspiciously short time before the supposed attack. The realisation almost sent her into another panic.

She had no choice now but to tell her husband that she had ordered Hallam to report to the house, and to blame her lapse of memory on her illness. They would no longer be looking for a stranger. If the guards had not already informed Ari, they soon would, and it was better it should come from her or he would be even more suspicious than he was already.

Even then, Philippa knew she was still far from being in the clear. If they caught Hallam, he would be killed, and if he was questioned and implicated her under torture, she would also die. It was the law. As a noble she would not be given over to the priests, she would be strangled. Ari would not do it himself as husbands were entitled. He would have one of the criminals perform the task, then the man would be put to death without pain as a reward. Her uncle would not protect her against his own laws. If he could allow the strangling of a cousin, why would he stop at a niece?

Philippa told her husband at the first opportunity, giving him no chance to question her first. 'A few people have been asking about the glass medallion,' she said. 'I wanted to see him to find out if any had been made. I didn't know he had been arrested.'

He studied his fingers as he listened to her explanation, then said, 'Yes, I was informed you had sent for him.' He did not elaborate, and Philippa tried to adopt the same casual manner as she steeled herself to ask what she had been so anxious to know. She tried not to make it sound like a question.

'Then he must surely have been captured.'

'Not yet,' he answered abruptly, and changed the subject. 'I have much on my mind with a new business. It will be best if you sleep at the palace with your mother until it is completed.'

Alerted by the shout from the galley watch, the pilot of the night patrol boat was alarmed to see a fishing craft drifting in the restricted area of the war galleys. Assyrian spies and saboteurs were a constant threat, so he urged his rowers to full speed as he rushed to investigate.

'Over there, Pilot!' called the watchman, 'A man swimming away!'

But only after towing the fishing boat clear and satisfying himself there were no fire bundles aboard did the pilot go after the swimmer.

Although exhausted, still the man had to be subdued with an oar before they were able to safely drag him aboard. He appeared to have suffered a severe beating. Hardly a place on his naked body was left unscathed.

The stunned swimmer was transferred back to the fishing boat and the pilot himself lashed his hands behind the mast, pondering as he did so, the implications of the discarded and torn breeches left lying in the filthy bilge water, and also the purple headband, which had slipped down around the man's neck. He draped the breeches around his prisoner's nakedness; tying the legs in a knot behind the mast.

Then the pilot made an error he was later to regret. He ordered the boat towed in to the fisherman's beach rather than going directly to the wharf and handing over his prisoner. He was not concerned about the man trying to escape. He had sufficient men and the prisoner was subdued and securely tied. He could hand him over as soon as he had returned the boat, but to make doubly sure, he stayed aboard the fishing boat to keep an eye on his charge.

The pilot jumped off as soon as the boat grated on the sand. With rope in hand he was looking for a suitable tethering point when an angry fisherman ran down the beach and leaped aboard the boat. Before the pilot had a chance to intervene, the fisherman attacked the dazed and helpless prisoner with his fists.

The pilot ran back and beat the fisherman off with a paddle, chasing him from the boat.' Get out you crazy fool or I'll crack your skull!'

'Get out yourself! It's my boat!' The fisherman dug into a bag tied to his belt and produced a knife. 'He stole my boat! I will kill him!'

'If you do I will have you arrested.'

'I have a right! I have a right!' Brandishing the knife, he danced about, trying to get back to the boat, but keeping out of range of the paddle.

A group of fishermen quickly gathered and the boat owner appealed to them. 'He stole my boat. Does the law not say I have a right to kill him?'

'He has a right to kill the thief!' One of them replied, and the others immediately added their support. 'Let him kill the thief, he has a right!'

'He has no right! Stay away, all of you, or you will be arrested!'

'It is not us who are thieves!'

'The council will decide.'

'The king will give him to me. It is the law!'

'Fetch the guards!' the pilot shouted to the slaves waiting in the galley, and they quickly pulled away.

The group of fishermen crowded closer. 'At least he should take an ear!'

'Yes, give me an ear!'

The pilot threatened them with the paddle. 'It is not mine to give. Now hold back!'

But the fishermen would not be put off. The theft of a boat was a serious matter, even more serious than the loss of a wife, which could be more easily replaced. Their anger was real, but so too was their fear of taking matters into their own hands. Council justice had a tendency towards favouring the rich, and none of them knew the culprit. Also, pilots were influential and to be respected. It was safer to give their support from a distance and not become directly involved. They crowded the pilot, keeping him from intervening, but did not lay hands on him, only on the paddle.

As the pilot fought to get it back, he was alarmed to see the boat owner scramble once more into the boat and, with the knife still in his fist, advance towards the man. The prisoner did not appear to notice. His head hung low and one of his eyes had already swollen closed.

Suddenly the boat owner's free hand darted forward and latched onto a fistful of hair and the lobe of the prisoner's left ear. He pulled the head over as far as it would go and placed the blade of the knife beneath the ear. With a triumphant screech he began sawing upward.

The prisoner attempted to jerk his head away, at the same time lashing out with his foot, but the grip on his ear remained firm and the blade followed the movements, jagging through the hair and slicing through the fleshy lobe as easily as it would gut the belly of a fish. The bound man shook his head, splattering blood, but he made no sound.

'I have an ear! I have an ear!' Proudly the boat owner held the dripping lobe aloft, waving it gleefully at his companions.

'It is only half an ear, take the rest!' someone called out.

'Stay away!' the pilot shouted back, but no one paid any attention, and attracted by the commotion, other people began arriving, among them a sailor.

'I know that man, Pilot!' the sailor called. 'He's the free slave who attacked the wife of Lord Arumah in Lamos. He would have been gelded but for his lordship's mercy.'

The news changed the mood of the crowd. Where before they had been noisily content to have his ear, now they were quieter. The smell of *real* blood was in the air. Not a man in Tyre had looked upon the beauty of the king's niece without a sigh of envy. Even the pilot was shocked and quieted by this new information. He had known Lady Philippa since she was a child, and more than once had guided her hand on the tiller of the king's galley boat.

'Do it now,' someone urged the boat owner. 'Cut off the rapist's yoni sticker and save his lordship the trouble.'

The suggestion was accepted enthusiastically. 'Yes! Cut it off! Cut off his yoni sticker!'

The pilot struggled to break away. Despite his misgivings, he was still a pilot; a man of authority and discipline. He would not be bullied by a rabble of fishermen. But there were too many of them. A glance towards the wharf showed the galley boat returning, but it was still a long way out.

Encouraged by his friends and this new mood, the boat owner went behind the mast and untied the knot holding the breeches. They fell away and the crowd jeered at the man's nakedness.

'It is too small for bait!' someone called out, and the crowd tittered before falling into an expectant silence.

The boat owner grinned and returned to the front to stare fixedly at the object he was about to remove. He took his time, placing the earlobe in the same bag as he had taken the knife, before moving cautiously forward with both hands extended; one ready to grab, and the other to cut.

For the first time the prisoner showed signs of protecting himself. He raised one leg and shifted his weight, preparing to kick, but the fisherman stopped his forward advance. Grinning craftily, he moved to stand behind where the prisoner's feet were blocked by the mast. He reached around and took a firm hold of the man's genitals, stretching them out, and the crowd began to voice their encouragement. 'Cut them off! Cut them off!'

The prisoner groaned as his testicles were squeezed, his knees buckling, but still he did not cry out. Blood trickled from his ear, spreading down through the hairs of his chest and over his stomach.

'Cut them off and throw them here!'

'If you do I will see you strung!' the pilot shouted. 'I know

133

every one of you! I will see you all strung!'

The boat owner reached around with the knife and tried to bring his two hands together, but with the mast between, he could not quite reach. The prisoner struggled against his bonds, shaking his head and sprinkling blood.

The fisherman cursed and moved once more to the side. Still holding firmly to the genitals with one hand, he attempted to bring the knife forward, but the man twisted around and kicked out, knocking him off balance, and he was forced to let go of his hold to prevent falling out of the boat.

The jeers of his friends wiped away the fisherman's grin. He went behind and picked up the wet breeches. With a flick of his wrist he wrapped them around the man's legs and pulled them hard against the mast, then he tied the legs of the breeches firmly together. This time there would be nothing to stop him.

The returning galley boat was close now, with two guards already standing in the bows ready to jump off. The group of fishermen saw them and began moving away, and the pilot suddenly found himself in full control of the paddle. He used it to disperse the last of the group standing between him and the boat.

The boat owner had not seen, or did not care about the arrival of the guards. He stood in front of the man, reaching forward and the pilot knew he could not get there in time. He shouted, trying to distract him, but to no avail. The boat owner grasped the man's genitals and stretched them out again, ready to saw, and the prisoner did the only thing possible in the circumstances. He spat in the boat owner's face.

But the boat owner did not let go of his intended trophy. Neither did he let go of the knife. He wiped away the spittle with his arm and the grin returned.

It had been a small distraction, but it was all the pilot

needed. He leaned into the boat and struck the boat owner in the back with the paddle, then leaped aboard and followed it up with several blows about the head, driving the owner from the boat to join his departing friends. At a safe distance the owner stopped to dig in his bag and hold aloft his smaller trophy, pinned on the point of his knife. 'He is mine,' he screamed defiantly. 'I have his ear!'

The cell was little more than a hollow formed by the removal of rocks from the inner city wall. Logs placed one atop the other, as in the sea-gate, barred the opening to form a narrow pen. The only way in or out was by crawling – or being shoved - through a gap made by the removal of the centre log. Lying down without bending the legs was impossible.

Hallam soon gave up any ideas of escape. Even if he found a way out of the cell, there was no way out of the passage between the walls except by a door at the city gate, which was guarded at all times by the Cilicians.

The section in which he was being held was for condemned prisoners only, Parak had triumphantly informed him, and the previous occupants had recently been executed. Common criminals were detained in cells on the opposite side of the gate.

He received water but no food, and was left alone in the darkness. His ear had stopped bleeding, but throbbed painfully and constantly, making coherent thought impossible, which was as well, for his plight was something he did not care to think about.

With the memory of thirst still fresh in his mind, and not sure if he would get more water, Hallam bathed his ear and swollen eye, but resisted using his meagre supply to wash the dried blood and filth streaking his body. Tentative examination revealed only the lobe of his ear had been lost, and similar cautious exploration of his genitals revealed they were scratched and swollen, but otherwise intact. Numbness gave them the unpleasant sensation of still being in the painful grip of the boat owner.

All he possessed was his headband. His breeches had gone. To hide his nakedness a guard had provided him with a filthy loincloth, which Hallam thought was probably the one previously owned by the slave they had strung in the square.

No light entered the passage except when the door at the end was opened, so the passing of time was marked mainly by the muted sound of the city or the arrival at dawn of the slave with his daily ration of food.

Hallam guessed he had been there for two days when the log was slid aside and a guard ordered him out. His arms were tied, a rope attached to his neck, and he was led – walking stiffly with legs apart like a goat with bloated udders - along the passage to a bright enclosure at the main gate. In the sudden glare he recognised the hazy image of Lord Arumah.

'Leave us,' Lord Arumah said to the guard.

The merchant studied Hallam silently for a moment, his quick eyes inspecting, and his old woman's face showing no expression other than a slight pinching of his nostrils.

'For what you have done you will be executed,' Lord Arumah said in a matter-of-fact tone, as if discussing the weather. 'It was a mistake not to have punished you in Lamos.'

'I did nothing in Lamos,' Hallam said.

Lord Arumah continued as if he had not heard. 'You attempted to defile not only my wife, but also the niece of the king. Such a crime must receive the worst punishment as an example. Both the king and I will rightly demand it.'

Hallam remained silent wondering, with a sudden chill,

what punishment could be worse than spiking.

'Why did you do it?' Lord Arumah persisted. 'You must have known you would be caught.' He turned away, shaking his head in disbelief. 'I have seen many acts of stupidity, but yours is the worst. I cannot imagine how you could think you could have your way with my wife with so many people close at hand to hear her cries.'

With his eye adjusting to the light, Hallam studied the man who was Philippa's husband. His presence inspired no guilt or remorse in him, only a deep resentment at the unjustness that would see him dead and Lord Arumah alive to possess what he had come to consider was his own. Lord Arumah had a sly manner, not looking at him as he paced around with his hands clasped in front like a priest, and Hallam wondered why he had come. Clearly not from idle curiosity. The merchant must be there only because he wanted to find out what had happened, which could only mean he did not believe whatever story Philippa had told him.

Hallam remained silent, his brain sluggish as it tried to unravel the implications of Lord Arumah's questioning. His mention of Philippa crying out for help was disturbing. She had not cried out. Could that be the reason?

'Will you not answer?'

'I was drunk. I would like lady Philippa to know I meant her no harm and to ask her forgiveness.'

Lord Arumah sniggered. 'Drunkenness will not excuse you. Why did you go to my house?'

'I was ordered to go there by a guard. I stopped at Jabez's stall to drink some wine I had left there.'

'The council will meet in three days to decide your fate. Is it the same story you will tell there?'

'It's the truth, so I will tell it.'

Lord Arumah left abruptly and, still wondering, Hallam was led back to his cell.

Philippa heard of Hallam's capture and imprisonment later that morning.

'I told you, didn't I?' her mother said, bustling into her room without so much as a greeting. 'He wanted to rape you and he almost did.'

Philippa felt suddenly faint. 'What...?'

'They caught him... that wild animal that attacked you. The one who nearly killed us on the beach. I told you and you would not believe me.'

'They caught him?' Philippa found it hard to breath. It had been two days. She had come to believe – to hope - he had escaped.

'He stole a boat and tried to sail away. They say he was almost killed by the fisherman. Too bad he wasn't!'

'Leave me alone, Mother, I don't want to talk about it. My head hurts and I need to sleep.'

For the next three days and nights Philippa received little in the way of sleep. She did not leave the palace, spending most of her daylight hours on the roof-garden with her uncle's children, where she had the sympathetic company of Milcah.

She saw nothing of her husband. It was not unusual for him to send her home when he had business meetings or guests staying, and she always enjoyed the reprieve, but now she felt as if she too was a prisoner awaiting execution.

Desperate to know what had happened, but unable to ask questions for fear of arousing suspicion, Philippa plagued Milcah for information, but the nurse baulked at repeating what she had heard. 'They are just silly rumours, mistress. Best if we not listen to them.'

Instead, Philippa tricked one of the other young nurses

into giving her the information she wanted. 'Somebody has been telling stories to the children about the man who attacked me,' she said to the nurse. 'It wasn't you, was it?'

'Me, mistress?' The girl looked shocked. 'I did not say anything to them about that, mistress.'

'Well, it must have been someone else then. I didn't think you would have known anything. Even so, when they do catch the man, I would rather you didn't say anything to the children. Especially the older ones. You know what they're like.'

'Of course, mistress, you can be sure I won't say anything about that. But mistress...' The nurse paused to frown in puzzlement. 'Haven't you heard? They did catch the man.'

'Oh?' Philippa feigned a puzzled frown of her own. 'Was he killed?'

'No, mistress,'

'What then?'

The nurse shuffled her feet and looked anxiously towards the children, as if searching for an excuse to leave. Finding none, she shrugged helplessly.

'Too bad he wasn't killed for what he tried to do.' Philippa all but choked on the words, but it would do no harm to start a few rumours of her own innocence. 'I hope something bad happens to him.'

'Yes, mistress. But they say the fisherman what caught him poked out his eye and cut off his ear.'

'Oh...?'

'Yes, mistress.' The girl glanced again towards the children and lowered her voice. 'If you will excuse me saying it, mistress, they also say that the fisherman cut off what was between his legs. I think it was because of you it was done, mistress.'

Philippa felt as if her body had suddenly detached itself from her mind. She glared at the nurse, repulsed by her smirk, wanting to slap it away, refusing to believe, yet filled with dread. 'That's rubbish!' she snapped at the dismayed girl. 'You should not be so stupid to believe it. If you repeat any of it...' Philippa lifted her hand, threatening. 'I will have you whipped!'

Throwing caution aside, Philippa went immediately to the palace gate and confronted one of the guards. 'I heard that the man they captured for attacking me has been tortured.'

'The guard was as perplexed as the nurse had been. 'No, Mistress Philippa. Torturing is not permitted until after a prisoner has been condemned by the council.'

'He was not harmed?'

'He lost some of his ear to the fisherman whose boat he stole. Nothing else, mistress, although I myself will be competing for the pleasure of cutting them off when the time comes.'

Philippa smiled weakly. 'I only wanted to be sure the law had not been broken. The man must be able to speak to the council.'

Every tenth day of the month was set aside by the council for the trying and punishment of suspected criminals. Two days before the meeting, Philippa's fears about her husband's suspicions were confirmed.

Needing a few personal items from her room, but wanting to be sure Ari was not there, she asked the same guard as to his whereabouts.

'Lord Arumah may still be at the main gate, mistress, I saw him there myself only a short while ago. He was speaking with the prisoner that attacked you.'

Although she refused to believe, even for a moment, that Hallam would betray her, Philippa waited apprehensively for her husband's return, and the summons she was sure would follow.

The summons did not come, but it gave her only small relief. Hallam had either refused to speak, or had told some other story to protect her. Yet she could do nothing for him in return, and the frustration of her utter helplessness, her inability to do anything, drove her to vow she would die with him rather than live with the guilt and suspicion. Hallam would suffer enough, so she would not declare their love to the council and burden him with the knowledge of her own suffering. She would wait until he was dead then jump from the wall onto the rocks.

Late that afternoon, after the children had been taken below by the nurses, Philippa climbed the stairs to the roof-garden. She did not go all the way to the top, but entered a short passage a flight below and went to the heavy emergency door at the end, which led onto the top of the wall. She examined the heavy locking bars, easing them up in their slots to test the weight, and was relieved to find she could lift them without too much difficulty. It was a long time since she had been through the door, and had never gone alone. It was forbidden.

She returned to the steps and continued up to the roof. From there, she looked down onto the top of the wall. The men working on the sea-gate had almost finished replacing the logs, which had become a daily task since the capture of the Assyrian spies. The activity had provided much entertainment for the children.

Philippa remembered the sea-gate being constructed when she was still a child herself, and recalled her own fascination at seeing the big logs raised and lowered into the gap by the creaking ropes and wheels attached to the pole structure above. Her uncle had taken a few of the older children with him to inspect it and she had been one of them. Afterwards, he had taken them for a short walk along the wall and shown them the wooden hatches of the grain silos, explaining how the grain was lifted by the same wheels and ropes as the sea-gate, and how the entire wall was filled so if ever there was a siege the people would not starve. Smaller hatches allowed access through the silos to the long passage at the bottom of the wall, her uncle had also told them, and were used for emergency or repairs.

The men at the sea-gate stacked their equipment and strolled along the wall towards the steps at the main gate, but still Philippa remained looking down. The prison cells were in the passage at the base of the wall this side of the gate, and the wall was seldom patrolled on top. A galley now circled the city during the night. If the hatches had not been permanently sealed, it may be possible to reach the cells, release a prisoner, and return to the wall without being seen. And she could get onto the wall through the heavy door below.

But Philippa's enthusiasm for her idea soon wilted. She would not have the strength to climb the full height of the wall, and a workman had once fallen into the silo and suffocated. When found some days later he had been half eaten by rats. She shuddered at the thought. She quailed also at the thought of walking through the dark passage, past cells full of criminals, not knowing which one was Hallam's, or if there were guards. It was impossible.

Philippa had no sleep that night, but her wakefulness was productive. In the morning, exhausted but resolved, she took special care with her dressing, wearing her most revealing robe and painting around her eyes with blue to conceal the effects of her sleepless night. Then she sent a guard to the gate to inform Captain Parak she wanted to see him at the palace. She waited on the roof-garden until she saw him approaching along King Street, then went down to meet him.

There had been a time when Parak's dog-like devotion had amused Philippa, but even long before the incident at Lamos, she had found it irksome. Now that she also knew of his treachery, she regarded him only with revulsion and contempt. What she was about to do sickened her, but she could think of no other way to save Hallam - and perhaps even herself.

Staunchly committed to her plan, Philippa met Parak outside and surprised him by asking if he would accompany her along King Street.

'I have been thinking of asking my husband to send you back to the palace,' Philippa explained. 'You accompanied me before and are much more efficient than the others. He should never have sent you to the gate.'

Parak grinned with delight. 'Thank you, my lady. Protecting you is my most pleasing duty.'

'You always were a charming man, captain,' Philippa said, smiling coyly, and Parak almost blushed.

Philippa put on a thoughtful expression, allowing a small frown to appear. 'What I said was true, captain, but perhaps I should be more truthful. I trust you more than the others, and there is something I would ask you to do for me. Something I would not trust to any other man.'

'You have only to ask it, my lady.'

Philippa maintained her thoughtful expression for a while longer, prolonging his anticipation, then she feigned a sigh of resignation. 'Maybe not. It is much too dangerous, even for a man of your courage.'

Parak's face fell. 'Please, my lady. I beg you to tell me...'

'You have been very loyal to me, haven't you, Parak?' Philippa smiled demurely. 'Perhaps some would say even more than was good for either of us.'

Parak was startled. 'Lady Philippa! I assure you. I have never...'

'There is no need to be concerned, Parak. It is flattering for a woman to have a handsome man pay her attention. I have no desire to speak of it with my husband, and I'm sure that what I tell you will not be repeated.'

Few men could resist a compliment from Lady Philippa, and Parak was certainly not one of them. He took a deep breath, as if to rid himself of his previous fumbling, then spoke with new strength. 'Even the promise of death would not loosen my tongue against you, Lady Philippa.'

'Thank you, my brave Parak, for what I am about to ask of you will put my life in your hands. It concerns the glassmaker's assistant, and what happened on the night of the king's feast.'

Parak scowled. 'You have no need to fear, my lady. The offal is safely imprisoned and will be executed tomorrow. I will be there myself to make sure he suffers fully for what he did to you... and to me.'

'He did nothing to me, Parak, but that is not what I mean. What I would ask is that you arrange his escape.'

Parak was clearly too stunned to reply immediately. He walked stiffly beside her with a puzzled expression for some distance before responding. 'Forgive me once more, Lady Philippa, but I am confused. Are you saying that you were not...' Parak coughed, searching for words. 'I mean no offence, my lady, but are you saying he is innocent of attacking you?'

'No, that is not what I'm saying, Parak, but sadly...' Philippa turned away to hide the tears that sprang suddenly into her eyes. So suddenly it surprised even her.

Even fewer men could resist her tears. 'Lady Philippa! You mustn't distress yourself... If there is something I can do...'

Philippa sniffed and wiped away the tears with a finger. 'My husband doesn't believe I was attacked either. He believes I went to meet the man secretly.'

'Lord Arumah thinks that? Surely, my lady, you must be mistaken!'

'No. My husband is very suspicious, as you know. It was I who encouraged him to spare the glassmaker in Lamos, and it was I who ordered the glassmaker sent to the house on the night of the feast. I wanted him to show his medallion to one of the guests. You must understand, Parak, my husband is an old man and he cannot... well, let me only say he does not have the desires of a younger man. Because of that he is jealous and does not trust me. Believe me, Parak, this is very painful to speak of, and I would never ask such a thing of you if my life did not depend on it.'

'Your life, my lady? But how can such a thing be possible? You are the niece of the king.'

'I already know that my husband has been to see the prisoner in private. Why do you think he would do such a thing if he was not suspicious?'

Parak frowned. 'I'm not sure....'

'Tomorrow the glassmaker will be given the opportunity to speak to the council. If he speaks against me in an attempt to save his life, my husband, being already jealous and suspicious, is likely to believe him. I could be condemned as an adulteress, even though I am innocent. It may be you who is chosen to strangle me, Parak. Is that something you would like?'

'Never! I would cut off both my hands first!'

'So what would you have me do then, Parak? Put my life in the hands of a desperate prisoner and a suspicious old man?'

'That will not be necessary, my lady,' Parak said confidently, 'and I am honoured by your trust. The answer is simple. I will kill the prisoner myself, before he has a chance to speak. It would not be difficult. All I have to do...'

'No!' Philippa was horrified. 'It would be... I do not want that to happen. I could not have his blood on my hands. He is.. he was drunk, and... no, Parak, I will not allow it.'

'Escape from the cells is impossible, my lady. There are five guards on gate duty at all times.'

'There is another way,' Philippa said. 'It's quite simple and without risk, and you will be well rewarded for the little you have to do.'

'Another way, my lady? I cannot think of any...'

'There is. I will explain, and if you agree, anything that is

145

in my power to give will be yours.' She laid a hand briefly on Parak's hairy arm, barely able to stifle a shiver. She forced a smile before looking away to hide the expression of distaste. 'I have little gold of my own to give, but I have noticed the way you look at me, Parak. Perhaps I can also bring myself to give you something more rewarding than just having your hands on my throat... if that is what you wish.'

It was a stunned Parak who later followed behind Philippa as they returned to the palace, but although his mind was numbed by her promise, his eyes never left the sensuous movement of her shapely buttocks beneath the clinging silk. Others spoke with awe of her beauty, but it was the soft melons behind that he had dreamed of having in his hands. He could not believe it was actually going to happen. He must still be dreaming. Nevertheless, his mind began to wander in that direction and he was forced to stop and pretend to adjust his sandal to hide the protruding bulge in his leather skirt. His need became so great he could think of nothing else, and thinking clearly was something he had to do soon if he ever hoped to get his hands on her incredible reward.

When Philippa entered the palace, Parak went into the privacy of the change cubicle. He latched the door and lifted his skirt. It was as rigid and thick in his fist as the shaft of his spear. He kneeled as he began, leaning his head against the wall for support.

With his mind clear, Parak sat, resting his back against the wall, and went over what she had asked of him. He could not blame Lord Arumah for being suspicious. He did not believe her either. For one thing, the offal could not have been drunk.

He had been tied to a pole all day and was only released a short while before the incident happened. There would have been no time to purchase wine, and he had no copper on him anyway, the scum had been searched. If anyone was drunk it was her.

It did not matter though. If anything it was a good sign. He had long ago decided she was cold and all show, but it seemed she had some fire down there after all. And if she could set it alight for the offal, she could do the same for him. He would show her how a *real* man could quench her noble flame.

Parak dragged his mind back to what he was supposed to be thinking about. She was right in saying that his part was simple, but she had not been so right about there being no risk. Someone would be blamed, and he had to make sure it wasn't him.

He did not worry about the offal, even though he had been looking forward to spiking him personally. That was a small pleasure compared to the one offered by her and, unlike hers, one that could not be repeated. And he did not have to worry about the offal escaping either. Many a prisoner working on the wall had tried to escape by jumping and none had survived, but to make doubly sure the offal didn't escape to tell the tale, he would advise him exactly where to jump.

Whatever happened, she would never see the glassmaker again. All he had to do then to get his reward was to find someone to take the blame for letting the scum out of his cell.

Before he was finally able to come up with the solution, Parak had to free his mind once again. This time he took it slower and enjoyed it more, visualising how it was going to be and, when he had finished, his left buttock had been squeezed and kneaded by his fingers to such an extent it ached when he walked.

Waiting for death, Hallam discovered, invoked strong visions of life. But there was little outward manifestation of that in the cell. Occasionally, the opening of the door at the end of the passage and a greying of the darkness would signal the arrival of the slave with water, stale bread and the slop jar, but no other activity broke the gloomy monotony, and little sound penetrated the thick walls. The only noise to disturb his troubled thoughts was the restless scurrying of rats and other vermin in the grain silos overhead.

The slave never spoke to him. It was either forbidden, or the man did not understand the few questions Hallam asked. Silently the slave would hand the pots through the small gap at the side, retrieve the empties, then shuffle away. The only guard he had seen was the one who had taken him to Lord Arumah. Not even Parak had visited, which was surprising, but perhaps the ape had lost interest with the lack of challenge.

As time passed in the gloom, periods of restless sleep and drowsy wakefulness joined to become one continuous twilight. Hallam could never be really sure if he was thinking or dreaming, and his thoughts - if that is what they were - took on an intensity and vividness he had never before experienced.

With little effort of will he could summon any vision he chose and dwell on it for long periods; seeing it clearly in his mind. The dank, grassy smell of the passage could be replaced by the pleasant one of sweating horses, or of cedar on a fire. Or his favourite; the intimate, pulse quickening visions and head spinning aromas of his love goddess.

The warm whispers she had breathed in his ear were

repeated a hundred times in his head, the taste and feel of her a thousand times on his lips, and the sea-fresh scent that was indelibly imprinted on his brain could be summoned simply by holding the hand that had touched her to his face. She had given him a delicious feast of herself, and he would die with the warmth of its sustenance. Everything of me, she had said. The gifts of his goddess, and Hallam clung to them, treasuring, as he had promised.

At first, the appearance of the slave provided a welcome diversion, but when Hallam estimated three days had passed, each opening of the door brought an expectation the time had come, and the rat in his belly began to gnaw in earnest.

He tried to prepare himself for the inevitable, rehearsing in his mind how he would act and what he would say, but when a guard finally did come, his legs were so weak he had to hold on to the logs for support and his mind rebelled.

The guard stood silently peering in, his presence marked only by the sound of his breathing and the slightly darker outline of his body filling the gaps between the logs. After long moments, when the guard had still not spoken, Hallam could stand the suspense no longer. 'Is it time?' he asked.

The guard chuckled softly. 'Are you in such a hurry to die, Offal? The council does not meet until tomorrow.'

Hallam sat down again. If Parak had come to gloat he would not give him the satisfaction. Parak's shadowy figure disappeared, moving farther down the passage. He returned a long while later, breathing heavily, and a few moments later the latch was removed and the log was slid aside. 'Out!' Parak ordered.

Hallam remained sitting. 'Why?'

Parak shot a hand through the opening and caught Hallam by the hair. His head was pulled through the logs. Another hand gripped him by the throat, holding him face up and helpless, with only his head and shoulders out, his legs kicking ineffectively inside the cell and his arms trapped.

'It would be a pleasure to kill you now, Offal,' Parak hissed down at him. 'It would be so easy, and I have promised myself the pleasure many times. All I have to do is this...' Parak squeezed, and Hallam writhed ineffectually, his legs kicking as he fought for breath. Parak chuckled and the pressure eased. 'I offered to strangle you, but that is not what my Lady Philippa wants. She does not trust you, Offal. She thinks you will speak against her at the council. She has asked me to set you free, and in return she has promised me a piece of her hot little yoni. You can be sure I will make good use of it. Much better use than you did, Offal.' Parak squeezed again. 'What do you think of that, Offal?'

'Stinking ape!' Hallam wheezed.

Parak squeezed again, slowly, his thick fingers digging and, beyond the blackness and spinning lights, Parak's gloating voice echoed from a distance. 'She won't know you are dead, Offal. I can tell her you have escaped, then I will have both the pleasure of your death *and* her noble yoni to enjoy.'

The pressure was released and Parak dragged him completely through the opening and dumped him on the ground. 'But that would be too risky.' He lashed out with his foot. 'Go, dog offal! Go to the end of the passage and climb the rope. When you reach the spikes climb to the trapdoor. When you are on the wall, go straight to the edge and jump over. It is safe there. A boat will be waiting. And remember, Offal, I will be thinking of you when I'm squeezing her plump little rump.'

Hallam stumbled along the passage, bumping against the rough walls. Nothing made sense. He crashed into the wall at the end and felt around for the rope, not really believing it was there, but it was. He climbed with difficulty, weakened by the lack of food, and he could go only a short distance before the strength in his arms gave out and he slithered down.

Hallam lay where he had fallen, closing his mind to everything except breathing and trying to summon his strength, shutting out Parak's lying words. He tried again, wrapping his feet into the rope as he climbed, forcing himself against the pain in his groin as he pulled upwards. The rope ended and he bumped against iron spikes set into the wall. He caught onto them with relief.

He climbed slowly, feeling for each spike, and testing it cautiously with his weight before pulling himself up with sweaty palms to the next. Sweat also stung his eyes, and his lungs fought for the hot musty air. His hands were pale blobs floating before his eyes.

He tried to concentrate on climbing, and not on freedom or what Parak had said, but the words kept echoing through his head, bringing emptiness, even though he knew Parak had lied.

Panic struck when his head bumped against solid wood at the top. He fumbled around urgently, feeling for an opening, then remembered the trapdoor. He paused to catch his breath and gather his strength.

When his arms and legs had stopped trembling, Hallam wedged his back against the door and pushed down with his feet on the spikes with all his remaining strength, knowing his life depended on the door opening. Pain knifed through his groin. He clenched his teeth to stop from screaming out and continued pushing, blood rushed to pound in his ears, making him dizzy.

When he thought he would pass out, the heavy door grated open just enough to let in a rush of cool air. He jammed his fist in the opening to hold it while he rested, then pushed again until he could scrape through.

He found himself on top of the wall - alone. The garden roof of the palace was close, not much more than a hundred cubits away. No light showed, but the tops of the olive trees glinted and he stared hard at them, looking for shadows or movement. It was a long way up from the top of the wall to the parapet of the roof-garden, she would need a rope, but it was the only way she could come. It was clear to him now what had happened. Parak had not been lying. The ape hated him too much to free him without the promise of reward, and what greater reward could she have offered? But he knew, as she had known, that she was not going to be around for Parak to collect. She would have to come. They would escape together.

But she did not come. Hallam waited long after the drying sweat had chilled before accepting, staring at the shadows on the roof-garden above, and the strength that had flowed back into his body began to ebb; replaced by a deep sense of loneliness. He fought to choke it back.

Lethargically, Hallam dragged the trapdoor back into place and latched it. He moved across the wall to look down at the sea where Parak had told him to jump. It was a terrifyingly long way. Much too far. Shifting specks of white immediately below warned of exposed rocks. Had his eyes not been so well adjusted to the dark he would not have seen them. He could not see the patrol galley, or any other boat. He moved back quickly. Parak had lied again.

He had only two choices; the city or the sea. The city was out of the question, even if he could reach it, which he couldn't. It had to be the sea. There was no other way. He had to jump.

Hallam could think of only one place where he could guarantee no rocks would be waiting below. He moved along the wall until he saw the logs, and the wheels and ropes that lowered them. He stood close to the edge, directly above the sea-gate. It was a calm night with no moon, and the sea below gleamed dark and forbidding.

The rat began moving in his belly. It was too far. At least three times the distance he had fallen from the spar, and that had been bad enough. There had to be some other way.

But he could think of none.

He looked again at the wall of the roof-garden, but no rope hung down, and no movement came from the parapet.

Gathering the shreds of his courage, Hallam adjusted the loincloth, pulled the headband down around his neck, and forced his reluctant feet closer, until he felt his toes creep over the edge. With his one good eye he looked straight ahead, far out over the Great Sea, to where the dark mass of it joined with the stars.

Then from far below he heard it. A brief, hoarse shout. It drifted up, barely audible above the sound of his own unsteady breathing; a shout that tried to be a whisper. 'Jump!'

Hallam jumped. A swooping, sickening, timeless plunge that forced the rat to claw up the inside of his chest to briefly stop his heart. The loincloth unwound, streaming out, flapping and whirring above him like the desperate wings of a flying insect, tugging and pulling, and with arms and legs flailing to stay upright, Hallam struck the water awkwardly with a thunderous splash and went under.

Philippa beat on the door with her clenched fists, giving way to squeals of anger and frustration. She checked the heavy latch again, disbelieving, jiggling it up and down in its slot at the same time as she pushed with her shoulder against the solid timbers, throwing the weight of her body against them, but the door remained as stubbornly immovable as the rock wall. It was either jammed or had been sealed from the other side. She leaned against it for a moment, sagging in defeat as she caught her breath. She had left it too late; delayed by her stupid mother. She tried the door once more, then snatched up the bag at her feet and ran with the hem of her robe lifted clear of her feet, stumbling in her haste, up the steps to the roof-garden.

More disappointment awaited her when she reached the parapet and looked down on the wall to see no sign of him. It was too far to climb down. She peered through the darkness willing the shadowy figure she had seen sitting at the trapdoor to emerge, but it did not. He had gone, jumped without her, perhaps already dead, and she clamped a hand to her mouth to stifle the sudden fear and isolation that engulfed her. She sank, gulping under the weight of it to the floor, sitting on the cold stones with her bag of jewellery clasped in her hand, the other still clamped, hot and wet, to her mouth.

A fishing boat left the deep shadow of the wall and drifted into the area of disturbed water. The man in the boat searched anxiously, concerned not only for the welfare of the person in the water, but also that the noisy splash may have been heard.

A loincloth appeared, floating languidly to the surface like an expired jellyfish. It was quickly retrieved with the aid of a paddle.

After several more anxious moments the man grunted and leaned over the side to grab at a mass of floating hair. With many more grunts the limp body was dragged over the side and draped belly down over the crude pole bench to purge the stomach of water.

When the coughing, retching and gasping had ceased, the man again took a handful of hair and, squatting clear of the stinking pool of fish slime, lifted the face for inspection. Two single eyes stared at each other from close range, then a low chuckle broke the silence. 'The gods have been kind to you, my friend. Big balls and all, you look just like me.'

Parak waited in the passage until he heard the trapdoor above close, then he flipped the rope to unhook it from the spike. He returned with the rope to the empty cell and sat beside it with his back against the logs, flicking idly at his foot with the end of the rope to pass the time.

He wondered idly if it had been a waste of energy to seal the emergency door. It was not likely she would take the chance of trying to smuggle him into the palace. It had few places she could hide him and he could never leave without being seen. Still, she was a conniving little bitch and you could never be too careful, so maybe it was just as well. And wasn't he also protecting her? With the door sealed she could not be blamed for unlatching the trapdoor. Some mystery would remain as to how the glassmaker had escaped, of course, but he would be the first to scratch his head and talk about the intervention of the gods.

When the slave arrived at dawn with the jars and slop pail, Parak strangled him with the rope. He bundled the slave's body into the cell and left, coiling the rope around his waist under his tunic as he walked to the exit door. He waited there for a few moments, listening, then slipped quickly through.

Zabby scuttled the fishing boat at dawn. With only a short period of darkness remaining they had not been able to sail far enough away to avoid detection once it got light. Hallam sat on the beach with the bag of clothing that Zabby had brought, while Zabby paddled the boat out to deeper water and smashed a hole in the bottom with the anchor rock. Hallam listened with mixed feelings. It sounded like the breaking of old bones. He and the boat had shared some unpleasant moments together. It was evil smelling and splattered with his blood, yet he felt a certain sadness at its passing. He consoled himself with the thought it was being put out of its misery; saved from a life of neglect and abuse at the hands of its bloodthirsty owner.

Their best hope of escape, Zabby informed Hallam, was to head south, staying as much as possible in the cover of the forested mountains until they reached the Salt Sea, then to follow the caravan road to Ezion-Geber.

Zabby had taken it upon himself to decide where they were going and how they would get there, and Hallam did not argue. Zabby knew the area and, without his knowledge and strength, Hallam knew he would stand little chance of surviving. His swollen groin and exhausted state meant Zabby had to either push, pull or lift him over the hard places as well as carry the bag of clothes. Fortunately, many of the wadis still held pools left over from the summer rains, so Zabby was spared the added burden of having to fill and carry the wine-skin he had brought for water.

It was not until much later in the day, after they had reached the relative security of the forest and could take a rest, that Zabby was able to explain what had taken place.

'Me and those blacks must have been the only ones who knew what really happened,' Zabby said with a wry grin. 'I should have known you wouldn't have been able to keep your hands off her. How far did you get? the rumour is that you had your breeches down when you were caught.'

'Just get on with it, Zabby,' Hallam growled.

'Nothing much to tell. The old black man came with Kabul to the factory and told me to steal a boat and pick you up when you jumped. I refused, of course. I told him he was mad, but with Kabul drooling on my leg, I didn't argue much. He said to wait in the factory until the second change of guard, when the patrol galley would also be changing. I would not have done it except I realised she must have been involved.' Zabby shook his head in admiration, looking at Hallam with a bemused smile. 'Whatever you did must have made a big impression for her to take such a risk.'

'She's a wonderful girl, Zabby. She has a clever head as well as a pretty one, and she's a loyal friend. I'm worried sick for her.' He did not repeat what Parak had said. He had suffered enough.

'That bad is it? Well, she must have used all her brains to get that pig, Parak, to help.'

Hallam scowled. 'How did you come to choose that boat?'

Zabby grinned. 'It just seemed the right thing to do. It was also the easiest one to steal. Some fools never learn. And talking of fools...' He fixed Hallam with warning look. 'I hope you have no ideas about going back there to visit your noble wench. If so, you'll be going alone. It's impossible. Everyone there is your enemy and there is nowhere to hide. You will only be putting her in more danger. She arranged for you to escape so the least you can do is oblige.' Zabby stood and picked up the bag. 'You'll never see her again, my friend, so forget her. She's not for you.'

Yes she is, Hallam disagreed silently, but even had the words been screamed aloud, the tone would have rung false in his ears.

F ifteen days later, they looked down on the caravan road from the side of a hill at the forest edge. 'The

King's Highway,' Zabby explained. 'From here it will be easier, but also more dangerous.'

Hallam looked without interest at the trampled series of interwoven paths that wound through the barren cliffs. Reaching the caravan road had been a major objective, but the long hike over the coastal plain, then the hard climb through the mountains, had sapped what little strength and enthusiasm he had for Zabby's plan. Each step took him farther from Philippa, and he would have been happier had they been going the other way, across the sea to Lamos.

Zabby pointed to a clump of dusty acacias in a wadi close to the road. 'We'll camp there until we can find the right caravan. It looks as if there is still some water, and we can keep out of sight but still have a good view both ways.'

Hallam followed him down. In contrast to his own mood, Zabby had never looked or sounded happier. And why not? Hallam thought morosely. The King's Road led past Ezion-Geber. Zabby was going home.

They forced themselves to eat the last of the dried fish - stolen by Zabby from the drying racks of a fishing village soon after leaving the beach, along with a small bag of dried barley. Without means of making a fire to boil it they had been eating the fish half raw, reinforced with barley mush and, when available, wild mushrooms and the occasional fig or berry. It took a considerable effort not to gag.

The first caravan arrived at noon. Dozing in the shade, Hallam heard the sing-song voice of a driver calling to his camel and the jingle and creaking of harness. Zabby scrutinised it from behind a bush, but it was only a small Egyptian caravan and he wanted something bigger, and preferably from Arabia. Small caravans, Zabby had informed him, showing off the knowledge acquired from seven years of escape research, would be less inclined to take on extra help, even if it was only for food, and the caravans of Egypt and Judaea did not pass through Edom. They turned south at the junction of Wadi-Bada, well before.

Arabian caravans, Zabby said, not only passed through Ezion-Geber, but were also less likely to be stopped by a tax patrol. With peace in the land and time on their hands, Judean soldiers regularly inspected caravans in the hope of discovering untaxed goods or other misdemeanours - such as the harbouring of runaway slaves. The penalty was usually the confiscation of part, or all of the caravan - a juicy incentive for the underpaid soldiers who stood to receive a useful percentage.

At Zabby's suggestion, they moved camp late in the afternoon, following the road until it reached one of the rest stops; a narrow protected canyon sparsely dotted with camel-grass and the blackened remains of old camp fires. 'It will be easier to speak to them if they are already stopped,' Zabby explained.

When still no Arabian caravan appeared the next day, the rumbling of their stomachs forced Zabby to admit defeat. They would approach the very next caravan, he vowed, regardless of where it came from.

It turned out to be Egyptian. They had already agreed that Zabby would take on the role of slave and Hallam that of an Edomite merchant. Hopefully, the purple headband would be a convincing touch.

'What reason do we give for being here?' Hallam asked. 'We look like beggars. And what about my ear, won't they think I'm a slave too?'

'We wouldn't be beggars and have to go through all this,' Zabby grumbled, 'if only you had been more trusting and not hidden your silver where I couldn't find it.' He studied Hallam critically, taking in the black eye - now faded to a becoming lilac to match his headband - the mutilated ear, and generally set-upon appearance. 'Better let me do the talking,' he advised.

They approached to where a kneeling camel with a reed

awning on its back had just dispatched a man in a white *kamis*. 'Peace be with thee.' Zabby greeted him, crossing his hands at his chest and bowing.

The Egyptian paused in his stretching and foot stamping to regard them both warily before responding with a tentative. 'And to thee...'

As was the custom, Zabby first paid eloquent homage to the Egyptian and his belongings before coming to business, complimenting him on the extraordinary quality of his camels, the unusually brilliant concept of the reed *houdah*, and the astounding beauty of the Egyptian's green slippers. It was all grossly overdone and unnecessary in Hallam's opinion.

The Egyptian listened with an expression of sleepy disinterest until Zabby got down to explaining how they had been set upon by thieves. Then the Egyptian's hooded eyes opened a little wider and he blinked several times, as if awakening from a doze.

'My esteemed master showed great courage by attacking the leader with his bare hands,' Zabby gushed, 'and even after he had been beaten by all four of them and his ear bitten off, he insisted on giving chase. But it was no use, they escaped with our two camels and all our food. We have not eaten so much as a dried fig in three days.' Zabby gave no explanation as to his own actions during the robbery.

Two younger men had joined the Egyptian, possibly his sons, for they listened to Zabby's story and gazed at Hallam with the same sleepy eyes and bemused expressions. Hallam accepted their gaze with a modestly bowed head and wished Zabby would shut up.

Zabby continued. 'So, it is only to where the road splits at Wadi-Bada that we ask to accompany you... no more than five days. We will work at whatever you say for only a small share of food.'

'Ah,' murmured the Egyptian.

'And there will be more of us to protect your valuable goods should the thieves return,' Zabby added.

'You said there were only four thieves,' said the elder of the sons. 'But we have three of ourselves and five strong camel drivers.'

'And little food,' added his brother.

The Egyptian partly lifted his weary arms in agreement. 'Regrettably, this is true. Perhaps another caravan....'

'If you paid us, it would be different,' said his son.

'Fifty coppers each would be a reasonable amount,' his father agreed.

Zabby held out his hands in a gesture of helplessness. 'Sadly, it was all stolen.'

'You were most fortunate the thieves did not also steal your jewellery, the son remarked, looking at the medallion that had somehow managed to negotiate the open neck of Hallam's tunic.

'It was hidden,' said Hallam. He demonstrated by returning the medallion to its customary place.

'Such jewellery could be more acceptable than copper.'

'No, it was a gift from my mother. I cannot....'

'Ah, this I can understand. A mother's gift is to be cherished. I myself could never trade such an attractive gift for only a few days of food. Even such food as freshly smoked goat, or date cakes that melted and tasted like honey on the tongue.'

'Perhaps...' ventured Zabby after a short silence. 'Perhaps his kind mother would understand if she knew her beloved son had not eaten for three days.' Hallam frowned furiously at him, but Zabby ignored him, pressing on. 'But as your vast experience and keen eye has told you, my lord, it has far more worth than a few bowls of food. Maybe if you were to include a camel it would appease his understanding mother further. Not one of your best, naturally, only your oldest, so my grievously injured master can continue his journey without his terrible pain.'

'A camel?' It was a shocked chorus. All three Egyptians looked at Zabby in astonishment. The younger son, a slim boy with delicate features and a shy smile, took a small step back, as if to exclude himself from the bargaining.

Zabby turned to Hallam with his hand extended. Unseen by the Egyptians he blinked his eye rapidly, obviously trying to convey a message. Hallam continued to glare at him, fingering the medallion protectively through his tunic. He had thought it lost until Zabby had produced it from the bag of clothing he had collected, and he had sworn not to remove it again.

Zabby wriggled his fingers impatiently, blinking and scowling furiously, and Hallam grudgingly removed the medallion from around his neck and handed it over.

'Forgive my good friend,' Zabby apologised, so involved with his new role of bargainer that he had forgotten his old one of slave. 'He has become very attached to it.' The Egyptian gave the medallion perfunctory inspection, passing it in silence from one to the other of his sons before handing it back to Zabby.

'Interesting, but a camel?' He smiled lazily. 'Surely it is a joke.' His sons nodded and smiled politely.

Zabby laughed. 'You misunderstand. I did not mean a camel to keep, but only to borrow.' Zabby lowered his voice, as if afraid of being overheard. 'You see, in fighting with the thieves my master also received a cowardly kick in the...' he paused, pointing to his crutch. 'It makes walking very difficult for him.'

'Ah...' the Egyptians switched their attention from Zabby's crutch to that of Hallam's, as if expecting him to prove Zabby's story by lowering his breeches and revealing the injured parts. Hallam shifted uncomfortably. They had already received more than their share of unwelcome attention.

'Surely,' Zabby pleaded. 'A man of such obvious kindness as yourself could not refuse an injured man a small ride and a paltry bowl of food in exchange for such a magnificent piece of jewellery?'

'Two bowls,' corrected the Egyptian.

'Two bowls.' Zabby amended. 'And perhaps two skins of wine each night to help us forget the unfortunate loss of our camels and goods?'

'One.'

'And no work?'

'Only your own.'

'My esteemed master will be greatly sorrowed by the loss of his mother's valuable gift,' Zabby said. 'But what choice have the hungry but to accept what is offered them? I envy your ability to make such a hard bargain, my lord, and we humbly agree to your terms.' He handed the medallion to the Egyptian, who then dangled it from the end of a heavily ringed finger, offering it casually to the elder of his two sons.

Hallam turned away impolitely and limped angrily towards the tree where they had left the bag, leaving Zabby to finalise the details of the arrangement before following.

Hallam was waiting for him. 'I cannot believe what you did!'

'Please! Not so loud, they will hear you.'

'I don't care! I thought you were a friend!'

Zabby adopted an injured look. 'Have I not provided you with good food and wine, and a camel to ride for the next five days?'

'You? It is my medallion that is providing it, you only gave it away and it was not yours to give.'

Zabby shrugged. 'You cannot eat glass.' He changed the subject before Hallam could answer. 'Did you see how they looked when I asked for a camel?' He grimaced with disgust. 'I gave up too easily. I should have asked for more. I should have asked for a nightly share of their women. After a full belly and a skin of wine there is nothing like....'

'I'm going to get it back. We can wait for another caravan.'

'You will only be wasting time. And it is I who should be offended by your lack of trust. Did you not see my signal?'

When he received no answer, Zabby gave a patient sigh. 'You are still inexperienced in these matters, my friend, whereas I have been a slave for many years and learned much about staying alive. The first thing you must learn is that when you have nothing your problems are many but your choices are few. You must start with the most important.'

Hallam frowned at him in confusion, and Zabby groaned. 'For now, I have solved the problem of food and transport. In five days, when we reach Wadi-Bada, I will solve the problem of the medallion. Meanwhile, it is in safe hands.'

In the face of such irrefutable logic, Hallam could only scowl.

After three days Hallam grudgingly admitted that Zabby may have been right. The food was the best he had eaten since leaving home, and not having to walk had given him a chance to regain his strength and for his groin to mend. He would have preferred a horse, but he quickly mastered the strange rocking motion of the camel and was able to doze fitfully for long periods in the sun.

For the first time since the darkness of the prison cell, Hallam was beginning to believe in his freedom and appreciate being alive. Two more precious gifts from his goddess. He thought of her often, though he tried not to, for the spectre of Parak intruded, taking much of the warmth from the sun. He prayed to the mother goddess Rhea to keep her safe.

The women accompanying the caravan had been chosen exclusively for their cooking and laundering skills, but Zabby was not fussy. He breached the flimsy canvas of the women's tents on the second night and squirmed his way into the bed of a cook, thereby ending his long period of enforced celibacy and, at the same time, greatly improving their diet. He had not as yet explained how he intended to recover the medallion, but knowing how Zabby's mind worked, Hallam suspected it was because the devious scoundrel hadn't yet given it a thought.

On the fourth day the caravan stopped as usual at dusk. A fire had been started, and the drivers were tending to their camels and loads when a large group of men rode into the camp.

'Soldiers!' whispered Zabby. 'Be ready to run... go for the cliffs where their horses can't follow.'

But they were given no chance to run. Within a few moments the caravan was surrounded. The horsemen ordered everyone to gather at the head of the caravan and sit on the ground, and Hallam and Zabby moved in amongst the five camel drivers, trying to look as if they belonged with them. Logs were added to the cooking fire to provide more light and a group of older men approached on foot, obviously the leaders. One of them, a man with a grey beard and a black cloak, addressed the Egyptian caravan owner.

'From whence do you come?'

'The city of David, my lord,' answered the Egyptian in a tremulous voice. 'We have no goods of value, only seed grain and iron.'

'We will see for ourselves... do you return to Egypt?'

'Yes, my lord.'

Another group rode up to join the man with the cloak. At their head was a young man, also in a dark cloak, but it was bordered with purple. The horse he rode was the most magnificent beast Hallam had ever seen; taller than a man at the shoulder, and as black and shiny as a ripe olive. It did not walk, but pranced daintily with the weightless steps of a dancing girl. The youth dismounted and spoke quietly for a few moments to the man with the grey beard, then the questioning was resumed.

'Have you been inspected by soldiers since leaving Judaea?'

'My lord?' The Egyptian acted confused, playing for time. In the continued silence he decided to play it safe. 'I do not believe so, my lord.' A ripple of laughter from the soldiers caused him to hastily amend his answer. 'That is, not since leaving Judaea, my lord.'

The group of camel drivers had become restless, muttering complaints in anticipation of the arduous task of having to untie their loads and display the goods for inspection. Zabby had become strangely still since the arrival of the young man with the black horse. But now he too became restless, then, to Hallam's consternation, Zabby stood and moved forward.

The movement drew immediate attention. 'Sit down!' commanded the man with the beard, and the two men flanking him stepped forward with their spears. But Zabby ignored the order. He reached the front then threw himself full length on the ground at the young man's feet.

The man with the beard stepped forward and prodded Zabby with a foot. 'Get up, slave, and speak while you can!'

Zabby scrambled to a kneeling position and bowed his head. 'Peace unto thee, father, and your forgiveness, but are you not Abdon, whose good friend was Zabud the shipwright?'

The man with the beard stiffened with surprise. 'And who asks the question?'

'I am Zabudesha, the son of the shipwright.'

'Mother of Zeus!' the old man bent down to peer closely at Zabby. 'But there is no resemblance! Speak the names of others to prove yourself.'

'Is your good wife not mistress, Tirzah, who made the best sweetened meats in all of Ezion-Geber? And who gave them freely to myself and... ' Zabby's voice grew soft and Hallam had to strain forward to catch the words. '...forgive me, it brings me pain to speak of it, and there will be pain for you in the hearing.'

'No, continue.'

'My closest friend... your son, Jetha, was killed by the dogs of Judaea on the same day of my capture. We fought together.'

The old man remained unmoving for a long time after Zabby had finished, his face like stone, then he placed a hand on Zabby's shoulder. 'And forgive me, Zabudesha, but it has been a long time, and you are much changed. We thought you also dead.' He lifted Zabby to his feet and the two of them embraced.

When they turned to face the youth waiting patiently to the side, Hallam was astonished to see in the light of the fire that one side of Zabby's face glistened, as if tears had streaked the dust on his cheek.

They rode away on spare horses supplied by Prince Hadad and his men; Zabby bouncing awkwardly to the unaccustomed rhythm, and Hallam doing much the same as he tried out the foot-loops the Edomites had attached to their saddlecloths. He soon discovered that as long as he applied weight evenly on both sides he could stand in them, relieving the strain on his knees and, even more comforting, easing the pressure on his groin. It took less time to master the two reins - one either side - which passed through the horse's mouth; an arrangement so simple he wondered why he had not thought of it himself.

They rode south along the King's Highway, spread out in groups of four, and they held a slow but steady pace that the tall desert horses were able to maintain for most of the night without seeming to tire. They paused at regular intervals to listen ahead for a whistle that cleared the way, then, as they continued, a rider would appear at the side of the road, waiting for them to pass. The men of Prince Hadad were obviously well trained and disciplined.

With each stride forward, Hallam's spirits rose. It was good to feel safe again and on a horse and, although he had met only a few of the men, he felt among friends.

The old man with the beard, introduced as Councillor Abdon, had embraced him as he had Zabby, welcoming him as a friend, and when he had been trying to make up his mind whether or not to prostrate himself as Zabby had done, the prince solved his dilemma by clasping his hand and smiling the most dazzling smile. And to make things even sweeter, was the familiar thumping of the medallion against his chest.

Grinning to himself in the dark, Hallam recalled the haste with which the Egyptian had removed it from his son's neck after Zabby had craftily informed him that he was trying to talk the prince out of searching the caravan. 'I have told him of your extreme kindness in helping us,' Zabby had said, giving Hallam several unseen nudges in the back. 'And such kindness should not be repaid by having you part with half your goods.' Then Zabby had paused dramatically, as if suddenly remembering. 'Although... I do believe my friend's medallion, given him by his dear mother...'

When the old man with the beard also thanked the Egyptian for taking care of his friends and paid him two pieces of silver for their passage, the Egyptian was so overcome with gratitude he had taken Zabby's hand in both of his and kissed the fingers. Hallam thought it was time he reviewed his opinion of his friend.

They left the King's Highway before dawn, taking a less defined trail that led through the rugged mountains of Edom to the Narrow Sea. At sunrise they stopped by a stream for food and rest. Apparently there was no further need for caution, for the groups joined to make a single large band of at least a hundred men, and the talk was free and jovial.

Zabby disappeared to meet up with old comrades, and Hallam led his horse to the stream. While it drank, he took a handful of dry grass and rubbed down the sweaty patch on the animal's back, enjoying the familiar smell of its sweat and the twitching of its skin. It brought back fond memories of his own horse. 'I think Piko would be much impressed by you,' he told the tall brown mare, and felt a sudden pang as he realised he may never see Piko again.

'Her name is Ishka,' said a soft voice behind.

Hallam turned to see Prince Hadad at the head of the black stallion. It was the first time he had seen the prince since the night before, and then it had been only briefly and in the light of the fire. He had not noticed then how young the prince was - much younger than himself - or how large and girlish were the dark eyes and lashes against the unblemished cheeks. Yet for all his youth and girlish looks, the prince exuded an aura of quiet authority. A little surprised, it was a few moments before Hallam became aware that he was staring. 'Forgive me, my lord, I did not hear...'

Prince Hadad interrupted by holding up a hand. 'There is no need for formality, we are all brothers here. I will be happy if you just call me, Prince, like everyone else... and this is Fire Dancer.'

'A fitting name,' Hallam said, relieved by the friendly manner. 'When I saw him last night he looked to be dancing.'

Prince Hadad's cheeks dimpled with his smile. 'Yes, he only does it when he is near a fire. I think he must have stood in one when he was a foal and still remembers.' He slapped affectionately at the stallion's neck and it lifted its head from the water to nuzzle him wetly. Hallam laughed and stretched out a hand, wanting to touch the silken nose, but the stallion immediately laid back his ears. 'It's all right, Dancer,' the prince soothed, 'he is a friend.'

The stallion sniffed cautiously at Hallam's outstretched fingers, then continued up his arm to his face. Hallam stiffened as the wet nose touched his undamaged ear, but the stallion's ears had come forward again, and the sniffing was even and gentle. Hallam kept a wary eye on the ears though as a mix of water and saliva was dribbled over his neck. The stallion nibbled daintily at his cheek, then suddenly snorted, and they both jerked away.

This time it was Prince Hadad who laughed, while Hallam grinned foolishly and wiped at his soggy cheek. 'I think he likes you,' the prince said. 'Come, you must share some food with me, then later we will ride together and you can tell me more about where you come from. Your friend, Zabudesha, has already told me that you are descended from the kings of Crete, so we have much in common.'

Hallam grinned as he followed the prince. He would *definitely* have to review his opinion of Zabby.

Riding at the side of Prince Hadad gave Hallam an exalted feeling to go with his unexpected rise to nobility. His ready acceptance by the prince also accorded him the recognition of all the men, and he was treated to smiles and friendly assistance whenever he was in their company. Rather than deny Zabby's creative report of his lineage - which would have made them both look foolish - Hallam skipped modestly over the details when asked, and tried instead to live up to expectations.

He adopted the same tidy habits as his new friend - a task made simpler after the prince had loaned him some of his own clothes. Included was a warm cloak with a woollen collar to keep out the chilly mountain air. To complement it and, to some extent influenced by recollections of Philippa,

Hallam also worked hard at adopting the prince's quiet but confident manner of speaking. In return, it was noticed by many that the prince had developed a new habit of rolling his eyes.

Even Zabby was impressed with Hallam's new attitude and status. 'I know the prince likes you,' Zabby told him. 'But shouldn't you treat him with a bit more respect?'

'Oh, Haddy doesn't mind, he gets plenty of that already.'

'Haddy?' Zabby's eye bulged. 'You call Prince Hadad, *Haddy?*'

'Of course!' Hallam replied, turning aside to hide the smile at Zabby's flabbergasted expression. 'Us nobles always call each other by pet names.'

For the first time since Hallam had known him, Zabby was speechless.

But in truth, Hallam had a great deal of respect for the prince, and not because of his princely status. Prince Hadad may have had the face of a lamb, but not the heart of one. He rode the black stallion with the same carefree assurance with which he commanded his men, and that alone was enough to convince Hallam of the prince's courage. No one else, he had heard, had ever ridden the black stallion.

'I would allow you to ride him,' the prince said, when Hallam made subtle overtures in that direction. 'But he would not. You may try if you wish, he likes you, so I may be wrong. Only be careful of your foot. The last man who tried lost a toe.'

Hallam did not try. The stallion allowed him the privilege of rubbing his nose, patting his neck, and even tugging on his forelock, but any movement to the side brought an instant flattening of the ears, and a certain intimidating stillness. Hallam was thankful the prince had not mentioned the toe while the stallion had been snuffling around his ear.

Being in the company of the prince soon made Hallam aware he had shortcomings in areas other than dress and manner. He measured himself against the younger man and was not pleased with the shortfall. His mother had taught him much to be thankful for, and he had also learned from Philippa, but they were women in a man's world. Lamos had provided no incentive to learn more than was necessary for daily living, and while Tyre had been a mine of information, there had been no opportunity or time to dig further. But he had ample time now as they rode through the mountains, visiting the villages, especially around the prince's fire at night, when they were joined by the councillors, and Hallam determined to make the most of it.

For the moment he had nowhere to go, and no plans other than the vague idea of one day returning to Philippa, but even that unlikely dream was beginning to fade with reality. And although he was happy to be in good company, he was not one of the prince's men, and things could change. He could not return home, so knowledge of the world outside was going to be essential to his survival. He could do worse than ask questions and listen to the knowledgeable Edomites with both ears and mind open.

'But if both countries had the same father, why is there war?' Hallam asked one evening as they were discussing the history of Edom and Judaea. 'Brothers should not fight each other.' Yet even as he spoke the words, Hallam remembered his own battles with his brother, Ethan.

'It can easily happen,' answered Councillor Abdon, 'if a man steals from his brother in the belief his brother has been given more than he.'

'And if a man does steal from his brother,' said one of the other councillors. 'He must find a reason other than greed to excuse his theft, and what better reason than hate?'

'We are both descended from the twin sons of Isaac,' Prince Hadad explained. 'The Edomites from Esau, and the Judeans from Jacob. The birthright should have gone to Esau, who was the elder twin, but Jacob used a bowl of stew to trick his brother and father into giving it to him, making them believe the exchange was only a joke, but then forcing them into keeping their word.'

'A bowl of stew?' Hallam was incredulous. 'You mean the war started because of a bowl of stew?'

Councillor Abdon sighed. 'Such are the foolish ways of men.'

Prince Hadad's father had been killed in a futile battle with the Judeans when the prince was still a child - the same battle which saw Zabby put into slavery. Fearing the young prince would meet the same fate as his father, the councillors had fled with him to the mountains and they had been in exile ever since. They went from village to village, accompanied by a constantly changing band of volunteers, and the villagers provided them with food and shelter, looked after their horses, and kept them informed on the whereabouts of Judean patrols.

From what Hallam saw and learned, the loyalty of the villagers was unquestionable. They would gladly have rallied behind their prince in battle, but Edom did not have the resources of Judaea. They had no powerful allies to call on, no chariots or horses, and no gold. And Solomon was careful to follow in the steps of his father and keep it that way. He maintained his governors in the Edomite cities, and subjugated the citizens with high taxes, taking over the copper, iron and shipping industries of Ezion-Geber, and controlling the strategic trade routes to Egypt, Arabia and India via King David's Highway.

The only area over which King Solomon did not have complete control was in the hearts and minds of the people. And not only the Edomite people, but also the Judeans. While Solomon grew richer and more powerful, the people themselves stayed poor, and it was to this weakness in Solomon's armour that the prince and his men were applying pressure: sowing the seeds of revolution in the fertile ground of discontent, and nurturing the results with tenderness. It was a process at which they had become adept.

'It will take a long time, and exile makes it difficult,' the prince explained. 'Maybe I will never be free to rule in my own land and lead my people to a better life, but at least we are doing what we can now, and are making friends while Solomon makes enemies.'

'If you kill an enemy who has a family of three,' councillor Abdon philosophised to Hallam. 'You will lose one enemy but gain three more. But if you show mercy and give him his life, do you not stand to gain four friends?'

Hallam was to see a variation of this philosophy graphically demonstrated a few days later while on their way to another village. They came unexpectedly on a cohort of Judean soldiers resting on the crest of a hill after a steep climb. The soldiers had shucked their leather patrol armour and were lying bunched up in the shade of a single tree in a most unmilitary fashion; their rein-hobbled horses scattered about in the search for something to nibble.

Approaching from the opposite direction, the well-armed and disciplined men of Prince Hadad could have taken the soldiers and their horses easily, but they rode past without even changing pace, showing no more attention to the alarmed and scrambling Judeans than if they had been a group of locals minding their herd. Some of the prince's men lifted their spears in casual salute, chuckling quietly to themselves when they received a few bewildered salutes in return.

Hallam was as surprised as the Judean soldiers. Riding at the head of the column beside the prince, he turned to look behind, but nothing had changed. The column had maintained its neat order and not moved from the path, and the soldiers under the tree - now all standing and gaping after them - had not moved either. Hallam was almost reluctant to ask the question. 'Were they not enemy soldiers?'

Prince Hadad gave him one of his dimpled smiles and rolled his eyes. 'Enemy? I saw no enemy, Hallam, only a few lazy soldiers.'

Questioned by a still puzzled Hallam, the prince elaborated on what had happened later that evening.

'Our men have strict orders not to fight except in self defence. It will only bring more soldiers. This way, they have no reason. The commander of that group is aware we could easily have taken them and will be grateful, not only for his life, but also because we did not treat them with scorn and allowed him to keep face. That is the reason for the salutes. With nothing to fear, his patrolling will be made easier and he will treat our villagers more kindly.'

In the weeks that followed, Hallam saw many such examples of Edomite diplomacy, and learned much from the often philosophical discussions of the councillors.

'You come from a wise people.' he told Zabby one morning as they shared sentry duty from a lookout above the camp.

Zabby pulled a sour face. 'And I thought you were only attracted by my beauty.'

Hallam laughed. 'Never that! But if Councillor Abdon and his friends can succeed, the prince will make a great king.'

'We will succeed,' Zabby said positively.

'I am sure you will. And you will stay to help?' It was a rhetorical question. Hallam knew Zabby would not leave, even if he had a choice.

Zabby nodded. 'And you?'

Hallam had been asking himself the same question repeatedly over the past weeks and he still had no answer. He liked and admired the Edomites, and as the prince's friend he enjoyed special privileges - except when it came to the young females of the villages, which Hallam was not interested in anyway. It could have been a lot worse. He had good friends, horses to ride and mountains to climb. They were not the mountains of Lamos, but ruggedly beautiful nonetheless, especially now, with every fissure in their barren slopes sharpened by the crisp air of approaching winter.

Hallam pulled the collar up further around his ears. 'I don't know what I'm going to do, Zabby,' he answered truthfully.

Zabby nodded again, as if it was the answer he had expected.

'But I feel I should be doing something in return for my keep.'

'There is nothing to do. The prince enjoys your company, and it is Solomon you must thank for your food.' None of the Edomites, Hallam had noticed, could ever bring themselves to call Solomon 'King'.

'I did forget.' Hallam laughed. 'I don't think I'll be going to thank him though.'

The councillors had long ago decided that as Solomon was responsible for their exile, he should pay for their upkeep. In the guise of Judean soldiers, the prince's volunteers extracted a toll from all the caravans that passed through Edom, which was, after all, their own country. The scheme worked well. Prince Hadad got the toll and King Solomon got the blame.

A useful bonus to the scheme was discovered by accident. The caravans from India and Arabia were usually left alone by Solomon's roving tax collectors for diplomatic reasons, and the prince's men discovered that by dropping the name of a particularly unpleasant local commander during a toll collecting exercise, especially on one of the Arabian caravans, they could virtually guarantee the commander's removal - and sometimes even his execution.

Egyptian caravans suffered the most. Pharaoh's despotic predecessors had, for centuries, made life unpleasant for their neighbours, but Egypt's waning power now made it vulnerable to those with long memories. As well as being heavily taxed, it was not unusual for Solomon, or his friend, Khiram of Tyre, to keep the envoys of Pharaoh waiting for weeks before sending them back with demands for more gold in exchange for the timber or other desperately needed goods they came to buy. The fangs of the asp had decayed, and goading it had become a safe and satisfying diversion, even for the men of Prince Hadad.

In a country where a spy or informer lurked behind every tuft of camel-grass, it was eloquent testimony to the prince's popularity that the toll scheme had worked for several years without discovery.

As they were leaving the lookout at the end of their guard duty, Zabby once again broached the subject of Hallam's own popularity with Prince Hadad. It had obviously been worrying him. 'Call me interfering, if you like,' he mumbled, looking as if he had swallowed something unpleasant. 'But you need to be careful of Councillor Jotham's son, Lemek.' Zabby paused to give Hallam a sideways look. 'I heard him talking to his father about you. He was saying he did not believe your ancestors were um... from Crete, and that you should not be trusted so close to the prince.'

Hallam stopped in alarm. 'But that's wrong! Did you not tell him?'

'Tell him what?'

'That I could be trusted, of course.'

'How could I? Then he would know I had been listening.'

'Councillor Jotham is the one with the funny hair, isn't he? I'll talk to him and tell him the truth.'

Zabby looked as if the unpleasant thing he had swallowed was about to come up. 'Maybe that would not be a good idea. Anyway, I have also heard that Lemek used to be more in the prince's company before you came, so maybe that is the reason for his dislike.'

'You mean he's jealous?'

'Can't you tell? Lemek is not one for the girls.'

'You mean he thinks the prince and me...?'

'Not surprising, the way you primp around rolling your eyes at each other,' Zabby muttered.

'It sounds to me like it's you that is jealous.'

'Maybe if you remove the lump and grow something soft in front to hold on to,' Zabby responded.

The news about Lemek worried Hallam. He would have to find a way to dispel their fears. He did not want to be the cause of a rift in what otherwise seemed to be a perfect all-round relationship. 'What do you suggest I do then?' he asked. He had a feeling Zabby was holding something back.

'Some time away will be good. The next village we visit is the closest one to Ezion-Geber, and I am told that my mother is still alive. If you were to come with me to visit her....?'

'Won't that be dangerous?'

'No one will know you there.'

'I was thinking of you.'

Zabby gave a cynical snort. 'What is one more slave among so many?'

When Hallam told Prince Hadad of their intentions, the prince was quick to offer support. 'I envy you, friend Hallam, and it grieves me that I am unable to accompany you to my own city. I would give much to visit the tomb of my father. I hope he understands in his afterlife that it is the people's welfare I fear to risk and not my own.'

'I'm sure your father would be proud to hear those words.' Hallam replied. 'Perhaps while I am there I can visit in your place and pass your respects?'

'Sadly, that would not be possible. The location of the tomb is a secret known only to a few. I myself have only seen it once. However, it would mean a great deal to me if you could visit the temple and pass some gold to a certain old priest who cares for it. I will give you his name, and we will also talk to Councillor Abdon and arrange for you to have some silver. I do not want you to remember my city as a place of hardship.'

In the friendly atmosphere of the moment, Hallam was tempted to bring up the subject of his discussion with Zabby concerning the fears of councillor Jotham and his son, but he held back. Sleeping wolves should be left in peace.

Accompanied by two of Prince Hadad's men, Zabby and Hallam left the village and negotiated the last of the jagged red hills bordering the sea on foot. The terrain was too rough for the desert horses, which in any case would have attracted too much attention in the city.

From barren cliffs they looked down on the clear water of the gulf and Ezion-Geber. The stone buildings looked drab and hot. Behind the city to the north could be seen a thin line of dust, which marked the King's Highway. Even more disappointing was the sea. It was wonderfully clear and blue, with patches of brilliant white beach, but so narrow that the naked brown cliffs on the other side could be seen clearly.

'Is that it? Hallam asked in surprise. 'I know it is called the Narrow Sea, but I thought it would be a lot wider than that. There is barely enough water to have a good swim.'

The men laughed. One of them pointed to the south, down the length of the narrow gulf to a distant haze. 'The sea is down there. Not very far, but I fear it is too far to swim.'.

Hallam and Zabby started down the path, leaving the two men at the top where they were to act as lookouts for the prince.

The city looked bigger once they reached the bottom. From the top, most of it had been hidden by the shoulder of a hill, and they had not had a view of the long stretch of wharves and docks. Fishing boats and sailing craft littered the harbour, evoking unpleasant memories of Tyre for Hallam. It was not as large or as busy as Tyre though, and it had no wall.

Wearing a respectable robe and a white *kufiyeh* around his head to hide his ears, Zabby led the way with a jaunty step, pointing out places of interest, including the temple where Hallam had promised the prince he would leave the gold.

'That place over there is now called the dog house,' Zabby

explained, lifting his chin disdainfully in the direction of an imposing white building standing alone on a hillock. Regimental pennants fluttered from the roof, and an army bivouac encircled the base of the hill. Large statues of reclining lions with abnormally long snouts guarded the entrance to the avenue leading up to the house. 'It used to be Prince Hadad's palace,' Zabby said. 'Now it is occupied by Solomon's watch-dog governor.'

Ezion-Geber was a major port with a constant influx of thirsty sailors, so it was not surprising that it abounded with taverns. Zabby poked his head into many of those they passed, searching the interior briefly before hurrying on. This did not surprise Hallam either. Prince Hadad's camps were all dry. Zabby must have been steaming at the mouth.

'Looking for something in particular?' Hallam asked. 'Or just checking to see if they have enough to keep you going before you start?'

Zabby disdained to answer. He crossed over an alleyway then stopped. 'Ah! I knew it was still here!' Hallam followed him down the alley and into a tavern. It was obviously popular for there was hardly room to stand. 'Over here,' Zabby said, pushing through the crowd to the back wall. He paid some copper to a fat man sitting on a stool and was given two strange looking yellow mugs. 'Indian tree cane,' Zabby explained proudly, as if they were his own creation. He passed one to Hallam. It was surprisingly light and smooth.

'You fill it here,' Zabby directed, grinning with anticipation. He held the mug under one of a line of wooden spouts protruding from the stone wall and removed the plug to allow a clear liquid to run into the mug. When it was full to the brim, he passed it carefully. 'Try *that* for camel piss!' He watched, smiling expectantly, his eye gleaming as Hallam took a tentative sip. 'Well?'

'Not bad... nice and cold. What is it?'

'Not bad?' Zabby looked offended. 'You will never taste palm wine as sweet or as cold.' He filled his own mug and took a long sip, then paused to close his eye and give a great sigh of contentment. 'I dreamed of this every day at that god-cursed glass factory.' Zabby's language had moderated considerably since joining the prince.

Zabby explained the secret of the cold wine. It came from a cave deep in the hill where large clay jars were buried in the cool earth. Lengths of Indian cane filled with hollow reeds delivered the palm wine underground to the tavern after passing through a spring.

Hallam was thinking of a way he could cut short the nostalgic drinking session before it became a drunken spree when, surprisingly, Zabby suggested it himself. 'If you don't mind,' he apologised, peering longingly into the bottom of his empty mug. 'I have to see my mother. Perhaps I should have seen her first...'

'No, I would feel the same way,' Hallam agreed, taking the mug from Zabby's hand. 'We can always come back later. Best camel piss I've ever had.'

They stopped at the entrance to a dilapidated looking cottage in a street full of red fowls, dogs, and screeching children.

Zabby tugged indecisively on the lobe of his good ear. 'Are you sure you won't come with me?'

Hallam slapped Zabby on the shoulder. 'She will be happy to see you. To her you will always be beautiful... and tell her you love her, mothers always like that.'

The prince had told Hallam to go to the temple at dusk, when the head priest would be there, so he had the whole afternoon free. He spent it at the docks, watching the boats coming and going and listening to the sailors. He bought a bowl of fish stew and a round of bread and sat outside in the sun near the water where he could enjoy the atmosphere.

With the palm wine sitting warm and mellow in his belly,

and silver to spend, Hallam could not remember feeling in better physical condition. His groin had returned to normal and everything seemed to be in working order, and months of hard riding and climbing had put the bounce back in his step.

A group of apprentice pilots was sitting nearby, boasting about where they had been. Strange names and places rolled off their tongues, as if they were talking about old friends. '...two brail ropes and a yard line to tie the old cow's nose to her fat backside so she wouldn't bend in the middle,' one of the young pilots was saying in a voice tinged with disbelief. 'Can you believe such stupidity?'

'My pilot refused to sail one from Myos,' reported one of the others. 'Said he would rather paddle there on a bloated camel.' His companions laughed. 'They must think the Narrow Sea is like the Nile.'

Hallam surmised they were talking about Egyptian boats, and he had a sudden yearning to meet them. 'Have any of you met a Pilot called Meldek, from Tyre?' he asked.

None of them had. One of them returned Hallam's question. 'Are you a pilot?'

'No, they tell me it is a good life, being a sailor.'

'Only if you are not tied to an oar.'

Hallam joined in their laughter, remembering the good times with Meldek and his crew. There existed a camaraderie among sailors he found appealing. Like the prince's men, they all seemed to belong to the same side, no matter where they came from.

'How do you become a pilot?' he asked.

'The easiest way is to own a boat.' It barely raised a smile. They were becoming bored with the outsider.

Hallam finished his stew and left the apprentices to their wild and unlikely stories. He spent another pleasant hour looking for, and buying a woollen skullcap of a type that could be pulled down over the ears, then it was time to go to the temple.

The head priest was a stooped old man who listened with head cocked as Hallam passed the prince's brief message, and the gold minas wrapped in a piece of cloth. A clasp of the priest's hand - the little finger in particular - and his duty was done.

Hallam walked towards the doorway. Through the opening he could see two soldiers coming across the square towards the temple. Walking close behind them was a man who looked as if he was trying to use the soldiers as a shield. The secretive behaviour caused Hallam to stop while still in the shadow. The soldiers parted as they reached the steps, leaving the man uncovered for a moment and, with a start, Hallam recognised Lemek, the son of councillor Jotham.

Hallam caught up with the priest as he was about to enter a room at the back of the temple. 'Do not be alarmed,' Hallam reassured him, 'but I think I have been followed. Is there another way out?'

The priest regarded him anxiously for a moment, then nodded. He led the way into the room, then through another door into a passage. At the end of it was a door leading out.

Hallam watched from the cover of a stall across the square. A soldier appeared in the doorway to look around in a bored manner before disappearing back inside, and Hallam waited no longer. He pulled the skullcap low and strode swiftly to Zabby's cottage.

A dog sniffed cautiously at his leg as he hammered on the door. It opened and a child looked silently up at him.

'Is Zabby... Zabudesha here?' he asked loudly, peering over the child's head into the gloomy interior. Thankfully, Zabby heard him and came quickly.

Hallam told him what had happened. 'Does he know where you live?'

'No, I don't think so, but we should not stay... I'll kill the traitor myself!'

Hallam did not doubt his sincerity, or his ability, but he did not think it would be wise for Zabby to take matters into his own hands. 'You will have to let the prince and the council decide,' he cautioned. 'Lemek's father is one of them, and it would not be wise to act on your own.'

'Are you now a councillor as well as a noble?'

'Neither, but I would be wise enough not take the chance of losing the respect of your friends... and there is also a mother to think of.'

'Who needs a mother when he has you to tell him what to do? Zabby grumbled. 'But maybe you are right.' He took Hallam by the arm and pulled him inside. 'Come, first you must meet with my mother, then we will take some food and leave. I know of another way through the hills. We can be with the prince before dawn. Lemek will have a surprise waiting for him.'

'No, I will meet your mother, but I don't think I will be returning with you.'

Zabby stopped to glare at him. 'What do you mean? If it is Lemek that concerns you...'

'No, it is not Lemek.' The thought had crossed his mind earlier when he was talking to the apprentices. Although it had been more of a feeling than a thought, it felt right. He could not see himself wandering in the mountains for the rest of his life. There had to be more.

'What then?'

'I do not want to be the cause of trouble. You and your countrymen have done much for me, and I won't forget, but this is your country, not mine. There are other things I want to do.'

'What things? The prince will be disappointed.'

'No, he will understand. You said your father was a shipwright. Does he have any friends who are still in the trade?'

'My uncle and his son still run the business.' Zabby

scowled. 'But now they are forced to make boats for the governor with little reward. Do you not see this broken down pile of mud they are forced to live in?'

'They live here with your mother?'

'They will be here after work is finished... but why are you interested?'

'Do you think they will know someone who can take me on as an apprentice pilot?'

'We can ask them when they get home. My uncle is well known as the best shipwright in Ezion-Geber.' Zabby looked dubiously at Hallam. 'Are you sure it is what you want?'

'No,' Hallam answered with a smile. 'But my problems are many and my choices are few.'

The apprentice who had jokingly said to Hallam that the easiest way to become a pilot was to own a boat, had spoken truer words than he probably realised. It made no difference that Zabby's uncle knew everyone who mattered on the waterfront. There were only two ways to become a pilot or an apprentice, and both were hard won. You had to have either wealth or experience.

Pilots enjoyed considerable prestige and were a close-knit fraternity. Most achieved the position only after many years at sea as a deck captain or paying apprentice, and they guarded their knowledge as jealously as the merchants who employed them guarded their trading secrets. If a pilot was famous enough, such as those who had explored unknown coasts, the cost of an apprenticeship with him could easily exceed the cost of the boat itself.

Hallam would have been content to simply go to sea as a common sailor, but Zabby's uncle advised against it. 'Work with me for a while,' he advised. 'I could use the help of someone I can trust, and you will be safe here. I will say you are a relative learning the shipbuilding trade. There is always a demand for shipwrights at sea. You will get more respect and earn more copper than a sailor.'

Hallam was more than happy with the arrangement. He worked in exchange for his food, and slept in a shelter beside the half-completed hull of the boat they were building for the governor. The remains of the silver given him by the prince helped pay for his food and, after purchasing a mattress and a few other necessary items, even an occasional beer in the waterfront taverns, where he could listen and talk to sailors.

Living on the waterfront with its atmosphere of ships and travel was pleasant, but the work itself was tedious. Each short hull plank had to be carefully split from the cedar logs, carefully heated in the coals of a fire if a curve was required, then shaped with an assortment of chisels and scrapers. Zabby's uncle demanded perfection, and was not content until each plank fitted its neighbour so closely that not even a hair plucked from his beard could pass between them.

But it was satisfying work, and he was not a slave. It was a time for more learning. And it was also a time of healing.

Zabby's uncle had prohibited the making of a fire anywhere near the boat or the timber, so Hallam had made his cooking area in the same place on the pebbly beach where they shaped the timber.

He was sitting there late one afternoon, crouched over the fire as he waited for the pot of stew he had concocted to heat through. It seemed to be taking forever. A rare drizzle had turned the evening cold, and he held a piece of sail over his head to keep himself and the fire dry. As he knelt to blow on the coals, he noticed a young woman watching him from the road that ran between the beach and the shipyard. Hallam returned his attention to the fire. It was not unusual for anyone to be there. The road serviced many of the small waterfront industries, and led to the causeway and wharves.

When he judged the stew ready, Hallam hurried with it towards his shelter and was surprised to see the young woman had not moved. Her head was uncovered and her ears poked through strings of wet hair. The flimsy robe she wore was stretched tight across a swollen stomach. Hallam nodded and smiled a greeting as he strode past her.

'If you will leave me a little, I can wash the pot,' she said.

Hallam stopped. Had it been a man, he may simply have told him he had nothing to spare, or left a little in the pot as requested, but a pregnant woman was another matter. He could not leave her to wait or eat in the rain, yet there was no other suitable place close by except his shelter, which was barely large enough to accommodate himself. Not sure what to do, he hesitated, and she turned and started to walk away.

'There is no need to wait,' Hallam called after her. 'You may have as much as you want, but I cannot leave you to eat here. I have a spare bowl inside, but you will have to sit on the mattress.' He started towards the shelter, expecting her to follow, but she remained where she was, her shoulders hunched and hands pushed up into the sleeves of her saturated robe.

'I am too wet,' she said. 'I will wait here until you have finished, then I will wash the pot.'

There was nothing subservient in her manner. She spoke with only a faint tremor to show her uncertainty; holding stubbornly to her pride.

Hallam well remembered the feeling that came with hunger, and he had not been alone. Neither had he been wet and cold - or pregnant. She looked to be no more than fifteen years. He sensed she would not object if he were to take control of her life for a short while. He pointed to the shelter. 'Go in and sit on the end of the mattress. While you stand there I am also getting wet, and the food is getting cold.'

She looked along the road, as if about to move off, but either

her need was too great, or his smile must have reassured her, for after a moment of hesitation she walked swiftly to the shelter and ducked through the opening. Hallam followed and sat beside her on the mattress. He scooped half the stew into a bowl and gave it to her with a wooden scoop. 'Eat!' he commanded.

She took the bowl with shivering hands. 'So much?' Her eyes did not leave the steaming contents.

'Eat,' Hallam repeated. He took a round of bread from the food box and tore it in half. He put a half on her bowl. 'Dip it in the juice.'

She held the bowl close to her chin, scooping the food in as fast as she could swallow, and Hallam studied her from the corner of his eye, his lips twitching at her small grunts of appreciation. Occasionally she gave a little shudder, probably from the cold, but he preferred to think of it as ecstasy. He was very proud of his stew.

She was not pretty. Her face was too thin and her ears stuck out like the handles of an urn, but her features were delicate and her eyes large. Droplets of water clung to the long lashes and dripped from the tip of her nose. She glanced up, saw his smile, and quickly looked down, lowering the bowl.

Hallam laughed to cover her embarrassment. 'Do I not make the best stew you have ever tasted?'

She nodded, her mouth stuffed full.

'Give me your bowl.'

She passed it reluctantly. It was not quite empty. Hallam added what remained in his own bowl and handed it back with the rest of the bread. He was not that hungry anyway. 'Eat.'

When the bowl was empty and wiped clean with the last of the bread, she reached for the empty pot. 'Thank you, my lord.'

Hallam moved the pot away; pushing it outside in the

rain. He took the bowls and pushed them out as well 'They can wash themselves. My name is Hallam. I am not a lord. Where is the father of your child?'

She shrugged. 'Gone.' She did not offer her own name, or any further explanation.

'You are all alone?'

She nodded.

'Forgive me, It is not my business.'

'No, you are kind.' She got to her knees. 'I will leave now.'

'Where do you live?'

She remained silent. Not the most talkative girl he had known.

'If you have nowhere, you can stay here. You cannot afford to catch the fever, being with child.' Hallam dug in his bag and removed the thick coat Prince Hadad had given him. He placed it on the mattress beside her. 'Take off your wet robe and put that on. You will be quite safe here, I will not harm you, and I do not expect anything in return for the food.' He gave her a cloth on which she could dry herself then left the shelter before she could protest.

To give her time, Hallam went for his usual swim and wash in the rock pool at the end of the beach, keeping a wary eye on the road to make sure she did not leave with his coat. When he returned, her wet robe was hanging over a pole outside the shelter and she was asleep on the mattress, curled up in the coat with her head wrapped in the towel.

Hallam did not have the heart to wake her. He dried himself on a spare tunic, then sat on the free bit of mattress to ponder what he should do next. He was getting a bit cold and tired himself, and she was lying on his only blanket. He covered himself as best he could in the damp tunic and propped himself against one of the poles.

He half awoke to gentle tugging on his leg and a whisper. 'You must lie down.' He stretched out and she covered him with the blanket, and Hallam was asleep again within moments. He awoke again during the night, dimly aware of her warm body next to his, but it was only when he shifted to his back to get more comfortable and his hand touched naked flesh that he started coming fully awake.

He explored cautiously and discovered a bony hip. She had removed the coat and used it to cover them both. At the touch of his hand she snuggled close, her warm body pressing.

Hallam suffered an agony of indecision. His own body responded instantly, urgently, but his conscience could not adjust. He moved away and turned his back.

She sat up with a small cry. 'Forgive me... I will leave now.' She scrambled on hands and knees towards the opening and was outside before Hallam could stop her. By the time he had crawled out himself she was already trying to get into her wet robe, hopping on one leg while the other probed desperately among the clinging folds for the opening.

The drizzle had stopped, and the low cloud had moved across to let in the light of the stars and a sliver of moon. Her pale body with its swollen belly was clearly visible, and Hallam watched, fascinated, for a few moments, before going to her aid. She crouched down to cover herself, her foot still tangled in the robe.

'There is no need to be afraid. I do not mean you any harm.' Hallam untangled her foot and directed her back to the shelter, and she had no option but to go for he held the robe. She sat in the corner and pulled the coat up to her chin.

'Lie down and sleep,' Hallam said. 'I will not bother you.'

'I am not afraid. I wished only to pay for your kindness, but I have shamed myself.'

'No. I told you I did not expect payment, and I did not want to take advantage. And you have a husband.'

'I have no husband.'

'Is he dead?'

'No... a sailor.' She mumbled, obviously reluctant to talk

about it, so Hallam did not pursue the matter.

'What is your name?'

'Peta.'

'Why did you want to leave, Peta? Do you have somewhere to go?

'I thought you were angry.'

'No, I was not angry. If you wish to pay for the food, you can pay by staying. The rain will return and I will not feel good about your leaving.'

They sat in silence, listening to the splat of water dripping from the timber of the roof into one of the pots. Hallam found her presence strangely comforting.

'Do you have a wife?' she asked.

'No. He had no wish to unburden himself to a stranger.

She studied him for a while. 'There is sadness in your face.'

It was not something he wanted to think about. 'I am not sad.'

'Sometimes if you share a trouble it is easier.'

'You have enough troubles of your own.'He pulled up the blanket. 'You should sleep now.'

She curled up in the coat beside him, carefully keeping her distance, and soon Hallam could hear the deep sound of her breathing.

He could find only restlessness for himself. Her presence brought Philippa close. You are now my man and I am your woman. The words haunted him. He had tried to block her out but she refused to set him free, and his visions of her, reinforced in the darkness of the cell, were stronger than ever. And so were the new, disturbing visions he had created for himself. Visions which included the hairy ape who had set him free. It was too big a sacrifice she had made. It did not matter that he would never see her again. How could she expect him to live with such visions, and the guilt that went with them?

The thin silent girl was gone when Hallam woke in the morning. He looked for the coat, expecting it to be gone as well, but found it neatly folded at the foot of the mattress. The pot and bowls had been washed and stacked neatly by the dead fire.

Hallam kept a lookout for her during the day, and again while he was cooking on the beach that evening, but she did not appear, and he resigned himself to the fact she was gone - probably to a more accommodating bed. He felt deserted.

Then he saw her the following evening when he went for his regular bathe. It was an isolated spot at the end of the road, close to the rising cliffs. It was already dark, for he had worked later than usual, and as he approached he heard splashing not far from his own spot. He went to investigate and saw her washing something on a rock. She was stooped over with her back to him, her robe tucked up between her legs to keep it clear of the water. He could not mistake those skinny legs.

'Peta?'

She squealed and spun around.

'Sorry, I did not mean to frighten you. What are you doing here?'

'I thought you had finished.'

'How do you know this is where I come?'

'I have seen.'

'How ... when I have not seen you?'

'From my sleeping place. I wait for you to finish so you are not disturbed.'

'Show me,' Hallam said irritably. He had worried about her, yet she had been right here, watching him from cover, as if afraid. He waited while she wrung the water from the robe she had been washing, then followed her over the rocks. She had cleared a small area in an eroded gap in the cliff face.

'You have been sleeping here?' It was pitifully bare, only a single blanket, a scrap of reed matting and a few scattered articles of clothing. 'Where do you cook?'

'It is not safe to make a fire because someone might see. I work for food. It is not a bad place. Only when it is raining.'

'It's a terrible place,' Hallam said. 'And its not safe for you to be here alone. Bring your things. You can stay with me until this man of yours returns. We can make another shelter next to mine. There is no need to work. I have plenty of food.'

She stood meekly as Hallam angrily bundled up her meagre belongings into the blanket and slung it over his shoulder. He discarded the scrap of matting, flinging it contemptuously into the sea.

When they reached the yard, Hallam tossed her bundle into the shelter and began searching around for material to build another. 'Tomorrow you can go into the city and buy another mattress and another blanket,' he told her. 'I will give you the copper for it.'

'It will be a waste. If you do not wish me to share your mattress it will be best if I do not stay. I do not wish to be a trouble to you.'

'No, you can do the cooking. I will be glad of your company.'

'Then you will allow me to share your mattress?'

'No.'

'Is it because I am ugly and with child?'

'You are not ugly. You only need to eat more and put on some fat.'

'Then if you would not mind it, I would like to share your bed. A man should not sleep alone. I can be as a wife until my man returns. I am already with child, so it will not matter.'

She stayed for more than a month, and was the balm that healed the open wound left by Philippa. Zabby's uncle accepted her presence with a shrug and a wink, and Peta made herself useful around the yard, keeping it tidy and tending the long fire on the beach where they heated the planks. At night they bathed together and slept together, and they talked about trivial, uncomplicated things.

Their lovemaking was undemanding and quietly satisfying, fulfilling their physical needs without the entanglements of the emotional ones. The flame was kept low, and it was understood that she was not his woman, and that he was not her man. They were loving friends.

She left when her sailor failed to arrived when expected, deciding to return to her village and wait. Also, the boat was nearing completion, and Hallam hoped to sail with it. She kissed him passionately and left without looking back, and he watched her go with sadness, but without remorse. She had lightened his load, and the painful wound had begun to heal. In time only a scar would remain.

Never before had Philippa experienced such a complexity of emotions, and each came with such intensity that she could be flushed with happiness one moment, and listless with despair the next. She had no appetite for food, and no interest in anything but her secret thoughts and unlikely dreams. Her life had changed. What before she had meekly accepted as her role, she now came to resent with a passion that surprised her. She could no longer accept her life as it was. It came between her and her love, and she would rather die than submit to it.

The thought of jumping from the wall was always with her, lurking there with the uncertainty of Hallam's situation. She had conditioned herself to jumping from the moment of his escape, living each moment thereafter in dread, but still determined to go through with it should she hear of his death. Her unknowing love was all that kept her alive.

As the weeks passed into months and still no news came, the gnawing eased and Philippa began to hope. But hope came with companions, and the most persistent was loneliness. In her fear for both their lives she had felt close to him, but the diminishing fear and the possibility of his survival left her feeling somehow more isolated. She sought the company of Milcah as often as possible, so she could talk about him and speak his name aloud, but the sound of it rang hollow, and seemed only to distance him further. She felt more imprisoned than ever.

Tentatively, Philippa began planning her escape from Tyre. It became more than wishful thinking when Ari and her uncle left to visit Solomon in Judaea. It was the perfect opportunity, and when she discussed her plans with Milcah and the nurse agreed to accompany her, Philippa began planning their escape in earnest, and with growing excitement. She would find him.

Most of her valuable jewellery had already been gathered on the night she had hoped to escape with Hallam. Now she began selling off what she could to replace the gold given to Parak, and she also arranged with an unsuspecting slave master for Milcah to be transferred into her ownership, so she would not be treated as a runaway if they were caught. They would take little in the way of baggage, only a few of their plainest robes.

And to further strengthen her resolve to leave, there was the continuing problem of Parak. He had become unbearable. There seemed no way to avoid him, and he had long since given up pleading or showing any pretence of subservience. He was now threatening to take by force what he insisted she still owed him.

She seldom left the palace for fear of being caught alone, but even so, hardly a day passed that he did not find some way of accosting her. And with Ari and her uncle gone, even the roof-garden was no longer safe from his invasion, and no threat she used would stop him.

'You have no proof, only words,' he told her when she threatened to complain to her husband on his return. 'Whereas I have a much different tale for the suspicious ears of Lord Arumah. Whose tale will he find the most interesting, I wonder, yours or mine?'

'You have the gold and that is all you will get,' Philippa insisted. 'You killed the slave and blamed the glassmaker. That is not what we agreed.'

'A slave is nothing, and it was necessary to avoid suspicion. I did what you asked only because of your promise. That was the bargain.'

''I think you are mistaken. We had no such bargain.'

'Is it so precious you will not give it up for even one night? You told me your feeble old husband no longer used it, and I know you gave it to the stinking glassmaker. Tonight would be perfect. Your house is empty and I can change my duty.'

'How dare you talk to me like that… you disgusting pig!'

Parak laughed scornfully. 'Did you not say yourself that it would be more pleasing to have than my hands around your neck? I can promise you, one way or another you will be mine and, unlike you, my noble Philippa, I keep my promises.'

Then leaving Tyre suddenly become a matter of urgency, which had nothing to do with Parak or her yearning to find Hallam. When Ari and her uncle returned, four months would have passed, and Parak's threats would no longer be valid. Her guilt would be obvious. How could she explain to a husband who never slept with her that she was pregnant?

When the hull of the boat was completed it was covered on the inside with molten pitch to make it waterproof. Then the deck was laid and that too was covered with pitch. For several days after, Hallam scraped the sticky black substance from his skin and plucked it out of his hair.

With the heavy work done, the more interesting tasks of rigging and finishing began. Coarse linen soaked in pitch, followed by a protective sheet of lead, was laid over both stern and bows and tacked in place with copper nails. The outside of the hull was given several coatings of oil, and the hull was ready for launching.

Fifty burly soldiers were volunteered by the governor, and the boat was rolled slowly down to the water on logs, while Zabby's uncle and cousins ran from one side to the other anxiously giving instructions and monitoring the progress. The hull floated in perfectly upright with barely a ripple, and the onlookers applauded enthusiastically. Zabby's uncle beamed with relief.

The mast was stepped and Hallam moved aboard to help the sail maker with the rigging, and to attend to other finishing work that needed to be done. Under the expert tutelage of Zabby's uncle, he had become a reasonably proficient shipwright, and had come to develop a proprietary interest in the boat he had helped build.

When the railing was completed, Hallam turned his attention to the cooking arrangements. It seemed to him that the large bronze bowl the sailors normally used for cooking was unnecessarily primitive. He added a few innovations of his own, using fire clay bricks, as used in kilns, in place of sand. A small clay oven he had seen being used in an Indian food stall was bought, and a copper lined box made with special ventilation holes and lid so fire and food could be quickly protected from rain or sea. It was a trifle longer than was usual because of the system of racks which allowed pots to be suspended against the motion of the boat.

The governor himself inspected the boat, and Zabby's uncle took the opportunity to speak on Hallam's behalf. Repair work always had to be done aboard, he argued, and less costly if done by a member of the crew. It was agreed that Hallam would be taken on in that capacity pending the approval of the deck captain, a man by the name of Cirato.

There would be no pilot. The boat was to be used for trading the shores of the Narrow Sea only, probably no farther than the *Street of Tears* at the entrance to the Arabian Sea. Two trading emissaries of the governor would also be on board. If a pilot was ever needed, he would be taken from one of the other boats owned by the governor, or recruited locally by the agents.

Captain Cirato did not come aboard until a week after the boat had been launched and the first trials were due to take place. He was a short, grizzled man with arms as hairy and corded as rope, and what he lacked in height, he made up for in spirit. He came with four members of the new crew, and the first thing he saw was the odd looking fire tray.

'What is that?' he demanded aggressively

'Fire tray, captain,' Hallam answered.

'It is too big, get rid of it.' He glowered up at Hallam. 'Who are you?'

'I am Hallam, your shipwright.'

'By whose order?'

'The governor, captain,' Hallam answered, taking a chance.

'Huh! Another relative I suppose.'

'No, captain, I helped build the boat.'

While they had been talking the men had been inspecting the fire tray. One had removed the cover to reveal the row of pots. From one of them wafted the spicy aroma of goat stew flavoured with wild garlic and several large scoops of mixed spice, which Hallam had bought from an Indian trader. It was an interesting mix, and he had been looking forward to tasting it.

One of the men picked up an iron ladle, dipped it into the stew and, after blowing and sniffing cautiously, took a mouthful. For a few moments he savoured it, his expression registering the bliss promised by the rich aroma. Then the sailor's expression went through a succession of changes, beginning with mild surprise and ending in shock.

With an explosive blast he spat out what remained in his mouth and dived for the water jug. He poured water into his gaping mouth and over his face, then he clasped at his throat and ran to the rail where he made loud retching noises over the side.

Captain Cirato, the remaining sailors, and a bemused Hallam, stared after him in surprise. Hallam recovered first. He moved quickly to pick up the ladle and dip it in the stew. He tasted cautiously. The flavour was delicious. He rolled it around in his mouth and felt the first tingle on his tongue. The tingle became a burning that increased rapidly until it felt as if his mouth was on fire. The heat spread up his face, leaving tiny beads of sweat in its wake. It prickled at his scalp, as if the roots of his hair were glowing and about to set fire to his hair. He swallowed behind clenched teeth, refusing to spit out, and the burning gradually decreased, leaving behind a taste not altogether unpleasant.

He tried to speak, but seemed to have lost much of his voice. He tried again, smiling apologetically at his startled audience. 'A bit too much spice,' he rasped.

Before they could answer, and to allay the fears of the sailor who had returned from the rail and was now scowling at him in a distinctly unfriendly manner, Hallam took another mouthful. It may have been that his tongue was still numb from his first taste, but it did not seem so bad with the second and, this time, the flavour really was delicious. He nodded and licked his lips appreciatively.

'Let me try,' said a barrel-chested Persian. He swept his long moustaches aside, took a mouthful, and swallowed with barely a pause. He savoured it for a while then gave his opinion. 'Pah! It is nothing.' He turned to captain Cirato, offering the ladle. 'Captain...?'

Captain Cirato had been studying the face of the Persian for signs of distress. When he saw nothing more than perhaps a slight tightening around the eyes, he took the ladle and dipped it in. He was not the type to be outdone by a member of his crew. His expression did not change either, only the colour of his ears, which took on a pinkish hew. He nodded and passed the spoon to the next crew member.

'Bread?' Hallam offered. 'It is supposed to be eaten with bread.' He produced a round from his food box and tore off a piece before passing it on.

'It would go well with wine,' the Persian remarked.

'No wine allowed on my boat,' the captain wheezed.

The ladle was passed around again. Even the first sailor took another mouthful without complaint, although he swallowed quickly and seemed to hold his breath afterwards.

When the pot was empty and the bread finished, Hallam passed the water jug. There was an appreciative series of burps, and a collective sigh, which had more the sound of relief than appreciation.

Captain Cirato belched loudly. 'You can also be the cook,' he said. 'But please be less wasteful of the spice.'

Lord Arumah was silent for so long that Parak was sure the old fool had fallen asleep. But finally he looked up. 'Does anyone know where?'

'No, my lord, but it is my belief she has gone to the north, perhaps to Damascus.'

Parak was almost certain she had gone south, to Edom. She would have followed the glassmaker, and the slave master had established that the slave who had escaped with him was an Edomite. It was only natural they would go where they would have the help of friends. But he could not say that to Lord Arumah without explaining further and implicating himself.

'When?'

'I think only a few days, my lord.' Parak thought it may have been as long as eight, but he needed to convince the merchant it wasn't too late to go after her.

'And no one missed her or thought to look for her?'

Parak shifted uncomfortably, still smarting at how she and the nurse had fooled not only him, but everyone else, with her fake illness. 'It seems no one knew she had left, my lord. She had reported she was not well and had confined herself to her room in the palace. It was only after Lady Keziah returned from visiting and reported her missing that we made enquiries. I was hoping your lordship will allow me to go after her. I have been greatly concerned with Lady Philippa's safety.'

Lord Arumah sighed and looked distractedly at the large bundle of rolled papyri that had accumulated on his table in his absence. 'Take as many men and spare horses as you need. I will write you a message to give to her. Bring her back safely and I will reward you well.'

Parak took a spare horse but no men, and he burned the message after he had broken the seal and read it. There was no need for her to know that the old goat begged her forgiveness for his foolish ways. In future she would be learning the ways of one who was not so foolish. With the gold she had given him, and with what he had saved, he had more than enough to return to Cilicia and live the life of a lord. He may even take the tasty little black girl there as well. It did a man good to have an occasional change of diet. As for his reward, it had already been promised, and she would pay it a thousand times over.

The sea trials lasted only a day. It was simply a matter of testing the rigging and sailing qualities of the boat, and settling in the timbers and, as expected, the boat passed every test. Conditions in the gulf were not the same as they would encounter in the open sea, but the captain assured them the boat would not sink in the first storm. Hallam took it as a personal compliment.

Loading began the next day. Hallam was given the task of provisioning the boat and collecting the tools and equipment needed for repairs, including a full barrel of pitch, a roll of caulking linen, copper and bronze nails, lengths of deck and hull timber, and lead sheeting. He stored it on timber racks in the narrow space below the deck, along with a spare sail, extra ropes, sleeping mats and blankets, and some of the more perishable cargo, such as hulled wheat, barley, dried fruits, olives, figs and dates.

The boat had no rowing benches or galley ports as there had been on Lord Arumah's larger boat, but four long oars were lashed to the rail that could be used to manoeuvre the boat in emergencies, or when no towing galleys were available at the ports they visited.

They sailed with the tide and an early land breeze a week after the trials.

Hallam regretted not having the opportunity of saying his farewells to Zabby and the prince, but had left messages for them with Zabby's uncle. It would be half a year at least before the boat returned to Ezion-Geber, and he had no real desire to return with it. A new life awaited him, and he was not sorry to see the old one falling astern. Some things were best left behind and forgotten.

But they were not easily forgotten, and it was with a leaden heart that Hallam looked back and wondered if he would ever see his goddess again.

Two women stood well apart from the group of well-wishers gathered on the wharf. One of them was thin and noticeably pregnant, the other indistinguishable in a dark robe with a hood that shadowed her face.

The thin woman sniffed quietly, raising a hand to her face, and the other glanced across at her. 'Did your man leave on the boat?' Her voice held a note of sympathy, as if she understood the sadness of a loved-one's departure.

'No, only a friend... did yours?'

'No, I don't know anyone here.'

The thin woman nodded and turned away. The other stood a while longer, scrutinising the crowd, before also leaving.

The voyage south, first along the coast of Egypt, then across the sea to Saba, could not have been more pleasant. The wind blew steadily from the north, and the clear water flashed with brilliantly-hued life. Like a bee amongst flowers, the boat drifted from one port to the other, trading goods that would be turned into gold back in Edom and, like bees, they were never short of company. Too much company, the agents grumbled, for even the most basic of craft had been enticed out by the good weather conditions, and the increase in competition had forced the bargaining to ridiculous extremes.

A shade awning was slung forward of the mast for the captain and crew, and a smaller one to the rear for the two agents, and conditions were such that they remained erected for weeks at a time; coming down for cleaning only when the splatter of seabird droppings had reached unsightly proportions.

Duties were light with the new boat, and each port had its diversions. Bazaars clamoured for attention and taverns crowded every waterfront, offering to those who could afford it - and were not overly fussy or concerned about their health - food, drink or female company.

Hallam spent his free time on less risky ventures, such as gambling on the Arabian game of *wary*, and came to the conclusion that the life of a sailor surpassed that of a hunter by far.

The good weather and hard trading prompted the agents to look farther afield and, after much debate, they decided on Punt. Ivory and good quality chalcedony could be acquired there at less than one tenth the price asked in Saba, and it was also well out of the reach of the annoying pedlar boats.

Captain Cirato tried to dissuade them. Three times he had sailed into the Arabian sea, he told the agents, and each time he had struck bad weather and unfavourable winds. Only once, and then with an experienced pilot, had he sailed down the Zeng coast to Punt. The argument persisted for days.

'We have heard that the winds from India have begun,' argued one of the agents. 'There are many Sabaen boats preparing to make the journey.'

'If you are afraid,' said the other, using loss of face as a lever, 'we can ask to sail in their company. Or perhaps seek the services of a Sabaen pilot.'

'From the Arabian Sea the voyage will take forty days at least,' Captain Cirato countered, 'and it will be half a year before we are able to return, making a full year in all. Are you prepared to wait that long for a profit?'

'It will be less by the time we are ready and have made the journey there.' the agents persisted. 'It is not too long if we consider the gain.'

Captain Cirato had no choice. They were there to trade, and in trading matters he had no say. His only argument could be the wind, the weather, or the capability of the boat, and all three were against him. He could not tell them his real reason. Sailor's intuition was something they would not understand.

The good weather made Captain Cirato uneasy. It was unusual for it to last so long, and the storms that usually accompanied the change of wind had not occurred. Every seaman knew the gods liked to keep the weather in good balance. Fair winds must follow foul, wet must come after dry, hot after cold, as light came after dark. Any imbalance could only mean the gods were busy elsewhere or had fallen asleep. But eventually they would return or awake to hurriedly make up the deficit.

Against his better judgement and, on a morning so beautifully fashioned that not even angry Baal would have had the heart to disrupt it, they sailed unchallenged through the aptly named *Street of Tears* and into the Arabian Sea.

It soon became clear, especially to the agents, that the captain had been wrong. Each morning they left shore with a land breeze, and returned with the afternoon sea breeze, guided by one of two Sabaen boats whose pilot knew every safe night stop along the way. Even Captain Cerato began to relax, replacing his formal tunic with a loincloth to join the crew in making the best of the weather, which grew ever more warm and moist as they voyaged south. Not even when the clouds began building was he overly concerned. They were only two stops away from Serapio, the pilot of the Sabaen boat had informed him the night before, and the clouds were far in the distance, rising above the mountains behind Punt. Above and behind, the sky remained as clear and blue as the sea.

The storm developed with astonishing speed. The crew could do nothing but watch as a haze the colour of dried blood formed beneath the billowing clouds that towered above the land. As it swept towards them the sun dimmed and the pale sea darkened. Although the shore was temptingly close, so too were the lines of barely submerged rock that protected it, and Captain Cirato ordered Hallam to climb the mast and report if he saw a more likely place to beach. Meanwhile, all they could do was maintain their present course and try to keep the other two boats in sight. With luck the storm would move north and the wind hold long enough for them to reach their night stop with the incoming tide.

But even as they watched, the breeze that had been blowing steadily all morning slowed, puffed several times as if exhausted, then stopped. It took everyone by surprise.

They drifted in a heavy stillness, the crew silent at their posts, only the slapping of waves against the hull. At the top of the swaying mast, Hallam looked apprehensively towards the disappearing shore. A flash of lightning made him start, then the captain's bellow.

'Close sail!'

His voice was all but drowned in the crash of thunder that followed. The crew rushed for the brail ropes, and Hallam slithered hastily down the mast to join them.

The gods had awakened.

'Man the oars!' shouted the captain. 'And get those cursed awnings cleared away!'

The two long oars, one on each side, were quickly unlashed from the rails and jammed into their gimbals. Two men manned each oar, one team pushing, the other pulling to turn the boat quickly to meet the oncoming squall. The remaining crew hauled on the eight brail lines, closing the sail by hoisting it up from the base and bunching it at the top spar then securing the brail lines to hold it there. The two agents knelt at the mast and prayed, one in a thin wail , the other in a litany of incoherent sobs. Their plaintive entreaties to Baal doing little to ease the tension.

The first gusts that hit were light and brought with them the tantalising smell of the land; of wet earth and rotting seaweed. A brail line came loose and a section of sail at the end of the spar dropped down. The gusts increased, tugging and worrying at the fallen section of sail like a playful dog.

'Get that rope or I'll use it to remove your hide!' roared

the captain, and a sailor rushed to secure the line, but too late. A heavy gust shuddered the boat, setting it back on its haunches. It tore at the loose section of sail, twisting the spar and snapping the port brace. Then came the sound all sailors dreaded; the terrifying splintering of timber.

Hallam collided with the Persian as they fell against the rail and nearly went over. 'Tie yourself!' the Persian shouted, and Hallam snatched up the loose end of a brail rope and fastened it around his waist.

'Clear that brace! Back the oars!' screamed the captain, and he put all his weight on the tiller arms to help the rowers keep the boat from broaching.

But the brace line had snapped at the spar end and could not be reached.

Any further orders were muffled by the wall of hail that rushed towards them, erupting the surface of the sea in a white frenzy, its roar growing rapidly in intensity; the sound of a waterfall in full flood.

Hallam threw himself down beside the Persian. The watery roar turned to a terrifying clatter as the fist-sized hailstones struck the deck and thudded onto exposed flesh; smacking painfully against bare knuckles and hastily covered heads.

The hail passed swiftly, but no reprieve followed. The crew scrambled back to their posts, slipping and stumbling on the ice as cold stinging rain, whipped horizontal by up draughts, lashed their faces and filled their eyes.

The damaged spar with its attached sail tore free and slid down the backstay. It struck Captain Cirato and one of the crew as they clung to the tiller arms of the steering oars, tangling them in ropes and dragging them both over the stern.

Hallam saw them go but could do nothing to help. He hauled himself to his feet on the safety-rope, only to be knocked flat by a wave as the boat slid into the trough and broached. The rope sawed and cut into his skin, but held as the cascading water crushed him against a rail post.

Not so fortunate was a sailor and one of the agents. Their cries were cut off as both were tumbled over the rail in the boil of water. Hallam dragged himself back to the mast and clung to it in the company of two others while the boat rolled dangerously in the rising sea.

The mast swung like a pendulum, its weight heeling the boat and holding it down longer with each roll. It could not be long before it turned completely over, and Hallam held his knife in his teeth, ready to cut his safety-rope.

Ironically, they were spared from going over by the same broken spar and floating sail that had caused them to broach. Still attached by one brace and a tangle of brail lines, it drifted with the strong wind and dragged the stern around to face the bows into the waves.

Hallam glanced around the deck and was alarmed to see that only five men remained. Another seaman had been crushed by a loose bundle of timber as it smashed through the railing. Held by his safety-rope, the man rolled lifelessly about the heaving deck.

The rain eased with the passing of the storm cell, but the wind continued to blow strongly and the seas to climb, although less steeply now they were in deeper water. Hallam could see no sign of the other two boats.

The remaining crew had lashed themselves to the mast, as if its solid bulk alone could save them. They seemed unable to speak, or even look at one another. All eyes were on the dark rushing sea.

Hallam was angry with himself for not jumping overboard while the shore was still visible. He believed he could easily have made it to the rocks. Now he had no option, the boat was his only chance, as it was for them all. He tore his eyes away from the mesmerising waves and forced himself to concentrate on what was happening to the battered vessel.

Both long oars had gone. The sail and brail ropes that had snagged over the tall sternpost were now dragging the boat sideways, heeling it at the top of every wave, then tugging it back into a broach as they descended. He shouted to the Persian beside him. 'We have to cut those ropes!'

The Persian stared blankly at him through red-rimmed eyes, his long moustaches blowing forward and waving in the wind like probing feelers. Hallam pointed, but the Persian did not look, perhaps not wanting to see more than he already had.

Hallam was also reluctant to leave the security of the mast, especially now that the boat was beginning to roll, but the other two sailors and the remaining agent were crouched low at the base of the mast and seemed intent on remaining there no matter what happened.

Hallam waited until the boat came level, then cut himself free and ran for the tangle of ropes at the stern, scrambling up the elevated section of the steering deck. As the ropes pulled taught on the next rise he hacked feverishly at them and, one at a time, they twanged away like broken strings from a lyre.

One of the steering oars and tiller arm had broken away, but the long tiller handle of the other swung free, the oar still intact. He pulled on it, trying to get the boat to come around, but it had already gone too far and the wind had caught the beam. In desperation he pushed the other way and gradually, helped by the wind, the bows swung around, the momentum keeping them going until they had turned completely away from the wind.

Running with the wind and set free of the restraining ropes and sail, the boat swooped down the first wave with spray flying. The prow dug into the trough and kept going, the stern rising until it seemed the boat must catapult over. It shuddered, struggling to free itself from the grip of the sea. Swinging helplessly from the steering oar, Hallam prepared himself to go under a second time. Perhaps for the last time.

But they had built a courageous boat, he and Zabby's

uncle. The bows rose sluggishly, the timbers groaning and creaking as it shook itself free, rising heavily, ponderously up the wave, but Hallam knew it would not survive another such dunking. As they crested the wave he dragged on the tiller with the strength of desperation, pushing hard with his bare feet against the deck, and she responded reluctantly, barely turning at all, but enough to set her down the next wave at a slight angle. She took the trough easier, rolling and yawing violently, but not driving under, and climbing free without the burden of water to strain her back.

Hallam was not conscious of passing time, only of the passing waves. As each came he held the shuddering tiller arm hard over, praying it would not break, for each wave was different and seemed higher or more jagged than the one before. He took them as they came, going by instinct, much as he would have on a runaway horse, holding his breath as they careered down into the troughs, then breathing out at every swooping and twisting rise. A tenuous pattern began to form with the sailing, and Hallam allowed a small dose of hope to penetrate his fear. The storm could not last forever, and maybe they had come through the worst of it.

The Persian crawled across to the rail and cut the dead sailor free, and the two Moabite sailors began untangling the ropes around the mast and securing some of the broken timbers that threatened injury to unwary limbs. Seeing them, Hallam felt his confidence surge. Apparently they felt the same, that the worst was over and hope had replaced dull acceptance. Then he realised with a shock that they were trusting the boat to his hands. Their confidence appalled him. *They* were the sailors, not he. He was a hunter, more at home in the mountain forests than these treacherous mountains of water. Until now his own life had been his only concern. All his actions had been out of sheer desperation, but with the unwelcome responsibility of other lives thrust into his care, it was different. Renewed fear and uncertainty struck him like a blow in the pit of his stomach. Suddenly the boat seemed larger and more threatening. The immensity of it stretched far out before him, its ponderous rising and plunging and twisting a thing of unimaginable power. No single man could ever hope to master so large a beast in so unfriendly a place. It was impossible. Still, when he returned his full attention to the sea, it was with a firm grip on the slender arm of the tiller.

Towards evening the wind eased, but it grew cold with mist and light rain. In the gloom of approaching dark the waves took on an even more ominous look, seeming to tower into the low cloud and become a part of it, with the horizon gone, as if they had been trapped inside some immense boiling cauldron.

From the top of one wave, Hallam was alarmed to see the rounded shape of something floating two waves almost directly ahead. Although he had never seen one, he first thought it must be a whale, and hoped they would not collide, then he saw what appeared to be waving tentacles. It disappeared in the trough and he waited anxiously, the thought going through his mind that it may be some great sea monster searching for prey. It rose again, closer and, peering hard into the gloom, he saw it was a man with frantically waving arms sitting on an overturned boat.

Hallam was faced with yet another terrifying decision. His control of the boat was tenuous and still largely instinctive. The angle he was holding seemed to be working fairly well. Changing it could mean disaster, but he would have to make a small adjustment if he were to try saving the man. He hesitated, grappling with his fear, deciding he could not take the chance and risk more lives. He held grimly to his course, the man would have to take his chances. Then he pushed on the tiller handle. It was almost an involuntary action, without conscious decision. He had no choice. He shouted to catch the Persian's attention, beckoning urgently and pointing to the overturned boat. He cupped his hand to block the wind. 'We have to pick him up. When we come alongside throw him a rope. I will get as close as I can.'

The Persian gaped in disbelief, first at the waving man, then at Hallam and, for a disturbing moment, Hallam thought he had not understood or was refusing. 'Go!' he bawled. 'Or it will be too late!'

The Persian threw up his hands in a gesture of hopelessness and lurched along the deck to obey.

It was thirty cubits from where Hallam stood at the steering oar to the bows, and difficult to see in the fading light. With their erratic movement, it was more by luck than skill that he was able to bring them close to the upturned boat and its madly waving survivor. When he disappeared from view, Hallam thought he had pushed over him. It seemed to take a long time before the Persian finally leaned over the rail and hoisted what looked to be two long bundles over the rail. He passed them to the sailors then returned to help a large black man aboard.

Hallam glanced at the upturned hull as it drifted past. The bottom was laced with a tangle of rigging, and behind trailed a mess of torn sail bearing the distinctive red embroidery of the Sabaens. It was one of the boats that had accompanied them. The mast had obviously snapped and the capsized boat had rolled itself into the rigging.

The Persian finally pulled himself to the rear and gave Hallam the news. 'They are alive,' he panted. 'The slave is strong, but the two girls....' he shook his head. 'I do not think they will live for long.'

'Girls?' Hallam tore his eyes away from the sea long enough to give the Persian a startled glance. 'Are you sure?'

'Very young and sick. Nearly dead.'

Hallam had known that one of the Sabaen boats had on board the family and servant of a high Sabaen official in Serapio. but it had kept apart, so no one had seen them. 'Can you take the steering oar?' he asked.

The Persian pulled on one of his moustaches and took the handle cautiously, and Hallam was almost as reluctant to give it to him. He would not have, had the slight turn across the wave not given him the confidence. He felt as if he were handing the reins of a frisky but favourite horse to a stranger, but he had to see for himself, and he could not do all the steering alone. Sooner or later, he would need help, and the Persian was the only one he could trust. 'Keep it angled into the waves, exactly as it is now,' he advised.

They were indeed girls, and looked to be not more than eleven or twelve years old. Their flimsy summer robes were torn and twisted about their skinny limbs, and they had gone beyond shivering to violent shaking. The black was plump and tearfully thankful. 'O praise the gods, master!' he cried. 'And praise for your mercy and our lives. My poor mistresses...'

'They are not saved yet,' Hallam told him. Red welts of rope burn covered much of the girls' exposed flesh. Short lengths of rope were still fastened to their legs and arms. One of the girls struggled when Hallam tried to turn her over, clutching at the deck in panic and gasping for breath, as if she was still in the water.

'It's all right now,' Hallam soothed. He turned her over and removed the ropes, which must have held her to the overturned boat, and he felt a twinge of admiration for the black man and his presence of mind in what must have been terrifying circumstances. The other girl opened her eyes when he turned her over but her look was glazed and distant. He would have to get them warm soon or they would die of exposure. Hallam was struck by their similarity to each other and looked closer. They were more than similar, they were identical.

. The agent and the two sailors were huddled at the base of the mast with their backs to the wind, as unconcerned with events around them as sheep in the rain; trusting their fate to the gods.

The black slave fussed over the girls, removing the last of the ropes and covering their nakedness as best he could with the flimsy robes. He stripped to a loincloth and used his wet robe to further cover them. His own plump body, as sleek and hairless as a seal, was apparently impervious to the cold. A eunuch, Hallam surmised.

Thankfully, the Persian seemed to be controlling the boat fairly well, so Hallam looked at the remains of the deck cargo for something he could use for shelter or warmth. But there was only a bundle of timber, a few bales of leather sandals, and two crates of iron goods. Still it seemed to Hallam they could well do without the precarious-looking load. A stack of timber had already killed someone and it could easily happen again. And maybe the boat would sit higher in the water without the unnecessary weight. Fewer waves would wash over the deck, and it may give them a chance to open the hatch and bring out some dry clothing and blankets. It would be risky, but they would have to take the chance. Without some protection they may all perish.

The agent was horrified when Hallam squatted beside him and made the suggestion. 'No! I forbid it! You will have wasted half a year of trading!'

'It is already wasted,' Hallam reminded him. 'And there will be even more waste if the boat sinks and you drown like your friend.'

'But it will not! The storm is over now and tomorrow we will return!'

'Maybe you will show us the way,' Hallam retorted angrily.

'I say if it will help the boat then we should get rid of it,' said one of the sailors, and the other nodded his agreement.

They set about dumping it while the agent sulked at the mast, refusing to help. The reduced weight did not seem to make much difference, although Hallam was sure the boat rode a little higher. After discussing it with the Persian, Hallam removed the hatch cover with the help of the two sailors, then went below himself. The hatch was quickly closed after him, sealing him in the musty hull.

He felt his way around, thankful he had stacked most of the equipment himself so he knew roughly where to look. He found one of the smaller awnings, several blankets, his coat from the prince, and a smoked leg of meat. Only a small amount of water had leaked in, and he gave a grunt of satisfaction. They had built a fine boat, he and Zabby's uncle. He thumped urgently on the hatch to be let out.

With a following wind, the most sheltered place on deck was the wall of the steering deck immediately in front of the tiller. Hallam strung knotted ropes flat across the deck from one rail to the other, onto which safety-ropes could be tied, then he had everyone except the Persian, who was still on the tiller, move there. The awning was doubled over and they crawled between the folds with the blankets, securely held down by the ropes.

Before lashing them down with another rope, Hallam told the slave to remove the girls' wet clothes. 'And yours too,' he said, recalling the cold night he had spent with a dead sheep in the mountains of Lamos. 'You have fat and they do not. They need to share the heat of your body. Hold them close against you, one on either side.'

'Master, I beg you!' he pleaded. 'I could not...'

'Why, are you not gelded?'

'Yes, master, but even so, such a thing cannot be allowed.'

'It must be done, and quickly,' Hallam growled.

Still scowling furiously, and trying to ignore the four large eyes that stared accusingly at him, Hallam pushed and pulled their thin and shivering naked bodies in close against the reluctant slave, then covered them with several blankets. 'Now pull the awning over your head,' he ordered.

They ran before the wind all night. Hallam and the Persian took turns on the tiller arm, staying together for the company even when not steering. It was not a time to be alone. The night was as black as a hole, the only light coming from the luminescence of the sea itself and the lightning from a distant storm, the flashes of which, left them temporarily blinded against the perils of the heaving monster below. Hallam was convinced they were headed for another storm, but refrained from mentioning it to the Persian. He had no wish to further test the man's courage - or his own.

But the storm moved away, and the first grey light of dawn shrank the waves and brought a heady blend of relief, satisfaction, and exhilaration for Hallam. He smiled knowingly to himself as he observed the Persian, standing straddle-legged at the tiller with chest expanded, nonchalantly stroking his long moustaches as he looked contentedly out over the flattening sea.

The wind had fallen and shafts of sunlight pierced the cloud, but daylight revealed no land, and they were still a long way from being safe. Still, they were finally able to relax a little without fear of the boat capsizing, and their relief showed in a spurt of activity. The hatch was opened and more food and dry clothing brought out, the water barrel was checked and found to be almost full, and wet clothing was strung out to dry.

The girls had not stirred with the others, and Hallam lifted the end of the awning to uncover their faces, half expecting to find them dead. He felt their cheeks and was relieved to find them warm and glowing. He studied them for a few moments with almost paternal pride, taking in their delicate features, and marvelling at the similarities. He left them and the eunuch to sleep.

Nothing had been said, but it soon became evident that of the four remaining members of the crew, it was Hallam who was expected to show the lead. Circumstances had placed him in a position of responsibility and it seemed to have caught on. The Persian – who was simply called 'Persian' by the crew because no one could pronounce his real name - reinforced it by directing his questions only to Hallam, then treating his answers as if they were orders.

It was a new experience for Hallam, and one he had to admit was not without a certain appeal, but he was not all that sure if he could deliver. Of all the crew he was probably the least experienced. He had no idea of their position, where they were going, or even how to manage the boat. He knew only a little more about sailing now than when he had stolen the fishing boat and attempted to sail to Lamos. So far, he had been lucky.

He took stock of his crew. The agent could be discounted, and Persian, although he looked the part with his flowing moustaches, hairy chest, and theatrical flourishes, showed clearly he had no inclination to act the part. The two sailors were Moabite peasants all the way from their splayed toes to their rotting teeth, and it was one of them who was responsible for the loose brail that had caused the loss of the spar. Looking at them, Hallam felt his unwanted authority take a firmer hold.

Prince Hadad, he reminded himself, although younger, was still able to command the respect of a thousand tough men - men like Zabby. Servility that went beyond the fact he was a prince. He had accepted his responsibility with humility, acting like a leader and not like a noble. The prince inspired the men, and the men inspired the prince. Hallam decided that if the prince could do it, so could he.

They had plenty of food and water, so in that respect they

were fortunate. What they needed most urgently was a means of controlling the boat and making it safe.

'We have to make a sail,' Hallam informed the crew as they sat on the steering deck gnawing on bones and enjoying the warmth of the sun.

'Where would you have us sail to?' asked the agent, still smarting over the loss of his cargo.

'We have a spare sail,' said one of the sailors.

'Yes, but no timber to make a spar.'

'Perhaps if you had not thrown it over the side,' the agent muttered.

'And perhaps...' growled Persian, glowering at the agent. 'It is not all we will throw over the side.'

'That timber was too short and thick anyway,' Hallam said. 'We need something much longer. Maybe if we joined the spare oars together?'

They discussed the problem and decided the best solution was to splice the oars together for strength and cut the sail to fit. It would only be half a sail, but better than none. The remaining half would be kept in reserve, or for rigging in some other way, and they would have to make do with only one steering oar.

'We should use the Egyptian method of pulling the sail up with the spar instead of lowering it,' Hallam suggested. 'I don't think we have enough rope left for brails.'

They started immediately. While the spare sail and oars were being handed up from below, Hallam collected his wood tools. The splintered remnants of the spar had to be removed and a block attached with a hole through which the halyard could run.

Labouring in the warmth of the sun with the familiar contours of the tools in his hands brought a sense of normality, and Hallam worked happily, content to be doing something other than facing his doubts and fears.

His calm was shattered mid-morning by a series of indignant

squeals coming from under the awning, and he turned to see the eunuch being forcibly evicted by four thrashing legs. The slave released a squeal of his own as a slender foot caught him squarely between his plump buttocks.

'What's wrong?' Hallam asked, as the eunuch stumbled towards him, hands lowered to cover his deformed nakedness.

'My mistresses require their clothes.'

Hallam retrieved them from the backstay where they had been drying. 'And yours too?' he asked, grinning.

'Master, please!' He removed one hand to rub at several discoloured areas around his upper body.

'What did you do?'

'Nothing, master. They are angry at me for taking their clothes and sleeping beside them. Did I not tell you?'

Hallam gave him his loincloth then turned back in time to see two heads disappear under the awning. 'Here are your clothes,' Hallam said. 'I will try and find something to repair them.'

He received no answer, so he left the robes where they could reach them and returned to his tools, still smiling. They had obviously made a full recovery.

The sail was ready by mid-afternoon and made ready for lifting. With the breeze steady from behind, Hallam stood anxiously at the steering oar and gave his first real command; a raised arm with the palm of the hand outspread. The sail was quickly hauled up. It filled out and the boat surged forward. A few adjustments were made to the braces, and the leech ropes were made fast. When it was seen that their efforts were holding together, Persian slapped Hallam on the back with such enthusiasm he had to clutch at the backstay to avoid falling over.

For the time being, Hallam was content merely to run with the wind and get used to the boat under sail. He experimented with the makeshift spar, turning it fully on either side in turn and tentatively nudging the bows across the wind to see how far they could sail away from it. It was not much. They were going wherever the wind took them, and there was nothing they could do about it.

He tried to remember what Captain Cirato had done as they sailed close to the Zeng shore. The conditions had been much the same as they were now, with the sun on the left side in the morning, the wind behind and the waves on the port beam. And once the captain was out of the land breeze, he had shortened the port brace to keep them from coming too close to land. Then he had changed over in the afternoon to the starboard brace when they wanted to come in with the sea breeze.

Hallam figured if they were to have any chance of reaching land, that was how he would have to sail. They were obviously being blown down the length of the Zeng coast, but how far the coast went beyond Punt, and how far they had been blown out to sea, he had no way of knowing.

What he did know from listening to the talk of the pilots in Ezion-Geber, was that beyond the Sea of Zeng lay the Sea of Darkness and the edge of the world, and it was in that direction they were heading.

An unexpected source of information was the eunuch, who revealed his name was Phineas. Without disclosing his fears of where they were heading, Hallam had been discussing with Persian the possibility of lowering the sail and drifting while they waited for a wind that would blow them towards the land. Later, the slave approached when he was standing alone in the prow, looking anxiously ahead to the horizon.

'Forgive me, master. If you will command me, I will tell what I have heard spoken by the sailors who go to India. They speak often of this wind.'

Hallam was in the mood to listen to anyone who could tell him about the wind, and he nodded for the eunuch to continue.

'They say that each year it is the same, master, and this is the time they sail from India to Adana. They must wait half a year before the wind will change and allow them to return.'

'Half a year?' Hallam frowned, turning away to hide his disappointment. They would all be dead before then.

'Please forgive me, master. 'I repeat only what I have heard, but I am a stupid slave who is easily mistaken.'

He should have known. Captain Cirato obviously did, but had not spoken of it – no doubt assuming everyone already knew. The crew had been told they would be in Punt for three months, and Hallam had believed it was because the agents needed that long for their trading. It had never occurred to him that the reason could have been because of the wind, and yet it was obvious. Had he thought about it, he would have realised they could not sail back unless they had a wind from behind - from the south.

Hallam thumped the rail with his fist and the slave moved hastily out of harm's way. Three months was too long. They did not have enough food, and if it did not rain, they would not have enough water for more than a few weeks. He glared at the empty horizon.

'What else do the sailors speak of? Do they say what lies beyond the sea of Zeng... or where lies the end of the world?'

When he received no answer, Hallam looked round to find the slave had returned to his charges. He grunted philosophically. Perhaps it was as well not to know what lay beyond the horizon. Living with hope was better than living with fear.

A short while later the slave approached Hallam again, smiling a nervous apology. 'My mistresses wish to speak with you, master.'

Hallam gave the tiller over to Persian and presented himself. He had been meaning to talk to them anyway.

The two Moabites had slung the awning above the deck and spread the area with the sleeping mats belonging to their departed comrades. The girls had hung one of the mats from the awning as a screen and made a comfortable private place for themselves, even using his heavy coat as a rug. Hallam sat down, facing the slave who sat cross-legged at the entrance, like the guardian of a harem.

Hallam smiled at the girls. 'I am glad to see you are well.'

From behind the slave's plump shoulders, the four dark eyes peered intently at him, as if he were some interesting but potentially dangerous exhibit. They did not return his smile, or respond to his greeting. They had made an attempt to repair their clothes and tidy their hair, bunching the dark curls on their heads and tying it around with strips of cloth. He was struck once again by the likeness they had to each other.

One of the girls prodded the eunuch with a foot, and he cleared his throat. 'My mistresses beg that you...' He winced as a finger dug him sharply in the ribs. He began again. 'My mistresses *demand* to be taken home immediately.'

Hallam would have laughed had he not been so taken aback. Their arrogance was astounding. Obviously they did not understand their predicament. Or maybe they were so used to having their every wish granted they simply refused to accept the reality of it. In a way, he sympathised with them. The situation was something he also was finding hard to accept.

'Did you not explain to your mistresses that they came close to perishing, and that we are still in danger?'

'Oh, yes, master, they have spoken of it. When we were in the water they prayed to their gods to be saved and the gods listened. Now my mistresses wish to be returned home so they can thank them with sacrifices.'

'I would like nothing better,' Hallam said. 'But it would help more if they prayed to their gods to show us the way.' As yet, neither girl had spoken, their eyes unwavering, and he could not be sure if they spoke the same language. He addressed a question to them directly. 'What are your names?'

Again it was the slave who answered. 'Mistress Sophira and Mistress Jemimah.' He did not indicate who was which. It would have made no difference anyway.

'Can your mistresses not speak for themselves?'

'They are not permitted to speak with strangers who are not themselves noble, master.'

'Noble?'

'Yes, master, their father, Lord Shan, is Vizier for trade in Saba. They are cousins to the Queen.'

'I see.' Hallam studied the girls, and they stared back, unblinking. 'Well, you had better remind your noble mistresses that they are no longer in Saba. Their gods have put them in my care, so they had better do what I tell them.'

One leaned forward and whispered in the slave's ear, and he nodded in understanding.

'There is another matter my mistresses wish to...' he paused to search for words, looking uncomfortable. A dig in the ribs prompted him. 'They wish to have a place for doing their toilet.'

It was something Hallam had not thought about. The men simply stood at the rail, taking care the wind was blowing in the right direction, or, if the need was greater, standing astride the stern, holding to the post with both hands while suspending their nether region close above the waves. It was a disconcerting and dangerous manoeuvre in a following sea, and obviously unsuitable for young ladies of noble birth. Something safer and more private would have to be arranged - and soon, no doubt.

Hallam solved the problem by sacrificing one of his pots. It had a stout handle that could be attached to a rope and tossed in the sea for cleaning. He explained its operation to the slave and it apparently worked, for there were no complaints, and a short while later he saw the slave hauling the pot in on the rope.

Late in the afternoon, the sky thickened with cloud and thunder rumbled in the distance, but although the cloud flickered with light and the sea picked up, the storm did not reach them. As a precaution, the sail was shortened and the awning taken down and used as before. Everything perishable was stowed below and the hatch sealed.

The girls sullenly ignored their ration of bread and water in protest at losing their comfortable nest. They retired beneath the awning with the pot on one side and a bundled up sleeping mat on the other, effectively disassociating themselves from the lowly peasants. Hallam and Persian took their place at the tiller, partly protected from the elements by capes cut from the larger awning. They attached their safety-ropes and took turns sleeping at each others' feet, within easy reach of an alerting kick.

Another problem presented itself to Hallam when the clouds finally dissolved to reveal the stars for the first time. The bright star of the north, without which no sailor could be sure of his position, was not among them.

Hallam refused to accept its absence, and developed a stiff neck by spending half the night searching the heavens in a state of near panic, convinced he had made another mistake. It was inconceivable that something so familiar and steadfast could simply disappear. It was a betrayal of everything he had come to believe and trust in the firmament.

He knew from the position of the rising sun the approximate position the star should have been, but it was not there. Nor was it anywhere in the sky, and neither were many of the familiar star patterns he had come to know. Some of them *appeared* familiar, but they were in the wrong place, and there were so many he could not be sure if they were the ones he knew or if they only looked the same. It was as if they had sailed into a new world.

All the painfully acquired experiences Hallam had methodically welded together to bolster his confidence fell apart. He became confused and despondent. He was no longer sure they were sailing with the same wind, or if the Zeng coast was really in the direction of the setting sun. Perhaps in this new world the sun set in a different place.

In the absence of any positive plan, Hallam did nothing. He kept the sail up and the starboard brace shortened, and they continued as before. He could not think of anything else they could do, and the disquieting thought that they were being drawn towards the edge of the world hung over him like another dark and threatening cloud.

But the real clouds stayed away, and the weather remained fine, with the wind blowing steadily from behind. The days grew warmer, and the passing of each was recorded with a notch in the base of the mast.

Hallam tried to overcome his uncertainty by keeping himself busy and devising ways of making sure that everyone else was occupied as well. The two sailors shared in helm duty while Hallam enlisted Persian's help in constructing a second entrance to the hold. They made an opening in the wall of the steering deck and fitted a door that could be left open in good weather, but which could be sealed quickly if the weather changed. Clothes, sleeping equipment, fire tray, firewood and food became more easily accessible.

The slave was instructed in the safe use of the fire tray and given the task of providing one cooked meal a day; a duty he embraced with enthusiasm, for it turned out he was an even more accomplished cook than Hallam. The eunuch also had the task of trying to keep his wilful charges occupied and happy. And in this he was much less accomplished. Despite Hallam's insistence they address their needs directly to him, they continued to come in a steady stream via the slave.

'My mistresses complain their clothes are unfit and require the needle and thread you promised them.' And later. 'My mistresses request a private place to wash and demand you tell the men to stop staring and laughing at them.'

Hallam attended to all their needs as best he could except for the last. He was reluctant to talk to the men on such a touchy subject, and he had not seen or heard anything to suggest they were doing anything to cause concern. As for being laughed at, they had only themselves and their arrogant behaviour to blame. He often laughed at them himself.

. He questioned the slave, hoping to find a way of making the girls more approachable, but he was of little help, and surprisingly loyal considering the way he was treated.

'They are very frightened, master,' he explained. 'Their mother died when they were very young and Lord Shan is often away. They spend much time alone at the palace with the queen, and know little of the ways of ordinary men.'

'If they want to be treated with respect,' Hallam answered, 'they will first have to earn it. They will get no special treatment. We are all in this boat together.'

Despite his words, Hallam did make allowances because of their youth and sex. The good weather had allowed the erection of both awnings, and he moved the girls and slave to the forward section of the boat where it was more private. They were instructed to wash only at night, and were given ample material with which to make a screen so they could keep to themselves, even when eating. When they did venture out, they covered themselves with blankets, and were always in the company of the slave.

The weather continued to grow steadily warmer and the sea calmer as they moved south, the breeze doing little more than giving the sail a periodic shake, as if to keep it, and the helmsman, from falling asleep.

In the early hours of one morning, Hallam was leaning

against the sternpost, dozing at the helm in a languid stupor, and kept from sleep only by the sail and the snores of Persian. He lifted his head at the sound of several light thuds and squinted at the sail, but the moon had gone, and he could not make out if it was the spar that was knocking.

His head was nodding forward again when it was jerked up by the sharp sound of a slap, followed by a stifled cry, and he grunted in understanding. It seemed as if the slave was suffering another onslaught at the hands, or feet, of the noble brats.

Yet something bothered him. It seemed a strange time for an argument, even for them. Hallam nudged Persian with his foot, it was about time for a changeover anyway.

He waited until Persian was fully awake, then dropped lightly to the deck and looked under the awning that housed the crew. It was too dark to make out more than a few shapeless lumps. Someone was snoring. About to leave, he detected a smell he knew should not be there. He felt his way through, stumbling over a sleeping form that identified itself by way of grumbling to be that of the agent, Gabaal.

Following his nose, he found the jar of wine. The stopper was out and the jar propped up in one of the cooking pots. The two Moabites were absent. Ignoring the mumbled complaints of the agent, Hallam found his way out and walked quickly towards the awning that housed the girls and the slave.

Stooping under the sail, he almost fell over the large bulk of the eunuch. The slave's feet and hands were bound with rope, and his loincloth had been removed and part of it stuffed into his mouth. Dark stains showed on the cloth, and a stout piece of timber lay beside him.

Hallam did not stop to check further. From behind the awning came sounds that needed no thought to identify. He picked up the piece of timber and swept the awning aside.

He could see only one of the girls. Her robe had been

228

pulled over her head and her hands had been tied behind her back. One of the Moabites sat holding her doubled over while the other kneeled behind her. So involved was he with his pleasure, he did not become aware of the intrusion until the heavy timber was coming at him with the full force of Hallam's swing. He had barely time to open his mouth before the timber struck him in the face, and he collapsed back to lay writhing on the deck.

The second Moabite managed to duck his head enough to receive only a glancing blow from the back swing, but it was enough to stun him. He fell over, releasing the girl, and she rolled onto her side.

Hallam shouted for Persian, then looked around anxiously for the other girl. Muffled sounds came from a rolled up bundle of blankets. He unravelled them hastily to reveal her pale face and frightened eyes. She too had been gagged and bound.

Persian ducked under the sail and stopped in surprise when he saw the slave. Agent Gabaal pushed close behind him.

'This one first,' Hallam said. The sailor was trying to get up. Hallam pushed him over with his foot. 'Tie him up. Then tie the other one.' He spoke to the agent. 'We need light. Fetch the tallow pot - quickly!'

'What happened?'

'What do you think? Get moving!'

'Mother of gods!'

Hallam returned his attention to the first girl. The sailors had come well prepared. He cut through the strips of cloth that bound her wrists, and removed the wad of cloth that had been pushed into her mouth, easing it out through clenched teeth. She trembled with fear, her eyes screwed tight as he tried to soothe her. 'No need to fear... you are safe now.'

He covered her with a blanket before going to the aid of her sister, cutting away her bonds and removing the cloth from her mouth. 'Are you all right?'

She licked at her dry lips and looked towards her sister.

'She may be hurt,' Hallam said, 'you must see for yourself.'

The agent returned with the tallow pot as he was untying the unconscious eunuch. Blood oozed from a gash at the back of his head. 'Take one of his arms,' Hallam directed. They dragged the eunuch to his sleeping mat and Hallam instructed the agent to bathe the wound in fresh water and bind it with a cloth.

'Why me?' agent Gabaal whined. 'I do not like blood, and he is only a slave. He can wait until...' He broke off, backing away as Hallam moved towards him with the knife he still held in his hand, then he turned and hurried towards the water barrel.

Persian had finished tying the sailor and was inspecting his companion. 'I think he is dead.' he reported.

Hallam picked up the lamp and went to look for himself. The sailor's loincloth was around his ankles, his face a bloated, unrecognisable mess. Persian gave him a vicious kick 'Moabite pig!'

They dragged the dead sailor to the broken section of rail and pushed him under the rope into the sea.

Hallam was mildly surprised that he felt no remorse at killing his first man. He felt only cold anger and disgust. He turned the light towards the other sailor now tied securely to the mast, and Persian answered his unspoken question. 'Only a sore head.'

Hallam returned to kneel beside the girl who was tending to her abused sister. 'How is she?'

As the Persian and agent Gabaal were in the process of binding the eunuch's head, she had no option but to speak for herself. 'We wish to be alone.' It was barely a whisper.

'We'll take Phineas to the back awning and look after him there, Hallam said. 'I think he will be all right.'

Hallam left her with the light and a jar of water, arranging the awning so they would have privacy. Phineas had stopped groaning and had regained some of his senses. He resisted weakly as Hallam and Persian helped him to the rear awning, mumbling about his mistresses. They laid him on a mat and Hallam instructed a sullen agent Gabaal to take care of him.

The boat was still wallowing calmly, so Hallam and Persian went to inspect the Moabite sailor tied to the mast. He must have consumed a lot of wine. Despite the bump on the head he was snoring peacefully. Persian gave him a sharp slap in the face. 'Wake up, pig!'

'What are we going to do with him?' Hallam asked.

'Let him join his friend.'

'If the weather changes we may need him.'

The Moabite's head jerked up. 'Yes… you will need me to pull the sail.'

Persian gave him another slap. 'Swallow your tongue, pig, or I cut it from your mouth.'

'Why? I did nothing! Takan did it. He stole the wine and made me drunk so I would help him. It was his idea for the girls. You must let me go!'

'It is the lying tongue of a coward I will cut out. I saw you looking, and I heard you talking. You did it together, Moabite scum.'

Considering his perilous situation, the insult alone may not have been enough to provoke the Moabite, but wine gave him the courage to return the insult. 'And you are a Persian dog who would lie with his mother!'

Persian took a handful of the Moabite's hair and reached for the knife at his belt. Hallam caught his arm as he was about to insert the point between the man's teeth. 'No, let him keep until the morning. Enough has happened for now, and the sail is beginning to move. You had better take the tiller.'

Hallam felt no sympathy for the Moabite. Had he not been tied helplessly to the mast he may well have not interfered, but he remembered being in a similar situation not that long ago himself. Despite his anger, he could not see the man killed in cold blood.

Persian released the Moabite's hair and returned his knife to its sheath. 'Tomorrow, pig.'

'We are all going to die anyway,' the Moabite said. 'They are only Sabaen whores and should not be here.'

'Shut your mouth or I'll call him back,' Hallam warned.

'We can share them. Why should we not enjoy ourselves before we die?'

Hallam gagged him with a piece of rope and tied it firmly behind the mast, giving it an extra tug when he heard a small cry of pain from the girl. He rummaged around in the dark of the steering hatch for the pot of balsam and passed it around the side of the awning. 'Do you need help... is she all right?'

She took the balsam but did not answer, and Hallam returned to the steering deck and the company of Persian. They talked until dawn, trying to decide what they were going to do with the Moabite. Persian was still in favour of throwing him overboard - after he had cut out his tongue as promised. 'He will only cause trouble,' he insisted. 'We can train the slave to take his place and Gabaal can also help.'

Hallam was more in favour of giving him a flogging. Once sober, the Moabite may regret what he had done.

Neither punishment was required. When it became light enough to see, Hallam returned to the mast and found the Moabite dead. His stomach had been ripped open and his entrails spilled onto the deck.

Hallam went to the awning and, after calling out quietly, pulled it aside. Both girls were asleep, one cradled in the arms of the other. The tallow pot was still burning. Hallam extinguished the flame and went to check the slave. He appeared to be asleep as well. Hallam called down Persian and they cut the Moabite free and pushed him over.

'Who do you think did it?' Hallam asked. 'The eunuch or one of the girls?'

Persian shook his head and spat several times over the rail. 'Whoever it was should clean the deck.'

Although Hallam had his suspicions, they never did find out who killed the Moabite. The girls' awning was taken down and they were moved back to the rear. Hallam carried the girl there, fussing over her and making sure she was warm and comfortable, talking kindly to her, feeling responsible, but she would not even look at him.

From now on, Hallam ordered, they would all sleep in the same place. A small screen that could be quickly removed was erected in the bows for washing. Hallam scrubbed the deck and included the uninjured girl in the proceedings.

Apart from a few scratches and bruises, especially about the wrists, which still bore the previous scars from her ordeal on the overturned boat, she seemed unharmed. To his surprise, she took the swab and pail he handed her and went to it without complaint.

'Was it you that killed the Moabite?' Hallam asked, thinking he may have made a breakthrough.

She ignored him, not looking up from her work.

Hallam asked the same question of the slave, who looked horrified at the suggestion. 'My mistresses would never kill anyone, master Hallam!'

'What about you? There is no need to be afraid, it saved us the trouble of doing it ourselves.'

'I never kill him either, master Hallam, too sick to get up, but it is a good thing. They were very bad men.'

The mystery continued unsolved, but Hallam had been watching the uninjured girl carefully and noticed a quiet determination in the way she went about things. Neither girl ever spoke in anything much above a whisper, and then only to the slave, so it was impossible to tell what they thought, but their eyes were alert and quick, and he suspected they missed little of what was going on around them. More than once, Hallam caught them looking at him as they whispered, as if they were discussing him, and it gave him an uneasy feeling. He began to review his opinion. They were hiding a lot more intelligence than they showed.

Hallam approached the unharmed girl late the next day when the slave was not around to answer for her. 'Why is your sister refusing to eat?'

'She is not hungry.'

'If she is hurt you must tell me… so I can help.'

'There is nothing.'

Hallam did not push it further, but he had his suspicions and was well aware of the preferences of some men. For the meal next day he made a rich broth from a flying fish that had landed on the deck, and lentils that had been soaked into a pulp. Instead of the usual spices, he put in a good dash of olive oil and another of wine. He took a bowl of it to the girl and placed it close to her nose as she lay on her stomach in the shade of the awning. 'Eat!' he commanded.

She turned her face away, but Hallam detected a certain reluctance.

'She is not hungry,' her sister said.

'Yes, she is,' Hallam insisted, 'and she must eat all of it or I'll have to force her. I have enough trouble without a sick girl to look after.'

'You do not understand.'

'Yes, I do.' Hallam glanced across to the other end of the awning where the slave was still sleeping off his sore head. He lowered his voice. 'What happened to her is painful, but it happens to boys all the time who are much younger. It will heal quicker if she is strong, and there is no spice, so it will not burn.'

Her uncomfortable silence was all he needed to confirm his suspicions. He left them with the bowl and a short time later was happy to see the girl sitting up and drinking his delicious broth straight from the bowl. He took her another and placed it in front of her without asking and she picked it up. He turned to go, then changed his mind and sat down. It was time to stop the pantomime once and for all while he had them to himself.

He studied them frankly, looking for some distinguishing feature to tell them apart, but the only difference as far as he could see was that one had a small bruise on her forehead, probably received during the struggle. She also seemed a little more confident in her manner compared to her sister.

'Which one are you?' he asked. 'Jemimah or Sophira?'

'Jemimah.'

'Are you girls afraid of talking to me?'

They glanced at each other, then Sophira shook her head. Jemimah hesitated briefly, then asked. 'Is it true we are going to die?'

Hallam gave it some serious thought before answering. 'To which god did you pray in the storm?'

'The sun goddess, Shams.'

'I do not think she saved you only to let you die.'

'But she is angry that we did not give a sacrifice in thanks. That is why she sent those men to attack us.'

Hallam was getting rapidly out of his depth. Understanding the whims of the gods was not one of his strong points. 'I'll have to think about it,' he said. He stood and paced in front of the them, hands clasped behind back and a thoughtful frown creasing his brow. It was important to look the part, he thought, and establish himself in their eyes as a person of authority, even if he wasn't.

The girls watched and waited expectantly, but Hallam was in no hurry to lose the advantage, and they were not the only audience. The slave was also listening, although he closed his eyes and made theatrical snoring sounds when Hallam stopped to examine the cloth on his head for signs of blood.

He returned to stand and look down at the girls. 'I think you are right,' he said. 'You will have to make a sacrifice. I did not think of it until you spoke, but then it came to me that your sun goddess saved you by allowing the last of the sun's rays to shine on Phineas so I could see him. Even though it was cloudy,' he added hastily. 'Had I not seen him waving you would undoubtedly have perished. Do you not agree?'

They nodded in unison, their dark eyes following his every movement, and Sophira's broth forgotten. 'Your goddess allowed me to save you from the storm,' Hallam continued shamelessly, warming to his subject. '... then I believe she spoke to my own goddess, Astarte, who is queen of the heavens, to send me a message through the stars.'

Hallam paused to remove the medallion from around his neck. 'This was passed to me by my ancestors who were the ancient kings of Crete,' he explained, and felt a twinge of guilt at his lie when the girls looked at each other in shared surprise. He dropped the medallion casually into the lap of Jemimah. 'It is a talisman for journeyers, and the stars you see on it are called the seven doves. It is through them that the messages are sent.'

Hallam paused to pace in an absent-minded fashion, pretending not to notice as the girls examined the medallion, and whispered excitedly together. The slave, Phineas, had raised up on his elbow, craning for a better look, and Hallam pretended not to notice him either.

It could do no harm to believe in something different, and the stories his mother had recounted to him of the seven doves of Crete had held him spellbound when he was much the same age as the girls were now. And the spell still seemed to be working. He returned to frown thoughtfully down at the girls, arms folded, and they looked up at him expectantly, trusting, and Hallam felt a second twinge of guilt. He put it quickly behind him.

'The seven doves do not speak words,' he explained, 'they only make whispering sounds, but I knew they were telling me you were in trouble with those two Moabites, even though I could see nothing and hear no sounds of it. I think you are right, Jemimah, it was a warning, but your goddess was kind and did not allow Sophira to lose her girlhood, only her pride, and both men are now dead. I think a small sacrifice should be made, but of course, only you can decide if you wish to sacrifice and what it must be.'

'Oh, yes, we must!' exclaimed Jemimah.

'But what?' asked Sophira. 'We have nothing.'

'No prized possessions?'

'Everything was lost. Everything!'

'It does not have to be of great value, only what you value the most of what you have left.'

The girls looked at each other with puzzled expressions, then went into whispered conference for several moments. At the end of it, Sophira gasped. 'No! I could not, it will have to be you.'

'No, Sophie, it has to be both of us!' More whispering followed, with both girls throwing anxious glances in Hallam's direction, so he moved out of earshot, making a show of checking a nearby brace. Phineas had given up all pretence of sleep and was sitting up, watching and trying to listen.

'We have decided,' Jemimah declared finally in a resigned voice, and Sophira rolled onto her stomach and hid her face in her arms.

'What will it be?'

Jemimah stared fixedly at the medallion now back on Hallam's chest. She looked pale, her mouth quivering and fingers restless, and Hallam was concerned he had overdone it.

'We believe that the men who attacked us were not only sent as a warning, but also as a signal. The gods always send signals'

'Oh?'

'The goddess Sham knew we had nothing to sacrifice, and it has to be a big one for saving our lives. We have to exchange them for the second most important thing we own.' She stopped to look down at her twisting fingers, and Hallam experienced a sudden uneasiness.

'Yes?'

Jemimah spoke reluctantly, almost mumbling, and she kept her head lowered. 'The signal she sent was that we must sacrifice our girlhood.'

Even though he had all but guessed, Hallam was still flabbergasted.

'Mistress! You must not even think such a thing!' Phineas exclaimed. 'Master Hallam, please tell her you will not allow it... they are virgins!'

Jemimah turned to scowl at Phineas before returning her attention to her fingers and continuing. 'We also believe that because it was you who she spoke to, it must be you takes our sacrifice.'

'Master Hallam, please!'

Hallam was impressed by their courage, and not a little humbled by their faith. It could not have been easy to come to such a decision after what had happened.

'I am greatly honoured,' he said sincerely. 'But that would be too great a sacrifice, and I do not believe it is what your goddess had in mind.'

Sophira looked up and Jemimah breathed out, seeming to sink lower by a full head. Phineas smiled weakly.

'Is there nothing else you can think of?' Hallam asked.

They looked blankly at each other.

'Do you not own a slave?'

'You want us to sacrifice Phineas?'

'Not me. The sun goddess, Sham.'

'No, master... I beg you! The goddess Sham needs me to stay here and take care of my mistresses. I'm sure if you spoke to your stars they would say you are mistaken. I am not a whole man. I am unworthy of being sacrificed...'

Jemimah had turned pale again. 'I would not like to

sacrifice Phineas. I would not know how to do it.'

'Not only you, Jemma, both of us have to do it.'

'Mistress Sophi...'

'Fortunately,' Hallam interrupted. 'It will not be necessary to make a blood sacrifice of Phineas. There has been enough spilled already. All you have to do is sacrifice what he means to you. Do you value him much?'

'Oh, yes, we do!' cried Sophira.

'It pleases me to hear it. But if you value him so much, why do you kick and slap him?'

They looked first at each other, then at Hallam in bewilderment. 'Because he is our slave,' Jemimah answered in a tone that suggested he should have known better than to ask such a question.

'Well, as from tonight, he will no longer be your slave. At the last rays of the sun... which is obviously the best time for the goddess Sham... we will have a ceremony, and you will sacrifice Phineas by giving him to me. You will have to do everything for yourself. We are now two men short, so you girls and Phineas will have to help with the boat. From now on you are members of the crew and will take orders and not give them, even to Phineas. Do you understand?'

They nodded in unison.

'Good! Sophira, your first order is to eat and get well, and Jemimah, yours is to take care of Phineas as well as Sophira... use plenty of balsam, and mix it with a some palm oil.'

They gathered at sundown. Hallam had briefed Persian and agent Gabaal, and told them to treat it as a solemn occasion, which he believed it was. The girls needed to feel they had made a meaningful sacrifice, and he did not want to belittle their gesture, for he also believed they considered it genuine. He needed to put an end to the pettiness and bickering, and with something positive to do it would take their minds off their situation and give them a feeling of self esteem.

They repeated his litany as he gave it, tearfully sacrificing a reluctant Phineas into the care of Hallam in thanks to the goddess Sham for saving their lives. Phineas spilled as many tears as both girls together, and Hallam was convinced the slave would have protested more strongly had he not felt reprieved from death.

To celebrate the occasion further, Hallam allowed them all a mug of the smuggled wine with their food, and they retired drowsily to their blankets with self- righteous smiles.

Standing alone at the helm, Hallam listened to their contented chatter and giggling with a smile of his own. He looked up thankfully at his stars, wishing he really could understand their whispering, and that they would tell him the way to land.

While Sophira and Phineas recovered, Jemimah busied herself with finding clothes more suitable for crew duties. Persian produced the sea-bags of all five missing men, and she raided them for items that had potential for conversion. Tunics seemed to be the most adaptable. She selected four and cut them down to size, then she and Sophira stitched them while an excluded Phineas lurked hopefully in the background.

The completed garments reached to their knees, as opposed to the deck, and afforded more freedom of movement and, when belted at the waist with a plaited cord made from the leftover material, were quite becoming. Phineas protested at the length, which he said showed too much of their legs, but his objections were ignored.

With the wardrobe completed and Sophira recovered, the girls declared themselves ready for duty and they began their training. Handling the cut-down sail was not all that difficult with the modified version of the Egyptian rig, but speed was essential, and Hallam was aware that in a stiff breeze the girls would not have the strength.

He had them rub tallow on their hands and went through only the easiest exercises, aware also, that despite their keenness, they would quickly become disillusioned if he pushed them too hard. As the weather was fine he taught them the basics of steering, and although they bickered over every wave, they enjoyed that more than anything.

Captain Cirato's sea-bag produced a head cloth of fine white silk - perhaps a gift for a loved one - and Hallam reserved it for a special purpose of his own. In the calm nights without a moon, the stars shone brilliantly, and several had become so familiar he was able to judge the time of night by where they were in the sky.

One pattern in particular drew his attention. It had seven stars closely resembling the pattern on the medallion. Where many of the other stars seemed to move in a confusing manner, the seven always followed the same path, rising on the port side, and setting on the starboard side, as did the sun. Almost, it seemed, as if they were following it. Hallam soon came to think of them as the seven doves, and felt better knowing there were stars above he could trust.

He made a frame for the scarf and attempted to make a map of the sky by lying beneath it and marking their positions with thin splinters of wood and fish bones, but the rocking of the boat made it difficult and he soon lost interest. However, when he explained what he was doing to the curious - and more patient - girls, they enthusiastically took over.

'We should give them names,' Sophira suggested, and they did, calling them after people they knew. All on board were honoured with the brightest stars, and Hallam's seven doves were placed in the centre of the scarf.

'If they follow the sun it must be a sign from the sun goddess, Sham,' Jemimah stated. 'She is telling Pilot Hallam

241

which way to go. If we follow them we will be saved.'

Hallam smiled at his promotion to pilot and gave her a quizzical look. 'You are right, Jemma. They go from east to west, so if we follow them we should find land, but for now the wind will not allow it.'

'Then the wind will change,' Sophira declared positively.

The wind did change, but not until the twenty sixth day, and then it changed in the wrong direction. For two days it did not blow at all. The air was heavy, and the sea and sky dull. On the third day a light rain fell, and they all rushed to take advantage of the fresh water, washing hair and clothes, and spreading out the awning to replenish the water barrel, which had become perilously low.

Two whales with splashes of white on their heads played alongside for a while, providing them with welcome entertainment before suddenly disappearing, leaving them more alone than ever.

Hallam prepared the boat for the worst. The sail was lowered and safety-ropes checked, the awning lashed down and all equipment stowed in the hatch. A last hot meal was eaten in silence.

The lightning began during the night; a flickering on the horizon so far away they could not be sure of the thunder that followed. A cool breeze sprang up, blowing towards the storm, and Hallam felt the rats begin to gnaw in his stomach. The friendly stars disappeared, taking the direction with them, so he had no way of knowing, but he was sure they were still going south - towards the edge of the world.

Dawn was a uniform grey, with only a vague indication of direction, but it seemed they were actually heading east. The sea and wind had picked up, but not too much, so Hallam decided it would be worth lifting the sail to try and close the distance more swiftly if they were heading towards land. They lifted it only halfway, but it was enough to set the boat skimming down the waves in a dampening spray, and they continued in the same exhilarating fashion for most of the day.

Late in the afternoon a falcon settled on the lookout ring at the top of the mast, huddling down in its feathers to rest. The girls were excited. 'It is an important omen,' Sophira whispered to Hallam as they stared up at the bird. 'The falcon of Athar is one of our gods. I think he has come to show us the way.'

The falcon stayed until almost dark, then it swooped low over the sea and sped away on the wind ahead of the boat. No one spoke for fear they may be wrong, but everyone cast anxious glances ahead for the first sight of land.

As night fell, the wind strengthened and the sea became choppy. They lowered the sail completely, but it seemed to make little difference, and Hallam could do nothing but try to hold the boat steady as they sped through the night. Lightning flashed on the starboard bow, then on the port, and then, alarmingly, from behind, revealing brief, startling glimpses of a sea speckled with foam.

In the silent company of Persian, Hallam stood exhausted at the steering oar, his salt-crusted and burning eyes straining ahead. He was no longer sure about the falcon. It may not have been flying towards land. It may only have been flying with the wind to gather speed and height before turning. Had they been going towards land they should have reached it long ago. Falcons did not fly so far out to sea. And the boat felt as if it was in the grip of some giant force from which it could not be turned away, as if they were caught in the strong current before a monstrous waterfall – the sort of waterfall that could be expected where the sea plunged over the edge of the world.

Then ahead in the dark he heard the sound of it. At first he thought it was only the wind, but it grew steadily louder, increasing to a thunderous roar, and the speed of the boat seemed to have increased even more.

In a flash of lightning Hallam saw it. A mass of white water and spray directly ahead. His heart leapt. 'Cut the ropes!' he yelled, and Persian slashed through both their safety-ropes.

A wave broke over the stern, cascading over them and swamping the others where they lay lashed down under the awning below.

One of the girls screamed. Another wave struck from behind, shoving the boat sharply forward. The steering oar snapped, leaving the tiller handle limp in Hallam's hand. Waves were breaking now on all sides, thundering and filling their eyes with spray, but through it, Hallam could see that not far ahead the white water ended abruptly against a solid black void. The edge of the world and the Sea of Darkness.

'Mother of Zeus protect us,' Persian chanted. 'Mother of Baal protect us.'

The deck beneath his feet began to shudder and, clinging to the backstay, Hallam braced himself for when they went over.

A wave struck them from the side, spinning the boat and tilting it over sharply, and Hallam suddenly found himself in the water. A wave crashed on his head, driving him under, and he fought his way to the surface only to be lifted helplessly in the curl of another wave. It rushed him forward, rising above then crashing down, tumbling him in a swirl of foam.

The wave receded, sucking at his legs, and he staggered up to look around in dazed disbelief at the wide stretch of sand on either side. Persian waded from the surf not far away, and they looked at each other in astonishment.

The boat was lying on its side, a good fifty cubits out in the surf, the mast lifting then slapping down as each wave pounded over it. Above the crashing came a thin cry for help.

Hallam started at the sound, as if he had been slapped awake. He plunged back into the waves, diving under to escape their fury, allowing the backwash to take him. He reached the mast and clung to it, pulling himself along with each surge and, when it lifted him clear, he shook the water from his eyes and searched the deck. It was bare. Not believing, he struggled closer to look again, but he had not been wrong. The awning had gone, and so had all those who had been under it.

Sick with despair, Hallam clung to the mast, reluctant to move and face the truth. But he was too exhausted to hold on. The mast slipped from his grasp as it lifted and he fell below it. He caught a fleeting glance of it coming down towards him as he surfaced, gasping for air, then it struck him into dark oblivion.

When the first wave crashed over the steering deck onto their heads and Sophira screamed, Phineas cut all the safety-ropes within reach, and threw the awning aside. Cutting the ropes early was what had saved him and the mistresses the first time.

The girls clung to him, and the next wave sent them sliding forward on the reed sleeping mat to the mast. When the boat turned and capsized, Phineas found himself standing securely upright on the rail with his back against the deck, and with water up to his waist. He held the girls firmly at his side as the boat rocked, waiting for the right moment.

In a brief lull, Phineas saw the beach and waited no longer. 'Land, mistresses. Go! Go! On your backs, please, like I taught you.'

It was also how he had done it before, floating and kicking on his back, and keeping their heads from going under, but it was rougher now. Halfway in, a wave tumbled them and he lost his grip. One of the girls cried out and Phineas struggled towards her, then suddenly he found he could stand. He plucked Sophira from the backwash, gathered both girls around the waist and; one under each arm, carried them to the beach.

Phineas was relieved to see Pilot Hallam and Persian already on the sand. When he saw the pilot diving back into the sea, he set the girls down and watched in bewilderment. He knew he should help when he saw the pilot lose his hold on the mast and go under. He wanted to help, but he could not move. The water suddenly terrified him. He wanted to be away from it. As far away as possible.

A painful pinch in the tender flesh of his side made him yelp. 'Quickly, Phineas! Help him!'

Still, he held back. Then, to his consternation, the girls ran past him and into the surf. 'Mistress Sophi! Mistress Jemma! Come back, please!' Phineas lumbered after them.

The girls stopped and looked about helplessly as the first breaker swirled around their hips. Phineas pushed past them. 'Get out, please!' He pushed through the next wave and caught the end of the mast.

The limp body collided with his legs. Phineas put an arm down and caught the pilot around the neck. Holding his head above the water, he kicked clear of the mast and allowed the waves to wash him in to the shallows, where the girls and Persian were waiting.

Water belched from the pilot's mouth as he was dumped face down in the sand, but he gave no other sign of recovery, and they stood looking down at the limp body, shocked and undecided.

'Is he dead?' asked Sophira.

'He can't be dead. Goddess Sham would not allow it,'

Jemimah answered, with little conviction. Pilot Hallam lay awfully still.

'I do not see him breathing,' Persian said.

'Drop him again, Phineas,' Jemimah ordered. 'On his belly, like before. Turn him around so his head is facing down.'

Phineas lifted the inert body by the seat of the breeches, spun it around, and dropped it again, but no more water came out.

'Keep doing it,' Jemimah ordered

Phineas dumped the pilot several more times, but although he made belching noises, no more water came out.

Jemimah turned his head. A large bump showed through the hair and watery blood trickled down his face. Blood also came from his nose. She brushed the sand from his eyes and mouth. 'Please…' she cried softly, looking up past the clearing clouds to the stars beyond. 'Please don't let Pilot Hallam die now…'

Philippa awoke with a start. She sat up quickly as the clatter of horses and the voices of men sounded close outside her window. It was still dark in the room, but grey showed through the gaps of the shutter. She threw aside the blankets and peered cautiously through one of the gaps.

A large group of men was dismounting on the track that ran past the cottage to the village. Both men and horses were almost obscured by their own steaming breath, but she could see enough to tell they all carried spears, and her heart began to thump painfully.

A door banged in the adjoining cottage and Philippa jumped. She felt the child stir within her and laid a hand to

247

her swollen belly, as if to reassure it. The farmer from whom she had rented the cottage came into view and called a loud greeting to the men, and Philippa drew back in alarm.

They had told her that the village was occasionally visited by Solomon's soldiers, but she had also been told that the houses were no longer searched, and that she would be given ample warning. But she had not been warned. And why was the farmer being so friendly towards them? He had been paid well for the cottage, a whole year in advance - long enough to see in the birth of her child. But she had been careless about covering her hair. Could someone have recognised her, even though she was using her mother's name?

With her mind in turmoil, Philippa threw on her heavy robe with the hood and walked quickly into the main living room, going towards Milcah's annex at the back, but she had gone only a few steps when a loud banging came on the front door and she jerked with fright.

'Mistress Keziah! Are you awake?'

Philippa stared at the door from across the room, trying to gather her thoughts. She had gone through her story many times in preparation for just such an emergency. The same reason she had told the farmer; about waiting for her husband who was at sea, but now it seemed so inadequate and feeble. No one could believe such an unlikely tale.

The banging came again. 'Mistress Keziah! Please open!'

She could not delay further. If they had to force their way in it would only make her look more guilty. She adjusted the hood and moved silently across the room to open the door. All she could think of as she lifted the bar was how cold were her bare feet on the mud floor.

The farmer and a man with a woollen cowl covering his head waited on the threshold. The others milled around on the track, stamping their feet and blowing steam on their clenched hands. 'Forgive the early awakening, mistress,' the farmer said. 'You have an important...'

'No need for introductions,' the visitor interrupted. 'Would you leave us? I wish to speak to Mistress Keziah alone.' Without waiting for a reply, he turned to Philippa. 'May I enter?'

Philippa stepped aside and he came in, closing the door behind.

'An unusually cold morning for this time of year,' he said pleasantly. He crossed to the raised fire alcove and knelt to blow gently on the dying embers, feeding them with small kindling from the box alongside until he had it ablaze. He warmed his hands over the flame before lifting a burning piece of wood and pointing with it to the candle on the table. 'Do you mind?'

He went past her to light the candle, then replaced the stick on the fire before removing his cowl to let free a mass of dark curls. He pulled a bench up to the fire and turned to smile, and Philippa saw his face for the first time. It was smooth and strikingly handsome. He gestured for her to take a seat. 'You will be comfortable here, and warm.'

'No... thank you. If you will just tell me...'

He remained with his open hand held towards the bench in invitation, smiling pleasantly, and Philippa moved forward, for it was not so much an invitation as it was a command. When she was seated, he sat beside her, keeping his distance, and Philippa began to relax. For a commander of soldiers he seemed remarkably young, but there was no mistaking the authority in his manner.

'Mistress Keziah, would you mind removing your head cloth so I can see your face?'

She could not refuse. If he wished, he could easily remove it himself, and she was not about to let that happen. She pushed back the hood, not looking at him, but she could tell he was staring at her.

He studied her for a long time before speaking. 'Yes, it is true. It has to be. But he chose poor words.'

Philippa glanced at him, her breath catching. Someone *had* recognised her. 'Forgive me... I don't understand. Perhaps if you explain...'

He reached across and briefly touched her hand. 'Later, but first there are some questions I must ask of you, and the first is...' he smiled disarmingly, 'why are you here... Lady Philippa?'

Philippa stared at the fire, suddenly feeling colder. The child moved again and she moved her arms to shield the unnoticeable movement. 'My name is Keziah,' she said woodenly. 'I'm waiting for my husband to return from sea.'

He stood and went to the door, and a short while later two other men entered, bringing with them the smell of damp leather and horse sweat. They looked curiously at her as they passed to warm their hands at the fire, one of them more curiously than the other, and when he spoke it was with a tone of disbelief. 'Yes, she has cut her hair short, but it is definitely Lady Philippa... how could I forget.'

'Good! Now all we have to discover is the truth. Will you not tell us, Lady Philippa?'

Philippa remained silent.

'Are you perhaps looking for Hallam?'

She glanced up quickly. 'Do you know...?' She stopped, realising she had given herself away.

'Why are you looking for him?'

They waited expectantly, and Philippa shifted uncomfortably on her seat. 'I don't know who you are.'

'Of course, please forgive our manners. I am Prince Hadad, and this is my chief councillor, Jotham, and this, ' he pointed to the man who had recognised her, 'is Zabudesha. I'm surprised you don't remember him. He used to be one of your husband's slaves.'

Philippa felt a rush of relief and hope as she looked intently at the man who had escaped with Hallam. If he was here... 'Forgive me, I did not see you that often. I must thank you for what you did for Hallam and me. He spoke of you often… as a good friend.'

Zabudesha tilted his head in modesty. 'I believe the thanks should be returned, my lady, for without your help, Hallam would be dead and I would still be roasting my ba ... self at the glass factory.'

'How did you find me?' Philippa asked.

'We hear many things,' the prince answered. 'We heard that Solomon himself ordered the searching of every house in Damascus when it was reported you had been seen there. It was a clever ploy of yours to set a false trail.'

Philippa frowned. 'But I didn't. I came straight to Ezion-Geber on an Arabian caravan. I was sure Hallam would come here with the slave…' Philippa stopped to smile apologetically at Zabudesha. 'Forgive me, you are no longer a slave. Hallam told me you were from Ezion-Geber. My nurse, Milcah, has been looking for you. She goes every week with the mule man to search for you or Hallam.'

'And has been asking too many questions,' the prince said. 'That is how we came to find you. One of our men followed her. Then, when the mule man mentioned your hair… we suspected it was you.' The prince paused to give Philippa a puzzled look. 'But how did you know Hallam had gone to sea?'

Philippa was also puzzled. 'Has he? I only said that to give a reason for my waiting.'

The prince laughed. 'A good reason then, for that is indeed where he is.'

Philippa's rising spirits sank. 'Will he return?'

'He did not say, but perhaps we can get word to him, if that is your wish.'

'If you could, I would be forever in your debt.'

'You have not said why you left Tyre,' the prince said. 'It seems strange to me, Lady Philippa, that a rich noblewoman should care so much for a poor and common man like

Hallam, and that she would risk her life to follow him.'

'My life was more at risk in Tyre. My husband was suspicious, and I am no longer rich.' Philippa's fingers searched automatically for the smooth, comforting feel of the gold butterfly clasp she kept concealed on the inside of her robe; her last piece of jewellery, and which she had vowed never to part with. She looked boldly at the prince. ' 'Please do not think badly of me, Prince Hadad. Lord Arumah was my husband by arrangement with my uncle, and was never a husband to me but in name. What I did was wrong, but it was done out of love, and I feel only happiness. I am pregnant with Hallam's child.'

Zabudesha broke the stunned silence with a loud guffaw. 'So! He did it after all and said nothing! If I don't give the rat a solid thudding when next I see him, the gods can…'

The prince scowled at Zabudesha, cutting him short, before turning an apologetic smile on Philippa. 'Forgive the uncouth rogue, my lady, and you need have no fear as to what we think. Hallam is a friend and he spoke of you also with love. You will be safe here. I will spread the word… mistress Keziah… that you are to be cared for as one of our own. In the meanwhile, I will try to get word to Hallam.'

Philippa was not sure whether she wanted to laugh or cry. 'Thank you, prince, you make me very happy.'

The prince sighed with resignation. 'I suppose I should be happy too, my lady, for I came close to betraying a friend. There are some who believe that in matters of love and war all means are fair, and for the first time in my life I was tempted to believe it myself.'

The roar of falling water became fainter, the dark abyss brighter as he floated up towards the light. Then the sound of voices in harmony. The sweet singing of the goddesses.

'This is the sound the donkey makes: heehaw, heehaw.
But what does the donkey say? He says, heehaw, heehaw.
This is the sound the camel makes: braargh, braargh.
But what does the camel say? He says, braargh, braargh,
This is the sound....

He tried to call to them, to tell them to be careful of falling in the abyss, but no sound came from his lips and they leaned in farther, blocking out the light and he cried out in fear.

'He must be awake, Jemma, he made a funny noise.'

'People often make funny noises in their sleep.'

'Well, his eyelashes moved, so he must be.'

Cool fingers touched his cheeks, moving his head gently from side to side. 'Are you awake, Pilot Hallam?'

'Sophi, look! I think he smiled...'

They had expected to die at sea; drowned in a storm or swept over the edge of the world into darkness, but instead found themselves on a gleaming, sun-drenched beach. It brought songs to the heart and smiles to the lips of them all.

The boat had struck a sandbank in the estuary of a wide river, close to the northern bank, and obviously at high tide, for it lay stranded on the sand, and the white lines of the surf were now a long way out. Muddy water, speckled with mangrove leaves and brown foam, drifted sluggishly past on either side.

While Hallam had been sleeping off his bump on the head,

253

the others had been busy since dawn, salvaging what they could from the stranded boat and carrying it higher up the sandpit to a clump of stunted mangroves.

As soon as he could stand without succumbing to dizziness, Hallam had a closer look at the boat. Some of the hull planks had split, allowing water and sand into the hold, and water had also entered the open hatch under the steering deck where Agent Gabaal had closeted himself. Unable to swim, he had crawled in unseen when the storm was at its worst and remained there, wedged in with the fire tray and pots. He had not emerged until daylight when the boat had stopped moving, stepping onto the sand without even getting his feet wet.

Hallam had the girls stuff the gaps in the hull planks with spare clothing to reduce further leaking. More planks would have to be shaped and fitted to the hull, but if there were no more storms, and if they could somehow get the boat upright, Hallam was sure it would float. His biggest worry was that once some of the weight was removed it would wash higher up on the spit with the next incoming tide, and it was not a good place. At high tide they would be marooned on a mangrove island with water lapping at their feet.

'We have to anchor the boat,' Hallam informed his bedraggled but happy crew. 'Find every rope you can and tie them together. Fix one end to the stern and run the other out to that small channel behind the boat. We'll carry the ballast there and bury it for an anchor. And pray that it holds. If it doesn't, we may lose the boat.'

They needed no further encouragement. The boat was their only security against whatever dangers lay waiting ashore. All had heard the stories of hairy man-eating apes and ferocious beasts that infested the land of the Zengi south of Punt, and they had talked in whispers about them during the night. It did not seem so threatening now with the sun shining, but they were a long way south of Punt and the visions persisted.

Carrying the heavy millstones over the soft sand was slow and exhausting work for their already tired bodies, especially so for the girls, who had to combine their strength, and work together. But other than a few squeals at scraped fingers, they did not complain, and Hallam encouraged them at every opportunity. For spoiled noble brats they were showing more initiative than he had expected.

By the time the boat was secured to the makeshift anchor, the tide was on the way in and, with the sound of approaching breakers spurring them on, they worked feverishly on emptying the hold of sand and water.

Hallam removed the mast to make floating easier, hacking desperately through the last support as the boat began shifting in the first incoming waves. They dragged the mast clear and tied it to a mangrove stump.

Hallam watched anxiously as the waves smacked against the boat's exposed belly, but the fury in them had gone and the planks held, and so did the anchor. Without the weight of the mast to pull her over, and with a lightened load, the boat straightened and, under a benevolent sky, floated free.

They clambered aboard the leaning boat, shortening the anchor rope with each receding wave, until they were clear of the first breakers and riding uncomfortably in the choppy swell. The boat leaked water and listed with the uneven weight of sand still in the hold, but she rode out the tide and settled back on the sand when it left, giving them time until the next tide to bale her out, improve the hasty repairs, replace the depleted cargo, and move the millstone anchor to allow her to swing into the channel. The mast was dragged back and tied alongside.

With the incoming tide, Hallam planned to float the boat up the river into calm water and, hopefully, beyond the reach of the tide into fresh water. The oars were relieved of spar duty and one was lashed to the stern quarter to act as a steering oar.

The south side of the river was out of sight, hidden by mangrove islands, but the closer north bank was wooded with stunted trees and bushes.

Hallam decided to take the chance and stay in a channel, as close to the bank as possible. Whatever the dangers, they would need to be on the bank to repair the boat and find food. It would do them no good to be stuck in the middle of the river.

When the tide finally came in and the boat swung into the channel, they hauled the millstones aboard and floated ponderously forward. Hallam steered tentatively with the makeshift oar, almost as nervous as he had been with the stormy waves at sea. Persian stood amidships with the spare oar, ready to dip it in on either side to help turn the boat should a sandbank suddenly appear. Phineas waited by the millstone anchor, which he was to toss over at Hallam's command, and Sophie and Jemma stood one either side of the prow, their young eyes given the task of seeking out any dangers ahead, not only in the water, but also on the bank.

No one spoke as they drifted slowly past the mangrove islands. And they were still silent when the river narrowed and the south bank came closer. The mangrove islands gradually gave way to islands of densely packed reeds, and uprooted trees with sun-bleached limbs that were festooned with flood debris, the height of which, caused a few sobering thoughts for Hallam.

When the tide turned, they dropped the anchor and sat waiting in mid channel for it to return, talking quietly to give themselves a feeling of normality, but their eyes seldom strayed from the trees along the bank.

They formed a chain and baled out the hold, and once the tide was out, Hallam filled one of the leather buckets with water and tasted it, but it was still brackish. They would have to go much farther upriver.

They floated with the tide for the next two days and, although the water became drinkable, no place on the bank appeared that looked suitable for an extended stay. It remained flat and thick with reeds.

As the sluggish tide began to compete with the flow of the river, their progress became painfully slow, but a good sea breeze blew in the afternoons, and it became clear they would have to rig a sail to get anywhere. A suitable place would have to be found soon. Food was becoming a serious problem, and the constant baling of water was depleting their strength further.

Hallam stared longingly at the mast floating alongside, but could see no way of raising it. They would have to find something smaller.

It took the rest of the day on one of the islands to find a suitable makeshift mast amongst the wedged in jumble of sticks and logs on an island. When erected next morning, it looked hopelessly inadequate and ugly, with so many stays and braces it was difficult to move on deck without tripping, but the timber was iron hard and it worked. It worked so well they had to stop again and devise a way of dropping the sail more quickly to avoid being driven up on a sandbank.

The country changed more rapidly once they were underway, and the water cleared, tasting sweet and fresh. They had seen no sign of life other than birds and fish, but as the bank steepened, beautiful tall trees appeared, and the reeds thinned to isolated clumps, giving way to tangled bushes, grass, and even ferns. Colourful birds screeched, and small apes leaped among the branches, peering curiously at them from the shaking foliage.

Crocodiles appeared on the sandbanks, at first only a few, then in alarming numbers, but it was Phineas who gave them the biggest fright of the day.

Hallam was engrossed with watching the apes when Sophira's warning shout rang out from the prow: 'Sea-elephants in the water!'

'They're sea-cows, not elephants, mistress,' Phineas corrected.

'Pilot Hallam! You're going straight towards them. Turn away, quickly!'

Hallam turned the boat but it made no difference, the sea-cows blocked the entire channel. Without waiting for the order, Phineas dropped the anchor. With the sail still up, the boat slowed and came to a halt in the middle of the herd.

'You fool!' Hallam shouted. 'Pull it up!'

'I can see one going under the boat!' Jemma screeched.

'Get away from the side!'

The sea-cows had all disappeared below the surface. The boat jarred as one bumped into the anchor rope and Phineas let it go with a yell. Persian ran to help. The beasts surfaced around them, blowing sprays of water, every massive head and pink-rimmed eye turned towards them, but none touched the boat, and it glided sedately through the herd.

That night was one of the longest. The wild country was noisy, and no one could sleep. Sea-cows moaned and splashed all around, and the bush crashed, hooted and screeched with unknown menace.

Hunger and fear was aboard the boat too.

'What was that?' whispered one of the girls in the darkness.

'It was a lion, mistress.'

It came again; a sound so deep and threatening that even the sea-cows stopped to listen. A long silence followed, then the whisper came again. 'I hate this place. Can't we fix the boat quickly and leave, Pilot Hallam?'

'That's what we are trying to do, Jemma, but we need time and we need food.'

'Maybe the lion will eat us first and we won't have to worry.'

'Maybe we can tempt him with the figs and dates,' Hallam intervened, trying to lighten the mood. 'I for one will not be needing more of them.'

'Or me,' said Jemma. 'My belly has not stopped rumbling all day.'

'I know, we all heard it. I think the lion heard it too.'

'It's not funny, Sophi.'

Most of the food they had left was spoiled, including the smoked meat, which had become green with mould. The diet of dates, olives and dried figs was, other than keeping them more regular than they would have liked, beginning to pall. Some barley and lentils were salvaged by spreading them out on the awning to dry in the sun, but they needed fresh meat. So far, all their efforts at catching or spearing fish had failed.

Fortunately, the gods intervened, perhaps moved to sympathy by the rumbling of Jemma's stomach, for it was she who jarred Hallam awake from a drugged sleep in the early hours of the morning with a hard dig in the ribs. ' Wake up, quickly! I think the lion is attacking the sea-cows.'

'What...? I told you not to dig.'

'Shush… listen!'

He heard it. Loud roars, deep grunting, and thunderous splashing, and so close that the boat rocked in the disturbed water.

'Get your spear!'

Hallam looked towards the sound, but the moon had gone and a heavy mist blanketed the river. He could see nothing. He listened to the roars. They did not sound like those a lion would make, but he had never heard one until earlier that evening, so could not tell for sure.

'I think it is the fighting of sea-bulls, Master Hallam,' Phineas said.

It was a more reasonable explanation, and gave some respite to their fears. Nevertheless, everyone stood anxiously peering into the mist until dawn, when the noise finally stopped.

When the mist lifted it revealed the brown body of a large sea-bull lying half out of the water on a nearby sandbank. A short way downstream the herd lazed on another exposed strip of sand.

'Is it dead?'

'I think so.'

'In Egypt it is a great delicacy,' said agent Gabaal.

'Perhaps we can float down to it,' suggested Persian.

'It's worth a try,' Hallam agreed. 'If we join the ropes together again, we should be able to reach it without lifting the anchor.'

By paying out the rope, and with the aid of the oar, they reached the dead bull. 'We have competition,' Hallam observed, pointing to the small crocodiles that were already at work, gnawing into the belly. They scattered as the boat grated alongside, darting like fish, and leaving the surrounding water muddied with blood.

The vision of a fat, juicy steak sizzling on a fire made Hallam's jaw ache with anticipation. Unfortunately, they would have to wait until dark. The light from the fire tray could be shielded, but the smoke could not, and he did not want any uninvited guests dropping in unexpectedly.

When Hallam was beginning to think he would never find the ideal spot and would have to settle for something less, it suddenly appeared. A high bank with large overhanging trees in the lee of a slight bend. A channel of dark, still water alongside the bank, and a protected sandpit afforded the perfect place for beaching the boat.

Hallam sailed the boat all the way in with Persian

frantically backing with his oar until the bottom scraped on the sand under the canopy of the trees. Hallam jumped over with his spear and climbed the bank.

The large trees reached back for at least fifty paces, giving plenty of screening and shade, and the ground was sandy and level, with patches of coarse dry grass and scrub that could easily be cleared. No flood debris festooned the lower branches as they had farther downstream.

Hallam climbed one of the trees near the edge for a look at what lay beyond. The dark tree line of the wide, meandering river stood out clearly from the grey-green of a seemingly limitless plain of small and grotesquely gnarled trees. He gazed long and hard at a herd of small goat-like animals grazing peacefully in a grassy clearing. The distance was too far to make out the details, but they looked harmless enough, and would no doubt be edible.

He could see no smoke or any other sign of humans, and the only paths were those of small animals. From the base of the tree the boat was obscured. He listened to the sounds of the birds, especially for those he could recognise, and heard amongst them the whistle of a fish eagle and the cooing of doves. Hearing the familiar sounds made the place seem even less menacing.

Hallam returned to the bank and looked at the overhanging tree. It was more than tall enough to suspend the mast from its branches when the time came to replace it. He dug the point of his spear into the trunk and peeled away a piece of bark to reveal red wood beneath. If he could find a few straight ones, they would be perfect for steering oars, and even a new spar for the sail.

He grinned down at the anxious faces peering silently up at him, feeling a sudden rush of warmth towards them. They had come through so much together. 'Welcome to your new home, my good friends,' he greeted them.

Not being able to make a fire was a serious disadvantage. The sea-cow steaks were delicious - better even, Persian swore, than sea turtle - but without a means of curing the mountain of succulent flesh, or rendering down the buttery fat, the bulk of what they had would soon be spoiled. The fire tray with its protective shields could handle only small amounts at a time, but even that was risky, and they used it sparingly. The glow was minimal, so too the smoke filtering through the overhead branches, but the delicious aroma of cooking meat would drift a long way on the light wind.

Other security problems plagued Hallam. Both girls refused to leave the boat, and nothing could get them to change their minds, even the promise of a reed hut of their own. 'There are crawly things on the ground,' Sophira complained.

'There is plenty of room in the hatch now it is empty,' suggested Jemma. 'If the lions come we can easily close the door.'

'No, it is too cramped in there. What if I build the hut in the tree?'

'Wild apes in the trees.'

'But they're only small, and they seem quite harmless. Maybe you can make friends of them.'

They looked at him with the bland but knowing expressions that the sane use in the company of imbeciles, and Hallam gave up. He could not blame them. The doleful chuckling of the sea-cows, and constant rustling of the undergrowth, had caused him to sit up with his spear on more than a few occasions during the night.

When Hallam noticed Phineas and agent Gabaal examining the main cargo hatch with more than just a passing interest,

Hallam knew he had to do something.

For the next three days, while the others occupied themselves with building a shelter for the stacked cargo and huts for themselves - which they obviously had no intention of using - Hallam devoted himself to the making of a set of javelins, and a bow, which he strung with a strip cut from the hide of the sea-bull.

He tested the weapons in the vicinity of the camp, and soon realised he would have to change his hunting methods. The animals were more wary of predators than the wild sheep of Lamos, and he was also badly out of practice, managing to shoot only one green wood pigeon, and then at the expense of two precious arrows, which sailed harmlessly through the branches and splashed far out into the river.

Disgusted with his efforts, he nevertheless decided it was time to scout farther afield. They could not hide forever, and he had climbed the tree regularly to scour the countryside for smoke, but had seen nothing. He was beginning to get the feeling he was worrying for no reason, and that they were the only humans in this place after all.

Exploring upriver in the cover of the large trees seemed the obvious place to start.

He took Phineas with him, hoping the black would have inherited some of the natural instincts of his ancestors and be of use, but he was wrong. Phineas had the lumbering grace of a sea-cow, and the nerves of a bird. He walked so close on his heels that Hallam could not hear any other sounds other than heavy breathing and weighty footfalls behind, and the sharp point of the spear Phineas clutched in his hand wavered alarmingly close to his ear. Hallam moved his own spear into the trail position to keep the slave at a respectable distance.

They stopped at regular intervals so Hallam could climb a tree and survey what lay ahead. After one such climb, he saw the same herd of animals he had seen on the day they had arrived. They looked to be in much the same place, and it was not too far from the river, from which they no doubt drank. If so, they may be content and unwary. A narrow watercourse, thick with bushes, ran close to where they grazed.

'We have come very far from the camp,' Phineas whispered after Hallam had climbed down. He pointed at the sun, which had barely moved since starting off. 'Better to start going back.'

'I saw a herd of small animals,' Hallam said. 'I want to see if I can get close enough to spear one.'

He set off before Phineas could protest further, heading away from the river and towards the cover of the gully. When he thought they were close, he motioned to Phineas to stay where he was, and crawled from the gully in the cover of small bushes and grass. He lifted his head slowly above and saw them.

They were very different to goats. Taller and more slender of leg, with beautiful honey and milk coloured hides and lyre shaped horns. They stood alert, as if they had heard or scented him, their heads still, but turned away, looking at some place to the right. A soft rustling in the grass behind made Hallam turn quickly. Phineas smiled apologetically.

Without warning, the herd exploded into action, leaping and scattering like dry leaves in a sudden gust. They floated weightless over bushes, slender legs folded, unleashing only at the moment of landing to spring them off in another direction.

Hallam raised up in the grass and watched in fascination, the javelin forgotten at his side. Two animals bounded directly towards him, and he ducked behind the bush as they sailed over his head. It was not a charge, they were in headlong flight, but still unsure, Hallam and Phineas cowered low in the grass until they had passed. Hallam stood to watch them go. Phineas did the same, and stepped directly into the path of a running man.

The impact knocked Phineas back a step, but the man's head collided with the point of Phineas's solid shoulder, and he stopped as if he had run into a tree. He flopped on his back, senseless even before hitting the ground. The bow he had been carrying flew into the grass, and the bark quiver strapped to his chest spilled its arrows around him.

With a yelp of fright, Phineas raised his spear and lunged at the unconscious man, and he would have speared him through his shining round stomach had Hallam not knocked the spear aside at the last moment. The point grazed the skin at the man's side and buried itself in the earth.

'Wait... be quiet!' Hallam elbowed Phineas in the stomach, cutting short his second yell of defiance. 'There may be others.'

The man was small, not much taller than the girls, but he had the face of an old man. He was all but naked, his penis enclosed in a sheath of bark, which suggested protection rather than modesty. His skin was pale in colour, not white, nor black, or even brown, but the yellow of tarnished gold, and his head was sparsely bristled with knots of dusty hair no larger than cloves.

His buttocks were impressively large, easily twice that of a normal man. A straight piece of jawbone belonging to some animal, and which Hallam took to be a knife, was tied to the quiver. The teeth had been ground down on both sides to form a jagged but sharp edge.

'Is it a wild ape, master Hallam?' Phineas spoke in a breathless whisper. 'We should kill it before it wakes up. It may call to others.'

'Apes do not have weapons, Phineas. No, we won't kill him, but you are right, we should hold him for a while in case there are others. Stay low. Collect the arrows and find his bow while I tie him up.'

Hallam used his headband as a gag and tied the heavily callused bare feet together with the man's quiver string. He used his own knife belt to tie the wrists.

While they waited for the man to waken, Hallam examined the weapons. The bow was smaller than his own, but much thicker and stronger, and the arrows were flightless and short, the heads protected by cylinders of bark. He removed one to reveal a carved bone head smeared with a sticky black substance. Closer inspection also showed the heads to be detachable.

When he thought about it, he could see it made sense. With a fixed head an arrow could easily be torn out as the animal fled through the bush, but if only the shaft fell off, the head would stay in and have time to work. It was probably the only way they could kill such alert and speedy animals. They would have to chase after the animal though, which was probably what the man had been doing.

'Wild man waking up, master Hallam,' Phineas warned, lifting his spear.

'Put it down, Phineas. We don't want to frighten him to death.'

The wild man's slanted eyes - not unlike those of a wild Mongol - blinked several times, then opened wide in shock. He scrabbled on the ground, making strange grunting sounds behind the gag as he tried desperately to get away from them, but he could not rise against the bonds.

'There is no need to fear.' Hallam told him, holding forward a placating hand.

At sound of his voice the man redoubled his efforts, writhing and rolling in the grass until he was brought up by a bush. They followed after him. 'Take an arm, Phineas.' They dragged him back under cover and sat him up against the trunk of a tree, holding him steady until he stopped struggling. Immediately he turned his head away and closed his eyes.

In an act of faith, Hallam untied the wrists and removed the gag. When he saw the wild man's eyes open a little, he nodded encouragingly and smiled. The man rubbed his wrists, his eyes moving from Hallam to Phineas and back. They also took in the knife stuck in the ground at Hallam's feet, and the javelin lying in the grass, and it was difficult to tell which he found the most interesting. Suddenly he jabbered loudly at them. It did not sound like any language. It was a strange whistling and clicking sound.

Phineas moved closer to his discarded spear. 'It's calling to others. We should kill it, Master Hallam. It's too wild for safety.'

'You already came too close to doing that, Phineas.' Hallam looked at the spear graze on the man's side, which had started to bleed with all his squirming around. 'Pass me the balsam from the bag... and one of those terrible barley cakes of yours.'

'You thinking of trying to tame it for a slave, Master Hallam?'

'It's worth a try, Phineas, but not as a slave. We need friends in this place, not enemies.'

The wild man was reluctant to have his wound treated. Hallam held his arm aside and smeared the graze with balsam, but as soon as he released his arm the man scraped it off. He jabbered at him, flicking the balsam from his finger in disgust and wiping it over a clump of dry grass.

Not discouraged, Hallam took a small bite of the barley cake, nodded in feigned appreciation then, smiling encouragement, tried to place it between the man's lips, but his hand was struck aside. The man made signs in the air with his hands, pointing first to his own fingers, then at Hallam's.

'I think it is too wild to be tamed, Master Hallam.'

'Perhaps you are right, Phineas, but maybe you are not.' Hallam looked at the black on his fingers and spat the few remaining crumbs from his mouth. He should have realised it was poison. Not knowing what else to do to convey his understanding, Hallam rolled his eyes. The man grunted then, surprisingly, his lips split open to reveal blackened teeth, and his eyes disappeared behind wrinkles.

'What's he doing at you, Master Hallam?'

'Can't you recognise a smile when you see one, Phineas? I'm going to untie his feet. Give him back his weapons.'

'Master Hallam! We should keep them away!'

'And smile while you are doing it. He should know that you are a friend as well.'

The man left his weapons on the ground while he stood to give what Hallam could only think was an angry speech. It was accompanied by arm waving, crouching, ducking, even hopping, and he pointed several times into the bush.

Still clicking furiously, the wild man gathered up his weapons and ran a short distance towards the gully. He stopped, turning to point and babble some more at them, as if still angrily telling them off, then he turned abruptly and ran in the direction taken by the animals.

Hallam noticed with some relief that it was not in the same direction as the camp. He had no idea what to make of all the angry miming and pointing. Maybe Phineas was right, and it was not a smile he had seen, but some kind of grimace, yet his warning about the poison seemed clear.

He looked at his sticky fingers and held them to his nose. The smell was not unlike that of stinking feet. He wiped it off on the grass. It was not something he would like pumping through his veins. He sincerely hoped Prince Hadad was right about sparing lives and making friends.

The news they were not alone in the wilderness caused a mixed reaction in camp. Fear, when Phineas gave his version of events; subdued hope, when Hallam told his side of the story.

'We should leave now,' Agent Gabaal suggested. 'If we take only what we need we can be back on the river before dark. Their arrows may not reach us once we're in the middle.'

Persian agreed with him. 'We can use the mast we already have and stop on one of those big islands farther down to repair the leaks.'

'It won't work,' Hallam said. 'The river may flood, and you saw what it was like at sea. If we don't have a good mast and replace the hull timbers, the boat will sink even before we hit a storm.'

Memories of the storms and the truth of what he said silenced them. Hope and the euphoria of finding themselves safely on land had sustained them thus far, but now they settled into a silence of uncertainty. No one, including Hallam, had given much thought to the return journey. It was something they preferred not to think about.

'You gave him back his arrows,' Jemma commented thoughtfully after a lengthy silence. She paused, and Hallam waited for the reproach he was sure would follow. She would be right. He had thoughtlessly put them all at risk on a foolish whim. A wild savage who carried only poisoned arrows, and went about naked in a land full of lions and other dangerous beasts, was not someone you could expect to be grateful after being knocked unconscious.

'He could easily have shot them at you if he had wanted to,' Jemma continued. 'Don't arrows go farther than spears? I think you were right, Hallam. Anyway, I would rather be killed on land than drowned at sea.'

'Me too,' agreed Sophi, shuddering.

Hallam could hardly believe it was not one of their silly jokes. But Jemma's uncharacteristic use of his name without the accompanying title, and their sombre, identical expressions, convinced him they were serious. Her faith

269

in his hazy judgement, and her astute reasoning about the travelling distance between an arrow and a spear impressed him. It was not something he had thought of himself.

'We have decided to sleep in the hut from now on, haven't we, Sophi?'

Sophi looked surprised.

'Is it all right to make a big fire now, Hallam, seeing as they know we are here?'

'I suppose so, Jemma,' Hallam answered distractedly. He was finding it hard to keep up with their constantly changing attitudes.

With all the excitement, the small news of what the girls had found while scouring a pot with river sand was almost forgotten. Only Agent Gabaal remembered, and later, sitting alone by the fire, he removed the plug from the hollow section of reed and tipped the contents of it into the palm of his hand. He admired the small gleaming mound, tilting his hand so it caught the light, then he replaced the grains carefully. It was the result of only a few hours work, and already he had enough to purchase a fine length of silk.

Jemimah roused Hallam shortly after dawn with an urgent shaking of his shoulder and a taut whisper. 'Hallam! Wake up... we think it is the wild people...'

Hallam opened his eyes to see both girls leaning over him. 'What?'

'It is a horrible clicking noise... like you told us the wild people make instead of speaking.'

They listened but heard only the bright chatter of early birds. 'I don't hear anything, it is probably just the...'

'Shush... listen!'

He heard it. The unmistakable clicking and whistling of the wild man shouting from some distance away. The noise stopped, and Hallam threw aside his blanket and picked up the spear, which always lay at his side. 'Stay here,' he told the girls.

The shouting resumed as soon as he appeared from the shadows of the camp area. He saw the man in the trees a few hundred paces away. Not far behind him stood a group of the wild people draped in animal skins. The man in front was gesticulating, pointing upriver, then at the ground by his feet. He bent to lift what seemed to be a heavy club and waved it in the air, then he strode to a nearby tree and placed the club-like object in a fork. He shouted some more then moved back to join the others, and they all disappeared into the trees.

Hallam hesitated. The skin blankets were reassuring, and he had not seen any weapons. It was too far to see what had been left in the tree, but the gesturing seemed to indicate that he was expected to go and fetch it. He stuck the spear in the ground and walked forward. They seemed to have found the camp easily enough. Had their intentions been hostile, they would not have given a warning.

'Hallam!'

'It's all right, Jemma. Wake the others.'

He walked normally, hiding the tension he felt. He was sure they would be watching, and a show of trust would be a sign of friendship - or so he hoped. If they were not friendly, Hallam thought cynically, now would be the perfect opportunity for them to reduce their enemy by one.

When he reached the tree and saw what the club-like object was, he felt an overwhelming sense of relief and gratitude.

The honey and cream coloured hide was still attached to the hindquarter. He took it down and raised it in the direction the wild people had gone. 'Thank you, Prince Haddy,' he murmured.

In response to the unexpected gift, Hallam left one of his own; a bronze-bladed knife that had belonged to one of the dead sailors. To go with it, he included the belt and leather sheath. He placed it in the fork of the tree and whistled, baulking at the idea of talking foolishly to the silent trees. The man did not appear then, but next morning the knife was gone, and in its place was a piece of curled bark covered with leaves, which, when cautiously removed, revealed a comb of dark honey.

The exchange of gifts became an almost daily ritual, testing the imagination of everyone. They had little in the way of spare food, but the wild people seemed to possess an endless supply, though not all of it appetising. Snakes, lizards, and hairy caterpillars were consigned to the fire with shivers of revulsion and at arm's length by the girls.

Occasionally the gifts were baffling, such as the delicious, giant-sized egg that fed all six of them, and which the girls insisted was the egg of a dragon. Their own gifts of unused clothing were never worn by the wild people, but were ripped up and converted into small shoulder bags for carrying whatever it was they carried, and which Hallam thought was such a good idea that he made one for himself, much to the amusement and delight of the wild men.

They named them the 'Click people'. There were five in all; an older male, who Hallam took to be the father of the one they had first met, three females and an infant. In the early morning chill they could usually be seen draped in their skin blankets, but as soon as the sun was on the ground they shed them and went about naked, the males wearing only the bark sheaths, and the females a small apron of strung shells or pods.

They appeared to have few other possessions, and their camp was nothing more than a small fire and two rude shelters; made by tying together the tops of saplings to form a dome then laying reeds and branches around the sides.

They had made their primitive camp amongst the small trees away from the river, in a spot Hallam would not even have considered, and he suspected the only reason for them being there was to study the strange-looking visitors. He was wrong.

Sitting alone at a particularly large fire at their own camp late one night, waiting for a large chunk of rancid fat to render down, he heard a sound and looked up to see the dark bulk of a sea-cow emerge from the dark. It came purposefully towards him and, thoroughly alarmed, he rolled backwards off his log seat and ran for the nearest tree.

But it was not him the sea-cow was interested in. With angry snorts, it plodded straight through the fire, kicking over the pot and scattering logs and coals in a shower of sparks, then it spun around and began stomping on them, grunting and snorting. It paused to lift its legs in turn, as if to ease the pain of burning, before resuming the onslaught.

Hallam watched in amazement from the branch of the tree as the sea-cow folded its stubby legs and collapsed on the embers. Its hide steamed and sizzled, but it did not stop until all the embers were extinguished. It rolled back to its feet and inspected the dead fire, sniffing and snorting up clouds of ash then, apparently satisfied with its work, it trotted back the way it had come.

Incredibly, and perhaps luckily, the others slept through the whole performance, and Hallam had only the scattered fire and a flattened pot to prove that he hadn't been dreaming.

From then on they only made large fires in the day, and shielded the coals at night.

Knowing he could learn much from the Click people, Hallam tried to encourage them into the camp, but despite their curiosity, they came no closer than the perimeter, and the two men always followed the same ritual when approaching. A hand was raised and a greeting shouted to everyone in turn and, if not acknowledged immediately, stubbornly repeated until it was. It was a lengthy process, and difficult to know who was being greeted unless they were paying attention.

It seemed important to the Click people that everyone know they were there - which would have been impossible unless they were deaf - and they looked disappointed if their noisy greetings were not returned with equal enthusiasm. It made no difference, Hallam discovered, if you tried to be polite and greet them first. You were simply ignored until it was your turn.

Once the lengthy ritual was over, they sat in the shade and waited to be entertained, watching with apparent awe whatever particular activity, object or person interested them most, and often moving vantage points to get a better view. The boat and the twins were their favourite, and it soon reached the stage where the girls' privacy could not be assured.

'We can't bathe or do anything any more,' Sophi complained to Hallam. 'They are always spying. Can't you do something?'

'They don't mean to spy, Sophi, it's just that they haven't seen people like us before and they're curious.'

'Well I wish they would stop. We don't sit and stare at them and I need to go. They're sitting on the path to our private place.'

Hallam found them another place and built a reed screen around it, but he could do nothing about the bathing.

The girls went to the same place all the time; a safe, shallow channel well away from the mainstream of the river and screened from the camp.

'They're used to seeing naked women,' Hallam told them. 'I don't think they'll follow you.' But he was wrong again.

Terrified screams from the river sent Hallam racing down the path with Phineas and Persian pounding after him. The screams, interspersed by angry shouts from one of the Click men, were coming from upstream; from an area usually shunned by the girls because of the thick banks of reeds.

Hallam and the men skidded to a stop on the riverbank. The naked girls were being propelled forcibly across the sand by the old man of the Click people. He held them firmly by the upper arm, one in each hand, and was clearly scolding them. When the old man saw Hallam and the others, he pushed the girls forward, and they scrambled up the bank to cower behind a bush.

The old man continued his tirade, shouting and pointed towards the river. He turned and strode to the reeds, pointing at them, and Hallam descended the bank to join him.

The girls' clothing was lying on the sand between two banks of reeds - a well screened and private place - but the reeds grew far into the water, turning it dark. The old man snatched up a piece of dry reed and pointed with it, and Hallam saw the snout and partly submerged bulk of the crocodile.

He could think of no way to express his thanks. He shrugged helplessly, shaking his head. He had warned the girls often enough. They should have known better. He picked up the clothes, preparing to leave, but the old man was not yet through.

Indicating that Hallam should follow, he led the way a short distance downriver and stopped in a wide stretch of sand, through which, ran a shallow stream of clear water. He made a great show of looking carefully around then, so suddenly that Hallam flinched, began shouting towards the empty bush on the bank. When the Click women appeared, he seemed to become even angrier, scowling and all but stamping his foot in agitation as they lingered coyly on the bank.

They came down reluctantly and he shook the stick at them, urging them to hurry, then he herded them towards the water like tame animals. As Hallam watched the pantomime in bewilderment, the old man spoke to the women, dropping the reed to scoop handfuls of sand over his body. The women giggled, which seemed to incense him further. He snatched up his reed and they stepped hastily into the water.

At the old man's urging they began self-consciously going through the motions of washing, and Hallam grinned. He called to the girls in the same angry tone used by the old man. 'Sophi! Jemma! Get down here!'

When, after a few moments they had still not appeared, he shouted again: 'If you don't hurry up I'll come and fetch you with a stick!' He glanced at the old man to see how he was doing, and was encouraged by his puzzled expression. For added effect, he took the reed from the old man's hand.

Covering themselves demurely with their hands, the girls approached, escorted in front by an anxious Phineas.

Hallam frowned at them and spoke severely. 'If you ever do a stupid thing like that again, I'll take a stick to your backsides!' He shook the reed at them for emphasis. 'A crocodile was right beside you. If it wasn't for the old man you would have been eaten.'

Their faces were pale, but held expressions that told they were not amused at being humiliated or spoken to in such a manner.

'There is no need to be frightened,' Hallam relented. 'I'm doing this for the benefit of the old man. He's just gone to great lengths to tell me that this is a safe place to bathe, and I agree. To show you understand, you should get in the water with the women. It will be a good way to make friends with them, don't you think?'

'What about you, Pilot Hallam?' Jemma asked frostily. 'Will you take your clothes off and show them you understand too?'

Before he could respond, she walked stiffly and unashamedly past him to the water, and Sophi followed in the same manner. Hallam frowned after them, feeling suddenly foolish.

The girls went directly to the baby, cooing with delight, and the Click women responded immediately, giggling shyly as they showed off the child, drawn together by the magnetism of the very young.

Hallam walked thoughtfully back to the camp. He would have to change his thinking. He was taking their welfare and youth too much for granted, thinking of them as children, but the downy shadows were showing dark, and boyish hips beginning to soften and flare. He had come to love them both, as he would younger sisters, but he was not the only man in camp, and the painful experience of Sophi at the hands of the Moabite sailors was an example he should be heeding more carefully.

Encouraged by the girls, and with the barriers removed by the bathing episode, the Click women entered the camp first, expressing their amazement by giggling and, not to be outdone, their men followed.

They showed particular interest in iron, and the sound of it clanging made them gape in wonder.

With a confusing display of hand signals, Hallam indicated he would give them salt, which they recognised, in exchange for meat or fish. He also presented each of the men with a bronze arrowhead, which they placed carefully in the small pouches hanging from thongs around their necks and, as far as Hallam was able to tell, never used them.

But what impressed them most was the medallion. Hallam had taken to wearing it again, and when the old man saw it hanging from his neck, he acted most strangely, hiding his face and looking only through his fingers. He called urgently to the others to do the same, and they talked excitedly to each other.

Hallam removed the medallion and held it towards them, inviting closer inspection, but they shied away, as if it were something dangerous he was offering. Only when he had hidden it under his tunic would they remove their hands from their faces.

The next day, the old man - after first checking through his fingers to ensure the medallion was not visible - approached Hallam with a large green insect perched on his finger. It was raised up in a sitting position with its two front legs held together, as if praying, and its large black eyes seemed to contemplate Hallam with an unusually perceptive interest for an insect. The old man pointed at the eye and then at Hallam's chest, and no further explanation was needed. The insect's black eye with its clear perimeter looked uncannily like his medallion.

The old man placed the insect reverently on the branch of a tree and it turned its head away, almost disdainfully, to inspect its new domain. It was obviously an insect of special importance to the Click people.

Hallam learned their names by listening as they called to each other. He worked out that the young male was called something that sounded like Kwai, and the old man something that sounded like Kwekwe. He repeated the names to them, but received only laughter in return, so could not be sure if he had got them right. He labelled them with those names anyway.

The girls had a much simpler method. They made up their own, calling the two young women Shell and Berry because of the materials used to make their small aprons. The old woman was simply named Mother, and the baby boy Baba. It seemed to work, for all were soon responding to their new names as if they had always had them.

At first, the men with their bark sheaths, which barely covered the essentials, had embarrassed Hallam on behalf of the girls, but they seemed not to notice. It was different with the women. The old woman was weather-worn and wrinkled, but the two young ones, with their slanted eyes and exquisitely delicate features, seemed not much older than the twins, and were unusually attractive. Their bodies were as smooth and golden as river pebbles, with narrow waists - accentuated almost to the extreme by their large buttocks - and petite breasts. As wild and strange as they were, their femininity was undeniable, and Hallam found it impossible to look at them and not feel a sudden sharpening of the senses.

Phineas showed his disapproval by ignoring them and trying to persuade the girls to do the same, but they were starved for feminine companionship and ignored him. Hallam tried to keep his eyes averted when they were close. Agent Gabaal was too busy with his gold to take much note of anything, but Persian, like Hallam, was not gelded or blinded by gold, and he followed their every movement with an expression that hinted of a busy imagination.

It worried Hallam. Despite Persian's vanity, he liked and trusted the man. The girls treated him like a favourite uncle, and he responded in kind. But the bodies of young girls changed quickly, and so too, Hallam believed, could the ways of a trusted uncle.

Work on the boat was progressing more slowly than Hallam would have liked. It was not simply a matter of sliding in new planks to replace those damaged. Zabby's uncle, like most of the better shipbuilders, had used the flush method for assembling the hull. The planks did not overlap, but were butted together to produce a smooth surface overall, each short plank being tongued on one edge and slotted on the other.

The hull was constructed from the bottom up, with the ribs being fitted last. It was a technique that made no sense to Hallam, for each plank had to be custom shaped to fit the curve of the hull at its allotted position, before being fixed in place with bronze nails.

It was a laborious process. To replace one plank meant removing all those above - an almost impossibly long task with the basic tools and expertise Hallam had at his disposal - and the problem caused him many a restless night. He was on the point of surrendering to patchwork when the solution was provided by Phineas.

'Forgive me for stupidly interfering, Master Hallam,' Phineas offered tentatively after Hallam had angrily thrown down the plank he had been trying to fit. 'But is it not possible to stitch it like cloth?'

'You *are* stupidly interfering,' Hallam snarled. 'Have you nothing better to do? What about that timber you're supposed to be collecting for the pitch?'

'All done like you said, master. Forgive me, please.' He moved away, but Hallam called him back, remembering that the slave's cautiously offered suggestions had not always been foolish.

'There is nothing to forgive, Phineas. I'm just frustrated. What did you mean?'

'I saw it in Punt, Master Hallam. The fishermen have no nails for the boats. They must stitch them with string from the coconut tree.'

'Oh?'

Phineas searched the sand for a piece of sharp stone and used it to mark one of the planks on the hull. 'First are made holes here.' He placed two marks close together near the edge of a plank, then another two opposite them on the adjacent plank. He drew lines to join the holes diagonally. 'In here is made cuts for the string to sit down. After the string is tied on the inside, all is covered with the pitch to make strong.'

'And, if we remove the outside half of the slot,' mused Hallam, getting the idea and following it through, 'and also the inside half of the tongue, the plank will fit in nice and flush but won't push through. We can then place a few more stitches on the tongue and....'

A frown of concentration creased his brow as he went through the process again in his mind. It would save months of frustrating labour, and the sound timbers above - already swollen firmly into place - would not have to be disturbed. He looked for the hidden catch. It all seemed too simple. But he could not find one, and the frown transformed itself into a grin.

'Phineas, my flabby friend, not only are you not stupid, you are also not going to escape until I give adequate thanks.' He advanced on the startled slave with arms outstretched, catching him in a hug and kissing him on the cheek.

Phineas squealed. 'Master Hallam... *please*!' But his grin of delight rivalled Hallam's in size.

Hallam turned him around and gave him a slap on the rump. 'Enough of that. To work! We need the hardest wood we can find for charcoal, and we need a skin to make bellows and, if you have any gods, ask them to please provide us with a coconut tree.'

Phineas's gods could not find a coconut tree, but they provided something better; the inner bark of a shrub that produced the fine tough threads on which the Click women strung the shells and berries for their aprons. In the company of Sophi and Jemma, the women sat in the shade and produced a seemingly endless supply, twisting the threads together by rolling them with their palms over the smooth skin of their thighs.

The waxen threads did not dry out and become as brittle as bark string, and when Hallam tested it, he found it needed nearly all his strength to break a double strand. More than enough was produced in only a few days, but the women seemed to enjoy making it, so he let them continue, using the surplus to lash together the new section of deck railing, and for repairing some of the frayed ropes.

Once the planks were in place, only the mast and new spar remained to be erected. Hallam climbed the tree overhanging the boat and eased himself along a branch to remove the bark from a fork. He greased it thoroughly with fat, then passed their thickest rope over it before climbing down to help with the lifting. Millstones were used to counterbalance the weight, and the mast was slowly raised.

While it hung suspended, and with the invaluable help of the Click men, the boat was pushed, pulled and cursed into position and the mast lowered and fixed into its step. The new spar, with the sail attached, was hauled up via its new block to check that everything worked as it should. The mast was shorter than before, and the spar a little crooked as they had not been able to find a straight branch in a suitably hard material, but it was stronger than the previous one, and gave the boat a certain jaunty air, as if she were wearing a cocked hat.

By mutual agreement, they had decided to stay with the Egyptian method and do away with the brails. It was more weight to pull up, but safer to let down in a hurry, and no one wanted to take a chance on the spar breaking a second time through delay.

The mast was much less trouble than any of them had expected, and the whole operation took only four days to complete. They gathered on the bank to admire their handiwork and congratulate themselves.

'It looks more like a boat now,' Hallam commented. 'Once the stays are on, she will be ready to sail.'

'I think we should leave as soon as she is ready,' Persian suggested. 'We can take our chances on the wind.'

'Perhaps,' Hallam answered evasively. He looked at Persian with concern. He had not been his usual cheerful self for the past few weeks.. 'Do you not feel well? You have not been eating.'

'My hunger will return with the sea,' Persian answered.

Hallam's calculations were largely guesswork, based only on their passage down, but he understood that to sail north, back up the Zeng coast to Arabia, they would obviously need a wind from the south. From discussions with Phineas, he also understood that in the Zeng Sea the big winds blew only twice a year- once from the south and once from the north - but they had been blown so far down he could not be sure it would still be the same. And they would not know for sure until they had committed themselves to its whims.

Hallam believed the wind had already changed. The

movement of the clouds seemed to back up his assumption, but it was difficult to tell for they often moved erratically. To help with his calculations, he made a new calendar on a piece of stretched hide. Since cutting the first notch in the mast at sea, he had methodically continued the practice, and these he now transferred onto the hide with a hot spike, burning one mark for each eight days.

They had left Saba in the summer, soon after the change of wind, and he calculated that if the wind blew as expected, they still had a long wait. They had been in the wilderness for one hundred and sixty four days. By the time the south wind returned, it would be a full year. For himself, he didn't mind. He was in no hurry to face the uncertainties of the voyage north, and he had come to love this wild and bountiful land and wanted to see more, but he could not say the same for the others.

It is the nature of man, Councillor Abdon had philosophised to Hallam when they were in the mountains of Edom, that idle thoughts turn more readily towards evil than good, and Hallam had cause to remember them now that work on the boat was completed. Boredom caused tempers to be short and complaints to be long.

For the twins, boredom was made worse by the absence of the Click people. They had often disappeared in the past, sometimes for several days, presumably on hunting trips, for they always returned with meat or skins, but this time they had been gone for almost a month, and even Hallam was wondering anxiously if they would return. Now that he had time, he hoped to somehow persuade them to take him on one of their nomadic excursions.

To fill in the time, Hallam organised excursions of his own. It was still too early to start collecting food for the return journey, but Agent Gabaal had spoken so much about gold that Hallam decided it was time to see for himself.

They took with them several of the eating bowls Phineas

had made from the clay of an anthill and walked upstream to a place Gabaal had not dared to venture on his own.

'The best places are along the bank where there is a bend in the river,' Gabaal explained. He showed them the correct method of swirling the dark mud from the bottom with a little water, and Hallam was surprised when, at the end of the first day, they had collected easily one minas worth of gold.

'There is more gold in this river than any I have heard of,' Gabaal enthused, excited at the prospect of substantially increasing his horde. 'With fifty slaves I could fill the jar in a day, and we cannot even see the hills from where it comes. Look how fine it is! Surely, the hills must be made of gold! Can we not sail up the river to reach them?'

Hallam was tempted. He wanted to see what lay beyond for reasons of his own, and the prospect of finding the source of the gold was an added incentive, but he was forced to reject the idea. The boat was too large, the wind too variable, and they would be going against the current, he explained. 'You will have to be content with what we have here, Gabaal, but remember, there must be no argument. As we have shared your work, so you must share the gold.'

But interest waned after the first week for everyone except Gabaal, despite the empty wine jar they used for storing the gold being already one third full.

'I'm bored with this,' Jemimah declared, dropping her bowl onto the sand in disgust. 'Can't we do something else for a change? Gold is so *boring*, and my feet are getting sore from being in the water all the time.'

'Hands too,' added Sophi.

Hallam swirled his bowl and slopped the bulk of it over the edge. 'But this is a good place, look at that streak of gold... don't you want to be rich?'

'We are already rich. Father is the richest man in Saba... after the queen.'

'Good, then we can have your share. What do you want to

do instead?'

'Anything.'

Hallam gave an exaggerated sigh. He was becoming bored himself. 'We are not too far from the place where we first met Kwai. Maybe we can see those beautiful animals I told you about.'

'Even hunting would be better than this,' Jemma conceded ungraciously.

'Not hunting, just looking, and you will have to be quiet, or you will see nothing, and tomorrow I want you to carry on with the star chart you started at sea. We may need it.'

They left Persian and Phineas in the care of the disgruntled Gabaal, and headed away from the river. It was not long before Hallam found a number of the small hoof-prints of the dainty animals on the sand. Their droppings were fresh, but he could see no sign of the animals themselves. They followed for a while then decided to give up when the marks scattered. 'They must have heard us coming,' he explained, pointing to the marks. 'See how they are more spread out and deeper? It shows they were running.'

'I don't like it out here, away from the river,' Sophi complained. 'Maybe we should go back and look for some more gold.'

'You are even worse than Phineas.'

They started back, but had gone only a short distance when Jemma, walking close behind Hallam, caught him suddenly by the arm. 'What's that?' she whispered. 'I heard a noise... over there!' She pointed to one of the small stunted trees not thirty paces away. Taller than the girls, Hallam could see clearly above the grass, and what he saw turned him cold.

The lion was sitting in the shade of the tree, looking directly at him, and it was not alone. Three lionesses and two cubs were close behind, feeding on the carcass of some animal.

'What is it?' Jemma whispered, craning up on her toes.

286

Hallam moved his spear to the front. 'Be quiet and move behind me... slowly.'

The lion stood and lifted its head to sniff and stare. Its mane was full and black.

Both girls drew in sharp breaths, and Sophi let out a thin squeal. It was barely audible, yet still enough to cause the lion to grunt and suddenly spin away. It trotted into the long grass and disappeared. The two cubs sprang after it, and all three lionesses lifted their heads to stare towards where Hallam and the girls stood frozen. One of the lionesses let out a warning growl and Sophie gasped.

'Be quiet and stand still,' Hallam whispered. Instinct told him if they tried to run the lions would pounce. They were in the open, with not even one of the small trees within reaching distance. Their only chance was to brazen it out. He tightened his grip on the shaft of the spear and glanced to the side, worried by the disappearance of the male, and wondering if it was circling to make an attack from behind.

Two of the lionesses rose and followed after the cubs, but the third lioness, greyer in colour than the others, remained crouching, growling deep from within her belly, nodding her head as she focused her yellow eyes and sniffed the air.

Hallam could sense the girls' panic rising with the ominous growling, and he willed them not to run. He longed to reach behind with a reassuring hand, but he dared not move.

The old lioness lifted her head and shook it, as if puzzled, then she stood and ambled slowly away, pausing every few steps to turn her head and look back with her face wrinkling in a silent snarl.

Hallam waited until she had disappeared before reaching behind. 'Move back slowly,' he whispered, 'and whatever you do, don't run or make a noise, even if you see them again.'

It was an unnecessary warning. The girls were so stiff with fright they could barely walk, let alone run. When they had doubled the distance between themselves and where the lions had been, he shepherded the girls close in front until they reached the tall trees of the river, then helped them up into the branches. He was not sure if lions could climb trees, but he felt a lot safer off the ground. And even more so, when he reached the top and could see the lions had returned to their interrupted meal. When they sauntered off to lie in the shade, he helped the reluctant girls down and they swiftly went to join the others.

That was the last of the excursions. The girls refused to leave the camp and would have moved back to the hatch on the boat had it not already been filled with timber.

Persian, also reluctant to leave camp, began carving a horse's head for the boat's prow from the hard roots of a dead tree. The gleam of gold had blinded Gabaal to most dangers and he returned to the river, but closer to the camp than before.

The girls went to work making bark string, using it to bind together the reed fish traps as taught them by the Click women. Hallam and Phineas set them in narrow channels amongst the reeds, and made a drying rack for the fish they caught, filleting, then dipping them in a brine mix before laying them on the rack in the sun.

The fish curled like pieces of dry bark, but softened in water and tasted better than those he and Zabby had stolen on the shore of the Great Sea. He stored them in one of the empty lentil barrels and, once it was filled, sealed the lid with pitch. He was more than happy with the result, and it was the first of their sea provisions.

His greatest success though, came with the return of the Click people.

Kwai pointed with the tip of his bow to the large imprint in the sand that looked not unlike that of an ox. Kwai's father put his own bow on the ground and held both hands to the side of his head like horns. He snorted and pawed at the sand with his foot.

Hallam looked at him with astonishment. 'A bull?'

Although he could not have understood, Kwai nodded vigorously. He made a series of his animated clicking sounds and walked on, following the prints. They soon found more, enough to show a large herd had passed and, to Hallam's continued astonishment, piles of fresh, ox-like dung. It did not seem possible there could be oxen in such a place, but the proof was there to see. He began to wonder if he may have been wrong. Perhaps they were not as isolated as he thought. He wore a puzzled frown as he followed after Kwai.

It was more than necessity that forced Hallam to seek the aid of the Click people. He wanted to see the country, but he also had to provision the boat, and he did not want to go alone. Like Phineas, Persian did not like hunting, and would have been more hindrance than help. Surprisingly, Kwai and his father seemed to understand his pantomime of leaping about with hands on the head for horns and belly patting.

Now he wondered if they had understood after all. He had meant to convey the graceful antelope, not an ox. Still, there was nothing wrong with an ox, as long as it did not belong to someone else.

The country had changed dramatically soon after leaving the river, becoming a flat woodland of short, twisted trees with leaves of copper and gold. They could barely go more than a hundred cubits without startling some animal. By noon, Hallam had seen more different species than he could count, some so strange he could only stop to gape in wonder.

When he saw the herd of black and white striped horses he could not help but let out a gasp of pleasure. They stood amongst the trees, their stripes blending with the shadows, and they stared back with equal curiosity at the two-legged intruders, alerted, but not alarmed by their presence.

Kwai and his father were delighted with his surprises. Kwai pointed with his bow to the still shapes of other animals watching their progress from the surrounding trees; tall animals with long twisted horns, and others the size and shape of hogs, which ran in a line with their tufted tails held stiff and high above the grass like the battle standards of a mounted cohort.

To Hallam's intense relief, they had not heard or seen any lions, and the other animals they passed seemed harmless enough, either watching curiously or moving hesitantly away. Any one of them would have been adequate for his needs, but he said nothing, content to follow and look, and to enjoy the vitality of this hunters paradise.

He began to relax. He stopped his quick, nervous scanning of the surrounding bush, and copied the slow, seemingly casual observing of his companions. He had always prided himself on his hunting ability, but in the company of Kwai and the old man he was a novice.

The Click men saw every small movement and heard every sound, but made no sound themselves. The whisper of their bare, apparently thorn-proof feet was hidden under the crunch of Hallam's new sea-cow sandals, and the brush of grass and small branches against their naked limbs was unheard below the tortured squeal of his breeches. He stopped and removed them and, while the Click men looked on in amazement, he cut the legs off at the thigh. It was a great improvement.

Hallam discovered the Click men also had a wicked sense of humour.

Kwai stopped suddenly and spoke quietly to his father, indicating a nearby thicket with a tilt of his head. Hallam looked, but could see nothing. Kwai bent to take a pinch of dust and toss it in the air, then he nodded to his father and they both looked at Hallam with their faces wrinkled in what looked suspiciously like mischievous grins.

Signalling for Hallam to follow, the old man pushed past Kwai and walked for a short distance in the direction they had been going. He stopped by a small tree and, when Hallam looked back, he saw that Kwai had remained behind. The old man nudged Hallam and pointed towards the thicket at the same time as Kwai began shouting at it in an angry voice. He shouted only a few words before running to join them.

No sooner had Kwai arrived when an angry snort came from the thicket, then the bushes erupted as if struck by a whirlwind. Branches waved and crackled, leaves flew, and the ugliest, most ferocious looking beast Hallam could have imagined exploded from the cover.

It was larger than a sea-cow, with a single curved horn as long as Kwai on its nose. It charged into the open, then stopped in a spray of dust, shedding torn branches and leaves from its wide back.

For long moments it stared towards where Kwai had been standing, its wide nostrils flaring, then it lowered its massive head and snorted on the ground, blowing up dust and dry grass. It stamped its front legs in fury, daring whatever had made the shouted challenge to appear. When no challenge was returned, it spun to the side and trotted forward a few steps, its drooping upper lip trembling as if in uncontrollable rage, then it spun again to face the opposite direction, ears twitching and turning as if a noise had been heard there. It reminded Hallam of an irate old man being called to his door by noisy ruffians who had since run away. It was the most ill-tempered beast, and looked as if it desperately wanted to kill something.

Hallam stood frozen, as he had with the lion, hardly daring to breathe, for they were not more than twenty good paces from the beast, and again, no suitable trees to climb. He searched for the beast's eyes but could see nothing until it blinked against the dust and he saw them far down the length of its elongated head, beside the massive horn. They were small and dark, and almost hidden in the wrinkles of its skin. Although it looked directly at them, it had not seen them, and Hallam surmised with relief that its eyesight must be very poor.

Finding nothing satisfying to kill, the beast vented its rage on a thorn bush, hooking viciously and ripping the bush from the ground. It tossed it irritably aside, then turned and trotted back to the thicket, lifting its thick, stubby legs in a surprisingly dainty manner, and snorting explosively with each step as if muttering curses.

When the beast's disgruntled departure had faded, Kwai and his father doubled over and staggered around as if drunk, stifling their laughter with hands over mouths, and renewing their efforts each time they looked at Hallam's pale face. They re-enacted the beast's rage time and again, and Hallam joined in their laughter, for they were accomplished mimics, but his grin became more strained as the morning wore on. It was not *that* funny, and would have been even less so had the beast seen or smelled them. But he forgave them. Kwai and the old man were showing off. Impressing him with their knowledge, as they had been awed by his.

The acrid stench of the herd reached them before they saw it. Kwai tossed a pinch of dust in the air, then pointed out the herd a short while later. It was large, but how large was impossible to tell, for they were spread throughout the trees, some lying in the shade, others meandering slowly about as they foraged.

From a distance they looked like a normal herd of cattle, but Hallam could see they were not. They looked more like a herd of stocky bulls with unusually flat horns. Kwai removed two arrows from his bark quiver and signalled to Hallam he must sit down and wait, then he and the old man disappeared into the grass, leaving him alone. More alone than he liked. He had only his spear and knife; flimsy protection against the animals he had seen, and he felt a flood of admiration and respect for the small naked men.

When the herd moved it sounded as if giant boulders were being rolled through the trees, and Hallam stood up quickly as the brown mass of animals thundered away through the bush. Kwai's father appeared in the dust, to beckon urgently, and Hallam ran to join him.

The old man led the way at a run, skipping lightly over dry branches and thorny bushes, and Hallam pounded close behind. They stopped next to the headless shaft of an arrow, and Kwai's father stooped to study the scuff of prints around it, grunting and clicking softly to himself, then he picked up the shaft and set off again at a trot. He studied the ground as he went, sometimes stopping to touch at the marks with the tip of the shaft while he grunted, either in satisfaction or frustration. Hallam could not tell which.

The prints were all around them, and Hallam thought it odd that the old man should be confused. He noted with some satisfaction that even when running, he could easily follow them himself. Then the old man stopped again to circle a particular print, and Hallam realised with sudden understanding that they had not been following the herd, but one beast. It awed him. He could see no difference in the print to the hundreds of others surrounding it.

He did not notice exactly when it was they moved away from the heavy trail. Sweat stung his eyes and he moved the headband down to block it. When he looked again the trail had gone and they were running over hard, seemingly unscathed earth. The pace increased and he started to lag.

The old man waited impatiently for him in the sandy bed

of a dry stream, and Hallam stumbled to a halt beside him, gasping for air. Apart from a sheen of perspiration and a gently heaving chest, Kwai's father looked no different from normal. He gave Hallam a gummy grin and pointed to the single set of hoof-prints in the sand. Close beside them were the small ones of Kwai.

They caught up with him late afternoon. He was dozing in the shade of a tree, and close-by, partly screened by the thick bush in which it stood, was the beast they had been following. It showed no reaction to their arrival. The poison had taken almost the full measure of its toll. The beast's heavily bossed head hung low between its splayed legs, and pink mucus drooled from its blown nostrils with each hoarse groan of breath. Spasms tugged at the bulging muscles, shaking its entire body from sagging ears to limp tail. It must have been in great pain, and the beast's agony reached out to Hallam. A quick thrust to the heart with his spear would relieve its misery.

He started towards it, but Kwai's sharp exclamation stopped him. He turned to look and Kwai waved him angrily away. When Hallam hesitated, Kwai took the spear from him and walked towards the stricken animal. He stopped a good few paces away and rattled the bush in front of the animal with the spear, and the beast lunged forward with startling speed. It stood on the bush, reaching forward with its drooling nose, swinging the great head, but its strength was gone. With a long groan it collapsed ponderously onto its knees and rolled over.

Kwai approached it cautiously. He placed the spear under its foreleg and thrust upward, and the beast shivered in death. Then Kwai did something odd. He began talking to the beast at length, in a tone of voice Hallam could only think of as apologetic. He sat on his haunches beside the great head and put his hand on it, as if to soothe it, then he stood and removed the knife Hallam had given him from its sheath.

Still talking animatedly to the dead beast, Kwai cut out the two arrow heads - one from the shoulder and one from the flank. He replaced them carefully in their bark containers, wiped his hands on the grass, then began expertly gutting the animal. He reached in and pulled out the liver, sliced a piece off, and popped it in his mouth, then he sliced a piece for the old man who did the same. A third chunk, impaled on the point was offered to Hallam..

While Kwai gutted the carcass and dragged what entrails he didn't want into the bush, the old man made a fire. He used the shaft of an arrow, rolling it rapidly between the palms of his hands onto a piece of soft, dry wood, placing a pinch of sand on the block first to grind a small hole. Within a few moments he had it smoking. A few crumbled dry leaves and splinters, a soft blow, and it began blazing. Kwai dragged in the branches of a dead tree to keep it going, and also several green ones, which he stacked alongside.

They camped beside the beast, Kwai and his father leaning against it while they grilled choice pieces from the entrails, tossing them about in the hot coals with fingers apparently impervious to heat. Hallam grilled his on the end of a stick, and wished they had camped a little farther away from the raw stench of the vermin infested animal.

A terrifying clamour of snarls and yelping jerked Hallam from a drugged doze. Another fire had been made on the other side of the beast and pungent smoke billowed from the green branches. Kwai and his father were still awake and, incredibly, still eating. Through the smoke, Hallam could see the shadowy forms of dog-like animals moving about outside the reach of the firelight.

As exhausted as he was from the long run, he found no further sleep until dawn when the animals departed.

The women arrived not long after the sun. How they managed to find the way, Hallam had no idea. The fire had long since settled to embers, so they would not have seen any smoke. It was one more mystery to contemplate, along with the many other uncanny abilities of the Click people.

No attempt was made to save the hide of the animal. The quarters were hacked into manageable portions with the hide intact, and the remainder - including much of the entrails - wrapped in the hide and buried in the sandy earth. A fire was made on top, some of the pungent green leaves and branches added then, when they were half burned away, the fire was spread to cover the excavated area and left to die out. The meat would be safe from predators until they could return to collect it.

While the work was in progress, Hallam searched for the head of the beast. He found it some way from the camp. Nothing remained except the jaw bone and the heavily bossed horns, which were deeply indented with teeth marks. Hallam put the deformed dog-like animals down on his growing list of beasts to stay well clear of.

They ferried the meat over the next two days, the Click women carrying large amounts on their heads, and the men slinging it on a pole between them. All the members of the camp were included except Persian, who complained of sickness. The girls showed none of their previous reluctance to venture out from the camp.

'We don't mind as long as Shell and Berry are with us,' Jemma explained. 'We feel safe with them. They know what they're doing.'

Hallam knew what she meant, but it did nothing for his self esteem. He thought he had done rather well with facing the lions.

Kwai made a small detour on the return trip. He left the load they were carrying under a tree in the care of Phineas, the old woman and the infant, then led the rest of them along a well used game trail. More trails soon appeared, crossing over each other in a confusing manner, but Kwai seemed to know where he was going. He paused on the way to find two sticks of roughly the same size and length, which he handed to the women before continuing on.

They stopped on the edge of an open grassy plain, in which lay a large expanse of muddy water, and the girls squealed with excitement. 'Elephants! Oh look! They have elephants here!'

'And not only elephants,' Hallam breathed. As the girls had pointed out, three elephants were indeed lounging idly near the centre of the shallow lake, and on the far side a herd of the striped horses grazed along the bank. Scattered among the trees were still other animals too far away to make out clearly, but which looked to Hallam like the graceful jumping antelope. But, as interesting as that was, it was apparently not what they had been brought there to see. Kwai signalled for them to sit down and wait, then he and the old man did their disappearing trick in the long grass.

While they waited, the Click women tied a clump of grass to one end of each stick, giggling secretively, and Hallam got the feeling they were about to experience another Click joke.

'What are they doing?' Sophi asked.

'They're your friends, why don't you ask them?'

Sophi screwed up her face to make it look puzzled, and made some shrugging motions, and the Click women held hands to their mouths to suppress their snorts of laughter.

'I suppose you will have to wait and find out,' Hallam remarked.

Kwai and his father reappeared to lead them around in a wide loop through the trees. They stopped beside an anthill, which Kwai indicated Hallam and the girls should stand on, then he took the sticks from the women, gave one to the old man, and they crept off through the grass and, much to the girls immediate consternation, so did the women. Suddenly they were alone.

'What's happening? Where are they going?' Sophi whispered sharply. 'Why are they leaving us?'

'I suppose they think you will be quite safe with me,' Hallam answered with the hint of a sneer. He climbed the anthill and the girls followed, nudging him and each other to stay close.

'What? What can you see?'

'Nothing.'

They looked down onto an expanse of long dry grass sparsely dotted with shrubs.

'Is it the elephants?'

'I don't think so.' If anything, they were farther away. One was lying in the water with only its trunk and two gleaming tusks showing.

'I love elephants,' Jemma whispered.

A wheezing sound came from below, immediately followed by a soft thumping. Looking towards the sound, Hallam saw one of the Click men weaving in a crouch through the grass, the stick with the clumpy head poking above.

'Look... over there.'

Something else had been attracted by the sound. An animal that had been lying concealed in the grass had raised up a birdlike head on a long neck to search around. Its head turned quickly from side to side, then it saw the weaving stick with the clumpy head and stood up on two long legs.

Jemma clutched Hallam by the arm. 'A monster bird!'

The bird-like animal lifted its long legs and thumped them several times on the ground, then it charged with astonishing speed towards the intruder, holding out stubby wings, and lifting its legs high through the grass.

But no sooner had it started its charge than the intruder disappeared. It popped up almost immediately in a different location to the accompaniment of wheezing and thumping.

The giant bird stopped in confusion. It turned in a circle, raising its legs high, running on the spot, then it saw the offender bobbing and twisting about and charged towards it, only to have it disappear and pop up somewhere else yet again.

'Why are they teasing the poor thing?' Sophi asked with a frown. 'Are they going to kill it?'

'I don't think so, they didn't take their bows.'

'Well, I hope it flies away.'

I don't think its wings are big enough.'

The animal seemed to have lost the elusive intruder. It stamped about in a haphazard fashion, its head turning as it searched in confusion.

Intrigued by its antics, Hallam and the girls did not see or hear the Click women arrive back until one of them called softly from behind. She beckoned to them to follow, and they ran into the cover of the trees. The Click women proudly displayed the two giant eggs they had stolen from the nest.

'I believe you have just seen your first dragon,' Hallam commented to the surprised girls.

When the flooding of her life river did not come for two seasons together, Morning Foot knew the seed in her belly had taken root and that death may be close.

She had thought about it with fear every day, and wondered why it was she did not speak out, for each day her silence went deeper, and the speaking of it harder. But then the seed in her belly was not that of a San, and no such thing had ever happened before.

She thought about it again as she knelt to blow gently on the dying embers of the fire, watching the small flame that blossomed, and seeing in its flickering how the seed in her belly would also come to life; brought into being by the breath of her body. It would grow with great strength and size, for the hairy Strange-One was all those things, and she wished she could dig out the rooted seed from her belly with her digging stick, as she did the young roots of the tree with four corners.

Morning Foot left the fire to grow, and went into the bushes to relieve herself, and to look for the star after which she had been named. She saw it in the usual place, low above the trees; the only one left now in the sky, and already fading as it ran to hide from the sun. She watched it leave in sadness, wondering if she would ever see it again, for surely, this would be the day she must find the courage to speak to Old Father.

Did you shoot him with love arrows from your eyes?' 'No, Old Father, he shot them to me many times, but I turned them aside.'

'But still you did not speak, even though he had planted his seed.'

'I was afraid you would hit me with the club of two sleeps.'

'Am I like the bone-eaters who eat their own cubs even when their bellies are full?'

Morning Foot gasped. Even to think of such a thing could bring bad omens. 'No, you are not like them, Old Father.'

'How is it you did not hear one who walks so noisily and casts such a big shadow?'

'My star was still running from the sun, and the Strange-One was hiding in the reeds where I get the water.

'Tell me the story of it.'

Morning Foot shifted uncomfortably. She had thought of it much, but had not spoken the words, and such words were not easy to find in the presence of Old Father. She could not tell him without shame how she had felt as he pushed it into her until it seemed to fill her whole belly. Or about the pain that was of a kind she had never experienced, even though Old Mother had prepared her for such times with the long fruit of the love tree. There had been much pain, but it had been one without fire.

Nor could she speak of how he had stayed inside her, covering her mouth with his own until his manhood grew large again. Especially she could not tell him how, even through her pain and fear, had come a strange feeling of pleasure, for despite his size, he had been gentle, so she had somehow known he was not going to kill her after he had finished.

'Is the story of it so shameful that it has no words?'

Morning Foot started guiltily as the arrow of Old Father's question struck deep into the heart of her thoughts. 'I fear only the shame of telling it to the ears of one who is not a woman, Old Father.'

'This you will speak of with your sister or mother, but how will I know in what direction to walk if you leave me no tracks to follow?'

'He jumped on me from the reeds, Old Father, while I bent to fill the gourd with water, then he took me into the thickness of the reeds and planted his seed.'

'You could not cry out?'

'He covered my mouth and lifted me from the ground. I could not cry out or run. For a long time I could not breathe, and even feared to be killed.'

'He did not club you to sleep?'

'I hoped many times he would, Old Father, for he was very big and strong, and gave me much pain.'

Old Father stood up. 'Come with me. Leave your blanket.'

Morning Foot pulled the blanket closer about a body suddenly gone cold. 'What is it, Old Father? What will you do with me?'

'Do not be stupid with me, Morning Foot. I see many

strange things when we go to the sleeping place of the long-haired ones, but they do not fill all my eyes. I have also seen the shooting of love arrows from the one who planted his seed. He shoots them also at Evening Heart, and I have seen you both turn them away with your eyes so they fall at your feet. Now come!'

Old Father led her into the bush, towards the stony patch of ground that had been the reason for them being in this part of the country, for what they sought was rare. He spoke to her as they walked, remonstrating with his free hand and talking loudly from the front while she listened attentively from behind. She had to break into a trot every so often to keep up with his angry stride.

'Long teeth and his two wives spend much time in the medicine water,' he told her. 'They have already heard the call from the high land. And did you not see how the ones who do not know what colour to be are looking to the sleeping place of the sun? They too have heard the roaring of Mantis and seen the flashing of his eyes, and are ready to heed his call.'

'Yes, I saw it, Old Father.' She had not, but was in a very agreeable mood.

'Soon they will leave, and we must follow to meet with our own family, and to find you a man, but first we will go to the cave of Eland and tell the one who wears the bracelet of teeth what we have seen. He will paint the story of the Strange-Ones for those that follow.'

'Thank you, Old Father, but what of the Strange-One's fruit that I carry there with me? And will a man not be afraid to go where a Strange-One has been?'

Even as her words were reaching into her ears, Morning Foot knew they were saying too much. Her relief had loosened and set free her tongue. She was not surprised when Old Father turned and gave her a stinging slap on her quickly raised arm. She took a few steps back as he threatened her with the shaft of an arrow, but he did not strike her with it.

'Do you think I am too stupid to think of these things?' He turned abruptly and walked on, and she ran to catch up.

'Like the trees, when your fruit is ripe it will drop on the ground and be left for the bone-eaters. It will not be looked upon or spoken of.'

'I understand, wise Old Father.'

When they reached the stony patch, the old man searched until he found what he was looking for in the shelter of a thorn bush; an irregular nest of silken threads with a tunnelled hole in the centre.

'Is it the night-one we seek, Old Father?'

'Only if it is female and shows the mark of blood on its tail, and take care. It must stay alive until near the time it is used.'

Although the question was in her mind, Morning Foot fastened her tongue and did not ask for the reason they collected the night-one when they had already plenty of juice from the sleep tree. She worked silently at her delicate task on the silken threads.

'I see you have learned one lesson at least,' he said. 'That is good. But there are more, and I will tell you of them, but first I will speak the words I see on your tongue. You wish to know if I will shoot my arrow of death at the Strange-One who planted his seed. Is it not so?'

'It is so, Old Father.'

'I will not shoot the arrow of death, nor even your brother, Flying Sticks, will shoot it. You must shoot the arrow yourself, but only if you wish it.'

'Me, Old Father?' Her heart stumbled

'Is it not the way of the San, that if a man wishes to take a woman he shoots her with an arrow of grass? And if the woman accepts, does she not shoot the grass arrow in return?'

'It is what I have learned, Old Father.'

'The Strange-One has shot you with a love arrow on which

has been the poison of his seed, and it will bring you much pain. Is it not the way that you may return what he has given you?'

'It would seem that is the way, Old Father, but I have not the strength or the skill to shoot it. And will the eye of Mantis that One- Ear wears around his neck not see me?'

'As he waited for you, so you will wait for him unseen, and you will be close.' He paused and turned away from her. 'If it is your wish to shoot the arrow, Morning Foot, you will find the strength.'

Hallam was almost certain the colour of the water in the river was changing. The channels were still clear, but the main stream was darker than usual, and may even be moving more swiftly. He marked the depth on a reed stuck in a pool, and next morning his suspicions were confirmed. The river was rising.

He went to consult Kwai on the matter, but the Click people's camp was deserted. Perhaps they had gone on another of their many excursions.

It had not rained for all the time they had been there. The sky had remained clear except for the occasional cloud coming in from the sea, and the air had been crisp and dry, but now he detected a heaviness in it and, although the sky remained clear, a certain dullness showed to the west.

Hallam watched the river carefully over the next few days, but could see no further rise, and the colour remained the same. Still, he was taking no chances. Most of the heavy cargo of millstones, spare timber, ropes and hardware had already been stowed on the boat. Now he organised the collecting of dry firewood, had the water barrel and empty wine jars filled with clear water and, finally, gathered the food.

Cut into strips as thick as a finger and as long as a hand, the salted meat on the drying racks had attained the brittle texture of kindling, but it softened when chewed and tasted delicious. Hallam packed them in the empty salt barrel and sealed the lid with wood pitch, as he had done with the fish. All that remained was what the twins had collected.

'Are you sure you want to take all of that?' Hallam asked, surveying the confusing array of roots, berries, wild fruit - most of it sour and unappetising - dried pods, sticks, and even beetles.

'We still have to get more,' Jemma replied.

'What are those?' He pointed to a pile of bright yellow berries that looked to have some food potential.

'Poison. You can't eat those.'

'Then why are you taking them?'

'The Click women said they are good to rub on stings, cuts and blisters. Also insect bites.'

'And those sticks?'

'We have to get more of those too. They're one of our best things. Come, I'll show you.' Jemma took one of the sticks and put it in the fire, then held her hands over the smoke. 'Smell.' She held her hands to his nose, and Hallam sniffed a pleasant fragrance not unlike sandalwood. 'The Click women use it to smoke the Baby. It makes him smell nice and it keeps away the bugs. Lasts all day.'

'You should get Gabaal to try some. And what about all these?' He picked up a green fruit the size of a husked coconut. It had already been broken open and he popped one of the fleshy white-coated seeds into his mouth. It was one of the few from their horde that he knew about, and the tart but refreshing flavour was almost addictive. Even the smooth pips were pleasant to suck. 'You have enough here to last a year.'

'That's our *very* favourite,' Sophi enthused. 'Do you know you can eat *everything* on the upside down tree... even the bark?'

'No, I didn't,' Hallam replied with a smile. He did not ask how they had come on the name, but it was an apt description for the giant tree that had branches like roots. 'But I hope you're not thinking of taking a tree.'

The Click women fixed our sore gums with these,' Jemma said, taking one of the seeds. 'Show him your gums, Sophi, yours were the worst.' Sophi bared her gums to show the healthy pink colour. 'They also wake you up.'

'What?'

'You know, when you're feeling tired. The Click people always carry them for when they get tired.'

Hallam was barely paying attention. He had forgotten about his sore gums. They had suddenly cleared after months of getting steadily worse, and now he thought about it, they had cleared soon after his hunting trip with Kwai and his father. They had stopped at one of the giant trees and he had tasted the seeds for the first time, enjoying the tart, thirst quenching flavour so much he had emptied the contents of several pods into his bag. He had been sucking them ever since.

'What about yours, Jemma?'

'Gone.' She gave him a gummy smile.

Hallam sought out the others and received the same result, except for Gabaal. 'I don't like the taste,' he replied in answer to Hallam's query.

'Do you have sore gums?'

'It is only because of the strange meat we are eating.'

'I think these will make them better, I would like you to try.' But Gabaal refused, until Hallam approached him a short while later with a small bowl of water in which he had soaked a handful of the creamy seeds. He took a swig himself then offered the rest to the agent. 'Drink,' he ordered.

'A bowl of wine would be more to my liking,' Gabaal said, but he drank it nonetheless, and did not shudder too convincingly.

After two days of forced medication, Gabaal's gums cleared, and Hallam knew he had found an important medicine. 'How are you feeling lately,' he asked the agent. 'Any better?'

'I will feel much happier when we are back at home,' Gabaal answered with his customary lack of humour, but Hallam noticed he had been sleeping less and measuring his gold more often.

'Take all your collection of magic potions,' he told the girls, 'and especially the fruit of the upside down tree. When you see your friends again we'll ask if they can find us some more. It's almost as good as my stick meat.'

But the girls did not see the Click people again.

Her star was still shining brightly when Morning Foot left the new sleeping place to go to the river. Old Father had warned her to be there before the sun, and well hidden, or the eye of Mantis may see her.

She took only her blanket and the small bow with its single arrow that Old Father had made for her. They were smaller than she had expected, so she no longer feared she would not have the strength. Now she was afraid it was the bow that would not be strong enough. With only one arrow and so small a bow she would have to be very close and silent. Even the small noise of her shell apron may be heard, so she had to remove it, placing it beside the still sleeping form of her sister. Old Father had also warned that they would wait for her only for as long as the passing of one sun. If she did not return, Evening Heart would take the apron and bury it in the cave of Eland at the High Land.

When she reached the river, Morning Foot hid herself amongst the reeds in the same place where the Strange One had waited for her; close to the path where they came to fetch water and bathe. She sat on her blanket, which softened the noise of the reeds beneath, and arranged the bow and arrow ready at her side, but she did not remove the bark tube from the head. The juice of the night-one would dry and weaken quickly when exposed to the air.

Morning Foot waited impatiently with her fear, casting anxious glances at the sun as it passed over the reeds, slowly changing the pattern of shadows on the blanket. It reached directly overhead, but still the one for whom she waited did not come.

The fat black one, who looked like a man, but who squatted like a woman, came to fetch water, and so did the sad one who stared at the sand in his bowl. But not the one she waited for, and she could not find the courage to leave and go to the sleeping place of the Strange Ones for fear of being seen by the eye of Mantis.

Long after the sun had passed over her head, her two friends with one face passed close as they went for their washing, and Morning Foot longed to call out to them, for she felt much happiness in their ways, but she could not, and sadness, the ugly sister of happiness, came to sit on her heart.

Then, soon after her friends with one face had returned, she heard the steps of Short Ear coming to take their place, and Morning Foot cowered low so as not to be seen by the eye of Mantis. She watched through the curtain of her fingers as Short Ear removed his coverings, and was relieved to see that he also removed the eye of Mantis and placed it so it stared up at the sky.

As he stood in the water, she marvelled once more at the smallness of his buttocks compared to that of the San, and also at the size of his shoulders and the length of his legs. It was the body of a man with great strength, but he had a softness in his heart, and much wisdom in his ways for one who did not have the ashes of many fires on his head.

Sadness sat even more heavily on Morning Foot. She would not live to enjoy a man for herself. She was small, and would surely die under the birthing tree from the size of the fruit she would have to bear. The bone-eaters would have them both.

With Short Ear involved with his washing and the eye of Mantis staring unseeing at the sky, and with the sun running faster with each passing moment to its sleeping place behind the High Land, Morning Foot finally found the courage to take up her bow, remove the cover from the head, and crawl silently from the reeds.

The horse's head Persian had carved for the boat was a perfect fit, if not a perfect likeness. One ear was shorter than the other due, Persian excused, to an awkwardly placed defect, and not, as Hallam suggested, a desire to make the horse resemble its owner. The eyes were glaringly determined, the nostrils angrily flared, and the teeth ferociously bared beneath a drooping upper lip reminiscent of the ill-tempered, one-horned beast Kwai had provoked in the thicket.

'A fair likeness would you say, Hallam?'

'It depends with what you make the comparison,' Hallam replied.

'He has nice teeth,' observed Jemma, tapping them with a fingernail.

'I'm sure my horse would be proud to be associated with

it,' Hallam said. 'From now on, the boat will take her name and be called *Piko*. She prances like a horse, and has the stout heart of one, so it is fitting she should have a horse's name. I'll leave you to secure her in the stable while I go for a wash. That is, if the girls have left any water in the river.'

'Be careful not to step on our crocodile,' Sophi called after him.

Persian removed the head to smear its long base with pitch before setting it in place and pegging it through the two holes he had cut in the prow. He sealed those too, after cutting them off flush and smoothing them with a coarse piece of stone, then he stepped back to admire his handiwork.

He saw her at the same instant she loosed the arrow.

It struck him in the right shoulder, and Persian stared at it for a moment in shocked disbelief before letting out a yelp of pain. He clutched at the shaft and it came away in his hand, and he flung it from him in horror. He cried out again, his voice rising in panic as the full implication of the empty shaft became clear. He clasped a hand over the small, dark hole in his shoulder and jumped, yelling, from the boat.

The alarmed girls ran towards him. 'What is it? What happened?'

'Poison... get something to cut it out... a knife... quickly!'

'Let me see,' Jemma demanded, pushing aside his hand. She looked closely, not touching. 'It's only a small hole and I can't see anything. What bit you?'

'Poison, there... under the skin. Quickly... Mother of Zeus! Don't you understand? Arrow. You have to get it out... she's trying to kill me....'

Sophira ran down the path to the river. Hallam was already stumbling across the sand towards her, fumbling in his haste to pull on his breeches. 'It's Persian!' she cried out. 'He thinks he's been shot with a poisoned arrow.'

It brought Hallam to a halt. 'He *what?*' He stared at her for a moment, then ran past her to the camp.

Persian was lying on the ground with Jemma bending over him, her lips about to close over a smear of blood on his shoulder. Hallam pushed her roughly aside. 'What are you doing?'

'Shouldn't I suck out the poison?'

'You little fool! You will also be poisoned... how do you know it is poison?'

'Hallam... my friend. Thank Zeus you are here! Please, you must cut it out, use your knife, but quickly. It burns like fire.'

'Bring water!' Hallam shouted to no one in particular. Then to Persian: 'Why do you say it is an arrow? The hole is too small.'

'It is! I saw the shaft... threw it away.'

Jemma brought the water and Hallam poured a good amount over the hole while pulling it apart with his fingers. He saw it close to the surface; a small circle of hollow reed surrounded by dark blood. It was much smaller than the normal socket of an arrow head, and Hallam stared at it with a puzzled frown.

'He said she wanted to kill him,' Jemma said quietly at his shoulder.

'She?'

'*Please*... my friend... It was long ago... I meant her no harm... use your knife.'

'I don't think the knife will do it unless I cut a big hole. I'll have to push from below and use my fingers. Sit on his middle, Phineas... hold his arms. Where's Gabaal?'

'Hiding in his shelter,' answered Jemma. 'He says whoever shot the arrow may still be here.'

Hallam looked up quickly, but the expression of both girls was coldly impassive, and he returned his attention to the wound. 'Who was it, Persian?'

'Not the one with the child, I swear... the way she looked... I knew she wanted me to...'

Sophira gasped. *'You forced Shell?'*

'No! I didn't harm her... no need to try to kill me...'

Sophira walked away. Without a word, Jemma stood and followed after her.

'You fool!' Hallam said to Persian. 'Do you know what you have done? You could have us all killed.'

'No! It was a long time... months... oh, Zeus! The pain... He began to shiver.

'Hold him down, Phineas....'

Persian squirmed and whimpered as Hallam spread the wound as wide as he could with the fingers of one hand, squeezing up at the same time. He forced a finger down the slippery shaft of the head until his finger pricked on a barb. He flinched, then moved his finger to cover the sharp sliver of reed. It bent easily under the pressure and he withdrew the head. Dark blood followed. Persian bellowed twice, drawing a hoarse breath between, then he lay quietly shivering.

'He wet himself on me, Master Hallam!'

'Never mind that. Get some more water and put the pitch on the fire to heat.' Hallam washed his hands thoroughly then sucked on the pricked finger, spitting repeatedly.

Without touching it, he examined the head lying where he had dropped it on the sand. It was a piece of fire hardened reed no longer than half the length of his little finger. The single barb was a sliver of the same material, bound on with the fine thread made by the women for their skirts. Thankfully, the tip of the barb was clean, but both the hollow of the point and the binding were smeared with what must have been poison, although it looked different to the usual substance. He flicked the head into the fire with a piece of stick.

Whatever the poison, it was extremely potent. Persian groaned and opened his eyes as Hallam poured water in and over the wound, but his eyes were glazed and rolling back; showing the whites. He began shaking, then convulsing so violently they could no longer hold him and were forced to stand clear of his thrashing arms and legs. Persian clawed at his face, pulling and jerking violently on one of his long moustaches, stretching his mouth grotesquely. Watery blood ran from his mouth and nose, and Hallam turned away, no longer able to watch.

It did not take long for Persian to die.

Hallam and Phineas carried his body to the river and buried him deep in the sand.

'It is a bad thing that happened, Master Hallam,' Phineas remarked, as they stood looking thoughtfully down at the smoothed-over patch of sand, and the pensive tone of his voice echoed Hallam's own unspoken thoughts. A scooped-out hole in the sand seemed so inadequate a reward for what they had been through together. And he had not been a bad man. A foolish one perhaps, but still a friend, and his presence was going to be sorely missed.

'Make a fire on top, Phineas, We don't want any animals digging him up.'

The girls were less sympathetic when Hallam gave them the news.

'He spoiled everything,' Sophira cried. 'We trusted him Why did he have to do it?'

Hallam had no answer.

'I'm glad he's dead,' Jemma said bitterly. 'I could never have looked at him again after what he did. Shell was our friend.'

'He said it happened months ago, and she never said anything. How do you know she didn't agree?'

'Because she killed him,' Jemma said, and Hallam had no answer to that either.

'I know why she didn't say anything,' Sophira said. 'I think she was frightened.'

'But why didn't she kill him long ago?'

'Maybe he made her pregnant,' Jemma said quietly.

'Poor Shell... why couldn't he leave her alone? Men are

such *animals*!'

'Thank you,' Hallam murmured.

'Come, Jemma, we should try and find her, maybe we can help.'

The girls walked away and Hallam looked after them in alarm. 'Where do you think you're going?'

'To their camp.'

'Don't be foolish. Anyway, they're not there, and even if they were, there is nothing you can do.' They ignored him, walking determinedly towards the camp, and Hallam went after them. 'Come on, girls, what you're doing is dangerous.'

'Shell was our friend. They won't harm us.'

'My friends too, remember.'

'Then why are you frightened?'

'I'm not....' Hallam gave up. Perhaps Jemma was right. If the Click people meant them harm they would already be dead, like Persian, and it was as well to know where they stood. 'All right, but I'll go first... if you don't mind.'

The camp looked as deserted as when he had checked it before, but he had not gone into it then. Now he did, and found it was not as empty as he had thought. The old clothing they had given the Click people had been discarded and lay strewn about in the dirt, including the cloth bags which had been so useful.

'They hate us now,' Sophira cried, close to tears.

Hallam searched for the bronze arrow heads but could not find them. At least that was a good sign.

Jemma called them to where she was standing before a neatly swept area of sand on which a circle had been drawn. Two small footprints had been carefully placed in the centre, and a single line had been drawn through each. Beside the footprints were two handprints, and in the palm of each lay identical bracelets of shells and red berries. They were clearly gifts to the girls; given by the hands of Shell and Berry.

The girls began to sniff. Sophi picked up the bracelets and gave one to Jemma, and Hallam moved to put a comforting arm around both the girls. 'You should be happy,' he said. 'It means they don't hate you after all.'

It was some while before he could get an answer. 'Look at the footprints. They have lines through them. We learned about that. It means....' Sophie stopped, unable to continue.

'It means,' Jemma finished, her own voice faltering, 'that we will never see their footprints... again...'

The river began to rise next morning. Throughout an evening made long by sadness and disturbing thoughts, they had watched the flicker of lightening far to the west. It was still going on many hours later, and in the morning the results could be clearly seen in the river. It rose steadily all day, and by nightfall was a full cubit higher.

'Don't you think we should leave now,' Sophira asked, 'before it's too late? There's nothing to stay for anyway, without our friends.'

'Friends wasn't the reason we were staying in the first place,' Hallam reminded her. 'It was to wait for the south wind, and I don't think we have to worry about the river. We have a safe place here.'

But next morning he was not so sure. It was one thing to judge the height of the flood by the flotsam in the trees, and quite another to see an expanse of swiftly flowing muddy water four times wider than before. It put everyone's already frayed nerves even further on edge.

The clear sky above removed some of the threat, but when Hallam went for a walk upriver later in the day, he was alarmed to see water creeping through the trees on his right.

He followed the line of its flow by eye and concluded that if it rose another half cubit their camp would be on an island.

Still, he decided he would wait and stick to his original plan to sit the flood out. It could not last for more than a week at the most, and they had all they needed stored safely on the boat. He returned to the camp to find everyone in a panic.

'Snakes!' Jemma screeched at him. 'Be careful! Snakes are everywhere!'

'Also rats and spiders and ... *things!*' Sophira squealed. 'Can't you *see* them? We can't sleep here. I'm going on the boat.'

'Me too!' declared Jemma.

They moved everything aboard and Hallam had Phineas smear sticky pitch on a section of the mooring ropes to discourage intruders. Climbing ashore to cook a meal for them all, Hallam found the small arrow shaft that Persian had thrown aside and wondered at its small size. Big enough to carry the message though. He burnt it on the fire.

It was a sleepless night for them all. The river roared, and swirling, tumbling water could be seen close in the moonlight. It became louder and rougher as the night wore on. The boat creaked and bumped in the eddies, and Hallam tried to judge the state of the river by the movement. A futile exercise that did nothing but increase his anxiety.

At dawn, another problem presented itself. The boat had risen so high that the top of the mast had become trapped between the branches of the tree overhead.

Hallam climbed the mast and threw down a rope to pull up the axe. He tied himself to the mast and lopped off the restraining branches, cursing Persian at each stroke for leaving him short-handed, and for betraying the trust of a friend.

Looking down on the four anxious faces peering up at him, Hallam was acutely aware that he would have to be extra careful from now on. Without him they stood no chance of surviving. And well they should be anxious, he thought morosely, for he had no idea what his next move would be.

It was a disturbing but spectacular view from where he perched. They were now surrounded by a sea of brown water cluttered with half submerged trees and quivering reed islands. Much of their camp was flooded, the swamped huts looking forlorn and derelict.

The main channel was much closer now; moved inward by the speeding volume of water unable to negotiate the bend, and an uprooted tree had lodged against the high bank behind which *Piko* sheltered. Diverted by the tree, a channel of water ate slowly away at the sandy soil, exposing the roots of a another tree, and causing it to lean threateningly in *Piko's* direction.

The threat of having the boat crushed by the tree forced the decision Hallam had been avoiding. He slid down the mast and confronted his depleted and pale-faced crew with a smile of confidence he was far from feeling. 'Fasten your safety lines and hold on for your life, fellow sailors,' he told them brightly. 'It's time to go home.'

It was easily said, but not easily done. *Piko* was nose in to the bank and beam on to the current. She would have to be turned around quickly or they would be going down the turbulent river backwards with no steering. And once they were in the current, there would be no stopping until they reached the sea – unless they struck an island. It was essential that everyone know clearly what was expected of them. Being able to turn the boat quickly to avoid the islands was imperative, so the oars were lashed in place at each stern quarter and instructions given on their use.

'As soon as we have pushed ourselves out, Phineas, you will push on the right oar, and Gabaal, you will pull on the left until we are facing downstream. Once we are moving, lift your oar and stand ready to dip it in when I shout your name, and to lift it out when I shout again. You have to keep watching me, understood?'

It would be better if they faced him, Hallam reasoned. They would not be able to see what dangers loomed ahead, and therefore would be less inclined to panic and do the wrong thing at the wrong time - as Phineas had done with the anchor amongst the sea-cows.

'What do you want us to do?' Jemma asked nervously.

Hallam gave the girls a reassuring smile. 'Stand beside me and enjoy the ride.'

Piko bolted down the river as her namesake had often slithered down the mountains of Lamos, and she was equally as sure-footed. She bucked in defiance each time an oar was dug in to turn her away from the treacherous islands with their sharp tree roots, skidding around the bends in the grip of the current. But on the good stretches she glided sedately along in company with slowly revolving trees, carpets of reeds, and the occasional dead animal; one of them the heavily bloated calf of a sea-cow.

Breathless with uncertainty at the start, Piko's crew soon became breathless with exhilaration when they realised she was responding well to control and did not have her head. The girls laughed and squealed with nervous excitement, their faces flushed and their eyes sparkling, and Hallam spurred them on with whoops and yells, overcoming their fear. Even Gabaal cracked a weak smile. It was what they all needed. A tonic to cure their depression and boost their confidence for the greater uncertainty that lay ahead.

The tall trees ended, giving way to the grey bush and mangroves, and their swift gallop eased to a gentle bobbing as the strength of the flood was spread through the flat expanse of the delta. Then suddenly they found themselves at sea.

'Raise the sail!' Hallam bellowed authoritatively, and they all turned to look at him in confusion.

He shrugged in defence. 'Well, now is as good a time as any, don't you think?'

A full day later they were still wallowing in muddy floodwater.

'I swear that's the same sea-cow we saw floating with us yesterday,' Hallam remarked. 'I think we'll have to get farther out and hope for a fair wind or we'll be here forever.'

Gabaal was dubious. 'Is it wise? We may not get back to land.'

'We can't get back anyway against the flood, even with the onshore breeze. We'll have to take the chance.'

Hallam said nothing to the others, but he also had a feeling a current was pushing them farther south. The shoreline was flat and featureless for as far as he could see on either side, so there was no way of telling for sure, but the feeling was strong.

He was reminded of when he tried to escape from Tyre in the fisherman's boat; sailing out in the night with a land breeze, only to be blown back to the war galleys by the stronger sea breeze. Perhaps the same would happen now, only this time he would know what to do.

'We sail out as far as we can tonight if there's an offshore breeze,' he informed his crew. 'At worst we will be blown back to where we are now when the breeze turns.'

And that became the pattern for the next five days; sailing

out to the limit of the soft offshore breeze in the dark early mornings, then returning with the fresh sea breeze later in the day. On each leg, Hallam faced *Piko's* flaring nostrils as far into the north as he could without her sail flapping and her beam shipping water, and in the evening he took her in as far as he dared on the tide.

His suspicions about the current were confirmed on the third day. They had sailed out of the muddy water on the way in, only to find themselves back in it in the morning. Twice they managed to beach *Piko* on a friendly sandbank at low tide, which gave them respite from the current and a chance to relax.

On the fifth day they sailed into more muddy water.

'We're going *backwards*,' Sophi wailed in despair. 'We're *never* going to leave here!'

'We should camp and wait for the right wind,' Jemma suggested, and the others gave their support to the idea. 'At least we'll be on land.'

But Hallam disagreed. 'No, we'll carry on. I have a feeling it may be another river.'

'Storm coming, Master Hallam,' Phineas called out the unwelcome news, and they all stared at the solid black line of clouds far out to sea.

'Pray to your gods it is not a bad one,' Hallam said.

The usual breeze did not come that night. The stars disappeared and it began to gust from the south, lightly at first, then with increasing strength and steadiness. Although the sea of mud became choppy, Hallam decided it was too good an opportunity to miss.

'Take your tiller handles, girls, we'll shorten the sail and go with it. If we don't take the chance we'll never get away.' He gave them the correct angle to steer, then left them to it.

In the past week he had assigned them to the tiller handles and encouraged them to steer at every opportunity, as the men were needed for more strenuous duties. They took to it like seasoned veterans, and being occupied with so important a task did much for their confidence and morale.

With a stiff breeze from dead astern, *Piko* had the run of her life. Although it was wet and uncomfortable, and not without incident. They narrowly missed colliding with an uprooted tree soon after setting the sail, and several times they were almost swamped by freak waves in the rising sea, but Hallam's confidence in both his and Piko's ability had grown. Day and night, he stuck tenaciously to his course, shortening sail a little only at night in deference to the unseen freak waves, or when the girls were at the tiller, and he dozed at their feet so they could kick him awake in a hurry if need be without leaving their post.

'You look horrible,' Jemma informed him. 'Your eyes are red and your hair looks like feathers. You should eat more and get some sleep.'

'Are you my mother? I will sleep when the wind stops. Then you can feed me as much as you like.'

On the tenth day of *Piko's* mad run, both the sea and the sky turned a pale blue, but still the wind held true. Coral reefs appeared close to the shore, and *Piko* nosed farther out to sea to stay well clear, heading towards the only white cloud in the expanse of blue, and next morning found them sailing between the mainland and a large island.

'Look!' exclaimed Jemma. 'Coconut trees!'

As if on cue, the wind eased and, in the lee of the island, the sea also calmed. With shortened sail, *Piko* drifted over water so clear that fish could be seen swimming close to the sandy bottom far below.

'It's so beautiful! Can't we stop? Think of all the coconuts we can collect.'

'Not yet,' Hallam said. Keep a sharp lookout for smoke. If we see nothing we'll stop for the night farther along.'

Piko grated her bottom on the white beach of a quiet lagoon late in the afternoon, and they stayed for five happy, carefree days of swimming, fishing and sleeping. And they saw no smoke, and heard no lions or unpredictable sea cows.

Hallam produced his javelin and they feasted on fresh coral fish steamed in coconut milk, succulent lobster baked with coconut milk, and tasty crab boiled in coconut milk. Even *Piko* had her fill of coconuts. Her deck became cluttered with them, and a carpet of palm fronds, which the girls insisted were needed for making hats, and also baskets to contain the growing mountain of coconut shell cups, bowls, sea-shells and smelly coral.

'If the pot was big enough I would bathe in coconut milk,' Jemma declared, belching in a most unladylike manner as she tossed a partly nibbled lobster leg on the fire. 'And I never thought I would get tired of eating those. I could stay here forever.'

They sailed away from the beautiful island with fond memories and many a backward glance. Memories they were to recall often in the trying days that lay ahead.

In fair weather and light winds that seemed at times to blow from four directions at once, Hallam continued his erratic pattern of sailing up the coast. The coral reefs stayed with them, and several more islands of varying sizes appeared - all of them smokeless, and one so large it took two days to sail its length. The knowledge the islands were there to fall back on if needed, gave Hallam some welcome peace of mind.

The current too, had changed in their favour, pushing them gently north as they lay waiting for the breeze to turn. Those were the most anxious times for Hallam, especially at night, when they were close to shore and the exposed reefs. It was also where the current was strongest, and it was not always possible to find a sandy beach where *Piko* could rest her weary bottom.

When they did manage to find such a place, Hallam and the girls worked on the star chart and the hide map of the coast, roughly estimating the distances by the time taken, and marking in the rivers, islands and reefs. On the same map, Hallam marked the position of the seven doves in relation to each place, for of all the stars, the doves remained steadfast, following faithfully after the sun, no matter how far to either side of them they happened to be.

The seven doves were directly overhead when the south wind finally arrived. It came with a rush, as if knowing it had been tardy and wished to make up for lost time. It caught them as they waited off the mainland for the sea breeze and pushed them steadily north, then it turned away from the mainland and pushed them out to sea.

Hallam shortened the windward braces and tried to hold as much to the north as possible, but could not hold enough to keep the mainland in sight. Although it was half expected, they watched apprehensively as the land gradually faded until only the high banks of clouds that hovered above it could be seen, then they too disappeared, and they were left with only the wind, the uncertainty, and the endless, empty sea.

I smail Sulemani was sitting in the stern of his outrigger, sopping up the last of the almond-flavoured oil in his bowl with a sticky ball of rice, when he glanced up and saw the boat looming out of the dark towards him. It was so close he could easily have tossed the rice-ball onto its deck. His hand froze halfway to his already parted lips, the spicy juices trickling through his fingers and onto his bare feet as he stared in shock. He was there to meet a boat, but this was not the boat he was expecting. It was too big. It was more the size of the Rajah's tax patrol boat.

Sulemani dropped the rice-ball and kicked at the sleeping body beside him. He whispered close to the groaning man's ear. 'Jusab... wake you up and be quiet. We have been betrayed!'

Sulemani stumbled clumsily down the narrow length of the outrigger, poking and trampling on the snoring bodies of his crew and whispering urgently to them. 'Hamid! Kabir! Rama! Wake you up and quickly take the paddles! We are betrayed!'

As the startled crew came awake and clattered noisily about in search of their paddles, Sulemani snatched one up and attempted to fend off the prow of the drifting boat. He almost dropped the paddle in fright when he looked up to see the flaring nostrils and bared teeth of a horse's head close above his own.

Sulemani gripped the nose to hold them away and the outrigger swung slowly alongside the strange boat, the hastily roused crew fending it off with their hands.

Standing precariously on the side of the outrigger, Sulemani raised his head cautiously above the deck and squinted through the dark in search of armed soldiers, but he saw only the lumps of sleeping bodies under an awning. He counted five. Above them the tiller handles were lashed together to hold the steering oars in a central position. The sail was raised, although it hung limp in the still air.

'What do you see?' The whispered question from below was accompanied by a sudden grip around Sulemani's ankle, causing him to jump with fright and almost lose his balance.

'You stupid person, you!' Sulemani hissed. He kicked the offender away and continued his observation. It was not the Rajah's tax patrol after all, only a foreign cargo vessel. Along the rail were tied roughly woven baskets. One of them was close to his hand and Sulemani poked an exploratory finger through the coarse weave to feel something hard and fibrous inside.

His legs began to tremble with the strain of balancing and he sat down to consider this new development, holding up his hand to still the whispered questions of his men.

It was a strange place for a cargo vessel to be. The port of Barigaza - from where the boat he was expecting to meet would come - was a long way to the south, and he had never seen a cargo boat of this size with so few crew and no soldier to protect it. Either it had lost its mooring, or it was on some illegal activity such as his own. This intriguing possibility prompted Sulemani to explore the idea further. Perhaps it was there to meet the very same boat he himself was waiting for!

He experienced a twinge of alarm, yet it did not make sense. The Kassim brothers could not be trusted, that was for certain, but not even they would be such stupid persons as to risk having their Rajah discover who it was had been stealing his peacocks. Especially as they were being sold to his sworn enemy, the Rajah of Suhar.

All of Sulemani's crew were now standing in the outrigger, holding onto the rail of the strange boat, and Sulemani joined them, his added bulk lifting the float clear of the water. A new idea was tweaking at his mind. Such a boat would be a great prize. It was sure to have a valuable cargo, and the Rajah would reward him handsomely for its delivery. Five men awake and with knives, against five unarmed and asleep, was only a small risk.

His brother, Jusab, was close beside, and Sulemani whispered quietly in his ear. 'Pass on that we will take this boat. Have knives ready, but no cutting of throats until we are sure they are not friends of Rajah.' He gave him an encouraging nudge. 'You go first.'

It was so easy that Sulemani did not even have to participate. The largest of the five - a black man who looked as if he could have been a problem - did not even wake up until his feet had been tied. The old man and the two girls were also quickly subdued and bound, and the third man, who looked to be sick, but who still managed to kick Jusab in the stomach, succumbed after two knives were held to his throat.

Sulemani also took the precaution of gagging them to ensure the Kassim brothers would not be warned away by hearing strange voices when they arrived. With all the prisoners secure, he sat cross-legged on the deck to inspect them at leisure.

Except for the one who had kicked Jusab, they did not look like sailors, and only the old one looked like a merchant, although his filthy robe told he must be a poor one. None looked important enough to be friends of Rajah. They would surely not be missed. He could sail the boat south, well out of Rajah's reach and keep it for himself. With such a boat he would be a rich man. He could hide it and sell the cargo a little at a time until empty, and the young girls he could easily sell to a harem. Looking alike would be a special attraction and should bring a high price.

But something about the girls was making Sulemani uneasy. Being closely involved with the profitable, but dangerous activity of outwitting Rajah, his survival instincts had become tuned to an extremely high pitch, and he had learned from painful experience not to ignore them.

What made Sulemani uncomfortable was the way they looked at him. Their clothing would not be worn by the poorest peasant, yet they did not lower their eyes respectfully as women should. They glared at him with the same arrogant expression used by Rajah's wives. Their stares disconcerted him so much that he was felt compelled to join in with the inspection of the cargo.

'Nothing.' Jusab answered in response to Sulemani's enquiry. 'Nothing but coconuts and rubbish.'

Sulemani went to the main hatch, which his men had finally opened, and looked into the dark, musty interior. He called to one of the men who had lowered himself in. 'Any good things inside, Kabir? What do you find?'

'Only empty coconuts.'

'Is it so? Surely you are mistaken!'

Kabir reappeared, sweating profusely, for it was a steamy night and even hotter below. He tossed one of the green pods on the deck and Sulemani smashed it open in a cascade of white seeds. He sniffed at one then touched it to his tongue. 'All dry of juices,' he commented, grimacing at the sour taste. He spat on the deck then stood to confront his prisoners.

'You are very stupid persons to have such things as dry coconuts. Where is your good cargo, please? If you do not show me to it, I will have to cut you by the throat one at a time until you speak. Only the young whores will be saved for the enjoyments of me and my men.'

Sulemani was interrupted by a low call from one of the men. 'Kassim is here!'

'Tell him to put the cages on the deck. We will pull this boat with our own. Hurry! Hurry!'

'He says he must come with us.'

'What?' Sulemani rushed to the rail as the second outrigger bumped alongside and the tall, thin figure of Kassim climbed over the rail. 'Why must you come?' Sulemani demanded. 'What is it you are saying?'

'It is my poor cousin.' Kassim whined. 'Rajah's men caught him stealing a bird. He will tell, I know it!' He looked around in distress, ringing his thin hands. 'You have a new boat?'

'You stupid snake of a person! Why did you come? We will all be killed!'

'But Ismail! What else could I do? I have the birds. You must take us!'

Sulemani was on the point of refusing when he realised he had no choice. Also, Kassim and his brothers would be useful in moving the boat. 'You are very lucky to deal with such a kind person as myself, Kassim, but do not think to trick me. We must leave here quickly. Put on the cages and tell your brothers to tie on your boat, then you must help with the big paddles over there.' He pointed to the long oars lashed to the rail. 'Hurry! Hurry!'

While the four cages of peacocks were being lifted on deck and the two outriggers tied to the stern, Sulemani organised the handling of the oars, putting four men on each, with Jusab on the tiller - which left himself free to consider a plan.

With the boat underway, Sulemani sat on the deck to remove the sticky rice stuck between his toes, and to think. Thanks to snaky Kassim, he had no choice now but to return to Suhar and hand the boat over to Rajah. But perhaps it was not such a bad thing. Hiding such a large boat would be difficult, and Rajah would pay him well for it. He would also be paid well for the captives, especially the females, and Rajah could deal with the others as he saw fit. Knowing the Rajah, Sulemani was thankful he was not one of them.

Hallam could not believe he had been so stupid. Even the excuse he gave himself that he was sick with a fever and did not know they were close to land, failed to salve his conscience. He should never have allowed everyone to fall asleep with no one on watch.

All he knew of their situation was that they had been captured by Indian pirates. He knew the fat one's name was Sulemani, and the thin one who had arrived with the peacocks was called Kassim. Other than that, he knew nothing, except that all of them were dirty and dangerous looking.

At dawn, after a night of isolation from the others, Hallam saw the mainland for the first time; a heavily wooded shore partly obscured by steaming mist. He felt no satisfaction or relief at having survived a long voyage on the unknown Sea of Zeng. All he felt was a crushing disappointment that he had allowed them to be caught unawares.

Soon after daylight, the fat one, Sulemani, came to remove their gags and ask a string of questions they could not understand. The only response he got was from Jemma, who spat on the deck as soon as her gag was removed, then called him a fat pig. It seemed to please Sulemani more than anger him. He laughed and stroked her gently on the cheek until she tried to bite his finger.

'Be careful,' Hallam warned her once the Indian had moved away.

'Pah! They are only filthy peasants. Our father deals with them all the time in Saba.'

'She is right,' said Sophi. 'You have to treat them like peasants or they don't respect you. Anyway, you must not worry. We will not be talking to them any more. Jemma only spoke because she was angry.'

Hallam was too taken aback to say anything further. He had all but forgotten their arrogant attitude and nudging of poor Phineas.

At mid-morning, *Piko* rounded a headland into a calm bay, and the peacocks - which had all been gagged by having their beaks tied - were removed to one of the outriggers and paddled away to some unknown destination. *Piko* was manoeuvred through a jam of small boats to a bamboo causeway that swayed ominously with the weight of the noisy crowd gathered to witness their arrival.

Sulemani stood importantly at the prow and tossed a rope to several willing hands and, as the argument raged over who would have the honour of making it fast, another was tossed from the stern. The ropes binding the captives ankles were removed, and Sulemani hustled them onto the creaking causeway, screaming at the crowd for a clear passage.

Accompanied by the noisy and gawking crowd, Hallam and his weary crew were escorted by the strutting Sulemani through a town of bamboo huts, along stinking muddy streets, the edges of which were fouled with rotting garbage, pools of stagnant urine, human faeces, and decaying animals.

'Now do you believe us?' asked Jemma, wrinkling her nose.

They climbed a short hill, leaving much of the crowd behind, then entered a courtyard through stone gates guarded by two men in sagging dhotis and greasy brocade waistcoats. One leaned tiredly on his spear, the other did not even bother to rise.

Sulemani left them in the courtyard in the care of his men and disappeared through another gate - presumably to report to whoever was in charge of the stinking town. He reappeared to beckon furiously. 'Hurry! Hurry! Rajah is waiting!'

Followed by all of Sulemani's men, and much of the remaining crowd, they were ushered through a garishly ornate doorway into a spacious room bare of all furnishing except a carved platform decorated with cushions.

'Sit! Sit!' Sulemani collapsed on the bare stone floor and indicated they should do the same.

Weakened by his fever, Hallam sat down thankfully, and Phineas and Gabaal followed his lead, but the girls remained standing. 'We do not lower ourselves before filthy peasants,' Jemma declared haughtily.

'Sit! Sit!' Sulemani tugged urgently at her robe.

Jemma jerked away and nudged Phineas with her foot. 'Tell the fat pig not to touch me,' she ordered.

Hallam looked at her in alarm. This was not the time to be playing at the noble mistress. He opened his mouth to tell her to sit down but she frowned at him, and Hallam surprised himself by remaining silent. He could not even begin to imagine how or why, but suddenly he knew he was no longer in control, and that Jemma was.

A murmur in the crowd, followed by someone making a long and obviously sycophantic announcement, heralded the arrival of Rajah. He strutted towards his raised platform on thin hairy legs, wearing a sagging dhoti like every other male, and a brocaded waistcoat like his guards, only not so greasy and threadbare. His hairy paunch protruded from the opening like the distended throat of a frog - which he strongly resembled, for his face was heavily pitted with the scars of pox. He hopped nimbly onto his platform and squatted on his cushions, arranging the dhoti carefully between his legs before looking up at his audience.

He saw the two girls standing alone at the forefront of the crowd and started with surprise. He spoke at length to Sulemani in a high-pitched, but authoritative voice, then listened carefully to the equally lengthy reply. He waved his hands in dismissal and shouted angrily at the crowd. With a low murmur of disappointment and much scuffling, they began crawling out through the door.

Rajah waited until the room was cleared of everyone but Sulemani, his men, and his prisoners. After a moment of hesitation, he dismissed the men as well. He called in four guards with red turbans and curved swords in gaudily decorated scabbards. At a terse command from Rajah, they unsheathed the swords and stood flanking the captives.

Rajah descended from his platform and strutted forward, looking grim, and Hallam tensed, willing Jemma to keep her mouth shut, which she did. After scrutinising each face carefully, the Rajah spoke angrily to both in turn and, when he had finished, Jemma nudged Phineas with her foot.

Phineas gulped several times and licked at his lips. 'My mistresses speak only the language of Saba.'

Rajah glared at Phineas, and the guard closest to him tapped the slave gently on the top of his bald head with the flat of his blade as a warning. 'Your mistresses have no tongue?' Rajah demanded, speaking, to Hallam's immense relief, in fluent Arabian. Phineas glanced nervously up at the guard and received a slight nod.

'Forgive my stupidity, Highness, but my mistresses are cousins to the Queen of Saba and not permitted to speak to ... strangers.'

Rajah stared at the girls for several moments, his eyes bulging in apparent shock, and Hallam was no less astonished at Jemma's bald-faced nerve. Then Rajah frowned at Phineas. 'Cousins, you say... to the Queen of Saba?'

'Yes, Highness.'

'Why are you here? And how do I know if you speak the truth? They do not look like cousins to me.'

Phineas began to answer then stopped when he saw Jemma touch her ear. 'Forgive me, Highness, but my mistress wishes to speak in my ear.' Without waiting for permission, and while Rajah and his equally flummoxed guards looked on in strained bewilderment, Jemma whispered at length to Phineas.

'My mistress wishes to know if your Highness is himself of royal blood, for if so, she will be permitted to speak with you, but only after she and all of us have been released of our bonds.'

It was a few more moments before Rajah was able to gather all his dignity, which he did by drawing himself up and placing his hands on his hips. 'I am the fifth eldest son to be Rajah of Suhar!'

Jemma simply nodded at the news and held out her wrists', and Sophi did the same. Confronted by this silent two pronged attack, Rajah nodded vaguely and the nearest guard stepped forward to carefully slice through the ropes, first the girls, and then the others.

'Thank you,' Jemma said, rubbing at the red marks. 'I shall inform my cousin of your kindness. I am sure she will insist on rewarding you in some way.'

Still speechless, and looking ill at ease, and perhaps even

a little miffed by having his customary title ignored, Rajah waved a deprecating hand. To put him at ease and allay his suspicions further, Sophi entered the fray. 'Do you not trade with Saba?'

'Of course, I send many ships there to trade. My peacocks are the best in India.'

'Then surely there must be an agent of Saba who is stationed here. If he is important enough he will know us.'

Rajah smiled for the first time and spoke rapidly to Sulemani, who then crawled to the door and disappeared. They heard his voice outside, urgently hurrying his men.

'While we are waiting,' said Jemma, 'and if it pleases you, we will tell you how we came to be here, and of the great and dangerous adventure we have had in the Sea of Zeng, far south of Punt. But first I must introduce you to our friends. This our slave, Phineas, and this is Gabaal, a trusted agent of the great King Solomon, who, of course, is also our friend, and this,' Jemma said, putting a hand on Hallam's shoulder, 'is Pilot Hallam, by far the greatest pilot in all the world.'

Still looking puzzled, but obviously softened by such glowing references, Rajah returned to his platform, where he sat on a cushion and patted those at his side for the girls. Hallam, Phineas and Gabaal were allowed the honour of sitting on the floor below.

Then followed one of the most startling displays of diplomacy, feminine wiles, storytelling, and embellished nonsense that Hallam was ever to witness, and Rajah devoured every word of it. His head swivelled from one girl to the other as they spoke, and his expressions mimicked theirs so closely it was almost too much for Hallam to watch. Several times, Rajah became so enthralled, he clapped his hands with excitement. In quick succession, he wiped away tears of laughter, then tears of sorrow. At one point, on hearing about the death of Persian and the bracelets left by the Click Women – which he examined with interest - he became so emotional, he had to leave the platform and stride about the floor until he managed to calm himself down.

On hearing of his own exploits, Hallam cringed with embarrassment and shrugged modestly in response to the Rajah's admiring looks and disbelieving shakes of the head.

Hallam watched the girl's performance with pride. His respect for them had increased steadily in the time he had known them. From spoiled noble brats they had adjusted to their rough and dangerous new environment with courage and without simpering complaint. Now the roles were reversed, and it was he who felt out of his element, while they were clearly back in theirs. They were natural courtiers, showing to the full that side which he had previously caught only a glimpse, and his respect turned to admiration.

Sulemani returned with an elderly man and they waited by the door for permission to enter, but the story was not yet finished. Rajah made them wait outside until it was, and until his guests had been served cool sherbet, and rice-balls in bowls of deliciously spicy almond-flavoured oil.

Finally, Sulemani and the other man were allowed to crawl across the floor and prostrated themselves. It took only a few moments for the Sabaen agent to prove the girls' credentials. Not that it would have made any difference. Rajah was by now so enamoured he would have accepted them had they been proved assassins.

He dismissed the agent, then spoke angrily to Sulemani in his Indian language, and the fat man began to quiver with fear. He began to whine and plead, but Rajah cut him short by gesturing to the guards. They pounced on Sulemani and dragged him, squealing, into the centre of the room. While three of the guards held him down, the fourth put the blade of his sword to Sulemani's throat.

'He treated you very badly,' The Rajah explained to the girls. 'He should be punished for offending such persons as yourselves. Surely you would not forgive me if he is not killed. When you say the word, it will be done.'

The girls looked at each other, their faces expressionless, but Hallam knew the look would communicate to the other what it was they were thinking. He waited, as breathless as the others, for their decision, praying it would be the right one.

Jemma did the talking as usual, and looked at Hallam with a peculiar smile on her lips and a glint in her eye as she spoke. 'A wise man once told us, Rajah, that if you kill an enemy you lose an enemy but gain more, but if you spare his life you not only lose an enemy but gain friends.'

It was some while before the Rajah realised she was finished, then a while longer before what she had said made sense, but finally, he smiled and tilted his head in agreement. 'A very wise man, perhaps.' He did not sound all that convinced, but nevertheless, waved his hand to the guards and they released the badly shaken Sulemani.

The Rajah spoke to Sulemani again in a tone suggesting how fortunate he was to have such forgiving friends, and tears of gratitude trickled down Sulemani's jowls. He scurried forward on hands and knees and, seemingly oblivious to the filth that caked them, kissed both of Jemma's feet. After only a short hesitation, he did the same for Sophi. It was clear they had made more than just a friend of Sulemani, they had acquired a devoted slave, perhaps even two devoted slaves, Hallam thought with relief, for he was fast becoming one himself.

What do you think of Rajah's gift, Hallam?' Sophi asked, turning herself around so he could inspect her from all sides.

'A gift from his harem, probably,' said Jemma. 'Do you

think they show too much?'

Hallam frowned and adopted a critical pose. The clothing *did* show too much for his liking, and accentuated their femininity in areas he would rather they didn't, but his pose was more to hide his feelings than to pass judgement, for he was stunned by the transformation. The girls looked almost like strangers. Beautiful strangers.

From low on their swelling hips, to high on their slim ankles, each was clad in shimmering silk; Jemma in brilliant green, and Sophi in an equally brilliant blue. Each leg was separately encased and the silk tied at the ankles so it billowed. The toenails of each foot bore a matching colour. Their flat midriffs were bare, and their almost equally flat breasts were concealed behind thick layers of gold-embroidered silk. Their hair had been freshly washed and swept up high to enhance the slenderness of their necks, held up by silver rings, and silver bracelets adorned their arms above the elbows. The bracelets of berries and shells given them by the Click women still adorned their wrists.

Hallam was relieved to note that their faces were free of paint, their belly dimples free of jewels, and that the silk was not transparent.

'Well?' asked Jemma, giving him a coy look.

'You are the most beautiful princesses I have ever seen.'

They beamed at him and spun away, and Hallam was left with the scent of jasmine wafting in the air, and the turmoil of his stirred emotions.

It would be at least two months, the Indian pilots informed Hallam, before he could expect a favourable wind for Saba. While he waited, it would be a great honour, they said, if he allowed them to arrange for the preparation and necessary repairs to the boat and, while this was being attended to by the most skilled workers in all of India, would he tell them of his experiences in the Sea of Zeng.

Hallam agreed reluctantly. Not because, like most pilots, he wanted to keep his knowledge secret, but because other than a few hazy ideas about the wind and stars, he didn't have much to give. And most of the pilots were old and experienced. He could probably learn more from them than they could from him.

While *Piko* went through a transformation, he lounged in the shade of an awning erected on the creaking bamboo causeway, drank a sweetened brew made from the leaves of a small bush that came from some island in the south, exchanged sea stories, and recovered from his fever.

The Rajah, seeing the opportunity of establishing good relations with powerful Saba, and thereby putting one over on his sworn enemy, the Rajah of Barigaza, had gone to great lengths to impress his important guests. Sumptuous accommodation was provided at the palace and every whim catered for. They could not move more than a few steps outside the palace courtyard without Sulemani and his men clamouring for the honour of carrying them on bamboo litters to whatever destination they chose. And wherever they went, they were accompanied by the palace guard to keep the throngs of onlookers at a respectful distance.

On hearing that the girls held perfumed squares of silk to their noses as they were carried through the town, the Rajah decreed it be cleaned up. A new area was designated on the edge of the town and defecating in the streets was forbidden.

'You have inspired me greatly to have the cleanest town in all of India,' Rajah declared to the girls. 'Much better than filthy Barigaza. We will give special attention to the great ships of Saba and good discounts to your traders. I long for the time you will convey to your illustrious father and your gracious queen my special efforts. When you leave you must take with you the gifts I have arranged for them. Your agent has already assured me he will tell of the very small amount of gold I have asked in exchange for silver and spices.'

'Perhaps a stronger causeway would also help,' suggested Hallam, making a mental note to speak to Gabaal about whose gold he was spending.

'Even at this very moment my people are cutting the bamboo for it,' Rajah assured him.

'We will speak of nothing but your kindness and generosity,' Jemma reassured him graciously. 'You have done many good things since we arrived.'

Rajah glowed. Already, he told them, he could see his new town blossoming to become the golden lotus of India. His rival in Barigaza, who had not even the brains of one of his peacocks, would shrivel and die.

'There is one more request I would impose upon you,' Rajah said to the girls, looking mysteriously smug.

'What is it, Rajah?'

'A new town must have a new name. I have decided, if you will honour me with agreement, that it should be named after those who inspired me to change it, which is your noble selves.'

'You wish the town to be given our names? That would be too great an honour!'

'Two such long names would be difficult for my people,' Rajah admitted, raising his hands in apology. 'Perhaps if you would agree to decide a name for yourselves....?'

'It should be called Sophira,' Jemma answered without hesitation. She put a hand on her sister's arm to stay her dissent while she explained. 'We were born in the same hour, but Sophi was the first born, so the honour must be hers.'

'You are a most wise and gracious princess,' Rajah said, taking her hand in both of his. 'I beg you to inform your queen of our new name.'

'Sophira is a name with a very memorable sound to it,'

Hallam said, smiling happily at the girls.'

But Sophie raised an objection. 'Unfortunately it will not be possible,' she said, smiling an apology at Rajah. 'Our names were given by the queen and cannot be used for the names of places without her permission.'

'Yes, that's true,' Jemma agreed. 'I had forgotten.'

Rajah looked crestfallen.

'Maybe we can change it slightly,' Hallam suggested after a few moments of thought. 'What if we removed the first and last letter to make it Ophir. Surely the queen wouldn't object to that?'

Piko sailed from Ophir in the company of two Sabaen boats, which had arrived during the time they were there. Rajah had provided a competent crew, one of his most experienced pilots, and two of his most elite guards for the personal protection of the girls. Sulemani, much to his disgust, was forced to remain behind.

Rajah saw them off with tears and fanfare from the sturdy new causeway on which the entire population had congregated. 'You take with you on your journey all our hearts,' Rajah sobbed, 'and we live only for the day you return them to us in your own hands. Please inform your father that my humble palace is waiting impatiently for the day he visits the beautiful city which is named after his elder daughter.'

Other than Rajah's bleeding hearts and the remains of her original cargo, *Piko* also carried two casks of the small brewing leaves, to which Hallam had become addicted, several chests of exquisite silver and ivory jewellery, carved bamboo beer mugs similar to those Hallam had seen in

Zabby's favourite tavern at Ezion-Geber, barrels of spices, sweet scented sandalwood, bolts of silk, and five ungagged peacocks - an oversight Hallam vowed to rectify each time their strident wailing shattered the tranquillity of the crossing to Saba.

It was decided that the profits would be split unevenly, with Hallam getting the largest share. 'It is only fair,' the girls argued when he protested. 'But for you there would be nothing, and we have no need for gold. Neither does Phineas. A slave is not permitted to own any, and he is well cared for. You will have our share.'

Gabaal also protested on the grounds he had found most of the gold and done all the bargaining - at which point Hallam reminded him again who had actually discovered the gold and who carried his load while he searched. Gabaal conceded reluctantly after Hallam agreed to double his share and pay the governor's commission himself.

It came as a mild shock to Hallam when he realised he would have more wealth than he could ever have expected to accrue in his lifetime, and thoughts of how he was going to spend it kept him happily preoccupied during the voyage.

The girls' excitement at returning home had, to some extent, been tempered by concern for their father. The two Sabaen boats which accompanied them had sailed from Zofar, so the pilots did not know if he was he still in Punt, or if he had returned to Saba after the girls had failed to arrive. He was an old man, and the shock of their assumed death may have speeded his own. 'If only we knew,' Sophi said wistfully. 'It's going to be a big surprise for everyone.'

But the Rajah had not missed the opportunity of scoring a few more points. Unbeknown to all, he had dispatched one of his boats with a trusted envoy at the first breath of the north west monsoon. It arrived at Adana four days ahead of *Piko*.

The first hint came as they entered the harbour, and any

doubts that may have lingered in Hallam's mind as to the importance of the girls were quickly dispelled. A fifty-oar war galley, streaming the red and gold banners of the Queen of Saba, sped across the harbour to meet them, followed, it seemed to an amazed Hallam, by every boat in Arabia.

As the war galley drew close, a man with grey hair blowing in the wind could be seen standing on the lookout platform in the prow, and the girls waved frenziedly and screamed out in unison.

A small tub was dispatched from the galley, and the grey-haired man stepped aboard *Piko* and into the arms of his daughters. There were too many tears being shed for Hallam's liking. He stayed well clear until a line had been attached and *Piko* was under tow. But eventually he was summoned by Jemma and introduced. The old man hugged Hallam and beat on his back until he managed to find his voice.

'You have returned my most precious treasures,' he told Hallam. 'Nothing can repay the debt I owe you.'

'The company of your lovely daughters has been reward enough, my lord,' Hallam replied.

The old man nodded, unable to speak further, and a red-eyed Jemma came to his aid. 'I'm sure we'll be able to think of something, Father.'

A h, the sweet wine of Izalia!' Agent Gabaal closed his eyes to more appreciate the taste and licked slowly at his lips. 'How I have missed it! And the good company of men such as yourself, Lemuel.'

They were sitting in the tiny office of the Judean agent's warehouse, taking a well earned rest after completing the inventory of *Piko's* unusual cargo. The Rajah of Suhar's gifts of peacocks, brewing leaves, and half the spices and silk, had already been removed by the Indian envoy and delivered to the queen. Gabaal had also managed to remove one of the chests of silver and ivory jewellery under cover of *Piko's* noisy welcome. It now rested securely under guard with his other belongings in the tavern at which he was staying. The remaining cargo occupied only a small section of the warehouse.

'I suppose the governor should be thankful the boat was not lost as well,' the Judean agent said. 'But as it was not, how will you explain the loss of his goods? I have them recorded as worth a full half talent in worth, and what remains will not bring even a quarter.'

'I agree, Lemuel, but everything was thrown overboard by the pilot. He said it was to lighten the boat, and even though I protested, he would not listen. There was nothing an old man like myself could do to stop him.'

'So all we have here was traded for with the gold you found in the river?'

'All of it,' said Gabaal. 'It was I who discovered the gold and risked wild animals and the poisoned arrows of wild men to collect it, yet only one fifth part of what you see is to be mine, and out of that small share must also come a share for the governor. The rest will go to the pilot.'

'But surely you must be mistaken, Gabaal? Such distribution seems hardly to be just after what you have done.'

Gabaal shrugged helplessly. 'Naturally, I will make a full report to the governor in person when we return to Ezion-Geber. He will not be pleased, but as you say, he at least has his boat, I have almost nothing to show for a year of hardship and danger. It seems there will only be one who will profit.'

'I hear he has already been rewarded handsomely by the queen and received the gold falcon for bravery,' said the Judean agent.

Gabaal spread his hands in a helpless gesture and sighed. 'Rewards do not always go to the deserving.'

They sat in silence for a while, sipping thoughtfully at their wine as each pondered in his own way the unjust vagaries of wealth and the important role it played in their lives.

'Perhaps we can find a way to amend this unjust state of affairs,' the Judean agent said finally, and Gabaal smiled. He had been thinking along the same lines himself, but had been loath to mention it.

'What do you suggest?'

'I think you should return to Ezion-Geber as soon as possible. There is a boat leaving tomorrow. I can arrange for you to sail with it.'

'Should I not return with the governor's boat?'

'From what we hear the pilot is too busy enjoying his rewards. Who can say how long it will be? I must also find a crew to sail it and...' the agent paused to smile knowingly at Gabaal, 'good sailors are hard to find. It could take a long time. You should report what happened to the governor as soon as possible.'

'I'm not sure...'

'I mentioned earlier that King Solomon was in Ezion-Geber to arrange a campaign against the Edomite bandits.'

'So?'

The governor will be playing host to the king. He will be too busy to give much thought to the loss of his goods, especially if you can arrange for the king to be present when you also happen to mention finding the gold. The king has an appetite for gold that even exceeds his appetite for wives.'

Gabaal chuckled. 'You have a swift mind for such a devious path, Lemuel. Should I inform the pilot of my leaving, do you think?'

'No, I will arrange for him to be told after you have left. And for a very small commission, I will also arrange for... how should I say it... a more just distribution of rewards?'

Hallam was finding little time for himself. A constant stream of officials, courtiers, merchants, and noble mothers who wished to introduce their daughters, threaded their way through the maze of courtyards to his door. Fame, he discovered, was a full time occupation, and, apparently, as risky as a sea full of rocks.

.He had been lodged in spacious private quarters within the palace precincts and left in the care of Phineas. The girls and their father had retired to the seclusion of their family home at Mocha after the first week of hectic celebration.

'Be careful who you see,' Jemma had warned on the eve of their departure. 'And don't act too friendly with anyone in the company of others who may feel insulted, especially officials and priests.'

'Best if you stay hidden until Phineas introduces visitors,' Sophi advised. 'He knows who is important and will warn you. And you mustn't agree to any schemes of the merchants. Tell them you first have to speak with Father. That will frighten them off.'

'You have to be especially careful not to offend any of the mothers who want to introduce you to their daughters,' cautioned Jemma. 'If they try to leave them alone with you, pretend to have a headache or something. If you really *must* have... well, you know... feel like being with a woman, Phineas will arrange for someone safe to visit.'

'And never speak to the queen unless she speaks to you

first,' Jemma continued. 'If she does talk to you, try not to blush and stare at her like you did at the award ceremony.'

That was enough to chasten Hallam and convince him he would be wise to heed their advice. If Jemma had noticed, then so would have the young queen, for she had the same quick, perceptive manner as the girls, the same intelligent brow, and the same disconcerting way of letting you know she understood what you were saying even as you were saying it.

It was her remarkable similarity to the girls, more than her acclaimed beauty, which had made Hallam stare. She could easily have been mistaken for an older sister, rather than a cousin. Her unblemished complexion belied the fact she was several years older, and she was tall, with a way of moving that hinted of a lithesome body beneath the flowing layers of silk. She was not as beautiful as Philippa, in Hallam's eyes, but when he lowered his head for her to place the chain of the Golden Falcon around his neck, he gazed at the swell of her breasts beneath the clinging silk and, for a fleeting moment, could believe he had been transported back in time. He could tell by the prickling of his skin that he turned red.

That most of the eligible young daughters he was introduced to also changed colour, did nothing to ease his discomfort. Most were also pretty, and many showed in their coy glances a seductive willingness to be alone with him. As they were all rich, he could easily have secured a pleasant future for himself ten times over, but the girls' whispered warnings and clandestine nudges had held him in check.

'You would have risked the queen's displeasure had you agreed to see that woman,' Jemma whispered, after removing him from the enjoyable company of a particularly attractive young female. 'She only likes you because you're a man.'

Hallam suspected it would be Jemma's displeasure, rather than the queen's he would be incurring, but was out of his depth, so did not force the issue. It was only the beginning, he told himself, and who could tell what the future would bring? But until he could find his own way through the murky waters of noble intrigue, he decided it would be wise to take their advice.

And their father, Lord Shan, in his capacity as vizier for Saba's commercial interests, had hinted at an expedition of several boats to explore the region south of Punt and, if possible, as far as the River Saba - a name Hallam had chosen himself in a sudden rush of enlightened diplomacy.

Best of all though, had been Lord Shan's promised reward for saving the lives of his daughters.

He had approached Hallam alone as they were preparing to leave for Mocha. 'I have been ordered by my two advisers,' Lord Shan had explained with a smile – which was something he had done a lot of since their return - to purchase the boat on your behalf. They assured me it is what you would want.'

Hallam had been struck speechless. He had come to regard *Piko* as part of himself, and returning her to the governor was something he had been dreading. He had decided to say farewell to her in Adana, leaving her in the care of the Gabaal, rather than prolong the agony by taking her to Ezion-Geber himself.

'They know me only too well, my lord,' was all Hallam had been able to mumble.

'Do not bargain with the governor,' Lord Shan had advised, 'unless his price exceeds four talents of gold. Pay what he asks, then return without delay. I will make arrangements with the keeper of the queen's treasure to provide you with the necessary document of promise. It will have the queen's seal. All you must do to make it legal is fill in the amount and add your own mark. By the time you return, we should also have returned from Mocha, and we can arrange to do whatever repairs you think will be needed.'

Because of important appointments, Hallam could not find the time himself, but as soon as Lord Shan and the girls had departed, he sent a palace messenger to find Gabaal. He would need a crew and a pilot who knew the Narrow Sea. He would have preferred to find his own crew, but *Piko* was not yet his, and the responsibility of hiring still belonged to the agent.

The messenger returned at nightfall to report Gabaal had already left Saba.

'But he can't leave!' Hallam protested, feeling the first cold touch of alarm. 'His responsibility is to stay with the boat. Did you check with the Judean shipping agent?'

'It was he who told me, your lordship. Should I instruct him to come and see you?'

'No, it is all right, I will go and see him myself tomorrow.'

'Best if I come with you, master,' Phineas suggested when Hallam told him of his plan. 'You a rich man now with your own boat, and am I not your slave? Not fitting to be unattended.'

They checked on *Piko* first to ensure she was still there, then sought out the agent in his warehouse. He was a man with the mouth and eyes of a fish, and Hallam mistrusted him even before he spoke.

'I am here only as the agent of King Solomon,' the agent replied evasively to Hallam's query as to Gabaal's whereabouts.

'You told my messenger he had left, so you must know where he has gone.'

'What is done by other agents is not my affair, but he did say he wished to return to Ezion-Geber as soon as possible.'

'But is the cargo from the boat not here in your warehouse? Gabaal informed me you were to handle it.'

'Here?' The agent looked confused. 'I fear you are mistaken. I believe it was taken to the palace.'

'I can check for you, Master Hallam,' Phineas offered.

'Yes, I think you had better, Phineas,' Hallam replied, glaring at the agent.

It was as Hallam suspected. Only the gifts from Rajah, the few bags of coconuts, sour pods and other bits they had collected had been delivered to the palace. Everything traded and bought by the gold was missing.

'Find me four of the best Sabaen sailors you can, Phineas. Offer them double wages, and find a pilot who knows the ways of the Narrow Sea. *Piko* will also need some weight, so see what you can do. I'm going aboard first thing in the morning and will stay there until she is ready. I may be too late to catch Gabaal at sea, but I'll find the thieving rat in Ezion-Geber.'

'Sailors are easy, Master Hallam. For double wages they will leave other boats. Pilot's too. They will sail with you for nothing now you are famous. *Piko* will be ready tomorrow. But very important you get permission from the queen before leaving.'

It was a much less confident Phineas that confronted him later that night, not long after Hallam had crawled wearily into his bed. After a sharp tap on the door, the slave came in with a flickering candle. He closed the door softly behind him, then stood apparently undecided for a moment before placing the candle on the floor at his side. 'Are you sleeping, Master Hallam?' he whispered.

'If it's another problem, Phineas, I don't want to know about it.'

'Not a problem, Master Hallam. Boat almost ready, I think.'

Hallam sat up, puzzled by the slave's odd manner. 'What is it then?'

'Lady come to see you.'

'Now? A bit late don't you think?'

'Best if you see her, Master Hallam. She's a special lady.'

'Oh, one of those.' Hallam was tempted. It had been a long time, but his mind was too active with other things. 'I didn't ask you to find me a woman, Phineas. I need to sleep. Tell her I have a headache.' He lay down and pulled up the cover. 'Take the candle with you when you leave.'

Phineas came close to the bed and leaned over to whisper urgently. 'Master Hallam, *please!* You *must* see her!' She is the *queen!*'

Hallam jumped as though propelled by a heavy foot from below. *'What?'*

'She say not to wake you if you are sleeping, but that would not be right. She waiting outside.'

'Why didn't you say that in the beginning, you dumb ox!' He leaped naked from the bed and snatched up his clothes. 'Tell her I'll be with her in a moment.'

Hallam was still wrestling with a stubborn smock when another, more discreet tapping came at the door. He bounded across the room to pull it open. 'Your Majesty... forgive me, I was not...'

She lifted a hand from the dark folds of her robe to stop him. A bulky hood covered her head and most of her face, and once again Hallam was prodded by the past. 'It is I who must apologise for disturbing you so late, Lord Hallam, but it is important that I not be seen. I hope you understand... may I enter?'

Hallam stepped hastily aside, still tugging clumsily at his smock. She closed the door softly behind her, then threw back the hood to reveal her face, and Hallam was surprised to note that she seemed nervous, her breath quick and her fingers busy. 'There is a special favour I wish to ask of you.'

'Anything I can do will be an honour, your majesty.'

'Perhaps you will not think so after I have asked it, and

you may refuse if you wish.'

'I could not imagine such a thing.'

She smiled wistfully. 'It is my earnest wish that you do not, but it is important to me that you do not take my wish as a command. This is not a formal meeting, Lord Hallam.'

'It makes no difference to me, your majesty... forgive me, but you call me lord?'

She nodded. 'In the true sense, perhaps you are not, but I have a reason for that also, which I may explain later. I am told you will be leaving tomorrow?'

'Only if you permit it. I will stay if you wish, of course.'

'No, the reason you are leaving is why I am here. Had you been staying, I may not have found the courage.' She looked distractedly around the room, seeming ill at ease and lost for words. Her discomfort communicated itself to Hallam, and, more puzzled than ever, he fidgeted nervously with his smock.

'My young cousins speak of you with stars in their eyes, Lord Hallam. I fear they are both in love. They say you are a man of wisdom and honour, and that you can be trusted in all ways.'

'Hallam smiled with genuine delight. 'I have a great affection for Jemma and Sophi, but as your majesty knows, they have a tendency to exaggerate.'

'Maybe not as much as you think, Lord Hallam. Sophira has told me of the sailors and what happened to her, and how it could also have happened to Jemimah had you not arrived in time to kill the men. A lesser man may have been tempted to tell such a story to Lord Shan and gain further reward.'

'We have never spoken of the matter since it happened,' Hallam said. 'I had hoped she had left it in the past where it belongs.' The news he had been credited with both killings did not escape Hallam. Not that it mattered. He could not blame them. A young noblewoman of sensitivity would not want it known around the palace that she had ripped the bowels out of a bound sailor.

'You know, of course, that as Queen I can never marry?'

'No, I didn't...'

'But it does not prevent me from having a child. The lineage must continue, as long as the man is of noble blood and remains unknown. I would like you to be that man, Lord Hallam, if you will agree.'

She stood waiting as Hallam struggled with his surprise and emotions. Her figure was just another dark shadow in the dim light of the room. The pale oval of her face with its dark eyes and the slim entwining fingers protruding from the robe were all that showed, yet Hallam saw much more. He saw a queen renowned for her beauty; a symbol of power and influence far beyond his ability to comprehend.

He looked at her dark-robed figure as he had the white-robed one of Philippa on the temple steps in Tyre, and felt the same feeling of inadequacy. He could never hope to fulfil her expectations, just as he had not been able to fulfil Philippa's. She was asking too much.

But he also saw a nervous young woman waiting, as timid as any virgin bride, for his answer. A beautiful woman who had just offered him something he could not even have dared to dream about, and he knew he could not refuse. To do so would not only be an insult to her, but a lie to himself, for she was beautiful and desirable. Even more so in her demure uncertainty. And her nervousness gave him courage.

'I could dream of such a thing for the rest of my life, your majesty, but I am not of noble birth.'

'My cousins tell me that you are descended from the kings of Crete.'

Hallam laughed. 'I told them that so they would talk to me.'

She smiled. 'It's of no matter. In my eyes you are noble, Lord Hallam, and will also be in the eyes of our child, if you agree and the gods should grant us one. But there is one more condition I must impose before you answer, and I almost withhold it from you in selfishness. If there is a child, you will not be able to acknowledge it.'

'I will never see it?'

She hesitated a moment before answering. 'That I will not withhold. No one should be denied the right to see or speak to their own child, but you cannot acknowledge it as your own, and we can never speak of this night... not even to each other. Do you agree to these unfortunate conditions... my lord? And to my earnest request?'

'It is more than I can expect, your majesty, and I will swear my silence to you.'

'Thank you, my lord, you make me very happy. You have no idea how nervous I have been... talking to you like this.'

'Your majesty...' Hallam ran his fingers through his hair and scratched at the back of his head in frustration at trying to find the right words. 'If you will forgive me, but it has been a long time... I hope I am able to er... fulfil your majesty's needs.'

'I'm sure you will do more than that, and I am here for the night. We will shed all formality with our clothes. Tonight I am Aphra, your woman. An inexperienced one, for this is new to me, and I am also afraid of not being what you expect, but I do have strong desires, and you are a desirable man. You must promise to treat me as you would any other woman.'

Hallam managed a smile, though it tugged tentatively at the corners of his mouth. 'No, that I could never promise. I can promise only to treat you with the love and respect a man should feel for the woman who wants to have his child. We will make this a night of love... for the child.'

She laughed breathlessly and, with head lowered, began to fumble at the fastenings of her robe. Hallam went to her aid, his fingers moving swiftly, made nimble by the unsteadiness of hers. He slid the robe from her shoulders and let it fall to the floor, then he tilted her chin so he could look at her face. The face that stirred the hearts of princes and kings, and he could barely breathe against the tightness in his throat.

She closed her eyes and he kissed her softly on the lips, then held her close against him, feeling the sleek warmth of her through the flimsy silk of her gown, and knowing that this was a moment he would remember. She responded hesitantly, then her arms closed around and they clung to each other, allowing time for the shyness of strangers to pass slowly into the familiarity of lovers.

'I now know why my cousins love you,' she whispered. 'You think of the needs of others. I have chosen wisely. We will have a wonderful child... a love child.'

'Feel my heart beating against yours,' Hallam murmured. 'It beats with love.'

She gave a small giggle. 'It is not all I can feel against me. Should we put out the candle?'

'No, we have nothing to hide from each other, at least. We must have it all.'

They shed their clothes together, she glancing shyly at his nakedness, and Hallam gazing with awe at hers. Then they sank onto the bed and came together in a rush.

'Take me,' she breathed urgently. 'Fill my belly with your seed and give me a child that will be like his father. Take me on a voyage of love, my brave pilot.'

With the star of the north once more shining bright on her nose, *Piko* ran the length of the gulf under a slackening breeze and glided smoothly into the still harbour of Ezion-Geber. As the few remaining shore lights flickered close, Hallam relinquished the tiller to the hired Sabaen pilot and jumped to the deck. 'Prepare to lower the sail,' he ordered the waiting crew.

'A fair night for a landing, Pilot Hallam,' one of them called out. 'Are we not going in?'

'It is almost morning, Amos. But if you care to swim ashore and rouse up a tub…'

'He's more likely to rouse up a whore, Pilot. 'Two coppers says you won't do it, Amos.'

'I'll wager the same that the fish get him before the whore,' called out another, and the men laughed, happy at the prospect of time ashore with double pay. Phineas had done well with his selection of pilot and crew.

Hallam left them to their banter and made his way to *Piko's* head in the prow. He stood holding on to the defective wooden ear, peering into the darkness ahead. It was an odd sensation, being the only one of the original crew to return. Just he and *Piko*. And they would stay together. That was a good feeling. Almost as good as the feeling of being a prospective father. He had no doubt in his mind she would have a child. A night so full of tenderness and passion had to produce something more than a good sweat.

He put her from his mind and ran through again what he would say to the governor. He would know by now that his boat had survived. Gabaal would have told his story, probably well adorned with lies, but at least that would relieve him of the boredom of going through it all again.

His offer to buy the boat would come as a surprise to the governor, and he could only hope it would be a pleasant one. If he mentioned the goods Gabaal had bought with the gold, and offered his share as compensation for the loss of the cargo, it would not only encourage the governor to accept the offer, but put Gabaal at the losing end, which is where the treacherous swine deserved to be.

The rattle of the spar, followed by the splash of the anchor sounded behind and *Piko* came gently to rest. 'Well done, you old nag.' Hallam said into the wooden ear. 'And tomorrow you will be mine!' He patted her affectionately between the ears and, as he walked away, he could almost swear that *Piko's* ferocious grimace had turned into a toothy grin.

I don't understand,' Hallam said, looking at the governor in confusion. 'What has that thieving Gabaal been saying?'

'I believe it is you who is the thief, *Sailor* Hallam. Gabaal is my agent, and he hurried back to give me a full report of what happened, while you, a mere sailor, kept my boat and stayed to enjoy the comforts of Saba.'

'That's not true. I stayed because I had to, and Gabaal said he wanted to trade the goods we brought from India, yet he stole them and left without telling me.'

'Ah, yes, I have a report about those goods, and also about the gold my agent found, and which he used to purchase the goods on my behalf. The same goods, Sailor Hallam, which you yourself stole in Saba and sold through the queen's keeper of treasures.' The governor picked up the document of promise Hallam had given him from Lord Shan and waved it scornfully in the air. 'How else could a common sailor such as yourself afford to purchase a boat? You think me such a dolt as to agree to sell to you something which you are attempting to purchase with my own gold? If so, you are a fool as well as a thief and a liar.'

Hallam could only stare at the governor and the waving document in bewilderment.

'Your silence betrays you,' the governor continued. 'But there is also the matter of my cargo, which you threw in the sea, the murder of three sailors, and the threatening of my agent. You are nothing but a thieving pirate and will be treated as one. You will be spiked to the mast of the same boat you attempted to steal and left there to rot!' The governor signalled to his guards. 'Take him away and hold him. When I can find the time, I will witness his execution myself.'

The cell was more comfortable than the one he had been given in Tyre; large enough to walk around in, and that's what Hallam did for the remainder of the day and much of the night. It was all too unbelievable. The lies and injustice of it overwhelming. He would demand to be heard. He would demand to see Gabaal so he could confront him with the truth. Surely the governor could not be so stupid as to not see it for himself?

He did not even have a witness he could call on. The girls and Phineas were all he had, and they were a long way from being reached. But even had they been there, he doubted the testimony of two girls and a slave would carry any weight.

He tried to think of something Gabaal had forgotten, some incident that would force him into revealing his treachery and brand him for the liar he was. Gabaal had sewn his poisonous seeds and covered them over well, but Hallam could not dispel the strong feeling he was missing something.

When his anger subsided, he tried to forget Gabaal's treachery and concentrate on something else. That he had saved the governor's boat and returned it after surviving a long voyage to where no one else had been seemed to carry no weight either, and that seemed odd. In Saba it had been the main topic of interest. He had been besieged by pilots and merchants seeking his knowledge. Lord Shan was planning an expedition. So why had the governor, who was the richest merchant in Edom, not seen the opportunities?

On the second morning the heavy door was suddenly flung open and Hallam was summoned out.

'I wish to see the governor,' Hallam demanded of the two guards. 'There is something he should know.'

'A fortunate coincidence,' replied one of them, 'for the governor also wishes to see you, and he is with the king. It would be wise to hold your anger and show proper allegiance.'

Flanked and hurried by the guards, Hallam was given no time to reflect on the surprising news of the king's presence.

The king and governor were not alone in the room. Five others of advanced age sat together on a bench along one wall. Unfortunately, Gabaal was not among them. A younger man stood by himself, and Hallam's confident step faltered when he recognised Lemek, the son of councillor Jotham and supposed friend of Prince Hadad. His presence could only mean more bad news.

On a chair set apart from the others, the governor waited, and the king sat on the cleared table with his arms folded and legs swinging over the side. A vacant stool had been placed in the centre of the room, obviously there for Hallam's use, and he stopped beside it.

The conversation had subsided as soon as he entered. The king stopped swinging his legs and looked at Hallam with the remains of a laugh on his face; a smoothly plump and untroubled face, made rounder by the dark curls and short trimmed beard that framed it. Hallam was not inspired to throw himself on the floor. His mood was more inclined towards throwing himself on Lemek or the governor. He limited himself to a stiff nod and a quietly murmured, 'Your majesty.'

The governor spoke to Lemek. 'He is the one?'

'The same, my lord.' Lemek stared at the floor, refusing to meet Hallam's glare.

The governor nodded. 'Leave us.'

Lemek departed hurriedly, and the governor turned to Hallam. 'It seems you are much more than just a pirate, a thief and a liar, Sailor Hallam. I have heard many more interesting tales about you since last you stood before me. Of particular interest is one concerning the wife of Lord Arumah of Tyre and the niece of King Khiram, who is also a friend of our good King Solomon. Another concerns an enemy of our king, the so called Prince Hadad of Edom.'

Hallam's heart sank further. If they knew about Philippa as well as the prince, there was not much use in trying to appeal to the governor's greed by pointing out the advantages of his voyage as he had planned. Against the false accusation of piracy he had a chance, but against rape and treason he had none Tight-lipped, he stood silently staring at the kings hairless swinging legs; the only movement in the room.

'You have nothing to say?'

'Only that I meant no harm to Lady Philippa, and Prince Hadad is my friend. I will say nothing against either of them. As for Gabaal, he is a liar and a cheat. Against him I will say much, but it seems to me you are not interested in the truth.'

The governor frowned and sat forward in his chair. He opened his mouth to speak, but King Solomon silenced him with an imperious wave of his hand. 'In that you are mistaken, Master Hallam,' the king said mildly. 'The truth interests me greatly, and also these men...' he waved the same hand towards the men on the bench, '...who are wise in the ways of the sea and will know the truth when they hear it. They will question, and you must answer. So please sit down and tell us the truth, Master Hallam. Tell us of this strange voyage of yours in the Sea of Zeng.'

It took the rest of the day. Hallam did not tell it in the imaginative way the girls had told it to the Rajah, but as he had told it to the pilots in Saba; as one sailor to another. Armed by the experience of countless similar sessions, he knew what they wanted to hear and was able to give them enough to convince them he knew what he was talking about, without giving away too many of his secrets. His knowledge was his only weapon, and he told them so bluntly.

'The governor has threatened to have me spiked, so why would I tell you how to find the river?' He laughed scornfully. 'Maybe you should ask Gabaal.'

The king listened to the proceedings with interest, but took little part, and the governor soon excused himself to attend to other, more urgent matters. His place was taken by men summoned by the king at different stages of his talk, at which times Hallam was asked to repeat what he had just said.

The discussion ended abruptly at dusk. The king left without comment, and Hallam was taken back to his cell, where he was given food and, surprisingly, a jug of wine. He sipped thoughtfully at the wine, wondering about Prince Hadad, and cursing the impatience which had sent him directly to see the governor before calling at Zabby's house for information. Had Lemek betrayed him as well? And if so, what had been his fate and that of Zabby and the others?

Hallam forced the unpleasant thoughts from his mind. He had his own fate to worry about. His only chance was if the seeds he had planted were taking root. Seeds of greed he hoped would overpower Gabaal's seeds of poison.

The king had been quick to question him on his promise to lead a Sabaen expedition to the gold. Gabaal would not have been able to resist enthusing about how much was there. Perhaps in his hasty efforts to stab him in the back, Gabaal had also pierced himself on the point of his own spear.

When Hallam was returned to the governor's office in the morning, he already had a good idea what the king had in mind. He soon discovered that his seeds had not only taken root, but had blossomed into a plan. Only the king and two of the men from the previous day were present, and the king soon presented his suspiciously perfumed bouquet.

'My advisers have counselled me to accept what you say as the truth,' he said. 'You will lead an expedition. In return, I will instruct the governor to withhold his charges against you.'

Had it been anyone but the king, Hallam would not have been able to resist the sarcastic reply that came immediately to mind. But he did allow himself a wry smile. 'Withhold, your majesty?'

'If the expedition succeeds you will be free to go your own way.'

'But I have already promised such an expedition to the Queen of Saba.'

Hallam knew he was in dangerous water, but he also knew if he missed the opportunity now he would regret it later. He had to find out just how much the king was prepared to give in exchange for the promise of gold. Not that it mattered either way. No matter what was promised, when it came to gold, no one could be trusted. King Solomon and the governor would change the rules of their devious game to suit themselves.

But he could also play the game. At the first opportunity he would escape. Saba controlled access to the sea of Zeng and the Zeng coast. There he would be safe, even from the mighty Solomon.

But King Solomon knew the game too well. 'You will be free to do as you wish. I have no quarrel with Saba, but until then you will remain here at the governor's residence, until such time as the boats are ready to leave. Lead my pilots to the river, Master Hallam, and your life will be spared.'

Jonathan carefully studied the handful of dirt he held clenched in his tiny fist before trying to stuff it into his mouth. He screwed up his face at the taste.

'Joni!' Milcah pulled his fist away, and Jonathon obligingly opened his mouth and allowed Milcah to scoop the dirt off his tongue with her finger. 'You must not eat that... uk!'

'Be careful of your finger,' Philippa warned, 'he has six teeth.'

'I know, mistress, I've felt them!'

Philippa smiled fondly as her grubby son struggled impatiently in Milcah's grasp.

The prince himself had chosen Jonathan's name. 'It means "gift of the gods", he had informed Philippa, and that was what he seemed to be, for a new meaning had come into her life. Joni had appeared without fuss, wearing a tangle of dark hair and with his eyes open. He had attached himself hungrily to her breast while Milcah was still trying to clean him off.

'Look, Milcah, just like his father,' Philippa had murmured, and Milcah had been shocked.

'Mistress! You must not say such a wicked thing!'

'Me? I was talking about his hair.'

'Oh, Mistress Philippa! Forgive me!'

'No, he did that too. It's a wonderful sensation, Milcah, you should try it.'

'My bags all empty of milk, mistress.'

'That's not what I meant either.'

Philippa had never known such happiness. She missed nothing from the luxurious life she had in Tyre. In the village she lived a simple, almost carefree life, amongst simple but kindly people. She loved every moment of it. The prince had been true to his word, and the villagers treated her like one of their own, supplying her with mare or goat's milk and honey for Joni, and cheese, mutton and fowl for herself and Milcah. Fresh produce came in once a week by mules from

Ezion-Geber. All that she lacked in her life, Philippa thought often, was Joni's father.

She had prayed every day for his safe return, and the gods had listened. But the gods seldom gave freely. What they now demanded in return for his safety was faith, and Philippa had little to give. All she had was uncertainty.

'Look how fast he goes, Milcah. He will be walking soon.'

'Walking will be too slow for him, mistress, he will start by running. His father will be very proud of him.'

'I'm afraid, Milcah. What will I say to him? We know nothing of each other. It's been so long. I'm not even sure if he likes me any more. He probably thinks of me as a noble whore. That is, if he thinks of me at all.'

'You are a beautiful lady, mistress. He be mad not to like you, and you give him a son. Any man be proud to have all that.'

'He has a new life now, Milcah. He will probably die of shock when he finds out he has a son.'

'You going to tell him yourself, mistress?'

'Of course! Who else do you think?'

'If you will forgive me, mistress, it is not a good idea for you to be in Ezion-Geber. Too many people there from Tyre who can recognise you.'

'I'll borrow your old robe and wear a head cloth. If I put some dirt on my face and go down with the mules on their next trip, I will not be noticed.'

But before that could happen, the news that Hallam had been arrested and was facing execution reached the village. Philippa was devastated. She refused to leave the cottage and spoke to no one, and Milcah was left to tend to the needs of Jonathan on her own.

As if that was not enough, it was also reported by the same messenger that King Solomon was in Ezion-Geber with a regiment of soldiers to try and capture Prince Hadad. It seemed the prince's tax patrols had finally been compromised.

Further news drifted up from Ezion-Geber with agonising slowness and in frustrating snippets, and it was impossible to know if it was truth or rumour. Some of it was thrilling. It was apparently reported by sailors that Hallam had sailed a boat into the Sea of Zeng and discovered a new land rich in gold. It was also told that he had been awarded for bravery by the Queen of Saba. But the most important news to arrive was that Hallam had had been interviewed by King Solomon and was being held captive in the governor's residence.

Philippa clung tenaciously to hope. She prayed to Hallam's goddess, Astarte, for intervention, and was heard, but once again it was at a high price. Hallam was not going to be executed, but was to lead an expedition to the new land for the king, and would be away for at least one, and maybe even two, years.

'I have to see him,' Philippa said to Milcah with a mix of relief and despondency. 'It may be my last chance, and whatever the risk, I have to take it.'

What business is it that you wish to discuss with the king's emissary?'

'That is only for the emissary himself to hear, but it concerns the pirate you have in prison.'

The governor's aide frowned. 'Your name?'

'Captain Parak.'

'Emissary Ahinadab is very busy. You will have to wait.'

Parak was kept waiting outside the aide's office for half the day. Few people came to visit, and he had the distinct feeling he was kept waiting as a reprimand. All he had for company were two plump, shiny black, and totally bald children who, when they were not whispering to each other, stared at him.

It was much too long a wait for Parak's piece of mind, and several times he considered walking out. He was having second thoughts about seeing the emissary. It was risky, and if by some remote chance the pirate glassmaker had been contacted by his elusive Philippa, he was not likely to give away her whereabouts, no matter what he threatened. But after a year of frustration and failure he had run out of options, and almost out of silver. Not for the first time did he regret having stupidly burned Lord Arumah's letter. With it, he would have had more chance of convincing the emissary. Now all he had was his word.

Finally, the scowling aide condescended to call him, and Parak was shown into the emissary's office. Lord Ahinadab was alone, and as bald as the children Parak had seen outside. Were it not for the difference in colour, he would have taken them to be related. The emissary was also so fat that his head appeared attached to his body by his chin. He waved Parak in with a hand that must have been difficult to lift with the weight of his gold rings. 'Yes, what is it?'

Parak told his story and the emissary listened with a bored expression. It was made no easier when the emissary leaned back in his chair and closed his eyes, as if taking a nap. He must have been listening though, for when Parak paused in consternation, the emissary lifted a hand and waved it lethargically. When Parak had finished, the Ahinadab sat forward with a sigh. 'You have been wasting my time. Nothing of what you say is new to me.'

Parak was astounded. 'You knew of Lady Philippa's disappearance?'

'Of course. The king has briefed me fully. He was a friend of Lord Arumah. Why do you think he would not know?'

'But what of my suspicions... that she may try and contact the pirate you have in prison. I'm sure they had an arrangement to meet. If I could just speak to him alone I may be able to persuade him to tell me where she is.'

'He is not in prison, and your suspicions should be told to Lord Arumah. I am only here to oversee the king's expedition. Your request to see the pilot is refused.'

Parak's face darkened with anger. 'You call him a pilot? He is nothing but a stinking glassmaker and a rapist. I should have killed him when I had the chance. He is making fools of you all!'

The emissary's face paled and he stood up, his chin quivering. 'You call me a fool? You call the king a *fool?*'

Parak had realised his mistake immediately, and even as the emissary was rising he held up his hands in supplication. 'No! Forgive me, your lordship, of course, it is not what I mean. I would cut out my tongue before even thinking such a thing. I beg your forgiveness for the stumbling of it, my lord.'

The emissary sat down slowly, but continued to glare at Parak who, in turn, went to great lengths to fix what he hoped was an expression of remorse on his face. Such a slip could easily cost more than a tongue. He waited anxiously as the emissary rearranged his bulk in the chair and shuffled the documents on his table. He picked one up and began to study it, and Parak got the feeling he was being dismissed, then the emissary lifted the document and waved it. 'Do you know what this is?' he asked.

'No, my lord.'

'It has the seal of two kings,' the emissary explained. 'King Solomon and King Khiram.' He waved the document again with a smug smile. 'It allows me to requisition any ship, any goods, and any men I feel will be needed for the expedition.' The emissary put the document down and searched for another. 'A Cilician guard, you said... and what did you say was your name?'

Parak had a strong premonition of impending disaster. He mumbled his name and the emissary picked up a bare quill, dipped it into a small silver box, then scratched on the document. He blew gently on it then looked up with the same smile. 'I have need of experienced soldiers for the expedition, Parak. My aide will take you to the captain in charge and you will begin training immediately, but not as a captain. First you will have to prove yourself worthy.'

'But, My Lord! It's impossible for me to go! I have been ordered to look for Lady Philippa, and Lord Arumah will be expecting me to report to him. He even gave me a letter to give to her!'

'One man to search an entire country? Leave the letter with me and I will pass it to the commander of the king's regiment that is already searching for Prince Hadad. They can look for Lady Philippa at the same time. I will inform Lord Arumah with my next dispatch to Tyre. As he and King Khiram are lending their most experienced pilots for the expedition, I am sure they will be happy to have an experienced guard such as yourself to look after them.'

'But I hate the sea! I get sick, and I don't trust this pirate to...'

'Neither do I,' said the emissary in a menacing tone. 'But there are many unpleasant duties we must perform in life.' He paused to fix Parak with a meaningful glare. 'If we hope to survive.'

It was easy for Hallam to forget he was a prisoner. He had been given the rooms on the upper level normally given to distinguished visitors. Even the king had once slept there, a guard had informed him.

The open balcony had a view of the sea, and was large enough to accommodate a fourteen-place table. It was where Hallam spent most of his time. The living and sleeping rooms were spread with luxurious rugs, the bed large enough to sleep four people, and the walls were decorated with exotic artefacts. It even had a separate washing room with a tub and a throne-like chair with a hole cut in the seat; designed presumably, to keep distinguished buttocks comfortably elevated while the owner contemplated the affairs of state.

But Hallam discovered after searching for a way out that it was not because he was considered a distinguished guest, or that they were concerned for his comfort, that he had been accommodated there. It was because the rooms were perfectly secure, yet still allowed easy access to his steady stream of visitors, most of whom *were* distinguished. That he was precious to them was clearly evident by his treatment. He was never made to feel like a prisoner and was given everything he wanted.

It was not difficult for Hallam to understand why he was being treated so well. The king had made a big investment in him, and it was obviously to his advantage to have his full cooperation, rather than have him sullenly rebellious. Every boat capable of making the voyage - including *Piko* - was being requisitioned. Pilots, sailors and shipwrights were being brought in from Tyre, and a growing army of farmers, engineers and slaves were accumulating in the compound surrounding the residence. The king had ordered that everything be ready in three months so they could sail with the first change of winds and, Hallam suspected, to get in before the Sabaens. If he was allowed to escape, it would all be for nothing.

Knowing it was in his best interests, Hallam caused no problems and, at times, could almost convince himself he was enjoying the experience. He was kept busy for most of the day giving advice and answering questions that ranged from the colour of the sand in the River Saba, to the shape of the animals in the forest. With the shipwrights, he discussed masts and sails, and the size of the small river boats they would be taking in pieces to be assembled on arrival.

Only in one area did he not cooperate fully, and that was when it came to what he had learned of the stars and winds, especially on the return voyage. He did not trust Solomon, and particularly his fat overseer, Ahinadab. Once he had led them to the river - a feat that was beginning to cause him more sleepless nights the closer it came to departure - he wanted to be certain of returning, and not to be considered expendable.

One of Hallam's more frequent and most eagerly awaited visitors, was Zabby's uncle. Hungry for news of his friends, Hallam questioned him mercilessly, but the old man knew little more than Hallam had been able to find out for himself from other sources. Zabby had visited Ezion-Geber only once since Hallam had left, Zabby's uncle reported, and now that the prince was being hunted, he doubted he would see him at all. Nevertheless, Hallam gave his own story and asked the old man to pass it on if he could.

They also discussed *Piko* at length. Hallam had insisted the old man be the one responsible for her refitting, and shamelessly told him to double his charges and to spare no expense.

'*Piko* is mine now,' he told the old man, 'and I want her to have only the best. The governor has not returned my document of promise from Lord Shan, so as far as I am concerned, she has been paid for, and I'm also going to make sure the king pays me well for her use.'

'The overseer is still insisting we put rings in the deck for cargo. There is much that has to be taken.'

'Ignore it,' Hallam said. 'I've already told him if he puts any deck cargo on *Piko,* I'll throw it overboard as soon as I sail, no matter how important he thinks it is, and I have advised the other pilots to do the same. It is too dangerous.'

Only one other visitor came that he knew, and Hallam was unsure if he was pleased to see him or not. It was Meldek, the pilot he had sailed with from Lamos.

Meldek came alone, and seemed more impressed with Hallam's quarters than with Hallam himself.

'I was told it was you,' he said by way of greeting, 'but I found it hard to believe.'

'Quite understandable,' Hallam replied. 'I find it hard to believe myself.'

'You seem to have acquired a reputation for yourself.'

'To which one do you refer? My reputation as a rapist, or my reputation as an upstart pilot?'

Meldek laughed. 'What happened in Tyre is no concern of mine. And frankly, I don't think this is either. I know nothing of the Sea of Zeng. All my experience is with the Great Sea.'

'I know very little myself,' Hallam replied. Meldek was too wise a sailor to be impressed by false bravado. 'What happened was more good fortune than good piloting.'

'I appreciate your honesty, especially as I have been ordered by King Khiram to sail on the same boat as you. I hope you do not object.'

Hallam was tempted to object on principle. *Piko* was his boat, and he was determined to be in control, and Meldek had obviously been instructed by the king to learn all the secrets he could. But he was pleased at the prospect of sailing with Meldek. With everyone else a stranger, he was the closest he had to a friend, and he liked the old man. 'I will not object if you agree to my conditions,' Hallam told him.

Meldek looked surprised. 'Oh? What are they?'

'As I now own the boat, I will be in command. There will be no sacrifices made at sea, and the final condition is that you share with me all your knowledge.'

'Yes, I can see you have changed.'

'Do you agree?'

Meldek smiled. 'I will tell you after you have first shared some of your own knowledge with me.'

Hallam returned the pilot's smile. 'And I can see you have

not changed.'

It was only when Meldek was about to leave that Hallam asked the question he had been wanting to ask all afternoon. 'By the way, how is Lady Philippa?'

'You have not heard?'

A chill feeling came over Hallam. 'Heard what?'

'That she ran away from Tyre, soon after you escaped.'

Stunned, Hallam could only stare at the pilot as visions of Philippa flashed through his mind. Philippa running away from Tyre. Stumbling in the dark as she struggled to hold up the front of her robe. He had not thought of her for so long he was surprised at the sudden rush of feeling that came with the vision. His love goddess had run away from Tyre. And to… where? 'Why?' he finally managed to ask.

Meldek shrugged. 'No one knows. She left with one of the black nurses and hasn't been seen since.'

But Hallam knew. It had to be Parak. 'Do you know...' he began, then changed his mind. If Parak had left Tyre as well he really didn't want to know.

When Meldek had gone, Hallam told the guard he was ill and did not want to be disturbed. He took a full jug of wine out to the balcony, stared out to sea, and slowly drank himself into oblivion.

I told you,' Zabby's uncle said. 'I may not see him for a long time, maybe never. I have heard they are hiding in Egypt.'

'I know, but I want you to take them anyway, just in case.' Hallam placed the cloth bundle containing the medallion and his gold falcon in front of the old man, and Zabby's uncle reluctantly transferred the bundle to his pouch. 'I'll do what

I can, but you must understand, I may...'

'Yes, I know,' Hallam interrupted irritably, rubbing at his sore eyes in the hope it would ease his sore head. 'You've already told me, but you are the only one I can trust to do this for me, and Zabby is the only one who knows her. They must find her. If you don't see Zabby, or if you can't find someone you can trust to take the falcon to Mocha with the message for Lord Shan, then keep them until I return.'

As the sailing date of the expedition drew close, Philippa became increasingly more agitated. The mule man had reported that Ezion-Geber was busier than he had ever seen it. Twenty three ships were to sail with over two hundred men - many of them Tyrians - and King Solomon himself would see them off.

Philippa had thought she would be going on her own, with only Milcah and the mule-man, and perhaps one or two others, but it seemed that half the village was going. The sailing was a good excuse for a holiday.

With Jonathan perched happily on one of the mule-man's donkeys, Philippa walked alongside, gripping firmly to the cloth of his smock She wore Milcah's old robe and a head cloth, and her face, particularly her fair eyebrows, were darkened with red dust and charcoal. Her already chewed down fingernails were roughened further, and her hands ingrained with dirt. Between her stout sandals and the fair skin of her feet she wore coarse goat hair stockings. And with each step along the rugged mountain path, she became increasingly more nervous.

It was not so much the fear of being discovered that worried her. Each step was bringing her closer to reality.

In her isolation she had built a dream. A stone cottage in the peace and solitude of the mountains, where they could live together and watch their son growing up. But he knew nothing of her dream, or his son. He may have dreams of his own. What could she say to him? How could she tell him everything in the short time they would have together. She may not even get a chance to speak to him, and he would be gone for another year at least. He would miss so much joy in not seeing his son grow. The young changed so quickly. And without her dream to sustain her, where would she find the strength to wait another long year?

As they approached the edge of town the pace slowed and word was passed back from those at the front. 'Soldiers are checking ahead!'

Philippa lifted Jonathan from the donkey by his arms and swung him around onto her own back. He complained bitterly. 'Be quiet Joni! Tie him on with the shawl, Milcah, and put on his cap.' It was what they had planned. She was less likely to be recognised if carrying a child.

The soldiers lined either side of the path so the people had to pass between them, and Philippa lowered her eyes as she passed, but they seemed only interested in the men. She was almost through when a soldier caught her by the arm. 'Hold there!' He bent to pick up the cap, which Jonathan had thrown off. 'Unusual hair.' He ruffled it before replacing the cap, pulling it over Jonathon's ears and playfully tweaking his nose before waving her on, and Philippa stumbled forward with her heart racing.

They joined the crush on the wharf and she began pushing her way to the front, but it soon became clear they were not going to get close. A rope linked to barrels kept them well back from the water's edge, and King Solomon, flanked by dignitaries and soldiers, was moving through the cleared area, talking to those about to leave.

With her heart still racing, but for an entirely different

reason, Philippa moved slowly along the line of boats, searching through the groups for his tall figure. She was paying particular attention to those wearing the red insignia of pilots on their caps, and had reached halfway along the line when she recognised a face and stopped in surprise.

'What, mistress? Have you seen him?'

'It's my uncle's pilot,' Philippa whispered. 'Stand in front of me, Milcah. He knows me too well.'

Meldek was talking to another pilot, and Philippa looked at him carefully, for he was also a tall man, but it was not Hallam. 'Keep moving, Milcah, he has to be here somewhere.'

Then she saw him. He was not on the wharf, but standing on the boat immediately behind Meldek, and he wore not a red pilot's cap, but only the headband she had bought for him. It had faded almost to white. Stripped to the waist, he was rubbing oil into the ugly carving of a horse's head in the prow, and his muscles bulged and rippled with the effort.

He had changed so much. He was bigger than she remembered. More muscular, and his face more rugged and handsome, and she dug her fingers firmly into the soft flesh of Milcah's upper arm. 'Just look at him! Oh, Milcah, just look at him!'

'Where, mistress?'

'There! On the boat... working on the horse's head.'

'Is that our master? He's changed, mistress. Call to him, he will hear you from here.'

'No! He mustn't see me!' She dug her fingers even more firmly into Milcah's arm and pulled her in front.'

'But, Mistress!' Milcah squirmed in Philippa's painful grip. 'You must see him! I can ask one of the soldiers to call him while you wait here.'

'Don't argue with me, Milcah!' Philippa whispered angrily. 'Just stand there and be quiet!'

He had finished oiling the head and stood wiping his hands

on a cloth while he looked over at the crowd, and Philippa caught her breath and ducked behind Milcah's shoulder as his eyes passed over her. They stopped a little farther along, and he smiled at someone in the crowd. She heard his voice clearly as he called to one of the soldiers. It was deeper, more self-assured. He spoke to the soldier, pointing into the crowd, and the man went to the rope and held it up to allow someone through. It was a woman. A thin, strangely attractive woman with a child on her hip. A boy child only a little older than Jonathan, and Philippa was sure she had seen the woman before.

Hallam jumped down to greet her, grinning with pleasure as he hugged the woman and kissed her on the forehead. He held out his arms and the child went to him willingly, laughing with delight as Hallam lifted him high in the air.

Philippa's heart stopped in her throat, then plummeted low into her belly as she suddenly remembered the woman she had seen when she first arrived in Ezion-Geber. The woman had been crying as a boat was leaving. Not a husband, only a friend, she had said. Could Hallam have been the friend she was crying for? She had been pregnant then. Could Hallam be the father?

'I want to leave now,' Philippa said firmly, and without waiting to see if Milcah followed, she turned and pushed her way out of the crowd, going towards the mules. In her confusion she was not aware that Jonathan had thrown off his cap, or that Milcah had stopped to pick it up. She was also not aware that Jonathan had pulled back her head cloth to reveal her own fiery hair.

But Philippa did become aware when, for the second time that morning, she was gripped roughly by the arm and pulled to a stop. She jerked her arm away and turned angrily to look into the face of Parak.

He stared at her, and Philippa looked away quickly, dropping her eyes and trying to move on, but Parak caught

374

her again by the arm. 'Wait! It's you...' He seemed confused, looking from her to Jonathan and back, trying to look into her face, which she kept turned away.

'You, Soldier! Take your hand off my woman! Do you not see she has a child?' The mule man shoved his great bulk between them, and Parak reluctantly loosened his grip.

'I know her... the hair...'

'No, you do not know her. Leave her alone.'

At that moment, Milcah arrived with Jonathan's cap, and Parak switched his attention to her. 'I know you too!'

'What do you want with our women, Soldier?'

More of the villagers had arrived and began to protest angrily.

'Yes! Why do you not look in the tavern for your whores!'

'Her brother is leaving. Would you cause her more pain?'

A cohort captain shouldered his way towards them. 'Parak! Stop your whoring and get back to your boat!'

Parak moved away hesitantly, still looking, and Philippa was pushed back through the crowd of villagers. When she was through she kept going, stopping only long enough to unhitch the donkey and dump Jonathan on its back. He clung on desperately, and Milcah ran to steady him as Philippa pulled the donkey forward.

Some of the villagers followed in confusion, but Philippa was unaware. With her head still uncovered, she passed through the soldiers on the path and set off up the mountain, oblivious to their curious stares and comments. When the donkey dragged on the lead, she passed it silently to Milcah and went on ahead, driving herself hard.

Seeing Parak had given her a nasty shock, but she had already shut him out. It was not fear that drove her. Neither was it the woman with the child, for she had soon realised the child was older than Jonathan. Hallam could not be the father.

She was being carried along on a wave of conflicting

emotions she could not understand. Anger at herself for letting her dream take control, and also despair. It could so easily have been her he had kissed, and his own son he had held, but she had stood by and watched someone else playing her part. Why had she not found the courage to call out, or at least allowed Milcah to speak for her?

It was not until she reached the top of the bluff when, exhausted and fighting for breath, she looked down on the sea and understood that she was running away. Running to shore up the cracks in her dream that were starting to let in the harsh light of reality.

She sat to wait for Milcah and Jonathan, looking down on the ships spreading out under sail, and she prayed to his goddess, Astarte, yet again. 'Keep him safe, O goddess of love and queen of the heavens. Keep my love and my dream alive and my life will be yours.'

It was some weeks before Hallam discovered that Parak was sailing with them. After leaving Ezion-Geber, they did not touch land until they had passed through the *Street of Tears* and reached Zeilah, on the shores of the Arabian Sea. There they were to restock with fresh water, food, and firewood before rounding the horn into the Sea of Zeng.

A temporary camp had been set up on the beach for the overseer, and it was there, as he was walking towards the camp with Meldek, that Hallam saw Parak.

Like most of the crews, the Cilician, wore only a short skirt because of the heat, and it was his hairy body that first caught Hallam's attention. Parak was with a group filling water barrels, and Hallam was not sure until he came close, then it was Parak who identified himself.

'I was wondering when I was going to meet up with you again, Offal,' he sneered.

Hallam felt his blood begin to churn as he fought back his anger, and the disturbing visions that had returned with his knowledge that Philippa had escaped Tyre. 'What are you doing here, Ape?'

'I should ask the same of you, Offal.'

'You have no business being here, I'm going to have you thrown out.'

Parak laughed. 'You would be doing me a favour, Offal, but don't you first want to hear about your noble lady?'

'You stinking ape.'

Parak laughed again. 'That's not what she called me when I gave her some of this...' Parak lifted his skirt and took hold of his hairy genitals. He jiggled them. 'Why don't you bend over this barrel and I'll show you. Maybe you'll enjoy it as much as she did.'

Hallam charged at Parak, lowering his head and driving into him and, caught by surprise, Parak was forced back through a pyramid of spears stuck in the sand, scattering them. He caught Hallam around the waist and tried to lift him, but the momentum was too great. Before he could get his balance he was brought up short against a full barrel of water. The air exploded from his lungs as Hallam's head drove into his stomach, his knees buckled, and he collapsed, doubled over and gasping for breath.

Hallam dived for one of the fallen spears.

'Stop him!' Meldek bellowed, and the soldiers jumped on Hallam before he could lift the spear. He struggled to free himself, but there were too many. 'Put it down, Hallam,' Meldek said calmly, and Hallam relinquished the spear reluctantly.

'Get out of here, you stinking ape. If I see you again, I'll kill you.' Throwing of the hands that held him, he stormed towards the overseer's tent, shoving past the two surprised guards lounging at the entrance. He swept aside the curtain.

Ahinadab was sprawled naked on his sleeping rug, his great body glistening with sweat, and even with his rage, Hallam noticed that Ahinadab was as hairless as a slug. 'There is a soldier here called Parak, ' Hallam said without preamble. 'Get rid of him.'

Ahinadab struggled to sit up. 'Get out! Who are you to make demands? I will have you flogged! Get out! Get out!'

'If he stays, I will kill him. Or maybe he will kill me. If that happens, I've no doubt that Solomon will then kill you. Get rid of him!'

Hallam ducked out of the tent, then put his head back in again. 'Tell me, Ahinadab. Why is it you have no hair around your balls and Parak has nothing else... did he get your share?'

L ight the signal fire,' Hallam ordered the deck captain. 'Hold the sail as it is, but secure the boat. We're going out to sea and we're staying out.'

The deck captain relayed his orders quietly, almost reluctantly. Once committed to the sea, there would be no turning back. They would be at the mercy of the winds and the gods.

Hallam waited at *Piko's* helm for Meldek to approach, as he knew he would, and he studiously ignored the whispering and anxious glances cast in his direction by the sailors. Going out this early in the voyage had not been the original plan, but plans could be changed, and he was tired of the procrastination and bickering amongst the pilots. They would have to commit themselves eventually, and sooner, rather than later, was best as far as Hallam was concerned. And it would do Ahinadab no harm to forego the comfort and security of sleeping ashore.

He felt no guilt that his decision had been largely prompted by his anger at the refusal of the overseer to exclude Parak from the expedition. Ahinadab was showing his authority. But he was not the only one to have it. He was leading the expedition. If they didn't want to follow, they could stay behind.

'Are you sure, Hallam?' Meldek asked with a concerned frown when he arrived at the steering deck. 'I see no signs of a storm. I thought we agreed to make further landings before heading out.'

'No, I'm not sure,' Hallam replied. 'But the storms down here build quickly. If one catches us too close to land with nowhere to run we will lose ships and men. The safest place is away from land.'

But the next morning, and the two that followed, found the boats on a calm sea, well out of sight of land, and with barely enough movement in the air to bend the column of smoke rising from *Piko's* signal fire. It was not exactly what Hallam had hoped for. He had been almost certain they would have picked up the north wind.

The fleet could do nothing but wait, and waiting did not go well with uncertainty, especially now that the north star could no longer be seen. The pilots had no option but to rely on Hallam's judgement, and it was as well he could not hear the comments from the other boats, for none of them was complimentary.

'The fool is putting us all at risk,' complained one of the pilots to his deck captain. 'We must be mad to put our trust in so inexperienced a man. He has only been there once.'

'Let us pray to Baal he can improve his record,' the deck captain muttered.

Then, on the fourth evening they were treated to a display

of lightning to the west that was so awesome in its intensity, they could only stare in wonder and give thanks to Baal they were not any closer. And it seemed the gods must be at war, for no sooner had the display begun, when another commenced far to the north east, as if in answer to a challenge.

The contest raged for most of the night, each storm trying to outdo the ferocity of the other, and the distant rumbling and crashing of the contest kept heads turning and eyes open. Although the wind had not reached them, the creaking of timber and rigging began to change in tone, and the men could feel the swell thickening as they lay sleepless on their mats.

As if trying to escape the fray, the north wind arrived in a hesitant flurry, unsure of where it was going or if it should even be there, but it steadied after a few days, both in strength and direction and, for the next fifteen days, the flaring nostrils of *Piko* dripped water constantly as she ran before it.

With every boat in the fleet being different in size and sailing capability, it was not unusual to discover they had scattered during the night. *Piko* signalled her position each morning with black smoke and, if the wind allowed, a flaming torch at intervals during the night. Hallam shortened sail to allow the boats to gather, and a sailor would climb the mast to count them.

When the seven doves followed the sun directly overhead, Hallam knew they were approaching halfway. For another twenty days, during long periods of frustrating calm, he watched anxiously as the stars fell gradually behind, recalling with gratitude and love the painstaking work of Jemma and Sophi with their square of silk and collection of thorns - which had since been replaced with spots of purple dye. He kept the scarf and his piece of hide securely concealed in a pocket of his leather cape, and consulted it only when alone.

He could not trust his skimpy knowledge of the first

voyage south either, so had to rely on what he knew of the return voyage, and the most notable of that had been the current close to land. They could make good use of it, so when the doves moved, he told Meldek it was time to shorten the starboard braces and begin moving to the west.

'How do you know it is time?' Meldek asked.

'Perhaps the gods have favoured me with the brain of a turtle,' Hallam answered with a smile, remembering the time Meldek had told him exactly the same thing when sailing from Lamos.

Meldek had either forgotten, or his anxiety would not allow him to return the smile. 'If I am ever to return I should know.'

'I will tell you only if I am proved right, old friend. The gods may have made a mistake and given me the brain of an ass instead.'

But the gods had not made a mistake. Ten days later they entered the blue water of the corral reefs and passed the island where the girls had gathered the coconuts, and once again Hallam gave thanks to them and their benevolent goddess, Sham. He began to relax for the first time.

They sailed with the current, within sight of land, and only in daylight out of respect for the reefs. When the colour of the water changed, Hallam knew it must be the first big river. From then on, a lookout watched constantly from the mast, and a few days later the call Hallam had been praying for finally came. 'Water ahead changing colour, Pilot, I think it's another river.'

'Haul in the sail and drag an anchor,' Hallam ordered the deck captain. 'Signal the other boats to do the same. We have to wait for the breeze and the tide.'

Hallam took *Piko* in himself, staying close to the north bank, and she drifted sedately into the main channel as if returning to her stable.

'Drop the anchor and call the boats in, Captain. Welcome

to River Saba.'

The deck captain was a big Tyrian, hard and unforgiving, but his rugged face looked about to crumble as he thumped Hallam several times on the back. 'Thank you for bringing us here safe, Pilot. It was well done.'

Meldek said nothing, but his smile had returned, and Hallam made no objection when the old pilot suggested a small sacrifice in thanks.

It had been Hallam's idea to bring the small river boats, and he lost no time in getting two of them assembled and in the water. He had only four months. Then he would have to make the return voyage with the change of the wind and ten of the boats, and he wanted to see as much of the river and country as possible in the time remaining. He also wanted to be well away from Ahinadab and Parak. He had not seen either of them since leaving Zeilah, and that was how he intended to keep it.

Each riverboat was equipped with both sails and oars, and carried seven men. Hallam chose his big deck captain to helm the second boat. A third boat with farmers and engineers would accompany them as far as the old camp to see if the site was suitable for a permanent base, and Hallam made it his first stop.

The camp was almost unrecognisable. Gone was the channel where *Piko* had resided, and also the tree he had climbed to lift the mast. The camp itself was overgrown and the shelters gone, but the blackened stones of the fire were still in a circle as he had left them, and Hallam looked at them with memories flooding back.

He could see no sign that told the Click people had

returned. The flood had not reached the flat area where they had made their camp, so he suggested to the engineers and farmers it was where they should build the base. He warned them of the sea-cow's dislike of fires, and left quickly, taking his memories with him.

As they headed west along the river, he made a smoke fire at each camp and left a marker in a prominent position where they would see it on the way back. To make sure he would know if the Click people had visited, he placed a cross of stones beside the fire - to indicate the crossing of paths - and left a knife; a gift he was sure they would not be able to resist.

As they progressed up the river, small hills of gigantic boulders and beautiful spreading trees began appearing. Hallam climbed the hills to search the country around for smoke, but none was to be seen, only the seemingly endless forest of small, twisted trees and, with increasing abundance, the giant upside down trees with the sour white seeds.

It was from one of the hills that Hallam first saw the mountains. They were far to the north, hazy and blue with distance, capped with cloud and, regretfully, too far to reach in the short time they had. Smaller hills lay ahead however, and they made a permanent camp near a series of spectacular orange cliffs where the wide River Saba split into two. Then they set out on foot to hunt and explore the wild hinterland.

As usual, Morning Foot was the first to wake and tend the fire. She broke off a handful of dry twigs from a nearby branch, then knelt to blow on the still warm embers. Only when she had it ablaze did she remember what Old Father had said. There must be no fire. They were too close to the Strange Ones. Morning Foot scattered the twigs, quickly extinguishing the flame.

Shivering in the dawn, she pulled her skin blanket more snugly around and went into the bush to relieve herself. It was more habit than need, for she had nothing much to relieve. They had drunk little in the last four days of walking to reach the river. Most of what they carried in the shells of the three-stick birds was given to the children.

Before returning to the camp, Morning Foot looked for her star as she always did, but this morning it was not to be seen, and she frowned. Maybe it was hidden by the smoke from the Strange Ones' fires, which could be smelled clearly in the crisp air. She did not like to start a day without seeing her star. It was a bad omen, but it was the smoke of the Strange Ones that had brought them, so maybe it was not a bad omen but a good one, and the frown disappeared when she thought again of her two young friends with one face. The family that accompanied them had not believed her when she had told of their strange ways, but now they would see and hear for themselves she had not been lying.

Morning Foot was disappointed for a second time that morning when she heard from Old Father that they would not be going as far as the river that day.

'Only the young men will go,' he told her. 'The Strange Ones have too many fires to be only Short Ear and his friends. They will go and see, but will not be seen. We will stay with the children.'

'The water is finished. Will we not fetch more?'

'The watering place of Two Teeth and his wives is close. Take only yourself and Evening Heart to fill the eggs, and go soon, before the sun makes a shadow and you are easily seen.'

Morning Foot watched the men walk briskly away through the trees, her own man with them, and even in the chill of the morning, she felt the warmth of the sun inside her as she admired again the quick way he walked. Even quicker than her brother, Flying Sticks. She had not expected to have a man of her own after what had happened, or a new child to take the place of the Strange One's fruit, which Old Mother had removed with the dead fish berries.

When the men were out of sight, Morning Foot packed the empty shells into a reed bag and, leaving the children with the Old Ones and the two sisters of her man, set off with Evening Heart in the opposite direction, towards the watering place of Two Teeth.

They had already gone half the distance before they noticed with alarm that the two older children were following, and Morning Foot remonstrated with them. 'You must stay with your mother as you were told!'

'We wish to help with the water,' said the boy. He showed no guilt or remorse. Already seven seasons old, he did not like being ordered by women only twice his age.

'We do not need your help,' Morning Foot scolded. 'You were supposed to look after the young one. Go!'

The girl, who was one season younger than her brother, turned to go, pulling at his arm, but he jerked away and stood his ground.

'Let them come,' said Evening Heart. 'The others can look after Baba. We are close now, and they will follow anyway.'

'But you must stay behind and be quiet,' Morning Foot ordered.

'And be careful Two Teeth does not stand on you,' her sister joked.

Parak awoke stiff and irritable from an uncomfortable night on the damp ground. His mood did not improve when he discovered the sentry he had ordered to wake them at dawn had fallen asleep. And not only asleep but snoring. In Tyre, the man would be thrown in the sea to wake him up, then beaten by his fellow guards with spear shafts. But they were not in Tyre, and Parak was getting tired of the undisciplined rabble of so-called hunters the overseer had placed in his charge. He would have to improvise with the punishment.

He threw aside his blanket. Even in the chilly dawn he wore only a sleeveless jerkin and short skirt. He stood above the sleeping sentry, hoisted the skirt, and urinated on the sleeping sentry's face, aiming particularly for his open mouth.

The man awoke gasping and choking, and Parak delivered a solid kick to his ribs. 'Quiet, you lazy scum.' He chuckled, holding the squirming man down with his foot as he followed the frantic rolling of the sentry's head with a steady stream of urine.

He left the man to his quiet gagging and, with his mood improved, turned his attention to the others, kicking them awake one by one. Then he walked to the edge of the trees and looked across the stretch of grass to the lake.

Thankfully, the three elephants had not returned. He did not see any of the animals he was looking for, but what he did see caused him to gape in astonishment. Two naked children of an unusual yellow colour were stooped over, filling containers of some kind in the shallow water on the far side. Parak's surprise turned to disbelieving delight when one stood up to reveal not only breasts, but the largest, most protruding set of buttocks he could have imagined. Then the other stood up to reveal the same unmistakably feminine profile.

They were obviously two of the small wild people they had been warned about, and Parak examined the surrounding bush carefully for a signs of others, but they appeared to be alone. His pulse quickened. Two naked women could hardly pose a threat to seven armed soldiers

He withdrew quietly to confront his men. 'Bring your weapons,' he told them with a sly grin. 'We have some tasty meat to catch.'

They had gone through the same hunting exercise many times before, and with outstanding success. While the other groups of hunters given the task of feeding the base struggled to kill even birds, Parak's group seldom returned without at least one large beast, and often several. The strategy was simple, and owed its success to the three elephants that had churned the bottom of the lake into a quagmire.

When the unsuspecting herds of animals came to drink - usually late in the evening or early in the morning - Parak and his men rushed them from their hiding place, panicking them into the water. They were speared as they floundered in the mud, with some of the less aggressive animals, such as calves and those without horns, being pounced upon and drowned for the sport of it.

Two men had been killed. One impaled on a horn, and another when, after goading the seemingly docile elephants, he went too close and foolishly became stuck in the mud himself. No trace of him was found, which did not surprise Parak or his men. One of the elephants had first trodden the trapped man into the mud, then had rolled on top of him.

Parak and his men employed the same hunting technique on the unsuspecting women. Staying well in the cover of the trees, they circled the lake and came in from behind, concealed by the long grass. They were almost thrown into panic themselves when two children leaped from the grass like startled animals and ran towards the trees.

'After them! Bring them back alive!' Parak shouted to two of his men. At the same time he waved the others in towards the lake and the women.

Alarmed by the shout, the two women ran from the water,

only to be faced by the four men spread out and charging towards them. All they could do was run back into the water.

Parak threw off his skirt as he ran after them. He launched himself in a dive at the closest woman, catching her by the heel, and they both fell headlong into the stinking mix of animal droppings and mud. The woman was up first, and the soldier beside Parak raised his spear and poised to hurl it into her back.

Parak lunged at the soldier and knocked him down. 'Don't kill her, you fool!' He shouted to the others. 'Leave your spears. Take them alive!'

The women were faster than the clumsy men, and making good headway across the shallow lake until the man Parak had urinated on and left behind on the other side came running towards them.

Had they separated, one of them, or possibly even both, may have escaped, but they stayed together, running to the side and losing ground rapidly as they tired in the sticky mud.

Whooping and yelling with the excitement of the chase, Parak and his men ran to cut them off. When one of the women stumbled into a hole and the other stopped to help, Parak leaped on them both.

The women refused to walk, so were dragged across the lake with each of the four men holding a wrist. When they reached the bank, they pulled them through the grass to the trees. 'Find something to tie them,' Parak ordered.

A branch was quickly stripped of its bark and the women's hands and feet were bound.

Panting heavily, Parak squatted beside one of them and prodded her buttocks with a finger. 'Look at the size of them!' He spread his hand across one rounded cheek and clenched his fingers, squeezing hard and laughing at the squealed reaction, then he turned her over to examine and fondle her small breasts. 'Young and firm, just the way I like them.' He lifted the small skirt of shells to look beneath and grinned.

'What are we going to do with them, Captain?'

'What do you think, you imbecile?'

'We going to do it now?'

'If you want to roll around on some more mud you can jump back in the lake. We'll take them to the river and clean them up first.'

'Looks to me like you're about ready now, Captain,' sniggered one of the men.

Parak looked down at himself and grinned sheepishly. 'It can sniff out a yoni from a hundred cubits. Instead of standing there looking envious, why don't you go and find the others. Keep a sharp lookout. There will be wild men somewhere. I don't want a poisoned arrow in my tail when I've got it dancing in the air.'

The men arrived back with the two children, a pile of skin blankets, and an assortment of primitive artefacts. The children had also been bound, and each was led by a leash of bark string tied around their necks. They gaped at the men, their slanted eyes made wide with fear, and they walked stiffly, as if half stunned. When they saw the women on the ground, both began crying out in their strange tongue, and the men looked at each other in astonishment before breaking into guffaws of laughter.

When one of the women began talking back, Parak silenced her by placing a muddy foot over her mouth. 'No others?' he asked the two men.

'Another five,' one replied. 'We almost got there in time to catch them all, but they were warned by the children. Two women with a small child ran away, but we got the other two. A man and a woman.' He laughed. 'Too old to run fast enough.'

'You killed them?'

The soldier held up his spear in answer. The iron head was dark with blood.

'Fools! I told you to take them alive. Even old slaves are better than none.'

'We thought it more important to catch the children, Captain.'

'Never mind. Get the women on their feet and let's get moving before the ones you allowed to escape find their men.'

'What should we do with all this, Captain?' the man asked, indicating the pile of blankets. They look warmer than ours.'

'Leave them for later, unless you want to run with them. Untie the women's feet… what's this?' Parak relieved the man of a short length of horn attached to a thong.

'The old man was wearing it around his neck.'

The horn had been cut off near the tip and the hollow end plugged with a tuft of animal hair. Parak removed the plug and put his finger inside. It came out covered in a sticky black substance. He wiped it off in the grass. 'It's the poison they use for their arrows.' He replaced the plug and hung the horn around his neck. 'Might come in useful. Let's get moving.'

'The women refuse to get up, Captain.'

Parak snatched the bloody spear from the soldier and prodded the first woman sharply in the buttocks, instantly drawing blood. 'Up!' he shouted at her. He prodded the other woman in the same way, even more sharply, and she cried out and scrambled to her feet, the other following. Parak reversed the spear and gave both a swipe across the buttocks with the shaft. 'Move! Move!'

They began to run and Parak herded the children after them, threatening with the spear, and they scampered after the women. Parak paused to pick up his own spear and skirt before chasing after them. 'Lead the way.' he called to one of his men. 'And keep running.'

When they were halfway to the river and crossing a stretch of open grassland, they saw four wild men running to intercept them. The women saw them too and swerved aside, but Parak beat them back into line with his spear, then changed his plans. They would have to forego their frolicking in the river for a more suitable time. 'Head for the camp!' he shouted to the man in front.

The turn away gave them extra room, but the women could not run fast enough with their hands tied behind their backs and the wild men were gaining rapidly, leaping over the rough ground with their short bows held high.

Telling the man beside him to do the same, Parak removed the wrist binding from the woman in front of him. 'Put it around her neck and hold onto it,' he panted, 'If she slows down give her a jab.' Parak set the example, pushing her forward at a faster pace. With the strip looped around her neck and wrapped in his fist, she had no chance of escape. He gave her a jab with the point of his spear to let her know he meant business.

A wide area around the base had been cleared for planting, and by the time they reached it the wild men were almost within range. Parak moved the children to the back with one of the men to discourage any long shots.

The first group of farmers they met saw quickly what was happening and joined in the flight. They had also been seen by soldiers at the base, who came forward, but still the wild men came after them.

Parak was puzzled when he glanced over his shoulder and saw only three behind. Then he saw the other one running out to the side. The man suddenly dropped to one knee and fired two arrows in quick succession at the head of the group. The first arrow fell short, but the second hit the man in front between the shoulders. He screeched but kept running, and was still running when they passed through the group of soldiers coming to meet them. Then he fell over.

'Move! Keep going!' Parak bellowed, and they ran over the fallen man, jumping clear of the thrashing legs, Parak holding his woman up by the neck and half dragging her when she tripped.

The soldiers began shooting arrows back, and the wild men stopped, then moved into the trees, their short bows no match for the larger, more powerful weapons of the soldiers. Nobody followed after them. The soldiers crowded around Parak and his men, ogling the naked, mud smeared captives. Parak ignored the questions and went to look at his fallen comrade.

He was barely moving now. Other than an occasional violent convulsion, which kept everyone well back, all he did was twitch. Watery blood ran from his mouth and nose, and his bulging eyes were glazed. The shaft of the arrow had gone, leaving only a bulge under the skin and a small wound oozing sticky, dark blood.

But it was none of those interesting things that caught Parak's attention. One of the soldier's hands was clenched and partly hidden beneath him, and Parak pulled it clear with his foot. 'Look,' he said to the curious bystanders. 'He's nearly bitten off one of his fingers.'

Ahinadab was scornful. 'Are you telling me that with a full cohort of trained soldiers under your command, you are still not able to capture or kill four naked savages?'

'Naked savages with poisoned arrows, and we never see them. They crawl around in the grass like snakes and strike when we least expect it.'

'Obviously better trained than you and your men,' sneered the overseer. 'I promoted you back to captain because I thought you would be a competent leader, but I see now I was mistaken.'

Parak smarted under the rebuke, but managed to keep his temper, even though it had become increasingly short these last ten days. 'If we let the women and children go they may leave us alone.'

The overseer impatiently waved the suggestion aside. 'You should have thought of that before you captured them and allowed your men to stupidly kill two others. Now it is too late. We have already lost four of our farmers and three of our gold seekers... not to mention the nine soldiers under your command. We cannot afford to lose any more. There are few enough already for the work we have to complete, and now the farmers are refusing to work on this side of the river. I am also tired of eating fish. I want these savages dealt with immediately'

'The men...' Parak hesitated. If he complained about the poor quality of the men given him, he would no doubt be blamed for that as well. 'The men are refusing to leave camp unless they are given armour.'

'Armour?' The overseer was incredulous. 'But we have no armour.'

'We can make some, my lord.' Parak laid a handful of arrowheads on the table between them. They had been cleaned of their poison, but still the overseer moved back and eyed them suspiciously. 'As you can see,' Parak explained. 'The detachable heads are small and only made of bone or fire-hardened wood. I have tested some and found they will not penetrate two layers of dry hide. We can make breast and back plates from the skins we already have.'

'Well, if you think it is necessary.'

Parak nodded. 'It will make it safer for the men, and we can also use the captives as bait.'

'What do you mean?'

Parak explained what he had in mind and, after his initial shock, the overseer was thoughtful. The women captives were proving a liability. Despite several beatings they still refused to work, or even to eat. All they did was lie in their pens like sick animals. They also refused to wear any of the clothing he had arranged for them, so had to be kept out of view of the men. Naked females, even though wild, would only cause trouble.

He had considered letting them go as Parak had suggested, just to be free of them, but what sort of an example would that set for the other slaves? It was better to let them starve themselves to death like they seemed intent on doing. But if Parak's plan worked, it may solve both problems.

'Take the women then,' the overseer said. 'I do not care how you do it, as long as it works and you do it quickly.'

Parak studied the two children sitting in the corner of the tent. They looked like two golden seals fresh from the water. Their heads had been shaved and their bodies glistened with oil, the scent of which, he could smell from where he stood. 'Can I take the children as well?' he asked, barely able to hide the smirk.

'The women will be sufficient,' Ahinadab answered shortly.

The river boats were so low in the water that Hallam was afraid of making any sudden turns. The bounty of their upriver exploration filled every available space. It even hung from the masts in the form of raw hides and several pairs of gracefully curved horns- all of which could be smelled from a hundred paces, as insufficient salt had been carried for the purpose of curing. The men cursed as they stumbled over piles of wild fruits, colourful stones, and the pet baby monkey - rescued when he had fallen from a tree into the water and been abandoned by the troop.

It was good-natured grumbling though. 'Best holiday I ever had,' the deck captain said to Hallam more than once.

About the only thing they didn't have was gold. The engineers had found several good sources, but it needed mining. So far, the river was still the best. But gold was the least of Hallam's concerns. His greatest find had been the cave with the paintings of the Click people hunting animals. There could be no mistaking it was them, for they were depicted as running naked with their bows held high. Unfortunately, that was the only sign he saw of them.

For much of the return journey they drifted peacefully along with the current. 'Take it easy, men,' Hallam joked. 'You well deserve a rest after all that hard work fishing, swimming, hunting and snoring.'

'Makes me exhausted just thinking about it,' commented one of the men.

'And now you want us to do even more? You're a hard man, Hallam.'

'But who are we to argue?'

'We need to find some more fruit for Badaniha.'

'What sort of a name is that?' Hallam asked.

'The opposite of Ahinadab, Pilot,' answered the man who had adopted the monkey. 'Our overseer is fat, bald and ugly, and our monkey is thin, hairy and handsome.'

The men collapsed in laughter, including Hallam, although he had to caution them about rocking the boat.

They stopped at each of the camp sites where Hallam had left knives on the way up, but none had been touched, and he was beginning to accept that he would never see the Click people again. Then as they neared the base, he did see them.

Four of them suddenly appeared on the north bank. Hallam turned the boat towards them, waving, excited at the prospect of a meeting. Kwai must have brought friends. They appeared to return his greeting, for all four raised their bows, but it was not a greeting they sent.

The four arrows streaked high across the water towards them. Hallam ducked instinctively as one hummed close over his head and plopped into the water behind. Two fell short, and one clattered amongst the horns on the mast, causing the monkey to screech with fright and leap from its perch onto one of the men. The arrow dropped into the boat, glancing off the naked back of a sailor, and he also yelled with fright.

'I'm hit! I'm hit!'

'Get down and use your paddles as a shield!' Hallam shouted. He knew how quickly the Click men could fire their deadly missiles. He swung the boat away as four more arrows splashed around them.

'Am I hit? Am I hit?'

A sailor scooped a handful of water over the frightened man's back to wash away a smear of black. 'Nothing there.'

'Your friends are not being very friendly, Pilot!' the deck captain shouted from the other boat.

'Stay close to this bank.' Hallam called back. 'It's out of range.'

'Not out of range for me, Pilot,' said one of the hunters, stringing an arrow to his bow.

'No,' Hallam said. 'No shooting back.'

The Click men stopped firing arrows. They stood looking for a moment, then vanished into the trees.

Hallam tried to recall the shape of the river ahead, and if the main channel stayed close to the south bank and out of range. He thought it did, but was taking no chances. 'Holiday over, men. Paddles in the water and give it all you've got!'

They reached the camp a short while later without further incident, and Hallam steered the boat in towards a sandbank where a group of men were digging and panning for gold. The area around the camp had changed considerably in their absence. Only a few of the larger trees remained standing on the once thickly forested bank, and large areas behind had been totally cleared. Scattered amongst the few remaining trees were the tents and new log structures of the base. No men could be seen on the cleared fields, and the only activity seemed to be on the river itself.

Hallam wasted no time with pleasantries when they reached the men on the sandbank. 'Why are the Click people trying to kill us?' he asked.

'Click people?' The man he had addressed looked puzzled. 'You mean the wild men?'

'Yes.'

The group of men laughed, but without humour. 'They're not trying, Pilot. They've already killed more than a boat-full of men.'

Hallam was shocked. 'Why?'

The man looked at his companions, hoping one of them would answer, but they only returned his looks. 'Best if you ask the overseer, Pilot.'

'I'd rather hear the truth,' Hallam said.

'You can tell the pilot,' the deck captain said. 'He's not one of the overseer's men.'

The man answered reluctantly. 'Well, it is only what we believe, Pilot, and we mean no disrespect, but we think it is because of the women captives.'

'And the two killed by the soldiers,' added one of the other men.

Hallam looked from one to the other in dismayed silence.

'The overseer should let them go,' the man continued. 'Then maybe they will leave us alone.'

One of the other men snorted in derision. 'Can you see him letting go of his pet children?'

'If the women die as well it will only make it worse.'

Hallam listened with growing consternation. Stunned by what he heard. When the men's talk turned to their adventures upriver, he sat in the boat and looked at his trembling hands. He had gone to great lengths to explain how best to handle the Click people should they return. His advice had obviously been ignored. There could be no excuse for such stupidity. Handled correctly, the Click people could have been a tremendous help to the expedition.

He saw the arrow lying where it had fallen in the bottom of the boat, partly hidden in the jumble of equipment, and picked it up, turning it around in his hands and feeling the anger building. 'Take me across to the base,' he ordered.

'What you going to do, Pilot?'

'Just take me across.'

'You need to be careful,' the deck captain warned.

'We are with you, Pilot, but we don't want to see you killed... or any of us either.'

'Drop me on the other side, then take the boats down the river and load all this stuff aboard *Piko*.'

Hallam climbed the now well trodden and unfamiliar path up the bank, and strode through the cleared forest towards the overseer's tent. The front had been rolled up against the heat, and Ahinadab was at his table, talking to a group of men standing before it. Behind the overseer stood the children, and Hallam's step faltered with his surprise.

They stood close behind Ahinadab, stirring the air above his head with reed fans. Both were draped in silk loin cloths, one in purple and one in yellow, and a heavy gold ring hung from the distended lobe of each left ear.

Ahinadab did not see Hallam until the group of men at his table suddenly parted and the black head of the arrow appeared beneath his chin. He screeched in horror, pushing as far back as he could in his chair, his eyes fixed on the arrowhead as if it were the head of a snake.

'Get out!' Hallam said to the men. He caught one of them by the arm. 'You! Let down the sides of the tent.' The man hesitated, looking at Ahinadab, and Hallam touched the underneath of the overseer's quivering chin with the point. 'Tell him.'

Ahinadab could not speak. He lifted a hand, flicking

the fingers urgently, and the man hurried to obey, cutting them off from the growing crowd outside. Hallam moved behind the table and relieved the children of their fans. They were almost as frightened as the overseer. They obviously recognised the arrow, and their eyes seldom left it as they obeyed Hallam's signals to undress and remove the earrings. Hallam tossed them contemptuously on the table, then tapped the overseer lightly on the cheek with the arrow. 'You next. Remove your robe.'

'What are you doing?' Ahinadab wheezed, 'Get out of here with that!' He flinched, as if suddenly aware he had said the wrong thing, and he was right. Hallam pulled the chair over, dumping the overseer onto the floor with his plump legs waving ungracefully in the air. Before he could recover, Hallam jerked the robe over Ahinadab's head with a ripping of cloth. He shrieked, and Hallam touched the arrow to his bulging stomach. 'Keep your mouth shut or I'll stick it in your fat gut.'

Raised voices and the scuffling of feet came from outside. The tent opening was flung aside and heads appeared. 'My Lord, what...'

'Stand back!' Hallam barked. He prodded Ahinadab. 'Get up.' When the overseer was on his feet, Hallam motioned towards the opening.

'No! I cannot...'

'Out!' He threatened with the arrow, and Ahinadab shuffled to the opening, covering himself with his hands.

'You will be executed for this! I will see you staked!'

'You won't see anything. Tell your men to stand well back and not risk your life by trying anything stupid. And remember, you slug, I do not have to stick this in you. A scratch will kill you just the same, only more slowly, and I'm sure you know by now it is not a pleasant death.' Hallam signalled to the confused children to follow, then shoved the overseer out of the tent. 'Take me to the women.' he ordered.

With the head of the arrow resting on his shoulder - close to his neck so the barbs would prick him there if he tried to run forward - Ahinadab led the way through the camp, waving urgently at the soldiers to stay back. Even had he not, it is doubtful they would have done anything. The overseer waddling naked through the camp while holding his genitals was too astonishing a sight to move them. The only stir came from those wanting a better view, particularly from the front, where the overseer's small hands were incapable of concealing the fact he had no pubic hair. And the only sound to be heard above the overseer's heavy wheezing was the occasional anonymous snigger.

'Where are we going?' Hallam asked as they left the camp and approached a newly-erected pole fence on the perimeter. A group of soldiers wearing bulky vests made of hide, and carrying shields of the same partly cured material, stood on the inside of the fence.

'The women...' Ahinadab whined, 'you said you wanted the women.'

'Out here?' Beyond the fence was only the barren ground of the cleared field.

'It was not my idea. I had nothing to do with it.'

The overseer's agitated denials sent a twinge of apprehension through Hallam. He felt his anger rising again, but the heat had gone from it, leaving it cold and purposeful. 'Where are they?' he demanded. 'Whatever has happened to them, will be your fate also.'

'There... in the field. He wanted to use them as bait. I told him it wouldn't work. It's a stupid idea. I told him!'

Hallam could see nothing in the field, only a few scattered piles of smouldering brush. 'Take me there. Tell the men to move away.'

'No! We can't go there.. it's dangerous... close to the trees.'

Hallam placed a foot on the overseers large rump and

pushed hard, and Ahinadab stumbled forward.

'We need soldiers to protect us!'

'No soldiers. Keep moving. Quickly!'

He did not see them until they were close; two small figures lying in the full sun, and his jaw tightened. 'If they are dead, so will you be.'

'If they are dead it is not my fault. They refuse to eat, even though I gave them good food. I tried to help them, but they just lie down and refuse to do anything.'

When they reached the women Hallam ordered the overseer to sit down. 'Don't move, I can run faster than you,' he warned.

They lay in a foetal position on the bare earth, and Hallam was shocked by their appearance. It looked like Shell and Berry, but they wore no distinguishing aprons, and were so thin it was difficult to tell. Their hands had been tied, even the fingers bound so they could not work on each others' knots. A length of rope tethered them to the stump of a tree. It was a futile precaution. Neither would have been able to escape anyway. Their ankles had been either broken or clubbed to prevent walking and had swollen to twice their normal size.

'You filthy pig… why?'

'I told you it was not my idea. He wanted their men to come and take them. He said they would be easier to catch if they had to be carried.'

'Who?'

'Captain Parak.'

He should have known. Suddenly his anger left him, replaced by weary resignation, as if his life had already been ordered and nothing could change it. He drew his knife and knelt to cut the ropes. The children were standing nearby, anxious and unsure, and he indicated they should come and sit with the women and talk to them. He was relieved to hear them respond, although only in whispers, but at least it showed they still had control of their senses.

'I'm sending the children back to the camp,' he told Ahinadab. 'Call to your men and tell them I want water, food, and five blankets.. and a spear,' he added.

As the overseer was shouting his orders, Hallam made the signals for eating and drinking to the children, pointing to the girl's lips. He also pointed to the camp, smiling encouragement and waving them away, and they took off at an energetic run. He went to lift one of the girls and noticed the sleek skin of her back and buttocks was latticed across with the cuts and welts. He placed one of her arms around his neck and hefted her gently over his shoulder, then he picked up the arrow and spoke to Ahinadab. 'Lift the other girl... carefully.'

'Where are we going?'

Hallam inclined his head towards the nearby trees. 'Into the shade.'

'It is madness! They will kill us if we go in there.'

Hallam reversed the arrow and moved towards him, and Ahinadab scrambled to get out of his way, but he was not quick enough to avoid two swipes across his naked back, and another on the buttocks as he stumbled forward to pick up the girl. Wheezing with the effort, although she could not have weighed more than a talent, Ahinadab held her in both arms and staggered after Hallam, hastening to stay close behind the shield of his body.

Hallam did not go far into the trees. He wanted to keep a clear view of the base and the open field. The girl seemed comfortable on his shoulder, so he left her there while he stood and waited for the return of the children. He made the sweating overseer sit down with the other girl on his lap to protest her lacerated back from the rough ground.

When the children arrived with their load, he laid the girls on a blanket in the shade and lifted their heads on to the laps of the children. He gave them water, trickling it between their parched lips, then poured some over their heads. It almost sizzled as it ran over their burning skin.

Ahinadab stayed close, crouching and searching fearfully through the trees. 'What now,' he whined. 'I have done everything you wanted. What are you going to do with me?'

'Nothing,' Hallam said. 'Go.'

'What?' The overseer looked confused, as if Hallam had just made another impossible demand.

'You can leave,' Hallam repeated. 'Get out of my sight before I change my mind and kill you. And don't send any soldiers unless you want me to come and do it.'

Hallam watched the overseer's grotesque retreat, then covered the girls with a blanket and instructed the children with signs to give them food and water, and to talk to them. While they were thus occupied, he went into the field and brought back a smouldering log for a fire. He got it going then searched around for four branches of equal thickness and length, and began trimming them with his knife.

By dusk, he had made two rough but serviceable stretchers from the poles and remaining blankets. He lifted the girls into them to be sure they were right, then settled himself with his back against a tree and the spear at his side to wait. A spear was little protection against the wild animals of this country, and none against the Click people, but in a desperate situation even a single claw was better than none.

To pass the time he thought of the people he loved in his life, and his mood began to soften. He began to sing in a croaky, unpractised voice, hoping to stir memories in the minds of the two Click girls with the song the twins had tried so unsuccessfully to teach them:

'This is the sound the donkey makes; hee-haw, hee-haw.
   But what does the donkey say? He says....'

He gave up, his voice sounding foreign and raucous in his ears, and his heart not in it, but no sooner had he stopped when he was surprised by a giggle. He turned to look at the children. They were looking back at him with startled expressions, but it was not from them that the giggle had come. It was one of the women, although he could not tell which, as both had their heads turned away. 'Sorry, but it's the best I can do.' He patted them both affectionately on the head to express his relief.

He was still awake as dawn began to break, but he was not the only one. A movement under the blanket next to him caught his attention and he watched as one of the girls sat up. She sat still for a long time, coming awake and looking up at the sky, then she leaned across to wake the girl beside her. Some urgent whispering took place, then the other girl also sat up to look at the sky. Hallam followed their gaze but could see nothing, only the morning star shining bright above the trees.

They spoke in whispers for a while, then the girl who had awoken first suddenly placed a hand on the other to stop her talking. She appeared to be listening, and Hallam listened too, his nerves beginning to jump, but he heard nothing. Suddenly, the girl spoke out loud, causing Hallam to start. The other did the same, calling excitedly into the bush. The children sat up and the girls urged them to speak as well, and they added their voices, squeaky with excitement, to the one way conversation.

Six of the Click people appeared out of the dark, four men and two women, one of them holding a child, the sight of which, elicited small cries of endearment from one of the women beside him, and Hallam surmised it must be the boy named Baba, which Jemma and Sophi had tried so hard to spoil. He raised his hand in greeting but no hand was raised in return.

Isolated, he stood by and listened to them talking, the men asking questions in their direct, demanding way, and the women answering softly, almost apologetically. There were several long pauses, filled with the sympathetic clicking of tongues and, although their language was incomprehensible, the expressions of joy, relief and distress in the tone were painfully familiar to Hallam, and it saddened him deeply to be excluded from these people he had come to think of as friends. It was painfully obvious they no longer thought of him the same way.

Eventually, the men came forward and lifted the stretchers with their injured occupants, and Hallam recognised Kwai. He searched the faces of the strangers for that of the old man, but he was not among them, and neither did he see the old woman. He raised a hand, smiling a greeting, but Kwai refused to give him even a glance. He may as well not have been there.

Silently, the Click people departed, and Hallam watched their small figures fade into the pre-dawn greyness with deep regret and shame. They had given kindness and understanding, yet had received only cruelty in return. It was not they who were the wild savages. Suddenly he felt more alone than he had ever felt in his life.

Hallam knew he could not return to the base. Ahinadab would want his blood. They needed him to take the boats home, but he was not prepared to gamble that need against the indignities he had put the overseer through in front of his men. The pleasure of killing Parak would have to wait.

He skirted the camp, walking a long way through the bush before turning towards the river. When he reached it, he stood on a sandbank and whistled to attract the attention of a fishing boat on the far side, and it came reluctantly.

'You should not be on this side, Pilot,' the helmsman said, urgently waving him aboard. 'It is dangerous.'

'Don't worry, the Click people won't be bothering you again,' Hallam reassured him. They've gone for good. How much fish do you have under those reeds?'

'More than any of us would like to eat, I can tell you.'

'Good. I'll take the lot.'

The boat took him to *Piko,* where the deck captain greeted him with a relieved grin. 'Wasn't sure if we would be seeing you again, Pilot.'

'Sorry to disappoint you, Captain. Get the men to load this fish aboard, then prepare to sail. Also, find Pilot Meldek and bring him here... as quick as you can.'

'What's happening, Pilot?'

'Nothing you won't enjoy, Captain. We're going on another holiday.'

It was much bigger than River Saba. The mouth was wider, the islands larger, the channels deeper, and even the trees, once they had sailed clear of the mangroves, seemed taller. They sailed up it for three days before going ashore to hunt and explore. The mountains were closer, but still too far to reach without one of the river boats, which they had been forced to leave behind. They found no trace of gold, which Hallam considered no disadvantage, and no sign of Click people. They provisioned the boat with meat and left, Hallam promising himself he would one day return and explore the great river at leisure.

They continued north, hugging the coast and fighting the current until they reached the island of coconuts. Hallam sailed *Piko* into the same lagoon where he had spent so many happy days with Phineas and the girls. It was where he had agreed to wait for Meldek and the boats that would be returning, but that was still a good ten days away.

'Ever tasted lobster cooked in coconut milk, Captain?'

'Can't say I have, Pilot,' the deck captain answered with a grin. 'But it sounds to me like you are going to put us through some more terrible hardships.'

Parak could not believe his good fortune. 'You are sending me home?'

'Do not misunderstand me, Parak. It is not for you I am doing it. I have not forgotten that it was because of your stupidity we had all those problems with the wild savages, and what nearly got me killed. It will be a pleasure to see you go, but it is not for me either. It is for the king.'

Parak raised his eyebrows in surprise. 'The king?'

'He instructed me that if we found gold here it was to remain ours. He does not want the Sabaen dogs sniffing around and getting in the way.'

Ahinadab sat back with a smug expression, knowing he would have to explain further, but wanting to savour what was to come. He had waited a long time for this moment and was going to enjoy it to the full.

'I don't understand, my lord.'

Ahinadab smiled. 'That pilot...' He could not bring himself to say his name. 'The one who brought us... has already promised to lead a Sabaen expedition here. The king does not want that to happen, Parak, so you will have the honour of preventing it. You are to travel with the boats that are returning and kill the pilot as soon as you reach India, or at least before he can reach Saba. Until then, you must take pains to stay out of his way. I believe you have a few scores to settle with him?'

Parak grinned. 'It will not only be an honour but a pleasure, my lord.'

'And if you can arrange that he dies painfully.. as he would with one of the poisoned arrows that I'm sure you still have... so much the better.'

'I will stick it in his gut, as he threatened to do with you, my lord, and I won't give him the full amount, but only half, so it will take longer. I want to see the offal bite *all* his fingers off before he dies, not only one.'

Ahinadab smiled dreamily. 'Yes, that would be perfect.'

Ten boats sailed from River Saba on the return journey. Those remaining would be enough to remove all the men left behind should, if the gods so decide, no others arrive within two years. Meldek gave the remaining pilots Hallam's sailing instructions on the day he himself left, and they had been as surprised as he had by the simplicity of them.

'He told us the return voyage was much more complicated than that,' one of the pilots commented indignantly.

'He lied,' Meldek said with a smile, repeating almost exactly what Hallam had said to him. 'He has enemies here and wanted to be sure of returning home, and I'm sure most of you would have done the same. You should be relieved.'

'That we are, Meldek, but speaking for myself, I would have had a lot more sleep had I known earlier.'

For reasons of safety, the gold so far recovered from the river - some four talents in all - was divided equally among the returning boats. Meldek brought *Piko's* share aboard when he met up with Hallam at the coconut island.

After discussing the return voyage, two of the pilots said

they were going to continue sailing up the coast as they had been doing. 'I see no reason to go all the way to India,' one of them stated. 'By staying close to the shore we can reach the Arabian Sea at least two months before you, and be home that much earlier.'

'Try if you wish,' Hallam said. 'It is not for me to tell you what to do, only what I am going to do. But the current is strong and the reefs many. The summer storms close to land are fierce. I prefer more sea room and to put my trust in the winds.'

It was fortunate that most of the pilots agreed with Hallam, for neither of the two boats that attempted to sail up the coast arrived home.

With room to spare, and experienced sailors at the helm, the boats that stayed with *Piko* ran before the storms, and although they also suffered, it was mainly from sickness, for many of the sailors refused to eat Hallam's suggested daily dose of sour seeds, and two of those died. No boats were lost though. They sailed together into the Bay of Suhar and reached the new Ophir barely a month after leaving River Saba.

The arrival of the boats at Ophir caused consternation amongst the populace and wild panic at the palace.

'Your magnificent majesty! You must go quickly! We are being attacked by pirates!'

The cry brought the Rajah of Suhar running from his palace with the half-eaten leg of a peacock still clutched in his fist. He stared in horror. Eight large boats were coming across the bay towards his city. Men were waving from the mast-tops, obviously directing the ships into the attack.

Rajah dropped the leg and ran back into the palace, shouting to his servants. 'Quickly! Collect the palace treasure and alert the guards! Follow me into the forest!'

'Majesty, your wives...'

'Yes! Yes! Tell them to hurry!'

By the time the first boat dropped its anchor the city was deserted.

'Where is everybody?' asked a puzzled Meldek. 'A short while ago there were people running and shouting everywhere.'

'A very excitable bunch,' Hallam answered. 'Probably think they are being invaded.'

When it became apparent that no one was coming to meet them, Hallam ordered the anchor lifted again. With the aid of the two emergency oars he nudged *Piko* through the clutter of outriggers and pulled alongside the bamboo jetty.

From a tall tree in the forest, a lookout passed the information to Rajah below. ''The boats are anchored, your magnificence! Only one has come in. Two men are walking up the hill to the palace.'

'Only two? Are they armed?'

'No. They are talking to the old mad woman... she is pointing. I think they are waving at us. Must I wave back?'

'No, you crazy mad person!' The Rajah spoke to one of his servants. 'Go and see what they want.'

'But, Majesty, surely it would be better if we wait...'

'Am I surrounded by cowards and fools? They may be important guests and you are keeping them waiting. Go! Go!'

Once the good news was spread that it was not pirates, the city returned almost as rapidly as it had disappeared. Rajah was effusive in his apologies, his joy at discovering who the sailors were heightened by relief. 'I should have looked for myself,' he cried, holding Hallam's hand and all but wringing it free of blood. 'I would have seen immediately it was not pirates but the honoured and trusted pilot Hallam, friend of the princesses of Saba. The very ones after which my beautiful clean city is named. We will have a great feast for all the pilots. I long to hear of your voyage.'

The Rajah ordered boats sent immediately to ferry the crews, and instructed they were not to be cheated, on pain of death. 'Most honest city in all of India,' he boasted to Meldek. 'I am sure King Solomon will be very impressed when you tell him.'

It was the first time since Coconut Island that all the pilots were together in one place. A festive atmosphere, thick with the heady aroma of sweet wine, pervaded Rajah's feast. Now they could relax. From here it was plain sailing, and they could enjoy what all agreed was an outstanding success. The Sea of Zeng had been conquered, and with it, their fears of the unknown. They shared an elite brotherhood. Old grievances were forgotten, sailing secrets proudly exposed, and vows of eternal friendship declared. Hallam's back was slapped so many times he spilled more wine than he was able to drink and finished the evening sober, for which he was grateful, as his head was troubled enough without being dulled by wine.

Any one of the pilots could now take boats to River Saba. His usefulness to Solomon had ended, and he did not believe for a moment that the king would keep his word and leave him free to take the Sabaens there. Why would he, when he could keep all the gold for himself?

Meldek had told him that Solomon had ordered the pilots to give Saba a wide berth, and the reason was obvious to Hallam. Solomon did not want any of his pilots defecting or falling into Sabaen hands - as he had fallen into Solomon's.

Hallam had given the problem a lot of thought on the return trip, and knew what he had to do, but he was reluctant to do it. Reaching Saba was not difficult. It was a long voyage from India, and the boats would need provisioning along the way. And as they could not stop at Saba, they would have to stop at one of the first Egyptian ports. All he had to do was disappear there until the boats left, then buy passage across the Narrow Sea to Mocha on one of the many pedlar boats. Once there he would be safe, even from Solomon, but to do that he would have to sacrifice *Piko*. She would sail on to Ezion-Geber and he would never see her again.

It was one of the hardest decision Hallam had ever had to make. *Piko* was more than just a boat, she had become a part of him, and he felt a strong sense of betrayal at even thinking of deserting her.

With nothing much to do but wait for the change of wind, Hallam kept himself and the crew busy with maintenance and repairs. He anchored *Piko* apart from the other boats, rather than beach her, and threw himself into the physical work while he agonised over his dilemma. But in the end, he came to accept there was no alternative, and reluctantly began planning his defection.

All the pilots, including Hallam, had taken up Rajah's offer of accommodation at the palace. The opportunity to indulge in a bit of luxury did not come that often, and having to listen to the endless triumphs of Rajah over his rival in Barigaza was a fair exchange for the good food. But now Hallam returned to sleep aboard, giving the excuse of work to be done, but in reality because he wanted to be alone with *Piko*.

The crew spent most of their nights in more congenial places ashore, taking turns at watch duty - a necessary precaution against thieves, for each boat still held its contingent share of gold. Hallam took to doing many of the watchman's duties himself.

With the unpredictable movements of the crew, he was

not surprised when, late one night as he lay awake on his mat, he heard the splash of oars as one of the small tubs used for ferrying the crews rowed across from the jetty. Neither was he surprised at the drunken stumbling and muttered curses as the lone man came aboard. It was only when he sat up to silence him and saw who it was, that he received an unpleasant shock.

He reached for his spear, which normally lay at his side, then remembered with another stab of alarm that he had left it leaning against the mast - well out of reach.

'Is this what you're looking for?' Parak asked. He moved quickly to pick up the spear, and Hallam crouched in readiness, moving to try and put the mast between them. But Parak tossed the spear contemptuously over the side. 'Or is it this?' He ginned and held up one of the small poisoned arrows of the Click people. 'You left it behind, so Ahinadab sent me to give it back to you... in the gut.'

Hallam edged towards the side of the boat, to where Parak had left the tub, planning to jump over and use it as a shield as he swam away. He reached for his knife, then realised he had taken it off to lie down.

Parak laughed. 'Forgotten something else? You make it too easy, Offal.'

Hallam tensed himself to jump, but Parak blocked him, using the arrow as if it were a sword. 'Don't be in such a hurry to leave, Offal, we have plenty of time to enjoy ourselves.'

'You hairy Cilician ape. What animal did your mother rut with to conceive you?' Without a weapon, getting Parak angry was the only defence he could think of.

'Say what you like,' Parak sneered. 'It will only make watching you die more pleasurable.' He feinted with the arrow and laughed as Hallam jumped back. 'I want to tell you all about the little noble whore I have waiting for me in Edom. I know where she is, Offal. It's going to be a pleasure to see her again.'

'Your mother must have taught you the spear and the sword as well,' Hallam goaded. 'Is that the best you can do? You dance around like a woman.'

Parak lunged again, but this time, Hallam did not jump back. He sprang to the side and, with the Cilician's arm at full stretch, caught the shaft of the arrow. At the same time he struck at Parak's face, but he was too close for his blows to be effective and Parak simply ignored them. His free hand caught Hallam by the throat and drove him back against the rail.

'How do you like *this* dance, Offal?' Parak hissed. He squeezed, forcing Hallam's head back and arching his spine over the rail.

Hallam held onto the rail with one hand, the other gripping the arrow. He could feel the smooth wood slipping in his palm as Parak pulled on it, and he tried to snap the slender shaft, but his grip was still too close to that of Parak's and without leverage. He removed his hand from the rail to use both on the arrow, but Parak was quicker. He released his grip on Hallam's throat, put his knee against the stanchion for support and, with a grunt of effort, jerked on the shaft with both hands, pulling it through Hallam's sweaty grip and leaving the detachable head behind, stuck in his palm.

With the sudden release of his grip, Hallam toppled back over the rail. He felt the sting of the barb in his flesh and lifted his hand to see the head clinging to his palm like some venomous black spider. He flicked his hand in horror as he fell, tearing the barb free, before crashing into the tub, landing heavily on his shoulder and hearing the soft crack of bone. The bows of the small craft pushed under, shipping water, and the frayed painter rope snapped. Rocking dangerously, the tub drifted away from *Piko's* side towards the open sea.

Panting with the exertion, Parak glared after the rocking tub, lifting himself on the rail so he could look down on the squirming glassmaker as he thumped around in the bottom, and holding his own raucous breath to better hear the groans of agony that accompanied the writhing.

When he could no longer see into the tub, Parak threw the bare shaft of the arrow after it and slapped his hand on the rail in frustration. He had wanted to watch closely the satisfying end he had planned for so long. He would also have to swim ashore and he did not like the water. Then he laughed. The tub was still rocking violently and, although he could not see the glassmaker's agony, he could clearly hear the sounds of it. 'That's right, Offal,' he called out. 'Bite them off!'

Ismail Sulemani's cousin, Jusab, stood up in the outrigger to get a better view onto the deck of the boat they were approaching. He had been told it was deserted, but it was best to be sure. When he noticed his two companions were also looking, he whispered urgently to them. 'Kassim! Hamid! Why are you looking? I must do the looking. You must pretend the fishing. Throw again the net on that side and pull to bring us closer.'

Jusab remained standing until the outrigger had been slowly hauled to the far side of the boat where it was hidden from the jetty. He caught onto the rail and climbed swiftly aboard. 'Wait here.' he whispered unnecessarily.

The deck was clear, all the ropes neatly coiled, and the hatch sealed. Jusab padded up to the wall of the raised steering deck. A sleeping mat, blanket, sea bag and knife lay beside a partly open vertical hatch in the wall. He felt around inside the hatch. Nothing but more sea bags and iron pots. He crawled in, searching well behind the pots and came on a large bag of a different shape. It was heavy, and the neck of the bag was securely tied. He dragged it out and handed it over the rail to the waiting hands, then he hesitated, looking speculatively at the open hatch and the good things inside, but shook his head, realising there was barely enough room in the narrow outrigger for what he already had.

When they were safely away from the boat, Jusab untied the neck of the bag and peered inside.

'What, Jusab?' asked Kassim. 'What is inside?'

'Coconuts,' Jusab answered shortly, pushing the bag away in disgust. 'Only stinking coconuts.'

The entire city of Ophir was mobilised to search for the pilot. A distraught Rajah even offered a handsome reward. No one had ever disappeared in Ophir before, he assured Meldek. It could only be the work of the jealous Rajah of Barigaza seeking to ruin his enviable reputation.

Someone suggested the pilot may have fallen from his boat and drowned, so Rajah himself conducted the underwater search, standing at the end of the jetty and ordering everyone who could swim to jump in and feel along the bottom all the way to the pilot's boat. All they found was slimy rubbish and a spear.

Only Parak was not surprised by the pilot's strange disappearance. He had seen the tub drifting out into the bay, and the way it had been rocking left him in no doubt it had sunk, taking the glassmaker with it.

Nevertheless, years of experience as a guard had taught him never to overlook the obvious, so while the Rajah was conducting his search, Parak had one of his own, looking at all the small tubs around the jetty, and in particular for one that had a paddle with a split handle bound up with coarse fibre. But the boat was not there, or anywhere along the beach.

Rajah, with the help of his people and the men from the expedition, continued the search for several days, even delaying the departure of the boats, but no trace of the pilot was found.

Sulemani looked at the coconut he held in his hands with an expression that told he knew it was supposed to be a joke, but did not quite get the point of it. 'You wish to pay only with coconuts?'

'One now and another when you get the boat. Then two more when we arrive.'

Sulemani managed a weak laugh. 'You a very funny person.'

'Why don't you open it?'

Reluctantly going along with the joke, Sulemani cracked the inner shell of the husk against a rock, then prised it apart with the point of his knife. His disdainful expression changed to one of astonishment. He placed the pieces down carefully then looked up, smiling and shaking his head in admiration. 'You very clever person. Very, very clever.'

'You agree then?'

Sulemani nodded, his attention already drawn back to the

glittering contents of the coconut. 'My cousin will bring the boat tomorrow.'

'You can trust him fully?'

Sulemani looked hurt. 'My heart is saddened. Very saddened that you ask a question of my trust in such a thing. In all of India there is not more honest persons than the Sulemani's. You must ask anyone.'

'And I am sure they will agree, but it is not you or your cousins I question. There will be many other people in your cousin's village. He will have to make preparations, and some may ask the reason.'

'But he has done it many times. Many, many times, and who is to know?' Sulemani feigned a surprised expression. 'No one, of course!'

'Will you be coming?'

'Yes, yes, naturally. Also three of my most trusted cousins. You will pay in gold?' Before he could receive an answer, Sulemani raised a hand and wagged an admonishing finger at himself, smiling craftily. 'Of course, I mean coconuts.'

'Enough to buy the boat twice over, I'm sure.'

The provisioning port of Zeilah, which had been the expedition's first stop on the voyage out, was also to be the last stop on the return to Ezion-Geber, and the boat crews were in high spirits. They would be hailed as heroes, and each had been promised a full year's wages over and above what he had already earned. The Narrow Sea was almost as good as being home, and they were in the mood to celebrate.

Parak was in a good mood himself. His own coffers had run perilously low, and he could do with the bonus. Ahinadab had promised that the king would also reward him for taking care of the pilot and this, added to the gold he had managed to collect while supervising some of the river panning, would set him up well to continue his search.

And this time he knew where to find her. Seeing her as he was about to leave had been a cruel twist, but the tide had turned. Dressing in peasant clothes and using a baby as a disguise had been a clever ruse, but she had given herself away by leaving the crowd with her hair uncovered, and from the elevated deck of the boat he had seen her take a path up the mountain, leading a donkey. Then he had also seen the big ugly man who had claimed she was his wife leaving the same way, his mules loaded with fruit. Wherever they were going, it would not be far. A few questions asked in the right place would tell him where to find the man with the mules, and would also lead him to Philippa. The reward she had promised was as good as in his hands.

Zeilah boasted only one tavern, and it was filled to bursting with men from the boats. So too, the queue for the prostitutes, so Parak bought a jar of beer instead, and was pushing his way through the noisy crowd when he heard a name that made him pause. The man who spoke it was the deck captain of the dead glassmaker's boat, and he had a voice that could easily be used as a warning in a fog. He was speaking to the chief pilot, Meldek, and Parak turned his back to them, edging closer.

'....only a few days from here to Mocha, and he has a good boat for an Egyptian. Goes there often, he says… so should have… soon.... unless Lord Shan away...'

'What if he is?'

'... leave... in safe hands... Egyptian tomorrow before he sails. Don't know about you... this worst... ever tasted.'

'... beer… myself... good either.'

Parak moved away, puzzled by what he had heard. Why had they mentioned the glassmaker's name? And what was important about an Egyptian boat and Mocha? It sounded as if the two men were sending something there. But what?

Taking his jar of beer with him, Parak left the tavern and wandered across to one of the better stalls where he spoke to the merchant owner. 'Do you know a Lord Shan who lives in Mocha?' he asked.

'Everyone knows Lord Shan,' the merchant answered. 'I have some good goat cheese from Mocha if you would like to taste.'

'What does he do?'

'Lord Shan? He is vizier for trade in Saba. Look at this turquoise. Have you ever seen better?'

Parak ignored him and walked away thoughtfully. The chief pilot himself had ordered that no one was to have contact with Saba, so what could he be sending to the Sabaen vizier for trade? He began to get the distinct feeling that something was going on that he should know about, and that maybe even the king should know about.

Still carrying his jar of beer, which gave him the look of a casual observer with nothing better to do, Parak went to that section of the beach used by the locals. Only three boats looked capable of sailing across the Narrow Sea, and he learned from a fisherman that one was in fact leaving the next day.

It was a gamble, but the feeling that something illegal was going on would not go away. He returned to the boat and collected his sea bag and blanket roll, truthfully telling one of the other soldiers that he was sleeping ashore for the night.

He slept on the beach within sight of the Egyptian boat, and was awake when Meldek and the deck captain arrived. Their movements were crucial. If they waited to see the boat off, he would have to hire one of the fishing boats to try and catch up with it, which would be risky, and no doubt expensive.

Fortunately, they did not. Meldek spoke to the Egyptian

pilot for a while, handed him a leather message tube, and they left.

Parak waited until the boat was about to leave before running down the beach.

'There has been a change of plan,' he explained breathlessly to the surprised Egyptian pilot. 'I have been ordered to go with you and deliver the message to Lord Shan myself.'

'Why is it so? I was told nothing of this...'

'It is not because the pilot doesn't trust you, it is only because of the importance of the message.' Parak handed him a small bag of his precious silver. 'He asked me to give you this in payment for your trouble... If you will give me the message tube...'

While the Egyptian was occupied with getting the boat ready, Parak surreptitiously ripped off the seal and removed the single rolled sheet of papyri. He read it carefully, then read it again, not believing.

Parak replaced the message carefully in the tube, thanking the gods for his suspicious nature. It did not seem possible, but the proof was in his hands. The king would be extremely interested to see the message, and to know his chief pilot was a traitor. He would also, no doubt, be extremely grateful.

The mule man led his two animals more slowly than usual up the final rocky ridge before the village, reluctant to impart the bad news he carried. He passed by the cottage of the woman, hoping she would not see him, but he was unable to escape the sharp eyes of the boy.

He came running from the cottage with his hands held ready for a lift. 'Mule Man! Mule Man!'

His mother was close behind and, with a sigh of resignation, the mule man lifted the boy onto the front mule and waited for the questions he knew she would ask - and which he knew he must answer. She would know by now, as would the whole village, for they must have seen the boats from the cliff-top.

'You saw the boats?' she asked breathlessly.

The mule man nodded, busying himself unnecessarily with holding her son on the mule.

'And? What is the news... is he there?'

The mule man shook his head. 'No, mistress, I'm sorry. He did not arrive with the boats.'

'Oh...' She turned and walked away a few steps, then turned back. 'Did you ask? Do you know... anything else?'

The mule man shifted uncomfortably. 'They say he *was* with the boats, Mistress Keziah, but he did not arrive with them.'

'I don't understand...'

'There is talk he disappeared in India.'

'*Disappeared*?'

The mule man knew she was staring at him, but he could not look back at her. 'I'm sorry, mistress. They searched... a whole week. Some say he fell from the boat and was drowned, others say he did not want to return to Ezion-Geber as he feared the king.'

She began to walk away, then returned for her son. 'Come, Jonathan. We must go now...'

Jonathan began to complain and the mule man intervened. 'Let me take him for a while, mistress. He likes to be with the mules. I can bring him back on the donkey, if you wish...'

She walked away without answering, tripping on the rough ground and falling to her knees, and the mule man snatched the boy off the mule so he could go to her aid, but she was up before he could get there and hurried on without looking back.

They would not allow her to leave on her own, and were reluctant to let her go at all. With the mule already loaded with the few belonging she and Milcah had accumulated during their stay, and with Jonathan sitting precariously astride the donkey and trying to urge it on with vigorous kicking, the villagers still tried to dissuade her.

'At least you should wait for the prince to return,' the farmer from whom she had rented the cottage persisted. He was also the headman of the village, and spoke for all those who had gathered to see her off. They leaned shamelessly on Jonathan for support.

'Who will play with Zora when Joni is gone?' asked a young woman. She was only a little older than Philippa, and the children had brought them together in friendship.

'You should stay. Soon we will be free again and Joni will have a good future with Prince Hadad as his guardian. He thinks of Joni as his own. Surely, you must wait...'

'You still have rent already paid. If it is too much I will reduce it.'

'It will be us the prince will blame if you leave... and if something bad should happen to you or Joni... he will not forgive us.'

Philippa looked fondly at the people she had come to love, and her voice was thick when she answered. In Tyre she had never known that such people existed. 'No, it is time for me to go. It is not easy to leave such wonderful friends, but perhaps I can help your cause. My uncle has much influence with King Solomon, and now that Lord Arumah has taken another wife...'

The mule man took them down to Ezion-Geber; to the square on the edge of the city from where the caravans arrived and departed to and from Canaan, Egypt and Arabia. He waited until Philippa had spoken to the agents and confirmed the passage before leaving, and he left the donkey as a parting gift for Jonathan. 'They belong together,' he explained gruffly.

Of all the inducements Philippa had received to persuade her to stay, it was the one that came closest to changing her mind.

With time to spare, they sat in the shade to wait, but Philippa could not sit still. 'I want to see his boat again, Milcah. Maybe I can talk to some of the men that were with him. Stay with Jonathan. I won't be long.'

'Do you think it is a good idea, mistress? It would be safer if you stayed or we came with you.'

'It doesn't really matter any more, Milcah. We are returning to Tyre anyway.'

'But mistress…'

'No, Milcah, I want to be alone.'

Many of the boats had been returned to their owners, and men were already busy loading them with trading goods. Groups of workers were also beginning to extend the far end of the wharf in readiness for the boats that were being built for King Solomon by her uncle. It was rumoured that a fleet of three hundred were to sail to the river of gold.

Philippa found the one with the horse's head beached on its own at the other end of the wharf. It looked deserted. A ramp with strips of wood nailed across as grips was laid against the rail and, after a quick look around, Philippa climbed it and stepped onto the deck.

It was quite different from her Uncle Khiram's sleek boat. The deck was strewn with tools, pots of pitch and lengths of timber. The hatch was open and she peered into the gloom. It smelled musty and damp. She climbed onto the raised steering deck and looked at the tiller handles. They were worn smooth and darkened with sweat. His hands and his sweat. She took hold of them and looked out past the horse's head, trying to imagine what it had been like for him, steering the boat through a strange sea to a strange land. What had been his thoughts, she wondered, as he stood holding these handles? He would have had moments of fear, surely. Perhaps the same fear of the unknown as she was experiencing at this very moment.

Philippa left the tiller and walked the length of the deck to the horse's head. No trace remained of the oil she had seen him rubbing on it. The wood was cracked and bleached almost white from the sun and salt. It was the ugliest head she had ever seen. She ran a hand lovingly over the cracked surface and the deformed ear, feeling the emotion welling up within her, and suddenly she could stay no longer. She turned abruptly and bumped into a man who was standing close behind. Before Philippa could resist, he pulled back the hood to reveal her hair, then he chuckled with delight.

'Ah, what a pleasure it is to see you again, Lady Philippa.'

The horse plodded slowly up the sandy bank of the wadi and came to a halt of its own accord with a tired, rumbling snort. Its rider dismounted with a groan of relief. 'I know how you feel.' He slid a hand along the muscular neck, feeling the coarseness of sand stuck to sweat as he lifted off the string of water calabashes. He wet a corner of his *kufiyeh* and wiped the clogged sand from the horse's nostrils. 'Not far to go now.'

While they both rested and drank, he looked back the way they had come. But for the red colour, it was not unlike the sea. An unforgiving, endless expanse of featureless red earth carved into waves by the wind. The men who travelled it, he thought, were also not unlike those of the sea; weather-beaten and tough, forged by heat and tempered by cold. He was glad to have met them, but happy to be alone again.

Leading the horse, he climbed slowly through the foothills, past an increasing number of small villages, until he reached the top and saw the sea for the first time in almost three months. He stopped for a while to look out and breath deeply of the salty tang, and his spirits lifted. He mounted awkwardly, his shoulder and neck still stiff from the fall, although the pain had mostly now gone. The barb from the poisoned arrow-head had caused much less pain, and the small scar had all but disappeared. Either the barb itself had been free of poison, or his vigorous sucking in the bottom of the boat had drawn it out.

With a final look at the sea, he set the horse on the track down the hill towards the white buildings of Mocha.

They sat on the roof-garden of Lord Shan's two-storey house; the girls cross-legged on cushions, and he with his back against the wall in the sun. Phineas hovered nearby. It was like old times, except that he was doing most of the talking.

'I tried singing your song... you know... the one about the donkey, and I heard one of them giggle, so I knew they were all right.'

Sophira turned her head away to blow noisily into a small square of silk. 'Oh, Hallam... I wish I could have been there to help them.'

'Me too,' said Jemma. 'What a horrible man to do such a thing!'

'Were you not afraid?'

'To start with I was too angry, but when the Click men came sneaking up, I was so scared I nearly wet myself.'

'Tell us again about when you...'

'Later. I think it is your turn now. Tell me what you've been doing. Have you seen much of the queen?'

'Oh, yes,' Jemma said. 'We were with her only a short while ago, when her child was born.'

'The queen has a child?' Hallam sat forward, unable to keep the excitement from his voice.

'Should I fetch some more sherbet, mistress?' Phineas asked. He picked up the silver flask without waiting for a reply and hurried towards the stairs. The girls glanced at each other, smiling secretively.

'She had a girl.' Sophi said.

'Looks just like you,' Jemma added, and both girls giggled.

'What do you mean?' Hallam asked, flustered, but unable to hide his grin of delight.

'You were a very naughty man to take advantage of our queen like that, Hallam.'

'Listen, you two... I don't know where you get all this, but I can see you haven't changed a bit.'

Jemma pointed with a thumb over her shoulder towards the stairs. 'He told us. We tricked him into it. She spent the whole night with you, didn't she? Really, Hallam! I'm surprised she did not have twins like us.'

'Jemma, I'm warning you...'

'We can arrange for you to see your daughter if you wish.'

'You can? But I thought I wasn't supposed to...'

'So it *is* true!'

Hallam looked from one to the other in bewilderment. 'Is this another one of your games?'

They nodded in unison, snorting with suppressed laughter, and Hallam grinned in defeat. 'You are terrible... both of you.'

'Sarah will be coming to live with us as soon as the queen

returns to the palace,' Sophi informed him. 'As cousins, Jemma and I will look after her, so you must be nice to us or we won't let you hold her.'

'Sarah... it's a pretty name.'

'It means, "the princess",' explained Sophi.

Jemma began nervously picking at her fingers. 'Maybe we should ask him now, Sophi.'

Sophi shrugged, then blushed, occupying herself with studiously nibbling a fingernail.

'Ask me what?'

Jemma pulled Sophi's hand away and held it. She too was looking suspiciously pinker around the ears, but her eyes were steady when she looked at Hallam. 'Sophi and me. We decided that when you came back we would ask you if... well... we both like you, so we decided if you wanted to take us as your wives, we wouldn't mind.'

Hallam stared at Jemma with his mouth open.

'That is, if you like us as well,' Sophi added.

Hallam switched his stare to Sophi. 'What is this...?'

They both looked down and shook their heads, their expressions serious. 'No, we mean it,' said Jemma.

'But...' Hallam was dumbfounded. He loved them both. They were his dearest friends, and both had grown in the time he had been away. They were taller, and firm muscle showed where before had been only girlish flesh. Their faces were thinner and their bodies more shapely, looking even more like the queen. They were no longer girls but young women. Beautiful young women.

'Does your father know about this... this idea of yours?

'Father won't mind, he likes you.'

Had he not been so close to them, Hallam may have been tempted. They were clever, beautiful and rich, and would make wonderful wives, but although he saw them as women, he still thought of them as his girls. It would be like marrying his own sisters.

'It is the greatest honour I have ever received,' Hallam said sincerely. 'I love you both, but I value our friendship too much to take advantage of your tempting offer. You both deserve more than a friend for a husband.'

'Cannot a husband also be friend?'

'Yes, it is essential, but when you find someone you *really* love, you will know what I mean.'

Jemma sighed forlornly. 'I knew you would say something like that. We couldn't trick him that time, Sophi.'

'When are you going to find the one *you* really love, Hallam?'

'Maybe I never will Sophi. She left Tyre and nobody knows where she went. She may even be dead by now.'

'Oh, Hallam! Why didn't you tell us? It's that woman you told us about, isn't it? What's her name? I can't remember it.'

'Philippa.'

'Yes! We must send Phineas to look for her right away.'

'No, he will be wasting his time and it's too dangerous. I'll go myself when your father returns. I have friends who may be able to help.' Hallam got up to sit between them. He hugged them close. 'Promise me that neither of you will ever change, and when you do find someone you love, I want to see them first... to warn them.'

He ducked as a bombardment of cushions descended on his head.

It was a good morning to be alive. The horse snickered softly as he approached the stables with a pail of grain, the girls sung cheerily as they went about their tasks in the house - apparently not that heartbroken over their failed proposal - and he was a father. He would see his daughter soon. In only a few days, the girls had promised, and he could stay with them for as long as he liked, or at least until Lord Shan returned and they could plan his future. He hoped it did not entail another long voyage for a while.

Phineas came to see him while he was brushing the horse. 'A woman has come from the village and asks to speak with you, Master Hallam.'

'Me? But I don't know anyone here. Are you sure it is for me she asks?'

'She did not speak your name, only that she wishes to speak with the man who is a pilot.' Phineas looked doubtful. 'She is a strange woman, master. She asked me if you were a good man.'

Hallam feigned a scowl. 'And what did you tell her?'

'Master Hallam, *please*! I told her the truth!'

Hallam laughed. 'You have learned too much from your clever young mistresses, you old scoundrel. Where is she?'

'Waiting by the gate.'

The woman's lower face was covered by her head cloth, so he could see only her eyes. One was bruised and swollen shut; the other anxious.

'You wish to see me?'

'You are the one they call the pilot?'

Hallam nodded.

'Forgive me, my lord, I ask to speak with you only because of my fear. I beg you not to say you have seen me. I am afraid for myself and my daughter, and also my old mother if he finds I have spoken to you.'

Hallam frowned. 'Who?'

'He does not say his name to us. Only that we are to call him "Lord".'

'Why does it concern me? I do not know anyone in the village. Perhaps it is another pilot you mistake me for.'

She hesitated, looking down the road as if wanting to

430

leave, and Hallam took her by the arm and led her inside the courtyard where they could not be seen. She seemed greatly distressed by her problem. As governor of the village, Lord Shan would no doubt handle such domestic problems, but in his absence he may be able to help. 'Tell me more of this man who troubles you. He is not your husband or a relative?'

'My husband is dead, master. There is only his old mother and our daughter. It is for her that I fear most. He beats her and makes her do terrible things of shame with him in front of us, even though she is young. He is a cruel man.'

Hallam shook his head in sympathy. 'Why is he there? Can you not ask him to leave?'

'He paid us, master. We are poor, and I let it be known we could take a lodger. Now he will not leave and I have spent the copper. When I ask him to leave he beats me...' She placed a finger on her swollen eye. 'When I tell him there is no pilot, he gets more angry. But now I have heard there is a pilot, so I came to tell you.'

'Why does he want to know about a pilot... is he a sailor?'

She took a while to answer, seeming uncertain. 'Perhaps he is a sailor, master. He once boasted of a long voyage... I think to India, but he carries a spear and talks more like a soldier.'

Hallam began to get an uneasy feeling. 'Why did he say you were not to speak to the pilot?'

'I don't know, master. He said he would beat me if I did.'

'So why did you... speak to me?'

'It is because of my daughter, master. I am afraid for her. He said that even after he has finished with the pilot he will keep her to be sure I do not speak out.'

'What does this ruffian look like? Do you know where he comes from?'

'He is a big man with a dark face and much hair, and he spoke once of a village in Cilicia.' Her tone became bitter. 'He said that even the pigs there were more pretty than my daughter.'

Hallam's uneasy feeling blossomed into full blown suspicion. It did not seem possible that Parak knew he was still alive, and that he had found him. Something must have happened to give him away, but he could not think what. It was turning out to be not such a nice day after all.

'I will fetch a spear,' he said, 'then you had better take me to see this wild animal you have in your house.'

As they drew close to a group of cottages, her steps became hesitant, and finally she stopped. 'You should have soldiers to help you, master. He is a very dangerous man.'

'There are no soldiers,' he told her.

There were two who guarded Lord Shan's house at night, but both were asleep, and Hallam did not wanted to involve them in what was his own affair. He had surprise on his side and he had a spear. More than he had the last time they met. It should be enough.

'You can wait here. Show me which is your place, and where he will be.'

She pointed out the building. 'We have only three rooms. Two for sleeping and one for eating, which is the biggest. I cannot be sure, but I think he will be in the big room in the middle.'

'Where is his spear?'

'In his sleeping room, which is on this side.' She held out her left arm.

'No sword or arrows?'

'A sword, which is under his floor mattress.'

'By which door did you leave?'

'The front, master. It will be closed, but the bar will not be in place... my mother and daughter...'

'I will send them out.'

Three windows barred with stout pieces of stick, but otherwise unshielded, were along the side wall. Hallam avoided them by going back the way they had come for a short distance so he could use the cover of other houses to approach from the front. Several people, mainly women and children, watched from doorways and corners. Parak had obviously made a name for himself amongst the neighbours.

He walked across the open stretch of ground to the door, pushed it open and walked in.

Parak was sitting with his back to the wall on the far side of the room, peeling something with a knife. A girl was kneeling not far away from him, with her back to Hallam. She held a jar tilted in her hands, and he heard the sound of pouring water.

Parak looked up, squinting into the light coming through the open doorway, then he started with surprise. He acted quickly, dropping what was in his hand and reaching forward to grab a handful of the girl's hair. He pulled her, screeching, towards him. The jar rolled on the floor, spilling water, and the pot she had been filling was knocked aside.

Parak held the girl's face into his chest as he scrambled to his feet. He struck her on the head with the flat of the knife-blade. 'Silence!' She stopped suddenly, and he held the point into the nape of her neck.

'I see you have not changed your cowardly ways, Parak.'

'So! The bitch warned you.'

'How did you find me, Ape?'

Parak regained his composure. 'Because I am smarter than you, Offal.' He began edging towards a door on his right, and Hallam moved to intercept him.

'Let her go, Parak. Show me again how you can dance like a woman.'

Parak made a sudden dash for the doorway, dragging the whimpering girl with him, backing through while he held her in front as a shield.

Hallam followed, his spear held forward, and Parak suddenly pushed the girl away from him and towards the point of the spear. At the same time he dived across the small room and snatched up his own spear from where it leaned against the wall.

Hallam jerked his spearhead aside as the girl came flying backward, narrowly avoiding spearing her in the back. She crashed into him in the doorway and fell, and he stepped back to give her room. She scrambled to get up, hampered by the robe, and Parak put his foot against her buttocks and pushed her forward, and once again Hallam was forced to jump aside as she dived headlong towards him. She skidded across the wet clay of the floor, her robe around her waist, and Hallam noticed with a shock that her thin buttocks were covered with heavy bruising.

Parak saw his look and laughed from the doorway. He held up his free hand, making clutching movements. 'A good tip for you, Offal. Makes them squirm and squeal. Too bad you won't get a chance to use it.'

'It's going to be a pleasure to kill you, Parak.'

The girl stumbled out through the open front door and the two men circled warily, their spears held at guard.

'Did I tell you I saw her, Offal?' He chuckled without humour. 'It must have slipped my mind. She was at the wharf in Ezion-Geber. I had her in my hands. I would have worn her out by now if I had not been forced to go on your stupid voyage.' Parak held up his hand again and clenched the fingers. 'But I know where she is, Offal. Soon her delicious little rump will be all mine.'

Hallam felt a surge of elation. Parak had made a slip. Philippa had been alive and safe. He forced the possibilities from his mind, fighting to keep his concentration. He could not afford to lose it with a man of Parak's experience. Had it been a throwing spear in his hand like before it may have been different. 'Did you come all this way just to tell me that?'

'I came here to kill you, Offal. The king wants you dead, Ahinadab wants you dead, and I want you dead. The king

434

will reward me well. So will my lovely Philippa, but she will have to be patient.'

Parak gave no sign that he was about to make a move. His eyes had remained hooded throughout, his movements steady, almost casual, but suddenly he sprang into action. He lunged with his spear held low, aiming for the groin.

It was a standard move; a feint designed to throw the defender off guard, so that when the spear was suddenly reversed and the butt swung down at the enemy's head, he would automatically hold his spear up to block, and that would be the end. The attacker could simply reverse the spear again and slice upward through the groin or stomach unopposed.

It was one of the few moves that Hallam knew. He did not try to block, but stepped sideways to the left, keeping his own spear low and aimed at Parak's stomach, allowing the butt to strike him on the right shoulder instead of the head. It was a mistake.

He should have stepped the other way. He heard the soft crack as his recently broken collar-bone gave way again and pain sliced down his arm before he could thrust with the counter-move. Parak's own quick counter all but knocked the spear from his weakened grasp. He broke off and switched the spear to his left hand, staying crouched and trying to conceal the fact he was hurt, but he knew he was in deadly peril.

Parak was not fooled. He saw the change of hands and his eyes widened in surprise. He moved cautiously back towards the front door and closed it with his foot. He fumbled behind for the latch bar and dropped it into place, then he grinned. 'We don't want to be disturbed now, do we?'

Hallam knew he would never have a better chance. Against the wall and close to the corner, Parak would have little space in which to move. He charged at Parak, shifting his spear into a throwing position and launching it quickly before Parak could guess what was happening.

It almost worked.

The bronze head struck the stone wall close to Parak's neck and snapped, showering his face with chips of mud and stone. Hallam did not stop. Taking advantage of Parak's momentary surprise, he lowered his head and charged into him with his left shoulder, crushing him against the wall in a last desperate gamble. Parak grunted heavily as the wind was knocked out of him. His head banged against the wall and he dropped his spear.

Parak slid down and, for a moment, Hallam thought he had him, but Parak's slide was only to scrabble for the spear. Hallam managed to get a foot on it and kicked it away. He tried to knee Parak in the face, but the Cilician caught him around the waist and pushed himself off the wall, sending them both staggering and hopping across the floor. They slipped in the wet patch and both fell, with Hallam underneath, taking all the weight on his injured shoulder. He cried out involuntarily at the pain, as Parak quickly sat astride his chest and caught him by the throat.

Hallam could move only his left arm and his legs. When he tried to buck and roll, his feet skidded helplessly around in the wet clay, unable to find purchase. He lay still and simply tried to breathe.

Parak laughed. 'Enjoy the dance, Offal?' He released Hallam's throat to calmly tuck the limp right arm under his leg. Hallam punched with his left, but it was ineffective, and Parak used both his to wrench it down and clamp it with his knee. With both of Parak's hands free, Hallam was completely at his mercy. And Parak had no mercy.

He grinned down, breathing heavily, his sweat dripping down onto Hallam's face. 'Yes, this is much better!' He flexed his knuckles. Knuckles that were black with hair. 'Now it is you who is going to squirm and squeal like a woman, Offal. I will do it slowly, and when your eyes bulge, I will hook one out and stick my finger right down inside your head to see if you have any brains.' He wriggled his thick finger in front of Hallam's eyes.

Hallam relaxed and sucked in all the air he could under Parak's solid weight, trying to regain his strength. He tried desperately to think of something he could do. As Parak's fingers closed around his throat and began to slowly squeeze, Hallam saw what had fallen free of Parak's open vest. A small antelope horn, shiny black, and no longer than the length of a finger. A similar one had hung around the neck of the old Click man.

He did not have much time. The horn had already begun to blur, and Hallam closed his eyes, concentrating all his remaining strength into his left arm. He flexed the muscle and slowly pulled it free, then reached for the horn, struggling with clumsy fingers to pull out the tight plug while still holding the horn. His head began to spin and he jerked on the thong in desperation, trying to break it, but it held fast.

The pressure on his neck suddenly eased, and he saw the hazy image of Parak's grinning face. The horn was ripped from his grasp and he heard a taunting laugh. It seemed to come from the other side of the room.

'I am pleased to see you are still thinking, Offal. I must thank you for the idea. It is a much better one.'

Parak slipped the thong over his head, pulled out the plug, and pushed his finger deep inside the horn. He pulled it out covered with a glob of the sticky black poison and held it up to admire. 'I wonder what it tastes like?' He chuckled as he began forcing it between Hallam's lips. 'I'm sure you will soon tell me. I thought I had killed you, Offal. It was a good feeling. But I'm glad I didn't. Now I will experience the pleasure of killing you a second time.'

Hallam clenched his teeth and tried to turn his head away, but his firmed lips offered no resistance against the strength of Parak's squirming finger. It followed relentlessly, rubbing on his lips and gums, and Hallam tasted the bitterness of the poison on his tongue. His lips began to burn, then turn numb.

'What does it taste like... will you not tell me?'

The thick, hairy finger pushed against his clenched teeth, stretching apart his lips and moving around the back, seeking an opening into his mouth, and when the finger reached his back teeth, Hallam opened his mouth and bit down on the finger, clenching with all the strength in his jaw, grinding, and he felt the soft bones give, the flesh part, and warm, salty blood come into his mouth.

Parak yelled and tried to pull his hand away, lifting Hallam's head clear of the floor, but Hallam's teeth remained clamped. He held his breath and closed his throat to avoid swallowing, chewing on the finger, and Parak beat at his face with his fists and attempted to bang his head on the floor, but Hallam covered his face with his left arm and held on with his eyes screwed tight.

The weight on his chest lifted and he opened his eyes to see Parak stooped over and awkwardly trying to stamp on his face, and Hallam finally let go.

Parak staggered away, turning in agonised circles as he clutched his bleeding finger.

Hallam rolled away, spitting blood and black poison from his mouth. He stuck his own fingers deep down his throat and retched, spitting out more black blood, which he stared at in horror.

The broken jar was lying nearby. He picked it up and poured the remnants over his face and into his gaping mouth, swilling and spitting, but the burning on his tongue and the numbness of his lips was getting worse. He crawled towards the pot into which the girl had been pouring water, but Parak got there first. He pulled it away and put his hand inside, swilling it around, but the pot was empty.

For a brief moment they looked at each other in shared realisation of their fate, then Hallam grinned lopsidedly.

'Have a pleasant death, Ape,' he mumbled thickly.

Parak spun away, searching on the floor and finding the fallen spear. He picked it up and lunged at Hallam with a snarl. Hallam flung the empty pot at his head and rolled clear as Parak's lunge caused him to slip on the wet floor and fall with the spear still in his hand.

Hallam was up first. He put his foot on the spear and bent to wrestle it free, but he did not have the strength. He wavered, almost falling, then staggered towards the front door. Two doors appeared, and he bumped into the wall. With his mouth on fire, he felt for the other door and threw back the bar. The door opened and he fell into the swirling sunlight.

The old woman peered fearfully out from the doorway of her darkened room. She could hear him in the other room, cursing and roaring like a madman about things that made no sense. She hobbled on stiff legs towards the open front door, then saw the other man lying outside, blocking the way.

She turned to hurry back, then stopped again as the madman came rushing out of his room with a sword in his hand, and she shrank back in fear, but he did not seem to notice her. He held his other hand out in front and she saw it was smeared with something black and was dripping blood.

The man stared wildly about, searching for something. He ran to the fire alcove and placed his bleeding finger on a log. He raised the sword and, with a loud bellow, chopped off his finger. He dropped the sword and thrust his hand into the hot ashes, holding it there, steaming and sizzling while his body shook violently and he roared. He jerked his arm out and rolled on the floor, whimpering and squealing, then he suddenly lay still, only his blackened hand twitching and jumping as if it had a life of its own.

The old woman waited by her door for a while, undecided, then she shuffled closer to look down at the man who had brought such misery into their house, and caused her granddaughter such shame and pain. He was still breathing.

Holding a hand to the aching joint of her hip, the old woman bent stiffly to pick up the sword. With the flat of the blade she lifted the severed finger from beside the log and tossed it in the fire, then she straightened slowly, took the sword in both gnarled hands and raised it high above the madman's head.

Hallam would not want us to make a sacrifice, Sophi. He did not believe his goddess wanted them.'

'Well, we have to do something.'

They had overcome their earlier distress and now looked at each other and their patient in confusion. They had placed him on a separate mattress in their own room, which was bright and airy, and where they could keep a constant watch on him.

His body had been stripped and washed free of blood, examined for wounds, and even his head for bumps, but nothing had been found to explain his condition, only the broken shoulder, which they already knew about, and which they both agreed could not be the cause. The swollen lips they decided must have come from a hit in the mouth. What worried them most was the grey colour of his skin.

'If only we knew what happened.'

Summoned urgently by the woman, Phineas had run to

the house and carried the unconscious Hallam back on his shoulder. Now Jemma ordered Phineas back to the house. 'Take the guards with you,' she said. 'See if you can find out what happened.'

While he was gone, they carefully lifted their patient's head and tried to get him to drink, but his lips remained slack and the water ran out.

Phineas returned with the woman and her daughter. The woman had gathered all the dead stranger's belongings, and Phineas brought those too. 'Best if you speak with the woman yourselves, mistresses.' He looked pale.

Jemma and Sophi questioned the relieved woman and her daughter at length, but although they discovered a lot more than before, they were still none the wiser as to who the strange man was, or what had happened to Hallam. It was not until much later, when they were going through the stranger's belongings and found the message in the leather tube that they got the first clue.

'It's for father!'

They read it excitedly, but the short message did not tell them much more than they already knew either. It was from a pilot who called himself Meldek, and was only to inform their father that Hallam was alive and coming to Mocha overland from Zofar, and also that his boat would be in Ezion-Geber soon after he received this message.

Sophi found the second, and most vital clue, a short while later. She held up the short antelope horn and gasped with surprise. 'Jemma! Look!'

Jemma also recognised it instantly. 'Sophi, be careful! It's poison!'

'I know. It's the same as the old Click man wore around his neck.'

'It still has some poison inside... it's almost dry.'

'Maybe it's the same one.'

They looked at each other. 'If it is,' Jemma said, voicing

both their thoughts. 'It would mean he was the one who killed the old Click man.'

'The same one who captured Shell and Berry.'

'And who tried to kill Hallam...' Jemma looked at her sister with a horrified expression, '... with a poisoned arrow, Sophi...'

They examined Hallam again with more care, checking every scratch and mark that even looked remotely like it could have been the puncture mark of one of the Click arrows. They peered carefully again through his hair, and even searched the soles of his feet in case he had stood on one, but found nothing.

'There is only one place we haven't looked properly,' said Jemma.

'*Jemma!* That wouldn't be right! Anyway, I can't see him being stuck *there*!'

'How do you know? And we've looked everywhere else, so we may as well check there too... just in case.'

'Who will do it?'

'Both of us.'

They scratched through the thick bush of hair and lifted the flaccid penis to look underneath, but it was unscathed.

'I didn't think it would feel so soft,' murmured Sophi.

'Me neither.'

They sat back to contemplate what else could be done.

'We still have some of those yellow berries. Do you think we should try them?

'That was for snakes and spiders, not arrow poison.'

'It can't do any harm... can it?'

Jemma was thoughtful. 'I don't think so. I'll drink some first, just in case, and if it's too bitter, we won't use it.'

Jemma fetched her box of dried roots, leaves and berries and crushed several of the yellow berries in a bowl with water. She tasted it and pulled a face. 'Tastes like sour goat's milk, but it's not bitter.'

With the aid of Phineas, they lifted Hallam again and forced the lip of the bowl between his teeth. Most of it spilled down his chest, but some must have trickled down his throat for there were unmistakable signs of swallowing.

'He's drinking!'

'Keep pouring, Sophi!'

With every avenue covered that they could think of except the summoning of a priest - which would have entailed sacrifice - the girls could do nothing but wait and watch by the light of the tallow candle. On its flame, they burned an occasional fragrant stick from their dwindling supply, filling the room with memories of the camp on the River Saba.

It would have been easier for them if Hallam's breathing had remained constant, but the faint rasping of it was unsteady and often appeared to stop altogether. When that happened, one of them would have to rush to put an ear to his chest and listen for his heartbeat, while the other waited anxiously for the result. On one such occasion Sophi's ear came away wet.

'Jemma! Come quickly!'

Hallam's body was as wet as if it had been doused by a pail of water. His breathing had quickened and he tossed his head from side to side. Phineas was quickly summoned from the adjoining room for his opinion.

'Good sign, mistresses. Evil spirits and good spirits fighting inside. What comes out through skin is blood of evil ones.'

They sat beside him with renewed hope and wiped away the sweat with cool damp clothes as it oozed from his pores. Then finally it stopped and he began to shiver.

Phineas was summoned once more, but this time his diagnosis was not so encouraging.

'Evil spirits are the cold ones, mistresses. They winning now. Must use fire or blankets to help Master Hallam's good spirits keep warm, then we wait to see who wins.'

They piled him with blankets, but the shivering continued, and they looked at each other in despair. 'What can we do, Jemma?'

Jemma frowned in thought. 'Are you warm, Sophi?'

'Yes... why?'

Jemma stood up and began removing her robe. 'You remember when we were on the boat after being saved and couldn't stop shivering?'

'That was different, Jemma, and it was Phineas who kept us warm. It doesn't seem right.'

'Well, we have to do *something*, Sophi, or he will die!' Jemma was close to tears.

'But what if he wakes up?'

'That's what we want him to do, isn't it? We'll just have to get out quickly.'

They lay one on either side, covering as much of his shivering body as they could with their own warm ones. They lay silent and without moving for a long time.

'Are you asleep, Jemma?'

'No.'

'Do you think we did the right thing?'

Jemma took a while to answer. 'I think so, as long as we are careful not to... you know... touch him *there*, but I think I should move his hand. It's a bit close.'

'I mean what if the berries are too old or something, and we poisoned him by mistake? You only tasted it, you didn't actually *swallow* it, did you?'

'Don't talk like that! It tasted all right.'

'I'm boiling.'

'Me too. I think we should sing. He likes us singing. Maybe he will hear us.'

They sang all the love songs they knew, harmonising softly, and did not sing any of the happy songs for that was not their mood, and it did not seem right. When Hallam began sweating again they kneeled beside him, wiping him down as before and forcing water between his teeth, then, when the shivering returned, they crawled dejectedly in beside him.

And so it went throughout the night and for most of the next day. In the afternoon the shivering stopped and the sweating eased, but then the talking - or what sounded like talking - began. The words, if that is what they were, came in spasmodic bursts that made no sense, and the girls silently consulted each others' dark-ringed eyes and summoned Phineas. He listened for a while then nodded knowingly.

'Evil spirits losing now, mistress. Running away through his mouth before they also be killed.'

Still, they maintained their vigil, but exhaustion finally forced them to entrust Phineas with a share of the watching, and they snatched a few moments of sleep between Hallam's unintelligible outbursts.

Phineas reluctantly woke them at dawn with a message from the night guards. 'Boat coming close in to beach, mistresses. Maybe Lord Shan returning. I should go to meet him.'

Bleary-eyed, the girls checked their patient. He was sleeping peacefully, his skin dry and cool, so they took a chance on leaving him for a few moments and climbed the stairs to the roof garden to see the arriving boat. The sails were down and it was already nosing onto the beach.

'Is it Father?'

Jemma shrugged. It was too far to make out any details.

'We should get washed and properly dressed.'

'He won't mind. We have so much to tell him... and we have a good excuse.

'Yes, but he may have important guests, so we should.'

But they lingered, captivated by the beautiful fresh morning and the colours of the sea.

'You know, Sophi...'

'Yes, I know, Jemma, but it can't be, and we had better go down and dress... we've already been away too long from

Hallam.'

One of the shafts of sunlight coming into the room struck Phineas on the bald patch of his head, making it glisten like a wet olive. Another enveloped the still burning candle sitting on the stool nearby, shaming its pale light into insignificance.

He had been watching the steady yellow flame for a long time.

From somewhere came the muffled sound of voices and laughter. He had been listening to that for a long time as well. He was not sure about the singing. He was sure he had heard that too, but it did not fit with the laughter. Perhaps he had been dreaming.

Favouring his sore shoulder and stiff neck, he pulled himself into a sitting position and reached across with his hand to pat gently on the nodding head. It jerked upright and he smiled into the owlish eyes that confronted him. They blinked several times before widening in surprise.

'Master Hallam... you awake again!' Phineas stood up groggily. 'I knew you come back! You wait while I fetch mistresses.'

'Not yet, Phineas.' His voice croaked, and he signalled for the bowl of water. 'Tell me what happened... how did I get here?' He sipped as Phineas told him what he knew, which wasn't much.

'I've been here that long?'

'We thought you was going to die, Master Hallam. Terrible fighting inside you with evil spirits, but we find no injury on you.'

'I thought so too, Phineas, but we can talk about that later.

What happened to Parak?'

Phineas looked puzzled. 'Is that the man you fight with? He is dead, master. Don't you remember? You cut his head off.'

Hallam returned Phineas's puzzled expression. Maybe his memory had been affected by the poison. His sleep had been filled with so many strange dreams it was difficult to separate them from reality.

'What of the woman and her daughter... were they harmed?'

'They all right, master. Mistress Sophie and Jemma gave them the silver what they found in the man's bag, and say they can come and work here to help with looking after your... the queen's child.'

'Good. I hear voices... is Lord Shan here?'

'Friends, Master Hallam. Very important friends. All been in to see you, but you been sleeping. I better call mistresses now or they be angry with me. They warn me not to say anything if you wake up.'

'Oh? What tricks are they up to now?'

'I'm not allowed to say anything, master. They be *very* angry with me.'

'Never mind that. I don't like surprises... especially theirs. Tell me.'

Phineas glanced towards the open doorway and gave Hallam a conspiratorial grin, apparently more than happy about springing the surprise himself. 'I tell you, Master Hallam, but you must please act surprised for them.'

'They will never know,' Hallam promised.

Phineas leaned closer and lowered his voice. 'She is here, master. With your child.'

Hallam grinned. 'Thank you, Phineas. Bring me a robe and help me up.'

Ignoring Phineas's protests that he should remain in bed, Hallam directed him to bind his shoulder and put his arm in a sling, as one of Sulemani's more adept cousins had done, then he had him help with the loose fitting robe. He washed his face, and was attempting with little success to drag one of the girls' silver brushes through his hair when a voice spoke from the doorway.

'A lost cause, my friend.'

'Prince Hadad!'

The prince grinned boyishly as he clasped Hallam's hand. 'I thought I heard voices and sneaked away. It's a great relief to see you alive and on your feet.'

'What are you doing here, Haddy?'

'At the kind invitation of Lord Shan... which I believe I must thank you for... I am temporarily avoiding the wrath of Solomon. When your boat arrived soon after his invitation, and then your friend, Meldek told Zabby's uncle all the news, it was too good an opportunity to miss. With Zabby's help, and a few other friends, we relieved the governor of your boat and sailed it here. It will be another thorn for Solomon to pluck from his greedy hide.'

'*Piko* is here? *And* Zabby?'

'We have many tales to tell, but for now there is someone awaiting your attention even more eagerly than myself, and I am not brave enough to risk the anger of those two wonderfully charming and beautiful young women.'

'Innocent young women, Haddy...'

The prince laughed. 'It is my welfare you should be concerned about, my friend. I have enough trouble in my life already. Now... your lady awaits.'

Hallam grinned. 'It was supposed to be a secret.'

The prince held a finger to his lips. 'Not so loud. I am sworn to secrecy.'

'Is she beautiful, Haddy?'

'There are no words to describe such beauty. I am insanely jealous. You have much to be proud of, my friend, and not the least is your incredible voyage, which everyone is talking about. I have always feared the unpredictable ways of the sea. It must have taken great courage.'

'The courage of ignorance, Haddy, but it's not the ways of the sea we should fear, but the ways of men.'

The prince smiled, showing his dimples. 'True, and I would say the same for the ways of women who are kept waiting.'

Prince Hadad and Phineas helped him to the stairs. 'You sure you ready for climbing, Master Hallam?'

'Never felt better... but you had better stay close behind on the stairs... in case.'

When he was halfway up the steps, he heard the girls singing.

'This is the sound the donkey makes: heehaw, heehaw.

Hallam's grin of anticipation widened. The clearly enunciated, light-hearted tone of the words told they were singing to a child. His child. He reached the top and stood for a moment to catch his breath.

The girls were sitting with two other women under a silk awning. The girls were facing and saw him immediately.

'Hallam!' They scrambled up and hurried towards him. 'Phineas was supposed to call us... you should not be up!' They fussed over him, adjusting his robe, checking the sling, enquiring about his strength, and generally treating him like an ancient and decrepit invalid. Peering over their heads, Hallam could see the shadows of the other two women. Both were now standing.

'Come, we have a surprise for you,' Jemma said.

He went along with their game. 'I'm sorry to disappoint you, but I already know about *Piko* being here. Prince Hadad told me.'

Sophi pouted. 'He promised he wouldn't.'

'Men can never keep a secret,' Jemma said. 'Why didn't you tell us he was so beautiful, Hallam?'

'I've already warned him about you two. Go easy on him.'

'You're jealous... what else did he tell you?'

Hallam feigned surprise. 'You mean there's more?'

Sophi giggled and Jemma pushed him gently towards the awning. 'Someone very special has been waiting to see you, and we must not keep her waiting any longer.'

'Two someones,' Sophi added.

They left him to go forward on his own. As he approached the awning one of the women left it and hurried past. Something about her seemed familiar to Hallam, but her face was covered and turned away. Then the other woman appeared ahead, and he stood transfixed as she came hesitantly towards him, her hair glowing in the sun like the embers of a fire. She held a child on her hip. A boy with a tangled mass of the same colour hair, and his small fist was clenched firmly around the leather thong of the glass medallion.

S ophi, Jemma, and Milcah watched anxiously from the shadows at the top of the stairs. 'He looks just like he did when we saw the lions at the river,' observed Jemma. 'Maybe it was wrong to give him such a big surprise so soon.'

'Mistress Philippa has been afraid for a long time that he has forgotten and no longer wants her,' whispered Milcah.

'Maybe we should have kept Jonathan with us until later... to give them a chance.'

'No, he's talking to him now... talking to his son for the first time, Sophi... isn't it exciting?'

'Do you think he still loves her?'

'He loves her,' Jemma said with conviction, yet a touch of wistfulness sounded in the sigh that followed.

'We should leave them now.'

'No, I want to see them kissing.'

'*Jemma!*'

Reluctantly, Jemma allowed Sophi and Milcah to lead her away.